REDEYE

BOOK 2 OF THE WONDERLAND CYCLE

SEQUEL TO

SHADOW of a DEAD STAR

book one of the wonderland cycle

To Nina,

A fellow mind forever voyaging, wonderfully creative and who knows her own power. I consider myself very fortunate to call you a peer and a comrade.

— [illegible]

A Division of **Whampa, LLC**
P.O. Box 2540
Dulles, VA 20101
Tel/Fax: 800-998-2509
http://curiosityquills.com

Cover design by Michael Shean

ISBN: 978-1-62007-234-9 (ebook)
ISBN: 978-1-62007-235-6 (paperback)
ISBN: 978-1-62007-236-3 (hardcover)

TABLE OF CONTENTS

For Marita

CHAPTER 1

In the end, all Bobbi had left of him was a bloody coat.

It had been the one that he had worn when they had driven through the Old City, when they had searched for dead little girls in a concrete wasteland. He had driven them through a mass of insane feral killers to save them both. That was him, her knight in cheap black microfiber.

Tom. On nights like this, she missed him like crazy.

Bobbi had never thought of him as hers at the time. There was too much going on, too much insanity and Stadil's stupid goddamned quest. And he had followed that road to the end, into the bowels of that abandoned hospital. The hospital that she had destroyed, and probably him with it, at his own request. But he had said that he had forgotten all about the Bureau, and that had meant that he intended to come back. Didn't it?

Thomas Cooley Walken, agent of the American Industrial Security Bureau. It had not been love, she didn't think, but it had been something perhaps preceding it. Despite everything she had wanted, she had become fascinated with his vulnerability, his strangeness. Walken didn't trust this world that she had accepted as a matter of fact. And now he was gone, and had taken the secret of that disbelief with him.

All she had left of him was that black coat, pinned up in a shadow box on the far wall of her tiny bedroom by the door. It was the first thing she saw upon rising, the last thing she saw before going to bed. She stared at it now, stretched out like a skin. The stains had long since faded into the fabric, blood long since bonded with the synthetic fibers.

She tore her eyes away to look at the holographic clock hanging over the doorway, its digits declaring seven-thirty p.m. "All right, Bobbi girl," she murmured to herself, continuing her evening ritual. "Get your ass up and get to work."

And so she did, not being the kind to argue with the boss. Bobbi went into the little bathroom attached to her bedroom and splashed cold water on her face. When she thought of him in the dark like this she tried to imagine that she was him, or at least think like him. Wide-eyed and yet cynical, knowing the world was evil and yet being constantly surprised by it. She had never understood that, that seeming lack of an emotional callus.

She liked him because he was like that. Complex. A puzzle. A girl like Bobbi was a sucker for puzzles, and the truth was she never thought that she could solve him. It was, she had realized, the core of attraction for her.

Maybe that was why they worked; they were just different enough. Then she reminded herself that they had only 'worked' for a few weeks, that she had gotten crazy jealous over him for reasons she had yet to decipher and that they might very well have been just drunk on sex and adrenaline the whole goddamned time. She collected herself, pushed those memories into the back of her head, and prepared herself for the evening's toil.

Bobbi left the bedroom and walked out into her office, which was a shrine to another dead man. Two years ago, the office into which she now walked had belonged to a man named Anton Stadil. He and his fellows had burnt out their brains here, laid out under the flat blind eyes of deactivated wallscreens. She had inherited the Ballroom after Stadil's death, but it was no longer the hedonistic palace that it had been two years before. Now it was called The Temple; the marble floor was now full of datanauts and other questionable creatures, drinking at tables or crammed into booths. She'd done it as a way to put her own life in order after Tom's disappearance, being apparently unknown to the Bureau as his co-conspirator, but it was also a means to conduct her investigation.

Setting up the club had taken quite some time. She was slow to build her enterprise from her inheritance for a few very important reasons. One was the Bureau, which apparently had no knowledge of her where Tom was concerned; that was fine by her, because she had enough things to worry about without the Fed sending her into a cryogenic penitentiary. The other problem – and, in her opinion, by far the biggest – was the Genefex corporation. Perhaps Bobbi might have gone on with her life right then and there had she believed that Stadil actually wanted Tom dead. But she didn't. Old Anton had told her, sitting right where she did now, that he had wanted Tom to know the truth. To realize his instincts. The truth had been that Genefex, a vast and powerful genetics concern – the developers of clinical immortality – had discovered that their vaunted cure for aging had been weak tea. That they had been behind the black market technological juggernaut known as Wonderland, the dark side of Great Siam. This is what they had known without doubt. The data had all been there.

But despite her dropping anonymous information to no less than six different news outlets, and even having taken the extreme step of leaking the evidence to the Bureau, nothing had happened to Genefex at all. The company had enjoyed double-digit gains and its oldest customers had escaped their projected Doomsdays. Great Siam was an even stronger state than before with the annexation of Burma and Malaysia a year ago. Everything that had been set to fall apart had spat in the face of prophecy. Something had gone seriously wrong.

That damnable archive. Sent by Stadil to Annika Hunt, the controversial journalist – unable to be cracked by the Bureau, its contents had been unearthed when Tom had tried to access it himself via Bobbi's own brain-riding terminal. Since Tom's disappearance, it had occurred to her that the secret lay instead not in the archive itself,but in its source – most specifically, the way that Stadil had died. With Tom gone, she could only solve that mystery on her own, and it had seemed the next best likely avenue to pursue. But there was just no cracking that particular nut, no matter how hard she'd tried. Sources dried up or shrank away, and she couldn't afford to deplete her reputation if she wanted to live any semblance of a normal life. So she had abandoned the search, or at the very least put it off until it appeared that there might actually be some traction. It had been a year since she had last touched the data.

Bobbi sat down at Stadil's desk. She saw herself reflected in its pristine majority: her heart-shaped face with its mane of lavender hair styled in layers with a laser pencil. Startling green eyes that she would never change. Her curves, her hair, the crisp turn of her nose – these were all synthetic (or at the very least augmented) and not at all the way they had been when she was born. But her eyes, bottle-green and glittering with their motes of gold around the pupils, those she would never change. The flesh was the symbol of her vanity, she had always believed, and she could change it with fashion. But her eyes were her warning label. She wanted everyone to know what they were in for.

Bobbi shook her head and brushed strands of hair from her face. "Come on, come on," she called out to the open air. "Miss Bobbi, she is here!" She was calling to the computer, which she had named Paracelcus after an old alchemist she'd read about, turning lead into gold. The equivalent of what she did with data, really, most of her adult life. There was familiar comfort in bravado, the cowgirl's shield. She found she often needed it these days.

The massive telescreens that had hung on the walls had been replaced with holographic projectors, which conjured up legions of data all round her. Her standard worktop could wrap the whole room, obscuring the sight of Stadil's kitsch collection with solid-light panels or three-dimensional displays. Bobbi had, at least to her knowledge, the best setup of anything not military or top-tier corporate elite. Stadil's money and property had made sure of that. She had inherited Stadil's assets the morning after Tom had vanished, as if they were reparations made for his disappearance. Windows of light winked into existence, depicting the very spare and industrially-influenced furnishings of The Temple's bar floor; dubious people in dubious fashions sat at skeletal steel tables, drinking and doing business.

Standing behind the bar, watching like some monstrous gargoyle, was a thoroughly massive black man, his prodigious musculature a product of vat-grown muscle tissue attached to an already powerful frame. He wore a tight white t-shirt to show it off, a Six Red Rebels band tee that rippled with his body's topography. This was Marcus Scalli, the only person Bobbi really talked to anymore. Bobbi had known Scalli for years, and he was the closest thing to a friend she really had. She'd never been one for close-and-personals. He managed the bar for her as well as handling security, directing Sandy, the bartender and his bouncers. She was pretty happy with how things were going in that department. All the "specialty services" were her deal.

Among the security monitors her mailbox window sprang into being, hovering there with a battery of business minutiae. Most of these were bills, promotional adverts, the usual fare that a business owner had to deal with. These she ignored out of hand; she'd written expert systems to process them and keep things running. Another was an alarm notice from one of the ghost-boxes she kept on the premises as part of the club's "special services."

Among other pursuits, Bobbi ran a data deposit service at the Temple. She kept a battery bank of ghost-boxes in a back room; the small but spacious dedicated file-storage modules were kept isolated from the network and each other, ensuring that nobody could hack them without interfacing them directly. For a sizable hourly fee, customers could transfer sensitive data into one of Bobbi's ghost-boxes and keep it safe for a period of time before they either removed it or had someone else pick it up. Transfer was only to physical storage media, and only with an assigned cipher key. They worked very well; even without Stadil's fortune in her pocket, she could have supported the club and property on the revenue generated alone.

It was a relatively easy service to maintain, but sometimes there would be issues. Sometimes the data stored was toxic, like a virus-prog with "leaky" code, and there'd be some lingering transfer on the unit in which it was stored. Bobbi would sometimes have to go down and clean out a ghost-box on her own – and, from the look of the alarm message pulsing red and irritable on her mailbox display, this would be one of those times.

Bobbi got up and headed for the elevator. Hanging from the muzzle of an aluminum deer's head mounted on the wall nearby was her hack kit, the old Army medic's satchel she'd been using for years now. The red cross seemed to stare out at her; she hesitated for a moment, staring back at it before finally taking up the strap and stepping into the elevator. She had a lot of things to fix, she thought. She wondered if this kind of work would be the medicine she needed in the end.

The floor of the Temple trembled with the throbbing beat of manic-pulse music, a beat that shook the doors as they opened into the back room. Bobbi's nose wrinkled as she stepped out of the elevator and into the soup; it wasn't her kind of track, that shuddering, rapid drone. Manic-pulse had taken the crown of popular music twenty years ago, fusing weirdly fluted, atonal synths to a skeleton of rapid bass rhythms. It was supposed to be representative of the future, or so The Nightmen had said when they first invented the stuff back in the late fifties – she didn't know what kind of future they had envisioned save that it was strange as Hell. But then again, people liked all kinds of weird these days. There wasn't really any room for normalcy.

Bobbi stepped past the ghostly-lit cabinets of the coolers, pausing to pluck a Tsingtao from one as she went. No chill-tab on the beer; only glass bottles, primitivity as cachet. Bobbi twisted the lid free and took a swig of the chilled beer, felt it stream thin and tasty over her tongue, and stepped through the storeroom door to be assailed by the wall of sound.

Bobbi had done much more than simply change the name of the club. The biggest difference was the distinct lack of lighting on the walls. When it belonged to the Slav, the club was lined with pornographic holograms and neon rails twisted into all manner of configurations. Now, however, the vaulted expanse was lined with dark green hexagonal tiles uplit by the soft glow of spot lamps. Simple. Bobbi was all about simple, especially since her clientele were anything but.

Scalli loomed at the edge of the bar. "Evening," he called over the withering beat, a sound that carried itself into her ear through her earbud. "Glad to see you're up."

"Most people are," Bobbi quipped as the cowgirl act slipped into place. "Everything decent out here?"

"Same as usual," Scalli said. "Everyone more interested in doing biz than causing trouble. Not for you, anyway." His brows arched as he saw the bag hanging from her shoulder. "Unless there's something going on I haven't heard of?"

She snorted. "Sorry, Scalli," Bobbi said, "just one of the boxes needs prodding at. Sorry to disappoint ya."

"Disappointment I can handle," Scalli drawled. She knew he didn't like complications; it was one of the reasons he'd come to work for her, since with Tom's passing virtually any complication she'd ever even thought of having seemed to have evaporated. Funny how money did that for you.

Bobbi smiled at him faintly. "Yeah, well, I'm gonna go play nurse. See you in a bit." She left him frowning after her, doing her usual circuit across the floor toward the secure booths where the ghost-boxes could be accessed. Hack artists and their retinues, such as they were, looked up to watch her pass. Some of them leered – that would be the new kids, those who didn't know her on sight – but the vets and the usuals mostly gave her nods as she passed by. Familiar faces, most of them. Bobbi marked the few which weren't on her way to the booths, resolving to look them up later off security footage. Never knew who new folk were, after all.

Booth number seven was the one in question. Like its fellows, it was a small cubicle no larger than a narrow walk-in closet; the door was a flat pane of heavy alloy, magnetically sealed and extremely difficult to cut through. Normally she'd open the doors from her office, but she also had them rigged to open in proximity to her personal electromagnetic signature. As she approached, the door to the booth swung open.

The walls of the booth were covered with the ribbed grid work of soundproof plastics, and dim blue lighting was projected from narrow bioluminescent strips bordering the ceiling. The ghost-box itself, a cube of flat gray metal with faceted corners, sat on a clear plastic dais with a single chair parked in front of it. It had a small display mounted on the lower right half of its front face, which was currently reading "SYSTEM ALARM." "Damn," Bobbi murmured as she stepped inside and took her seat in front of the ailing machine, "what's gotten into you?"

There was a universal access port set into the face of the 'box below its display. Bobbi set her beer down on the floor next to her, then reached into her bag and withdrew a thin, silvery cord which had two short plugs on either end. One went into the machine and one went into the back of a sleek, device which looked something like a brushed nickel collar with a padded interior and its front half removed. This she fitted against the back of her neck before connecting it with another cable to the interface port behind her ear. The collar was a portable neural firewall, a device which served as a terminal and a security barrier; some models would protect against viruses and the like, others helped resist intrusion. Bobbi's was a heavily Lyricom unit which, already fitted to paramilitary specifications right out of the box, was the equivalent of tank armor against intrusions and attacks against the computer in her head.

Which was good, because all that silicon in her skull couldn't exactly be replaced very easily. She had gotten a new implant after Tom had disappeared; it was an Arashi Intuex-7, top of the line – bleeding edge even now with its custom-build modules and amped up hardware, especially its powerful holographic storage unit that allowed her to store short-term memories and expert data for a brief span. It had been extremely expensive, or would have been before she had taken Stadil's money. Now it was an investment, hard-wired throughout her brain in ways her old Telefunken unit had never been. She didn't want to risk major brain surgery again until the paradigm was sufficiently reinvented to make it necessary.

Bobbi closed her eyes and took a deep breath, counting backwards. She only needed ten seconds or so before she fell into the trance necessary to access the network; most people of her experience did. Some went as short of six, maybe seven, but those were people were screened and militarized anyway. With each backward count she felt herself slip out of the real and into an abyss that was like warm bathwater – millimeter by millimeter her consciousness turned inward, and then suddenly she was no longer constrained by the curvaceous meat that housed her in the living world. She fell from the sleep of the walking world into that of the network, and she joined the ranks of the Awake.

Her thoughts were liquid as they poured out of her skull and into the narrow band of the cable. There was no hallucinatory realm here, no virtual reality – it was knowledge, plain and simple. Cold facts. She knew the storage capacity of her skull terminal to twenty-six decimal places, knew how much memory each internal program took up as they ran in the background. There was no need for displays or graphical hallucinations; being Awake meant you were intimately aware not only of the status of your own system, but of the system surrounding you out to a radius that corresponded to the caliber of your hardware. Your body still was still reachable, of course, and at times the flesh did strange tricks when attempting to resolve stimuli; the ranks of the Awake often used drugs like phenocyclanol, also known as Cycle, to dampen that effect. Bobbi had always reckoned that this was what the Astral Plane was supposed to have been like, a plane of pure knowledge – and sitting there with eyes closed, the Lyricom collar cradling the base of her neck, she certainly looked to the observer as if she might have been reaching out with some invisible third eye into eternity.

Deep in trance of Awakening, Bobbi willed herself connected to the ghost-box. There was a moment's lag as she negotiated her firewall and the started up its decontamination protocols, another as she executed the connection protocols. She dove into the machine, communed with its system software, and started up the diagnostic cycle. Three minutes, thirty point three two seven seconds passed before she became aware of the problem: the ghost-box had been host to a file, a rather big one. This wasn't at all unusual, of course, but what was interesting to her was that it appeared to have a latent shell of viral code attached to it, bleeding irrational code into the system – not harmful in and of itself, but tying up the box's memory was keeping the thing from further operation. A prank, perhaps, or something that managed to execute before it was supposed to? This sort of thing always happened with shit programmers, of which there were far too many trying to pass themselves off as pros.

Amused, Bobbi ran the firewall's analytical software, and failing to get an ID on the virus's profile, ran the much more advanced analytical package in her skullcomp as well. Still she found she couldn't quite get a purchase on it; custom programming then, nothing the firewall could recognize. Abandoning these shortcuts, she stripped out a sample and picked over it herself. Alphanumerics flashed through the screen of her Awakened mind, understanding aided by the system in her head. The fabric of the code was simple enough, but then she spotted something that stopped her cold.

There, floating in her sensorium, a simple line of programming commentary flared like a blazing message from God Himself.

!--// HELLO THERE, BRAIN MOTHER. BE SO KIND AS TO CONTACT ME AT... \\--!

A network address followed. Brain Mother, her own chosen pseudonym. Her hack handle. A message meant for her. Bobbi flew through the rest of the code sample, which only confirmed what she now surmised – that the virus wasn't a virus at all, merely a very effective method of getting her attention. She grabbed at the file, assuming now that it was meant for her as well, and what she saw there shook her out of her trance with a wall of fear and incomprehension.

It was the archive. Stadil's archive.

Bobbi closed her eyes and drew a deep breath. "Shit," she muttered. This wasn't the way she wanted to start her morning at all.

She stared at the box for a minute or so, then dumped the file into a datacell from her bag before pulling the plug from the socket behind her ear. Bobbi switched off the ghost-box and got up slowly, backing away from the now unpowered unit as if it might lunge for her throat. She made the circuit back toward the bar in careful silence, keeping her expression casual, or so she hoped. Scalli peered at her as she walked past him into the back room but said nothing.

By the time she stepped through the door, the flash of panic that she so carefully hid for the trip across the club floor now threatened to rise up and drown her. Her chest tightened as she leaned against a cooler cabinet, her eyes staring blankly at the concrete floor. How in the hell had she been discovered? Had the Bureau spotted her when they were tracking Walken with satellites? Did somebody turn her in? Chin? Pierre, that damned spider of a Frenchman?

Her hands slick with sweat, Bobbi stepped past into the elevator. She should leave this. She shouldn't bother with it. She should sell the Temple, pack up and leave town with the rest of Stadil's money. Fuck this. Fuck all of it. That would be the single smartest thing to do, she thought as she stabbed the single button on the elevator panel.

And yet . . .

Even as the elevator rose, the old familiar curiosity rose with it. Wasn't this what Bobbi had been waiting for after two years? Just like she had tagged Walken in his hour of need, was this not some other strange messenger carrying a tantalizing clue for her to work on? The puzzle, again, looming out in front of her. Inviting her. Bobbi heaved a deep sigh, cursing herself as she resigned herself to what she already knew was going to take place. Of course she was going to contact whoever this person was. Of course she was going to reopen what should for all rational sense be better off left alone.

She would do it because she had to, even as she had to Stadil's job in the first place. Because she liked puzzles. She needed them. Otherwise, what was life worth in the first place?

"I am gonna get myself killed," she murmured to herself as she stared at the elevator's illuminated ceiling. "I just know it."

When the elevator opened again and she walked out into her office, Bobbi had already planned out a strategy for herself. By the time she'd sat down, she knew how to execute it. Ten minutes later she had not only hit up six different hack boards and come up with access codes to a battery of global telecomm nodes, but she had already plotted a skipback chain and was making one to connect. Despite the tension that flooded her, despite the pressure of the immediate need to know, Bobbi's cowgirl cool allowed her to perform. She counted backward without difficulty and was Awake once more, sublimating into the network.

The node was an old one, laggy. Maybe even a private machine rigged into a node. Bobbi felt her commands follow her thoughts by a delay of milliseconds. She didn't like that; if Bobbi ran into trouble here, she'd be at a disadvantage in throwing up defenses. She was using her portable terminal, whose defenses were much better than the firewall collar she'd worn – but even so, all the expensive barrier programs in the world weren't going to help her if she wasn't able to call them in time.

There was nothing in the system that she could determine, just the operating system and a single program running. Protected system, she saw now; the lag came from walls of intrusion barriers that she only now could see from the inside. Very stupid, Bobbi girl, she thought to herself as she brought her usual defenses online. Concurrent interlocking layers of programming snapped into being around her, rendering her into a tower of iron. Though it made her very obvious to whomever was watching the terminal, it would be foolish to enter a system naked when someone was likely waiting for her – and then, as if summoned by the appearance of these defenses, a new visitor arrived.

<Good Evening.> The words appeared without a voice, tethered to the name 'Mysteron.' It was cute. Pretentious, but cute.

<Yahey,> Bobbi projected as Brain Mother. <Nice little box you have here. Neat trick with the barriers.>

<It's the lag. People see the age of the operating system and assume I'm running an Ancient. People forget that old tech is still useful.>

<That seems to be the general theme of things these days, yeah,> Bobbi replied. <Next best all over. All right, you summoned me, and here I am. What's up?>

A few seconds' pause from Mysteron kindled new tension in her, but soon the reply came. <You got the archive, then?>

<I got AN archive, yeah.>

<And you looked at it?>

It was Bobbi's turn to pause. Whoever this was, there was no telling what they knew or at least thought they knew about her. <I did,> she replied. <Very stiff encryption. You want to hire me to crack it, is that it?>

Another long pause from Mysteron. In the world of meat, Bobbi's palms had begun to sweat as she constantly monitored the other presence for signs of an attack or other activity. <I want to talk to you about our mutual friend,> came the reply after a while. <His case has gone unanswered for too long. Meet me at the Via Fontanella, 1457 12th Avenue, saloon bar. Ten o'clock tonight. This will be your only opportunity to do so.> And just like that, the presence left.

The words shot through Bobbi's spine like a rod of iron. She sat up hard, tearing the plug from her skull-socket as her expression flattened into a mask of lead. "Via Fontanella," she repeated to herself. Her mental threatboard shuddered in alarm. "I don't know that place." She raked her fingers through holographic panels, running searches. The Via Fontanella was an Italian place in the New City, over a hundred years old now. Fine dining. She had a couple of appropriate outfits she could wear – but on the other hand, did she really want to wear one of the clinging numbers in her closet when she was about to meet some mysterious personage who could potentially be planning to shoot her in the face?

"Fuck it," she said out loud to herself. "I'll have to improvise."

CHAPTER 2

Bobbi's idea of improvisation meant cutting down a twelve-grand Miri Bendis she'd had hanging in her closet into something she could run in. In what would be considered a sacrilege in the courts of the fashion cult she'd taken the original dress – itself basically a shape-hugging tube made of woven straps of memory plastic – and cut it up with a thermal scalpel into something more mobile. With hip-high slits down each side of its knee-length skirt and the sleeves removed it looked like the tabard of a knight at a fetish ball. With this pulled over a gray lycra bodysuit and vents cut in the sides, she looked a little more ready to attend an underground club than to trawl the restaurant scene.

And so it was that Bobbi appeared in the saloon bar at the Via Fontanella, with her hair piled into a teased mane and her eyes swallowed with airbrushed red, and exactly opposite of the crowd's fashion paradigm – which was also how she liked it. She was a species of neon banshee among the somber suits as she headed into the bar, wading through the packed foyer and into its richly-paneled chamber. Stark white walls gave way to dark wood and polished brass, a study in pub fashion long since passed into history. Dark-suited grayfaces drank Mexican beer poured from ancient, ivory-handled taps. A pair of what she took to be Slavic hookers, thin creatures perched on stools like disaffected gazelles, stared at her as she stood there rocking on the heels of her calf-high boots. And then, without even the slightest sliver of doubt crystallizing in her brain, she proceeded across the floor toward a table in the corner.

"Hey," Bobbi said to the woman sitting there. "This seat taken?"

The woman looked up. Red hair, cut into a rough shag, surrounded her pale face like a halo of fresh blood. Gray shimmer on her eyelids, vivid blue eyes rimmed with purple liner. Red lips quirked into a smile as she saw Bobbi standing there. It must have been a surgical job; Bobbi could see where the bone structure had been shifted, perhaps to give it a hint of masculinity there. Tough girl.

"Brain Mother," she said in a soft, breathless voice, wielding Bobbi's hack handle.

"You got me at a disadvantage, honey," Bobbi said as she dropped into her seat, lips quirking as she did so; she sat slightly sprawled, both to affect a confident pose and to give her access to the nerve-crusher that she'd strapped to the inside of her thigh with a Velcro band. It was a homemade device, battery and emitter jammed into a small square box affixed to the grips of an antique revolver, but Bobbi was no slouch when it came to bootleg machines. She smiled across the table at the woman, the crusher's weight buoying her bravado. "You got a name, too?"

Where Bobbi was playing gangsterette, the woman opposite her wore something far more fitting the establishment's fashion code – an elegant suit, heather-gray jacket with exaggerated shoulders over a simple silk blouse. A simple golden brooch of interlocking hexagons shone at her lapel. "My name's Frieda," she said with a wide smile, and she leaned forward a bit to prop her chin upon the back of a broad, long-fingered hand. "Frieda Kelley. And you're Roberta January, also known as Brain Mother."

A flash of irritation shot up Bobbi's back. "Bobbi'll do. Roberta's just a name on a birth certificate. So what's this all about? You didn't call me down here with a spook-letter for a date, I'm sure."

"No." Freida's smile took on a smirking edge; her eyes wrinkled, glittering with amusement. "You're pretty hard-nosed, aren't you, Bobbi?" She shook her head and laughed. "I can see why you two got along."

Another flash of irritation, coupled with impatience. "Uh-huh," Bobbi grunted. "Who we talking about here?" The name 'Kelley' ticked the vaguest familiarity in her head, along with a sudden, inexplicable spike of paranoia.

"Tom," said Kelley, putting a name to Bobbi's sudden fear. "Tom Walken. He and I used to work together at the Bureau." She must have read the look in her eyes as Bobbi's hand slid under her skirt, clenching the crusher's grip in anticipation of ambush, because she lifted her manicured hands in a mollifying gesture. "Relax," Freida said, her voice matching her hands for tone. "There's no trouble here. It's the opposite in fact."

"Uh-huh," Bobbi repeated, letting the sound cover the faint crackle of Velcro as she pulled the crusher free. "Well let's hear it, then. I don't have patience for mysteries, and you sure as Hell don't have a lot of time to spill before I march my pretty ass outta here." Or make salad out of her CNS, Bobbi thought as she fingered the trigger on the grip of the crusher. Whatever worked.

Freida's face fell a little, and she hunched a bit in her jacket's wide shoulders. "I'm sorry," she said, looking down at her broad hands. "I'm not a field agent. I'm not exactly good at the cloak-and-dagger." She looked up, her blue eyes reflecting the apology. "It took me a long time to figure out who you were, you see. I had to do a lot of digging to figure out that he'd been hiding out with you the whole time."

Bobbi's eyes narrowed a bit more, silently watching the woman across the table. She said nothing.

Freida shifted a little bit in her seat. "Okay," she continued, "it's like this. I'm assuming that you were the one who sent in what was supposed to be the archive that your boss, Stadil, sent to Annika Hunt."

"Not supposed to be," Bobbi said flatly. "Was." Her finger stroked the firing stud, and she stared holes through the redhead's pretty face. Something clicked in the back of her head and a bulb somewhere in her memory lit up. "You said your name was Kelley, right?"

"Yes," she replied.

Bobbi leaned in then, reaching under the table – and met her gaze just as the blunt body of the crusher passed the hem of Freida's skirt and met the side of her knee. "Tom said Kelley was a man," she said, and her eyes flashed with her own sudden anger. "So don't you fuck with me."

The pressure of the crusher's business end against her skin froze Freida in her tracks. She licked her lips nervously as she met Bobbi's gaze, and after a long moment's silence drew a nervous breath as a faint blush rose to her cheeks. "That's because when he knew me, I was."

Bobbi was angry. Bad enough that she got dragged out to a Mysterious Meeting, even worse now that she began to fear that the Bureau might be lying in wait for her. And yet, Kelley's admission caused Bobbi to hesitate in calculating a sudden escape. Her eyes flickered over the other woman's body, such as she could see it. The large hands, the vaguely mannish bone structure – it could be possible. "Explain," she commanded, and pressed the crusher harder into the other woman's knee.

"Genetic reassignment surgery," Freida replied, and her eyes dipped to fix upon the table. "There was a girl, you see, and she..."

"Didn't like boys, huh?" Bobbi's expression still did not waver – she didn't know if she quite believed Freida yet, but the nagging spark of sympathy that had summoned itself up at least gave her hope.

"I guess he told, you, huh." Freida sat up, then swept her hand across the table in front of her in a flippant gesture. "Yeah, well. Doctor at the office, someone I worked with. Didn't want to be with me as I was, of course, but she'd let slip to Tom that if I ever got a gene-job put on me . . . " She shrugged. "It turns out she liked me just fine as a girl – more than I ever could have hoped for. But I just wasn't myself anymore. And you can't go back."

Bobbi wrinkled her nose. "I figure it's you if you say it is," she replied. "Lots of people make alterations all the time." She thought of her own body, the often drastic changes she'd had done to it over the years. The mousy, scrawny thing she'd been. "But I get it. Gotta make the change for yourself instead of for somebody else, right?"

"Yeah." Freida pursed her lips, then, and leaned forward also. "Look," she said, "you can put that thing away. The Bureau doesn't know I'm here, and I can't talk to you with a gun under my hood. I'm here to talk with you about what happened to him."

Bobbi stared at her for a hard moment before pulling the crusher back. It wasn't that she believed the other woman entirely – Freida could be some sneaky bitch that was just a little mannish around the edges – but she felt that, perhaps, she wasn't going to get put down by a paramilitary squad the moment she drew back to her own side of the table.

"All right," Bobbi said, keeping the crusher under the table and pointed at Freida's middle. "So let's hear it, then."

Freida paused, slowly reaching up to brush a few strands of red out of her face. She leaned back a bit in her chair, palms on the table, and took a deep breath. "All right," she said, "Tom didn't have – friends, I guess. I mean he had people as good as friends, or maybe could have been, but I don't know that he ever saw any of us as buddies." When Bobbi said nothing she continued, saying, "But I always liked him. He looked out for me, and he respected my abilities. He took me seriously, and that goes a long way with me. Longer than you might guess."

"You'd be surprised," Bobbi replied. "So Tom was a good guy, we both know that. What's it got to do with me?" But for all her bluster, Bobbi's nerves stood straight on edge – she felt the bristling of something enormous on the horizon, and inside she swirled with the storm of anticipation.

Freida stared at her for a moment, and perhaps forgetting the gun leaned forward all the way to look Bobbi straight in the eye. "Look," she said. "Tom was a good cop. He was a good agent, too – and he pretty much got fucked over by everybody he worked under. As far as I'm concerned, the Bureau killed him as surely as if one of our men had shot him in the face, and that's not right by half. I want to find out what the hell really happened to him."

Bobbi's guts clenched as she tried to contain the rising tide of mingled dread and excitement that rose within her. "We can agree on that," she replied, feeling her hand going slick on the checkered wood of the crusher's grip. "So, you called me here. I guess you figure I'll help you?"

"I know you will." Freida's eyes glittered with what Bobbi clearly saw was the light of victory. "You want to know as bad as I do, I think. And we both know things. I know what's happened on the Bureau's side, and believe that you were with Tom 'til he left you."

Bobbi stared at her now. "Go on," she said, and she heard the sternness in her voice being stripped away by the flood she so dearly tried to keep back.

It was a cue that Freida seemed to take to mean she could be comfortable, because the stiffness in her shoulders faded; she propped herself up on an elbow as she settled into a more comfortable position. She took a smokeless cigarette from a silver case produced from the inside of her jacket, crushed its tip, and was instantly surrounded by the faint odor of herbs as she began her tale.

"I guess you know," Freida began, gesturing with the cigarette like a magic wand, "that this all started with Tom flagging down this plane that had the Dolls in it – you know about the Dolls, right?"

"Yeah," Bobbi said with a nod. "First one got killed by Koreans," she said, "and then the second one got shot when his gun fucked up."

Freida's lips flattened a bit, and she nodded. "And the third, well, we never recovered her. By that time it didn't matter, because the Bureau had already decided that he was the one to put the blame on. There was just too much pressure on the Bureau, and too much that didn't shake out. Easier to turn him into a scapegoat than to admit they just didn't know what the hell was going on."

Bobbi shifted in her seat a bit. "I don't understand that," she told her. "You'd think they'd . . . I don't know, just hang him up for being ineffective and say he botched the investigation. Why label him as a criminal?"

"Well," said Freida, "because the evidence seemed to suggest that he very well might have had something to do with it. Take that gun you mentioned." She paused to take a draw from her cigarette. "There wasn't any evidence of hacking at all."

Bobbi's brows arched; she wasn't expecting that. "That doesn't mean that it didn't happen," she replied. Her thoughts in that instant were filled with Stadil, his plans for Tom and the truth. "Tom would never have just up and killed that girl."

A shrug rolled through Freida's shoulders. "Well, I agree with you there," she said. "But there was no evidence that it had been tampered with. The record shows that he selected nonlethal rounds, and then just before he squeezed the trigger dialed back to explosives. I mean that's possible, isn't it? She was attacking him, he said – I've always thought it was a reflex reaction."

Bobbi shook her head. "He swore up and down to me that he never touched the dial," she said, harshness rising in her voice, "and I believe him. You people took everything he had without entertaining the possibility of a mistake or malfunction."

"By 'you people' you're referring to the rest of the Bureau, I'm sure." Freida's eyes narrowed. "All I did was the analysis. I don't think he killed that girl on his own, either. But what could we have done? At the time it seemed a definite possibility, and then when he just took off—"

Bobbi shifted in her seat again; the momentary flash of anger that had shot up her spine was swiftly replaced with discomfort. "That was my fault," she said. "I was hired to meet up with him."

One slender red brow arched. "Hired by whom?" Kelley asked.

It took a long, tormented moment before the words left Bobbi's lips. "Anton Stadil."

There was silence between them for a long moment. "I'm glad they closed this case already," said Freida, looking soberly down at her hands. "Else we'd probably be continuing this conversation in an interrogation room."

Silence hung between the two of them. Finally Bobbi decided to bite the bullet, as curiosity and that maddening desire to solve things finally got the best of her. "You're for real, aren't you?"

Freida's eyes were grim when they lifted to behold her. "Yeah," she said. "I am."

"Look, I'm going to put this thing away. And then let's just talk plainly, all right?"

"All right."

"And when I do, we're going to lay things out, both of us, on the table." Bobbi's fingers tightened on the weapon's grip for a long moment, feeling its texture biting into her palm. "No shit."

"No shit."

"Well all right then." Bobbi pressed the crusher back into place, felt its weight again nestling against her thigh. She smiled, which looked strange beneath her banshee makeup. "Let's have ourselves some girl talk."

Sitting there in the restaurant's bar, the two women spoke about things that neither of them had dared talk about since Tom had disappeared. Bobbi didn't speak first; she had let the transgendered Kelley do most the initial talking, and she certainly seemed to have a lot to say.

First and foremost was Freida's assertion that the Bureau had never intended to throw Tom to the wolves. Not at first, anyway. But when he shot the Doll and then disappeared, the scenario that the Bureau had prepared in case he had decided to run. The Romeo was solved, and they had their criminal. And so that was it. Everything she and Tom did after that played directly into the paranoid construct the Bureau had whipped up to absolve itself. He was doomed the moment he left, the moment he met her at the Market that night. Her fault. Stadil's fault. That fucker.

Bobbi ordered a double scotch and was quiet for a while, feeling a blazing core of anger pour into her gut and seethe there. Silence hung between the two of them for a while, with Freida determinedly watching a pair of chatting businessmen and Bobbi trying to fight down the emotional steam pressure generated when sadness crashed down over that cinder of rage. She closed her eyes and took the scotch down in a chain of steady swallows. The heat of her anger was drowned by that of the single malt; she'd have time to mourn again later.

"So," Bobby finally said, and her voice was raspy from the drink. "You said you weren't ever able to crack the archive."

"I wasn't," Freida replied with a nod. "Still haven't, either – it's the damnedest thing I'd ever seen. We'd always gotten it down to a certain level, and then..."

Bobbi nodded. "Some kind of fractal encryption," she replied. "Gets more and more complex as you go along – we ran into it, as well." That damnable archive. Bobbi paused, and her tone dipped coyly. "Cracked it, though."

Freida was quiet for a long moment. She looked at Bobbi with renewed appreciation, and no small amount of suspicion. "Did you?"

"Uh-huh." Bobbi leaned forward. "Tried to share it with you Bureau folks after Tom disappeared. You know, try and get his name cleared at least. But nobody wanted to hear it. I did it through anonymous submission, through hack informants I knew you people had . . . all the same thing. Nobody wanted to even look at what I had on hand. Certainly put things into perspective."

Silence for a moment, then Freida spoke. Her voice was flat. "I didn't hear about that," she replied. "And I should have. I'm the technical specialist over there, so I see everything that comes in via the Bureau net." Her pretty face turned hard and cold, and she looked down at her nails. "When was this?"

"Two years ago. Right after Orleans Hospital burned down."

"Orleans . . . " Freida looked back up. "Why is that important?"

Bobbi's brows arched. "Because that's where he was last," she replied, and she found herself getting very angry, very fast. "You people really just threw your hands into the air and left him to get hung, didn't you? I mean, I know he'd disappeared with me, but you didn't even bother to track him after that, did you?"

Freida spread her long-fingered hands in supplication, and her blue eyes were wide. "Look," she said, "I didn't have anything to do with this. I came here to try and figure out what happened to him."

"He blew up and died," Bobbi said, and she was shocked at how hollow her voice sounded as she voiced these words. "Burned with the hospital."

"Can you be so sure?"

Bobbi pursed her lips. "Look," she says, "You're a nice . . . a nice girl, and I can see you give a shit. But I don't want anything to do with the Bureau. Your people hung him out to dry, and I have no interest in getting hung up with him. I'll find my answers on my own, I think."

Freida paused. "Wait, wait." She shifted in her seat a bit, a prim frown lining her lips. "You're misunderstanding me. I said the Bureau doesn't know I'm here, but I didn't go into a lot of detail."

"Uh-huh." Beneath the table, Bobbi's hand slid slowly back to the grip of her nerve crusher. "You wanna illuminate me?"

There was a moment of silence as Freida's eyes tracked Bobbi's shifting shoulder, reading her mood. "I left the Bureau four months ago, Bobbi," she finally said. "I burned any ties I had with it." She looked down at her glass, at the delicate nails that tipped her slightly mannish hands. Waited for a reply.

Bobbi squinted at her. "Say what?"

"I said I've quit the Bureau." Freida looked back up at Bobbi now, seeking her gaze. "Wolsey's out – they put Gerald Exley in charge of the whole thing, and that man's turned as cold as a mech since Tom went underground. He started making some seriously dodgy decisions."

"Like drilling his partner?"

Freida gave Bobbi a puzzled look. "I don't understand what you're talking about."

"His partner, Brighton." Bobbi arched her brows. "You know who I'm talking about."

"Agent Brighton was transferred to another office," Freida said, her nose wrinkling.

Bobbi leaned forward again, both hands coming up to rest on the table. "Agent Brighton got transferred straight to Hell," she said darkly. "And it was Exley who pulled the trigger. Tom was there, man. He played cat and mouse with him before letting him go."

The expression on Freida's face was stormy as she listened; Bobbi couldn't tell if it was disbelief or if the woman had some suspicion that had just been confirmed. "I don't know," Freida said, frowning down at her drink. "I have to check on some things. Look, I'll get in touch with you in the next day or so – we'll meet on the network again. You don't have to worry about putting up barriers while you're in there now, it's not like we aren't on the same side."

"That a fact?" Bobbi's brows arched. "I'll take your word for it, honey, at least for now. You go make your confirmations or whatever, and let me know when you want to meet." She rose, then canted her head as she gave Freida one last surveying gaze.

". . . what is it?" Freida looked down at herself.

"Nothing." Bobbi pursed her lips. "Just it's a good look on you. You make an okay lady, honey. Maybe you shouldn't sell yourself too short."

Then Bobbi left, and the woman that had once been Arnold Kelley felt her cheeks burn as she sat alone in the sudden silence at her table.

CHAPTER 3

Bobbi felt a knot of fire tie itself in her chest as she stalked down the street from the Via Bella. By the time she made it to the end of the block, hot tears ran down her cheeks, making rivers of blood from her artfully sprayed makeup. She didn't know how to feel about what Freida had said; she had always thought that the Bureau had set their sights on Tom out of a lack of other targets, but this was just . . . this was a setup too, engineered by that damned Exley and probably under orders of that bitch Merducci as well. How she wished she could have been standing there right now, so that Bobbi could unload the full battery of her nerve crusher into that smiling, perfect face and roast it right on its sculpted scaffold! God, how she'd like it right now. To see that bitch, or Exley –

She realized what she was thinking, and she had to collect herself. Bobbi stopped at the corner, standing just under the awning of a Vectrex Media, where the smiling faces of Annie Taiga and Lorna Chan and a legion of other entertainment figures smiled down upon her like saints, and she willed the cauldron of her heart to settle down from its sudden boil. She knew that there would be no profit from letting this drive her crazy. She knew that this might have been the kind of thing that she would learn if she kept digging. She'd done everything that she possibly could short of hacking a major network to send the story out, and even then that wouldn't be any guarantee – she had done all of this, and nothing had happened. Genefex had prospered, Wonderland was even bigger, and now that fucker Exley was running the local Bureau office. So what the hell could she do?

Bobbi leaned against the video store's gleaming facade, retreating from the river of people that flowed in neat, traffic-controlled spurts throughout the New City. She had lived in this city for twenty-eight years; she had fought hard to live in the city's glittering herd, fought hard for her money and her prestige. Bobbi stared out at the crowd which collected on the corner. A trio of lean girls in Melanie Harrick boots tottered precariously on their towering heels, giggling to one another. A few years ago, she'd had simply thought, 'Damn, nice boots,' and then promptly gone on about her business. But now they seemed empty, vapid. A man in a black Vianni suit complained loudly about stock prices into his earbud phone underneath the streetlight.

Was this was how Tom had seen things? She had never understood his point of view, not entirely. Certainly she had seen her share of horrible things, but it had always seemed part of how things were, a natural process. Nature was a cruel and vicious thing at times, after all. Tonight, though, the increasing weight of revelation had shifted her perceptions. It all seemed so very synthetic to her, in a way she had never before realized. Maybe the facade wasn't just plastic; maybe it was action-figure time all the way down. Tom had believed that, and standing in the glow of the media store's glowing holographic signs she wondered very strongly if he might not have been right on the goddamned money.

It certainly gave her a lot to think about on the train ride home.

When Bobbi got back to the Temple, the club was much quieter than it had been. Last call had been sounded, and the cowboys who remained were draining their glasses in preparation to flee. She didn't bother to look at their faces; she knew she looked more than a little mad in her banshee getup and the tracks of bloody red that had dried on her cheeks. She just hoped that she could make it upstairs before –

"Bobbi?" Too late; Scalli had sighted her, and called to her from his place behind the bar. With the lack of a crowd she knew it was likely that he would spot her before she could make her escape; the big man's face was etched with concern as he came to the end of the bar. "Everything all right, girl?"

She mumbled something like 'Yeah, no problem' as Bobbi marched past him through the back door. Numbness spread through her body as she took the elevator to the top floor, and by the time she had arrived in Stadil's office, she found her upset transmuted into an incandescent fury. This was bullshit. This was bullshit! There was no way in hell that she was going to be turned into some weepy little sorority girl over this. She had been used by a dead man to kill another man, this she believed. A man that she had come – perhaps more quickly than she was comfortable with – to care about. Stadil had used her like a pawn, and he was an arm of that bitch and her company. So what was she going to do?

As far as she was concerned, Bobbi had two choices. She could sit around sniffling over the whole fucking thing, being paranoid about invisible hands guiding the world for the next fifty years until she overdosed on pints of ice cream, or she could just get that much angrier than she already was and do something about it. It wasn't like her to get sniffly over this kind of bullshit; she had the tools and the resources to go find out what the fuck happened, didn't she? As she stormed past the desk and headed into her room, bathed in the light of the screens that sprang up in her wake, she tried hard to push back the tide of emotion that threatened to crush her. She knew what she wanted to do; it was more a matter of how the fuck to do it.

Bobbi stepped through the doorway, and stopped as she saw Tom's coat in its shadow-box to the right. She turned toward it, and looking at the stained microfiber remembered a chain of faces, all of them his. His face when she'd met him, guarded and serious; how white and drawn he'd been when they'd managed to survive the ferals; how he seemed so hollow and thin when he'd pulled the Doll out from underneath the trash pile. Had it all been Stadil's fault? No, she thought, not entirely. The job would have killed him on its own. But better that, she believed, than to be fast-forwarded into oblivion by some asshole and his corporate masters.

She turned away from his coat and looked at her room. Bobbi could have afforded an apartment. Several. Hell, a house somewhere, if she'd wanted. She still maintained the warehouse she used to live in when she worked for Stadil, on the other side of the industrial pier on which the Temple sat. But there had been too many memories there for her now, and she let Scalli bunk there instead.

She had enjoyed the sparseness of the quarters there, however, and while it wasn't filled with packing crates or hanging sheets of plastic, the room was fairly empty. Her platform bed, small but very soft, taking up the center of the back wall. Pale gray and ivory bedsheets, real Egyptian cotton. The overstuffed black duvet. The long, squat slab of a Marco Almai dresser with its face like a single piece of ink, the lines between its shelves so thin as to be imperceptible to the eye. The little bathroom and its shower booth with its variable-tinted walls, which she always kept clouded white. Color was kept constrained to her closet, which she'd converted the remainder of the lounge into. The only real decoration was Tom's coat on the wall; she had thought about adding more, and certainly had intended to, but she just hadn't taken the opportunity. She couldn't say why.

Bobbi dropped onto the bed again, drew a deep breath, and closed her eyes. Maybe, when she opened them again, some sort of revelation would come to her.

Instead, there was a knock at the door.

"Yeah, come in," Bobbi called. She sat up. The door slid open to reveal Scalli's massive frame there, blotting out the light from the still-glowing display panels beyond him. He looked somewhat like a terrible djinn there, lit up as he was at the edge of Bobbi's darkened room, and his expression was grim.

"Hey," Bobbi said, her voice signing her fatigue. She wished he'd just leave her alone.

"Hey," he replied. Scalli looked over his shoulder at something for a moment. "You doing all right in here?"

She shrugged. "I'm all right. Just had a bad date." Bobbi rubbed at one eye with the back of her hand. "Listen, baby, can you..."

"Hey, don't you 'baby' me." Scalli's expression darkened, made even more terrible by the blue light behind him. "I've known you too long for that shit to work. What's going on?"

Bobbi stared at him for a long moment, then shrugged. "Look," she said, "don't worry about it. It's just a thing I had to go do, that's it."

"You never just go do 'a thing', either." Scalli reached for the light, but Bobbi raised her hand to stop him.

"Look," Bobbi said, her voice taking on an edge as she did so. "You're one of my oldest friends, Scalli, so you should know better than to poke me when I don't want to talk about something."

But Scalli would not be denied. "It's that dude again, isn't it? That Fed of yours."

Bobbi's eyes narrowed, and her voice turned to lead. "Back off, okay?"

"Not even by a goddamned foot," Scalli rumbled. He filled the doorway entirely now, arms crossed over his chest as he stared down at her. Bobbi shrank a little despite herself. All that stapled-up muscle of his made him look very much like some kind of hornless minotaur; all he needed was a ring through his nose and a pair of brazen hooves. "Now you listen here. I've been around, you know? Every time you go around trying to find out something about that man, you come back sadder and sadder – and I'm tired of seeing it, you know? I'm real sorry that he's disappeared, I am, but –"

"Scalli, you really need to –"

"But you need to back the hell off and leave it alone. Who the hell knows what's happened to you? He could've gone back to them. They could've put him under protection, gave him a new face! Hell, for all you knew he could be –"

"Okay, you know what?" Before she knew it she was on her feet, trembling with anger. "You know what? You need to shut the fuck up, Scalli. Shut the fuck up, because you don't know a damned thing about this whole situation. You hear me? You don't know shit. So why don't you go back downstairs and leave me the fuck alone?" She'd never bothered to take off her dress, and standing there in its punk lines and her green eyes boiling with rage amongst the red ruin of her makeup, the little woman was every bit as fearsome as her massive friend. Waves of brilliant anger radiated from her like heat from baking concrete, expanding her presence as if to fill the room. Bobbi heard her voice, the snarl in it like a beast's, and she actually managed to frighten herself.

She was used to going off these days; the cheerful, Devil-may-care girl she had been had faded dramatically in the last two years. But she had never screamed at Scalli, not even at his most smothering. He didn't shrink from her when she exploded, but the look on his face was all she needed to know that she'd gone too far. "Well all right, then," he said with a slow nod, and his face had become blank. "I guess I'll head out for the night." Then he was gone, leaving her standing there like the furious little punker she was – and it was that fury which drained out of her as the big man made his exit.

"Well, shit," she muttered, and fell back onto the bed. "Things just get better and better."

Three days passed in which Bobbi found herself hard-pressed for society. She didn't hear from Freida, which she wasn't certain was either good or bad, and Scalli had become quiet and businesslike as he went along his business downstairs. It was very discomforting to see her friend suddenly morph outwardly into an employee, and she felt like a real bitch about it. Which she should, she knew. Bobbi had no business blowing up on someone who had her best interests at heart, however ham-handed they might be in expressing it. Scalli hadn't deserved it, but he wasn't hearing anything more than job orders, or at the very least he wasn't acknowledging anything else she was saying – apologies, that sort of thing. She felt pretty damned miserable.

So on the fourth day, stuck between angry silence from Scalli and no word at all from Freida Kelley, Bobbi found herself in a thoroughly black mood. She didn't get up until late in the evening, content to lie in bed and stare at Tom's coat hanging on the wall. And feel sorry for herself, of course. Couldn't forget that.

When she rose, Bobbi eschewed her usual 'morning' ritual and called up a giant-sized monitor panel in order to watch the news. The far end of the room was suddenly aglow as the enormous screen leapt into place, the panels of light that usually made up her data wall melting into one. NewsNetNow's local feed came on, and Maya Frail's poreless, perfect face looked down upon her like a stern maiden goddess. " . . . the former Nissan-Sterling assembly plant in the Renton sector of the Decommissioned Suburban Zone. It isn't certain as to her involvement, but once again the individual known as Redeye seems to have once again thrust herself into the spotlight."

The picture behind Maya displayed what was billed as live feed from a NewsNetNow VTOL circling a scene of destruction at a distance. The factory complex was a hexagonal structure in the middle of a vacant, walled-in lot, large enough to have housed several assembly and fabrication centers. Before the Collapse it must have been a magnificent industrial structure, but it had died and long since begun to decompose in earnest. What had been left of its corpse had now been transformed into a pit of smoking embers as the feed now showed, its bones roasting on camera amid the glow of fires rising out of its shattered roof, and columns of smoke twisted slowly from within toward the evening sky.

"Civil Protection representatives have refused to comment on the explosion, which took place at 7:30 p.m. on Wednesday evening. Though authorities had proclaimed it to be an accident, NewsNetNow has obtained footage depicting a party of individuals on the scene soon after the incident took place."

As she spoke, the camera zoomed in to focus on a group of people sitting on a collapsed section of the wall that marked the borders of the old factory complex. It had been easy to miss them at first; they were dressed in scrounged and faded clothes, a mass of dark and dirty cloth and flesh in the shadow of the carnage. Most of them looked in various stages of crazy, from the way their faces were lit up with ecstasy at the sight of the factory's flames. All, Bobbi noted, except for one. A woman sat to one side, her face in profile, her expression grim but victorious as she stared on at the ruined factory. Her features were sharp and pretty, and unlike her disheveled companions her dark hair was sleek and clean as it poured over her shoulders. It was surprising; for some crazy bomb-queen like the news was making her out to be, she sure looked like she had her shit together.

One of the others turned and called for her attention; she turned to look at him, and Bobbi found herself jumping slightly at what she saw. The girl's eyes were surrounded by what looked at first like tattoos, but were in fact starbursts of thin scars around her sockets. One eye was dark, maybe brown or hazel, but the other was a livid, burning red. That baleful iris wasn't just tinted – it actually glowed, a dim point of light that shone like the cherry end of a cigarette as she stared back at the one who called to her. Words were exchanged, and then the knot of them were up and moving, disappearing into the dark with a speed that Bobbi had very rarely seen. She recognized it in the ferals of the Old City, in the skittering human horrors that too often populated its crumbling blocks. Bobbi remembered the blood that had coated Tom's car and shuddered.

"Though it has yet to be confirmed that she or her group had anything to do with it, the urban terrorist figure has been present for the destruction of four other locations in the DSZ, and is suspected of being involved in the murder of what Civil Protection has described as illegal salvage crews operating in the area. What significance could this act have? And who is Redeye? Professor Manuel Gonzalez-Ortega of Santiago University says he has the answer. "

Bobbi wrinkled her nose at that. Illegal salvage indeed – this is what you got when you had poor folk squatting in the big bad place that was the Old City. Why had they not gone and rebuilt the place yet? She thought of the profits to be found in urban redevelopment, especially so many years since the collapse. The New City was rich enough, wasn't it? Why not rebuild in earnest? Now the Professor's head appeared on the screen, weathered and urbane. "It seems obvious to me," he began, "yhat the individual known popularly as Redeye is simply one more in a long line of provocateurs symptomatic of the greater cultural consciousness. She is called a terrorist, but what crimes has she truly committed? The acts of her group – those that have been proven, those that she has allowed herself to be recorded in attendance of – these are very clearly more for attention than any real violation of the law. One must –"

As Bobbi watched, the system chimed and a mailbox window appeared superimposed over the Professor's face. She saw another stampless, anonymous message appear in her mailbox, and her heart leapt. After three days of being ignored by Scalli, dangerous mystery was a welcome creature with which to distract herself. The message appeared to be from Freida, requesting that Bobbi meet with her on her private server once more; thrilled to have something other to do than dodging Scalli and listening to Professor Snore drone on about the red-eyed girl, Bobbi plugged herself in straight away.

<Good evening.> Kelley was there, the name-presence of her handle floating in Bobbi's mind.

<Hi there,> Bobbi replied as Brain Mother. <What's up?>

There was a pause, seconds which felt like hours through the strange alchemy of the link. Caution flooded through Bobbi as she waited for a response, and she quietly prepared her defenses once more.

<I've been checking out some things,> Mysteron finally replied. <Thinking about what we talked about.>

<All right,> Bobbi replied. Her caution abated, but only slightly.

<I wanted to talk to Brighton, but it turns out that he's dead.>

<I think we covered that, yeah.> Bobbi allowed herself the grimmest little inward smile.

<That is to say, according to his service record, Brighton died six months ago during a raid on a drug facility in Chicago.> Another pause. <How did you say that he was killed?>

<Shotgun,> she replied without the slightest hesitation. <Tom said he was nearly cut in half with a shotgun. Took out a good portion of his chest with it. Burst fire, I guess.>

More silence. Tonight, Kelley/Mysteron felt as old as the machine she was operating from, some ancient computer program that required whole jarring seconds of processing before formulating a response. <The report says the same thing. There are pictures, everything. Severe damage to upper torso caused by a military-grade combat shotgun.>

At this, Bobbi felt a sting of vindication. <I told you, didn't I?>

<You did.>

<And how do you feel about that?>

<I don't know,> Kelley/Mysteron said. <I have a hard time believing that someone like Exley could be operating an office of the Bureau and killing off its operatives without their finding out.>

A flash of impatience shot through Bobbi's spine. Kelley might be a woman now, but she sure as hell was thinking like a man. <Look,> she said, <I told you that I had cracked the archive. You didn't ask me what was in it.>

<I was too surprised by what you'd said about Exley, I guess. Not very good police work on my part.>

<I'd get distracted too if I thought someone I was just working with had aced one of the folks at the office. Don't worry about it. Only I think you need to come out to my place. It's important that you see what this is all about. But then again . . . maybe you shouldn't. This thing, it's pretty much no-return sort of stuff, you know?>

A sigh-icon from Mysteron/Kelley. <I'm a big girl, I can handle it. It's not like I'm not expecting trouble anyway, meeting with you.>

<You're sure?> Bobbi felt herself tensing up at the idea. Maybe she should just call this off. Maybe she should destroy the file, hack the Bureau, smash every single copy that existed –

<I'm sure,> said Mysteron/Kelley, cutting off her train of thought. <I . . . need to know, I think. Tom was my friend too, more than I think he realized. >

Well, that sounded suspect, Bobbi thought. <Fine, then. Come out to my place.>

<All right. You're still operating The Temple?>

<Until I get a better offer, sure. Or someone burns it down.>

<Jesus. Don't jinx yourself like that!>

<These days, honey? Let's just say I make sure my insurance is paid up.>

An hour or so later Bobbi was working at her desk, approving expenditures for the bar downstairs and working on her third cup of coffee. It was prime operating time, and the crowd on the floor was deep into its cups as they did business among themselves; Bobbi had briefly flirted with the idea of setting up listening cones in the maze of exposed ductwork that ran over the club floor, but she had ultimately decided against becoming The Man in her own right. She glanced at the security monitors; the bar was lined with people, boys and girls in leathers and street clothes jockeying with each other for Scalli's attention. Punks and street creatures, underground intelligentsia all. Heaven help the human race, she thought, when the smartest folks are the ones crammed into bars at night plotting all kinds of larceny.

"Bobbi." Scalli's voice sprang forth from hidden speakers in the room. "Are you up there?"

Bobbi reached for a display and keyed the intercom. "I'm here," she replied. "What's up?"

The big man's image shifted behind the bar; he had been serving a drink to a girl in ancient monobike racing leathers, black with faded yellow warning stripes spray-painted on the shoulder and elbow pads. A thick cable of black hair hung down her back. Now he looked straight up into Camera Seven, and grim irritation was plain on his face.

"I got a visitor down here for you," Scalli growled, and nodded toward the dark-haired girl. "Says she's expected."

"Have her turn around," Bobbi began, but as she said this the girl did just that. Grinning up at the camera was Freida Kelley. "Ah. Nevermind. Send her up."

"Sure." Scalli waved Freida on toward the back door, and now looked positively stormy. Bobbi sighed and shook her head – they were going to have to talk about the whole thing soon.

Bobbi had enough time to look back toward the elevator and take a sip of coffee before it opened, and Freida appeared. "I'm here," she announced, giving Bobbi a bit of a nod. "Sorry if I made you wait. Had to get tarted up a little."

Bobbi's lips quirked into a lopsided smile. "So I see," she said, amused. "Do you change your looks around a lot?"

"I do if I'm visiting a hack dive in the middle of the Verge," Freida said with a chuckle, then walked across to drop herself into one of the chairs that Stadil had set up in front of the desk for visitors. "My usual look's a little Sally Ready, don't you think?"

Bobbi snorted. "Yeah. You like your boutiques, that's for sure."

"Says the girl who showed up in Miri Bendis – or whatever was left of her." Freida's blue eyes seemed to sparkle when she smiled, which she did so in earnest now. "I read a lot of fashion magazines – they suggest you do so in therapy. When you go through the change, I mean."

"Ah." Bobbi paused, looking down at her own brick-colored jeans and her ancient Red Cross tank top. She was suddenly very aware that there was a hole in it near her navel. Self-conscious. "Well, you definitely got the New City look down, that's for sure," she said, looking back up to Kelley, "so good for you. We're all street beasts down this way."

Kelley gave her a look of playful exasperation and laughed. "Yes, well, you looked amazing the other night. You can't beat a lady's innate style with study, you know. At any rate, you got something you wanted to show me?"

Bobbi wondered at the shift in Kelley's personality from the other night, but she chalked it up to Kelley having her game face on. "Yeah," Bobbi said. "You want it visual, or do you want to wire up?"

"I'll take it directly," Freida said with a nod, and reached up to extract the dustplug from a socket that Bobbi now saw gleaming behind her ear.

She plugged the short, blunt cone of a wireless receiver into the socket and nodded. "Whenever you're ready."

"Set your skull rig to accept a link from a box named A7B7C7," she said, and when Kelley had nodded again she reached for a holographic panel. "Here you go." Bobbi keyed the cloistered server box she had prepared for this purpose; the little thing was like the ghost-boxes downstairs, autistic save for a wire terminal or a one-way, short ranged wireless unit. Instantly, Kelley stiffened as she felt the contact, and her eyes widened in that strange, faraway fashion that only the Awakened had. Well, the Awakened and the brain-dead. But Freida's brows were arched high as her brain accessed the data, her glassy eyes wide despite the fact they currently could not see. "Shit," she whispered, and in the quiet of the office the word sounded like a prayer. "How far does this all go?"

"You just keep looking, honey," Bobbi said with a sigh. "And you'll find out. Just remember that I warned you."

CHAPTER 4

No matter how strong one's words may be, there really is no warning people against revelation. Once she had finished going through the file, Freida just sat there for a while. Her expression was . . . awed. Pained and angry. Bobbi knew that look; she and Tom had both worn variations of it once they had first gone through the collection and realized that there had been a single invisible hand guiding the damnation of society. All of the dark technology coming out of Wonderland, all the maddening perversities that seemed like so much black magic – all of these were helmed by a single entity, a single woman at the helm of a massive corporation. Billions of dollars in funds, legal and illicit, all spiraling toward a company which promised not only all of these dark pleasures, but a virtual eternity thanks to telomeric lengthening.

It seemed impossible; it seemed like something out of fiction. And yet, spelled out in digitally signed, imprinted data copy, was the evidence. Evidence which, had Brighton not gotten blasted across the floor of the First Ebezener Baptist Church over it, could perhaps have been waved off as an extremely clever fake – something to cover the acts of some other, lesser organization. And yet she had last seen Tom at a Genefex installation, and the horrors inside as Civil Protection had attempted to clash with the laboratory's sentinels. She had made sure that Freida had witnessed the recordings that Bobbi had made of the pale, ghoul-like things which so readily threw themselves into the police guns, and tore apart the invading troopers. She had made sure that Freida realized precisely what she had come to believe, and that was this: that if there was a true force of active evil in this world it would be the Genefex corporation, and Ghia Merducci was the Devil.

"I can't believe it," Freida finally said, and her voice was tiny. "I just . . . I can't believe it."

Bobbi gave Freida a thin smile. She knew that reaction all too well, and pity welled up in her to see it. "Well, you'd better get started, honey," she told the now dark-haired woman. "Because as fucked up as it is, the truth ain't going away." Bobbi got up from her seat behind the desk and waved her hand; all at once the glowing panels of the displays surged and vanished, leaving them in the far feebler light of the overhead lamps. "Bet you'd like a drink."

"Yeah," Freida said softly. She looked at her hands a moment, which were folded in her lap, as if she had to will them to pluck the wireless receiver from the port in her skull and replace the dustplug. Dazed as she was, however, she had clarity enough to turn and watch Bobbi walk over to a low, ornate cabinet which turned out to be a mini bar. "Uh, whisky, please." She blinked herself into the world a little more. "Better make it a double."

Bobbi smiled to herself as she took out a plastic bottle of Suntory Old and began to pour it into a pair of heavy crystal tumblers. "Hope you don't mind the Japanese stuff," she said, "because I don't think I wanna leave you alone long enough to go down and get the 'Fiddich." Bobbi walked back to the desk and handed Freida one of the glasses, sipping from the other herself. "You gonna be okay?"

Freida didn't answer at first, instead taking a deep draught from her own glass. She shut her eyes as the stuff burned a path back to reality down the back of her throat. "I think I will be now," she said with a smack of her lips. "Fuck, lady. None of that was a hoax at all, was it?"

"Not a bit of it," Bobbi said with a shake of her head. "Sorry if you thought I was bullshitting you before. I definitely wish I was."

Freida took another, smaller sip. "I don't even want to believe it," she said with a grim shake of her head. "All that time, you know, we knew that Wonderland was helping ruin things. But we didn't realize that it was behind so much."

Bobbi nodded. "Yeah," she said, swirling her own scotch slowly in her glass, "it does sound like the scariest kind of bullshit story. But I don't think it is. I saw those Special Tactics cops getting torn apart by those horrible things – and you saw that one girl. The one that looked like Merducci."

"She killed those troops with her bare hands," Freida said, and again her voice was quiet with awe. "And she moved so fast . . . I mean, I've seen augmented, but that . . . "

"Like something out of a goddamned nightmare," Bobbi said with a shake of her head. "I know. Tom said he killed another one like her in the underlevels."

"He must have been very lucky." After saying this, Freida sat up sharply and stared at Bobbi. Her eyes blazed, fierce and bright with sudden fury. "We can't let them get away with it, Bobbi," she said, her voice hard. "We can't. We can tell the Bureau – "

"And get you shot in the face, yes," Bobbi said with a rueful smile. "And at the very least get me put into a cryoprison. Career criminal over here, remember? Seems to me that going to the authorities is the absolutely worst thing that we could do. Besides, I sent the contents of the archive to the Bureau, and it didn't make so much as a blip – with Exley in charge it's most likely been suppressed. Which means he's just waiting for someone to show up and claim they had the information."

Freida's eyes widened a little, and she looked as if she were about to protest – but instead she deflated, sagging against the back of her chair, and nodded. "I guess you're right," she said softly, and looked down into what was left of her scotch. "And if Exley's connected to all this, then he's just waiting for someone to put their head out."

"So you can see my position." Bobbi drained the rest of her glass and set it aside. "Or our position, now, I suppose. Well congratulations, Alice, you're at my end of the rabbit hole."

With a shake of her head, Freida got up and began to pace in a slow circle. "The question is, of course, this: where do we go with this? What do we do? Genefex is the largest biotechnological concern on the planet, and it's obviously got resources that far outstrip the reaches of an everyday corporation. Shall we found a revolution? Take out Merducci with a rifle at a press conference? How do you discredit a creature like this?"

The two were silent for a long time, Bobbi moving to give them both another double. She was right, of course. How could they fight something like this? They'd already dug up a great deal of information on the situation; they could just let the whole thing go, content with knowing an already horrible truth, and live out their lives in the shadow of it. They'd killed anyone who'd had anything to do with it. They'd killed . . .

"They haven't killed me yet," Bobbi said finally.

"I'm sorry?" Freida looked at her from across the room, looking startled.

"They haven't killed me yet." Bobbi took her seat behind the desk again, setting her glass down in front of her and cradling it both hands.

"No, look. This whole conspiracy has gone around killing off whomever it was who was attached to it. Thinking about it now, I'm the only part of the whole thing – that is, who wasn't a willing part of it – who hasn't ended up dead or vanished. What do you think about that? Why do you think that is?"

"I don't know." Freida shook her head, frowning again at her glass. "I mean, it's possible that you just weren't necessary to remove, right? Or maybe Stadil protected you."

Bobbi made a soft growl in the bottom of her throat at that. "Old Anton," she muttered. "Yeah, that's entirely possible. You'd think that after two years I'd have thought about this but I honestly hadn't considered it. Anton was a planner – a real spider, you know. Maybe he had some other plan for me here. But I've scanned this whole office, the whole building in fact, and I couldn't find anything concerning this whole revelation that he had worked out for Tom. It's like he was waiting for us to figure it out for ourselves."

"Yeah, maybe." Freida shook her head. "Well, what do you want to do about it?"

"Well, I know what I'm going to do," said Bobbi. "But you don't have to do a damned thing. You wanted to know the truth, and I've shown it to you. That's all you really have to worry about." She shook her head and tilted her head back, letting the renewed flood of whiskey burn itself down her throat in a steady, pulsing tide; she felt her head buzz as the alcohol tried to kick in and her cranial implants cut in to take the edge off. Yes, she'd have to dig deeper, wouldn't she? It's not as if her mind would let her do anything else. She had to know what had happened to Tom, and what Stadil had truly planned for them. Something still tickled in the back of her mind; she could not accept that all that he had done was simply send Tom into the hands of the company.

Freida stared at her for a long moment. The fierceness in her eyes was there again, and Bobbi knew the decision which she had been expecting had been made. "No way in hell am I leaving this alone now," Freida said with a shake of her head. "Besides, we live in the city where Genefex is headquartered, right? We're actually in a better position to affect the corporation here. Merducci is here, too. The board must be here, as well – or at least they have to meet here. If we can operate without falling afoul of the Bureau or Civil Protection there's no reason why we couldn't do real and permanent damage to the whole thing."

"We're most likely going to get killed," Bobbi pointed out. "I need you to be realistic about that. I'm doing this because I got a score to settle, and I'm obsessive about mysteries anyway. But you . . . "

"I worked with the Bureau for four years," Freida rumbled. "And in that time I've dealt with enough of the dark shit that comes out of Wonderland to want to burn the whole fucking thing down. Fuck 'em all. If I can help tear the heart out of that place then you bet I'll stand up to be counted. It's not like I've never had my life endangered in the field before."

There was no arguing with her, Bobbi saw. The fire in her eyes was the same as what burned in Bobbi's heart, reflected in clear, sharp blue. "All right then," she said with a slow nod, "I guess that we're in business. I suppose first things first: where do we go from here?"

"We start with Orleans." Freida reached for her glass and held it out to Bobbi in a toast. "Pick up the trail from there. Slainte."

"Yeah, cheers," Bobbi said with a nod, clinking her glass against Freida's. "So all right. It sounds like you still have some access to the Bureau, from what you've said. Getting Brighton's records and such."

"Something like that," Freida said with a nod. "So I'll dig up what the Bureau has on the situation. I can tell you now, there was nothing in the report about any load of Civil Protection troopers getting ripped to pieces."

Bobbi nodded; she'd heard this story before. "I know," she said. "Nothing but the explosion, which they blamed on the incinerators going up. Accident, they said. Which, of course, was me. They didn't explain why there was a mass of cops down there either – in fact, as I recall, they didn't even mention that the cops were there at all."

Freida drained her glass and put it down hard on the desk, getting up at the same time. "Well, that does it. I've got to see what's going on there. I'll see what I can find, and you . . . do whatever it is you plan on doing."

"I have a few ideas." Bobbi gave her another ghost of a smile. "We will see what we can come up with."

When she had said "a few ideas," the truth was that Bobbi had zero. But this was no problem, really; once she said it, her brain tended to work in such a way that an answer would soon conjure itself into being. Freida had left soon after that, and Bobbi found herself alone in her office again as the rumbling beat of the music downstairs was a dim and distant storm. Bobbi listened to the sound echo softly up the elevator shaft, then decided to drown herself in the network again. She would return to the source, which meant to go back over the data she had compiled about Stadil. With Freida having revealed herself, though, Bobbi felt like she had some kind of a partner. Some kind of a chance. This was assuming, of course, that the comely transgendered woman was not some kind of plant meant to dig into the conspiracy using Bobbi as her contact. Bobbi thought about that as she shuffled through the Stadil data, building a precis.

When the computer was ready, she sat down and began to go over it. There were the summaries detailing the structure of the whole web, from the black laboratories to the research companies and plantations to their controlling subsidiaries and Genefex atop them. The corporation was the capstone of the pyramid, constantly looking down upon the operation like a vast and terrible eye. There were the reports, signed by Merducci's hand. There were the balance sheets, detailing transactions worth billions. Never the names of clients, of course, just middle-men and criminal outfits. Should she contact them? How vulnerable would that make her? Should she start down the same path that Anton did, running things for the horrible corporation while she attempted to destroy it from the inside? It was possible, after all. It could be done.

But Bobbi the Kingpin wasn't a role that she could see herself being placed in. Gray though her interests might be, she didn't do things that she outright knew would harm innocent people. She might be a little bent, but she wasn't broken. Not yet. Heaving a deep sigh she called up more data on the battery of floating displays, sitting at her desk, a sorceress calling up evil spirits. One of them had a list of all Genefex properties in the Seattle area, upon which Orleans Hospital had been prominent. There were a good deal of them, twenty or thirty. Many of them were in the Old City, which surprised Bobbi at first, but in the end made sense. The company could afford security, after all, and even the horrible crazies out there could provide some measure of experimental material. They were well out of the sight of Civil Protection as well. All that space to get lost in . . . yes, she could see why Merducci would choose to roost in the wilds.

Bobbi turned her attention to another window as the list scrolled on, frowning at a letter from a Genefex executive to some criminal fucker over in Wonderland. Lots of messages going to Bangkok and Phuket. There was the order for the Princess Dolls, for whom Bobbi also had the schematics but no means of understanding them. She wasn't scientific, after all, just technical. The horror presented by those little girls had been in the fact that they hadn't been little girls at all, not for a long time; they had been once, then they had been snatched off the street and had their brains entirely removed – not simply replaced in part by biosynthetic computer modules but entirely swapped for massive memory constructs meant to try and host human personalities. They had been not simply sexual creations but an attempt to completely get around the body question, immortality through consciousness transfer. It would have changed the world if it had worked, but the personalities transferred didn't change or grow beyond their initial limits. The company had given them up for failures, transferred them to a Wonderland broker, who in turn sold the three girls to a very high-profile executive here in Seattle. Stadil had handled the sale. Stadil, for whom she had worked. Stadil, who had sent her to see to Tom when his investigation into the Dolls began here in the city.

It always came back to this. The giant question mark. Bobbi scowled at the data floating before her. Something about it bothered her, something new that she could not put her finger on. What was it about the data that seemed different to her now? She leaned back in her seat, reaching for the bottle of Suntory that she'd left on the desk after Freida left, and was in the process of screwing off the top when realization came singing to her. Her eyes were drawn back to the slowly scrolling list of facility locations; she reached for the window, dipping her fingers into it, 'pulling' it so that it scrolled the other way. Addresses scrolled past, addresses she didn't recognize, and then – there it was.

Bobbi sat back hard and frowned. Surely this wasn't right. It couldn't be. And yet there it was, an entry for what was listed as 'TISSUE PROCESSOR 017.' The name was bad enough; Orleans had also been marked as a 'tissue processor', and from what little Tom had said from the premises, it had apparently been like something out of nightmare. But it was the address that truly gave her a shock – it was the address of the automotive complex that had been on the news earlier that very evening.

No way in hell was that right, Bobbi thought at first, and yet when she looked up the story on the NewsNetNow nexus and cross-referenced it with a pre-Collapse municipal index, she had no choice but to believe. Suddenly this woman had become her new focus, and she accessed the NewsNetNow nexus again to track through the news outlet's archive of material concerning her.

As Maya Frail said in her broadcast, Redeye and her group – whose numbers seemed to be growing with every appearance – had struck four other locations in the Old City since the year before. Bobbi went back through the list of secret facilities, comparing them with the addresses of the locations that had been bombed. Sure enough, they matched. A thrill of something that was best described as horrified delight shot up her spine as she went over their locations. Two more tissue processors, numbered 07 and 012, hidden in an old bodega and an abandoned garage. A warehouse had concealed Data Nexus 231. Now they had bombed the factory, which had been listed simply as Assembly Plant 29.

What purpose did these facilities have? How was Redeye and her group – who looked from Bobbi's point of view to be nothing but a band of crazy nomads – capable of destroying such facilities? And what about what was inside them? She had seen what had defended Orleans, the white ghouls and the quicksilver devils that were their champions. If fully armed and armored police troopers were massacred at a single site, then how the Hell were these people able to bomb four different ones on their own? Bobbi remembered the woman's expression, that look of grim victory, and she shook her head. There was something really nasty to learn there, and a wave of chill crashed down over her – not because it would be terrible, but because she knew that she would not be able to avoid finding out what it was.

CHAPTER 5

That night she dreamt about the jungle, about a thin, dirty girl carrying a spear made of swirling alphanumerics. The foliage was lurid and vaguely pixelated, like the scenery of an old computer game. Bobbi recognized herself in the girl, had recognized the way she walked, the way she tracked a trail through the undergrowth as she made her way toward her quarry – which had been a massive old beast of a tiger lurking in the undergrowth. It came out from under an overgrown outcropping to meet her dream self, who drew the spear back in readiness, and Bobbi had seen that the beast was beautiful. Radiantly so, a real thing in the synthetic forest; white fur and silver eyes, gleaming with hate and superiority. She was staggered by the sight of it, the awesome complexity and grace of its form, long enough for it to bare fangs made of glimmering fractals . . . .

Bobbi awoke in her bed, sweating in the darkness. Dreams were so goddamned stupid. Jungles? Really? Goddamned horrible silver eyes? Leave it to her imagination to choose this time to start dreaming mysteries.

But of course, she told herself as she rose and padded toward the shower, she knew what the dream was about. It was obvious. She was diving into this whole thing once again, and she knew that would put her eventually at odds with Genefex. More to the point, it would put her at odds with the company's silver-eyed ghoul of a founder. And then there was the girl . . .

With a sigh, Bobbi stripped and stepped into the shower booth, turning on the water. Instantly she was drowned in heat, allowing it to wash away the memory of the traitorous dream and the thin girl she'd seen there. She would not let her subconscious ruin things. She had to be better than that. Bobbi closed her eyes tightly, let the water do its work, and soon had emerged refreshed and pink with the heat and with new determination.

Checking the news yielded nothing that had anything to do with her investigation, though it looked like Germany had finally solved the takeover crisis and had solidified into an independent corporate state once again. Civil Protection was out in force after a string of robberies in Belltown. NewsNetNow's local feed was pretty mum on anything that happened in the Verge, of course, unless it was really newsworthy. Tim Angle's turn on screen today, chiseled features and white teeth. He'd been an actor a few years ago but he'd given it up for news. Weirdest damned thing.

Bobbi went down to the bar floor to see Scalli. He was looming behind the bar as usual, stalwart against the dull thrum of whatever it was playing on the sound system. Kings of Clemency, an old band. Liberty-rock from the fifties, the last gasps of American jingoist culture. Strange choice. Sandy was pouring pints of Tsingtao from gleaming taps, favoring her with a smile.

"Hey, Scalli," Bobbi called, looking past Sandy after returning the smile and fixing her eyes on the enormous man. "Got a minute?"

Scalli looked at her, his expression artfully casual. "Yeah, boss," he replied with a shrug, and followed after her when Bobbi ducked back into the storeroom. She felt his dark eyes on her back as she walked, felt tension mount between them like a tether. She was ready for an altercation, and so was he. At least if they got into a shouting match, they couldn't be heard over the guitar choruses of the Kings.

"All right," he said as the door sealed behind them, "what did you want?"

It was a challenge, and no mistake. Bobbi took a deep breath before she turned on him, brushing a few strands of violet out of her eyes. "All right," she began, "listen. I want to apologize. I want you to listen to me, please."

Scalli said nothing, filling up the room with a silence that made his bulk seem tiny by comparison. Bobbi took that to be her cue and so she kept on. "Now I know we've been friends for years."

"Ten years," Scalli said grimly.

"Right. Ten years."

"Since you hit town, in fact."

". . . . okay, yes, since I got to town." Bobbi wrinkled her nose. "Look. We've known each other a long damned time, it's true. I know we've not always been best buddies or whatever, but we've always looked out for each other. And I know you've got..." She paused, selecting her words carefully. "...sentiments, and I appreciate that. But I just haven't wanted to get you involved with this thing with Tom. I know you're trying to look out for me, but it's just..."

Scalli shifted, his arms crossing over his massive chest. "Yeah?"

Bobbi drew a breath. "Okay, look. Tom and I, we had a thing." She closed her eyes a moment, trying to put it into words. "And I don't know that I can describe it as more than that. We had strong feelings for each other, and we got into a lot of shit. You know a little about it."

"I know you two came out of the Old City looking like you drove through a slaughterhouse," Scalli said. "And that you wouldn't tell me why. Don't think I believe anything about body retrieval, because that little girl was more than that. I'm not stupid. I know what she was."

It was like a slap in the face. Bobbi stood there a moment, stunned. "Okay," she said, unable to really reply more to that. "So, I guess you kind of know what were up to a little."

"And I know he was being hunted by the Feds."

". . . yeah, that's true." Bobbi felt her back stiffen as she spoke; this wasn't going well. Scalli had never told her half of what he knew or didn't know about the situation, and these revelations were only throwing her off balance even more. She might have initiated the conversation, but she was hardly master of it now. "Look," said Bobbi in an attempt to rectify that, "the point is, I didn't want to drag you into it. There's a lot of unanswered questions. I know you think that he's still around, and maybe he is, but I . . . if he's still alive, it ain't in any form or fashion that he'd be comfortable with." The words were like hooks in her heart as she said them, but they needed to be said for both their sakes. "This ain't about saving him, Scalli, it's about finding out what the hell happened to him. This is for me. I can't just let it flap in the wind, here. I gotta know." She hoped that his would calm him, or at the very least smooth things out a little; the questions his words had sparked in her mind would have to wait until a later time to be processed.

Scalli said nothing again; he leaned against the concrete wall, looming as if he were an extrusion of it. His expression was still as flat as it was before she'd spoken in the first place. Finally he spoke, with a kind of tired voice that she'd heard other kids' fathers use. Resigned. "All right," said Scalli, shaking his head. "All right. I guess I understand. And I wasn't exactly being fair to you by bringing it up, either – just I worry about you, honey, you know? I worry that you're gonna get killed over what seemed to me like courting a cryopen, or worse."

He shook his head, and Bobbi knew that she was off the hook. She came up and put her arms around Scalli's massive torso, hands stopping just past his kidneys, and sighed. "You're good people, baby," she said, and she meant it. "I'm really sorry I went batshit on you. It's just been hard, you know? He just vanished, and the circumstances were fucking awful, and I just . . . " And she was hugging him hard before she knew it, not crying but close, mad at herself and at Scalli and his pushiness, and even more so at Stadil and his ridiculous plots. She was mad at the world, and at that bitch and her company, and all the horrible things that had happened under her watch. Most of all, though, she was mad at Tom – for vanishing, for leaving her with his puzzle that she absolutely had to solve. It took a lot for her not to break down again, the maddened, wailing beast that was her temper swirling around inside of her, but she managed it down just as Scalli put his wide hand upon her back.

"It's all right, Bobbi," he murmured, his voice deep and gentle. "I get it now. You need help, you just ask me."

She took a step back, surprise bringing forth a laugh that sounded more like half a sob. "Jesus, Scalli," Bobbi said, shaking her head, "Didn't I just tell you? I didn't want to drag you into this before, and I sure as hell don't want to now. Even if you do know more than I thought you did, which I must admit I'm awfully damned curious about."

Scalli scowled faintly and shook his head. "Relax," he said, stepping over to a nearby beverage case and taking out a can of Coca-Cola. He smacked the base against the side of the case to chill it, pulled the tab and took a deep swig before continuing. "Before you start putting me into any of your conspiracy theories, chalk it up to my past experiences. You know how I used to do security before I came to work for you, right?"

Bobbi nodded. "Freelance," she said. "I remember."

"Right." Scalli gestured faintly with his busy hand, the Coke can like a baton. "I saw Princess Dolls before when I was working as a body man for a Mitsubishi exec. It's the skin, you know, the artificial blood gives them away. No big mystery there."

She hadn't thought about that. "All right," Bobbi said, "I can see that. What about the rest?"

"Well, that's the more interesting part." He tilted the can back, draining the remainder of his Coke down that enormous throat of his. He let out a loud sound of pleasure and tossed it into a waste bin, shook his head, and sighed. "Right. Okay, so just around the time he disappeared, you remember when you said he got a new face? When I urged you to go and get a makeover, make yourself feel better?"

"Yeah." Bobbi frowned a little bit and took a seat on the edge of a counter. She'd forgotten she had told him that. "I thought you were just trying to help."

"Well, I was," he said with a nod. "I was. See, I still keep up with the underground boards, you see? Mostly so if I ever start working again I don't lose any opportunities, but also because I like to keep an eye out for trouble."

"And you found it, I guess."

Scalli nodded again. "Yeah. Around that time, someone put out a pretty sizable contract on your boy. Capture or nonlethal incapacitation, three hundred thousand straight up. They'd included the description of a woman with him that sounded suspiciously like someone that I knew. And before you ask, no, the contract isn't still open. Almost as soon as it had it was retracted, on account of your man disappearing." He spread his hands. "So you're in the clear."

Bobbi stared at him for a long moment. She wasn't sure how she should feel, if she should be angry or touched, or what – so she settled on irritated gratitude. ". . . well thank you very much, Marcus," she said, using his first name to show how she felt, "but I sure wish you'd have told me this before. Do you know who it was that put it up?"

"Yeah," Scalli said, turning to pick through bottles of beer. "But the name didn't ring a bell."

"Try me."

Scalli plucked a bottle of Heineken from the rack, gave her a look that said 'well, I told you so.' "'Cagliostro', the name was."

Bobbi frowned a little bit. "Cagliostro," she repeated, mulling it over. "Cagliostro. What is that?"

"Italian," Scalli said.

"What's it mean?"

He shrugged. "I don't know. It's just a name."

Bobbi wrinkled her nose. "Isn't 'Scalli' Italian?"

He made a face, reached inside the drinks case for another Coke. "Doesn't give me access to the vast racial memory of my mother's people, girl." He shook his head. "So anyway, that's what I know. What are you gonna do with it?"

"Gonna go drill that black board you were talking about, see what I can find." She shrugged. "Gonna need the address, of course."

"Yeah," said Scalli with the slightest hint of a sigh, "I figured that'd be the case."

Cagliostro. The name was unfamiliar to her, another bogeyman. What was it? A name? A hack handle? Some cute little alias? Bobbi sat at her desk, drinking from a tumbler of Suntory and feeling very curious indeed as she plowed through fields of data. Screens floated everywhere around her, each of them filled with some detail or another – some of it from the archive, some of it more mundane information.

Scalli had given her the network address of the black workboard that he still frequented, which was disguised as a discussion forum for old Horizon Rangers action toys; she had ghosted in on the back of some other dude who was logged in at the time, piggybacking his access profile. She had rode it Awake, getting her money's worth out of the latest version of Hyoong Lance, the subtle knife of modern underground intrusion software, guiding its hand personally, ensuring that she wasn't detected.

Bobbi was still mad at him for not telling her about the contract before, but considering the situation she didn't exactly blame him either – no, she appreciated it, the care he felt for her. It was nice to have a friend, especially when you were digging into a mile of black-magic crazy like this was turning out to be. She wondered if Freida knew about it, and if not, if she should tell her. Well, Bobbi had told her the rest, hadn't she? Unless it turned out that she was the enemy after all it could only help efforts to inform her. As she had made contact with the workboard's databases and unplugged herself from direct connection, she had wondered what it was that Freida might be finding out on her own.

It didn't take long before she found what she was looking for. Black workboards were supposed to erase records cleanly so as not to endanger contracting parties. But as Bobbi had hoped, there were no less than ten years' worth of contracting data in storage. Well, thought Bobbi, that's good luck for me then. And after a little bit of searching there it was, just as Scalli had said. The terms were as he had laid them out, too: capture or nonlethal incapacitation, Tom and an unknown associate. Only the face was his original, and the description of the woman supposed to be her was pretty sketchy – but then again you didn't need much to point her out, big pink cockatiel hairstyle like she had back then. 'Nice ass', it had said. She liked that. The contract had run for exactly three days, then it was retracted without anyone reporting in.

Bobbi considered it all. Three hundred thousand dollars . . . well, it was expensive enough for professionals, though she imagined that it would have been more expensive to try and corral a federal agent and keep him locked up than it would be just to dust him. There was no record of a node of origin, or even a trail that she could extrapolate – the message was a mystery, a ghost letter that appeared and disappeared without the slightest trace. And that was very interesting to Bobbi, because she'd done the ghost-job before. There was always some kind of a trace. You didn't just appear out of thin air, or data as the case might be.

Maybe it was new technology, some kind of hardware module or even a heretofore unknown stealthing program. However it was done, it meant that this Cagliostro character was either a datanaut of supreme ability, or had access to such a person. Bobbi shivered internally; it would be like challenging Michelangelo to an art contest, going against someone like that. As good as she was, Bobbi didn't see herself as a contemporary of any equivalent of the Great Mikey. At least, not yet.

Bobbi sat up, pursing her lips and reaching for her interface jack. Too many strange people – Frieda, Redeye, and now this Cagliostro fellow. Too many unknown elements. Inquiries would have to be made; people would have to be spoken to. She'd need to get some information on this guy, the best way to do it would be to speak to Pierre about him. Her fingers hovered there, floating just over the edges of the dustplug stuck in her socket. It had been a very long time since she'd used Pierre for anything, and egotist that he was, he'd probably assume she'd been using someone else and refuse to work with her. She figured have to do some convincing, and she wasn't going to kiss his boots. Conflict would probably arise.

When she finally went to see him, however, there was little in the way of a problem. Tense moments showing up, some sass thrown her way by Pierre's belle du jour, but ultimately a little coyness and a bit of an apology worked wonders to get the Frenchman leaning her way again, especially when she produced her account balance. The relationship patched, Bobbi had Pierre run a go-to on Cagliostro in an attempt to try and get some info on this mysterious bogeyman, and also to try and drum up some information on Redeye; the former would probably be more difficult than the latter, but she left it in his hands to see what could be drummed up. The smirking bastard made sure she paid dearly for it, too, but she figured it was better than the alternative.

Scalli had decided to play chauffeur for her, which had annoyed Bobbi at first. He drove a streamlined tank of a Mitsubishi Flare that he had modded up to accept his bulk; no passenger seat, the wheel in the middle and the canopy jacked up to fit him. He still looked like an ogre in a go-kart, but he'd given up his old transport truck in order to look more refined. The idea of her riding around in the back of his absurdity-mobile softened her enough that she agreed, though they stopped at a Rocket Chef drive-thru for some Maxi-Buns and Coke Ultras. She sat in the back of Scalli's ridiculous car, munching at her sloppy, print-protein burger and sipping melon cola through a twisted straw, watching the city loom past her as he drove her back toward Alki Point and home. It really was like a different place, this city she had called her home since she was old enough to remember. It had always been a bad old town, she knew that. It had always been sinful and selfish, but people had just always been like that. She'd done more work for rich, sinful people than she could remember. History was like that, if you cared enough to read it – full of people wanting to get illegal shit done.

And yet, as they drove along the freeway past the city, and Bobbi watched the Waters district rise like a glittering palatial complex from the New City's neon heart, it seemed to her that history's old patterns had given rise to something new and empty. She thought about how plastic the world had seemed to her, just after having met with Freida for the first time, how the towers they now passed appeared more like malevolent giants than mere structures. Humanity was a bad animal, she already knew – but there was Wonderland now, a whole goddamned parallel nation of black market laboratories and vice, built to bring out the worst in the species. And worse still, there was a goddamned corporation behind it. Bobbi had heard once that if you applied psychological standards to the corporation as an individual, as a person which corporations were still legally considered as being, they'd rack up as the worst of psychopaths every time. She'd never given that much credit, being a theory from over a hundred years ago, but it sure as hell seemed right on the bead to her now.

Put psychopaths in charge of the world, and you get a world that's eventually ruled by psychopathic behavior.

And there she was, sipping a Coke in a society possibly dominated not just by corporate concerns, but possibly by a single corporate master in the most mustache-twirling way possible. Thinking like that made Bobbi's head hurt – she couldn't imagine how Tom must have felt, meditating on it the way he did. Jesus, it was no wonder that he was so goddamned grim; it had certainly sobered her up.

She was roused from these deep, depressing thoughts by Scalli, who she realized was watching her from the rearview as they stopped at a traffic light. "Hey," she said, looking up into the reflection of his large black eyes. "You look like you're all kinds of serious."

"Speak for yourself, girl," he said, his heavy brows arching. "You been looking out the window like you got the world on your shoulders since we left your man Pierre's."

"Yeah," she said, looking down at herself. "I guess I have been."

Scalli's eyes turned back to the road, watching a line of pedestrians as they marched across the crosswalk. "More bad news about your boy?"

She shook her head. "No," she said, "just something about him. Pierre, I mean." Bobbi pursed her lips. "Scalli? Do you think the world's fucked?"

He snorted. "You gotta ask?"

"No, I'm serious." Bobbi paused to take another sip; the light turned green and Scalli picked up speed again. "You ever think that we were kinda done for?"

Scalli was quiet for a moment as he pulled the car beyond the light and onto the on-ramp toward the highway that led to the shore; in the distance the Field could be seen, and beyond its legion of gray warehouses the Temple loomed beyond. "I don't know," he finally said once they were on their way again. "I guess that you could say that at any time in history. If you're asking me if I think we're going to destroy ourselves? No. If we didn't do it with nukes and we didn't do it during the Eurowar, I don't think we're gonna. I'd like to think we've outgrown the concept of Apocalypse."

"Huh." Bobbi wrinkled her nose and looked back out the window. "But there are fates worse than getting blown the fuck up."

He gave a bark of a laugh. "Spoken like a true child of the modern age," he said as he muscled the car through traffic. "What do you think, girl? You seem to have an opinion on the subject."

Bobbi sighed and shook her head. Lunatics running the asylum, indeed. "I don't know," she said. "Tom always had a pretty dim view of people in general. I didn't used to, but . . . "

"But your opinion's changed since you've been with him."

"Pretty much." Bobbi looked back to find him frowning at the road ahead of him. "It's not because he's gone, either. Just that . . . I've seen things, being with him." Dead little girls, pale monsters tearing people apart. Sledgehammered reporters. Blood everywhere. "Changed my way of thinking I guess."

"Maybe you should tell me about what you've seen, then."

"Maybe." Bobbi heaved another sigh. Moments like these made her feel about a million years old. "I guess I need to see how things are gonna go, Scalli. Gotta find out what Pierre has to say about Cagliostro and that other girl."

"Mmmm." He shook his head, though the meaning of this gesture was vague to her. They drove on in silence.

Bobbi let her dark thoughts settle until the two of them got back. When she arrived at the Temple she found Sandy tending bar and the nighttime crowd in full effect – and, since Scalli wasn't there to dictate the musical selections, there was actually some modern tunes on the sound system. Aisha Nann was thumping out of the speakers from on high, Bobbi's favorite hypno-jazz artist. She let the music enfold her like a warm bath. Home again, home again, and even though it had been made from the works of a dead man she felt all the better for it.

She went straight upstairs and dropped into the chair behind her desk. Instantly the computer sprang to life, windows of data appearing everywhere. The contents of her mailbox manifested right in front of her, filled to the brim with the usual messages. Bills and invoices. Nothing from Freida or Pierre, though honestly she didn't expect anything from the latter – but then Bobbi recalled her new comrade's face when she went through Stadil's archive, and sighed. Poor thing, she thought. I hope she's doing all right.

You mean you hope she hasn't run off and left you, said a much smaller voice from the far back of her head, or gone off to wave this information at the Bureau and get you all shot in the face. Well, she couldn't argue with that, but she still hoped that Freida was okay.

Bobbi opened a new mail window and drafted a message, addressing it to the root account Freida's slow-ass server. < Hey, girl, > she wrote, < checking up to see if you're all right. Did you find that thing that you were looking for? Call me. > With that done, there was nothing else to do but get a drink and relax – or possibly do a lot more philosophizing, considering the roads that her mind had been traveling of late. But the dark thoughts didn't come straight away; she had sat there for a solid hour behind Stadil's desk, sipping Suntory and listening to the musical feed from downstairs, until the Worldbusters came on playing 'The Other'. The words came coiling out of the speakers, Johnny Morley's gruff, spoken-word lament laid over a slow pulsing beat:

Now she won't call my phone

And she won't be my lover
Yeah, it's a cold, black day
'Cause she's down with the Other

Bobbi sighed, suddenly awash in nostalgia. She loved this song; it wasn't very old, but it felt as if she had been listening to it for ages. She leaned way back in her chair, her bare feet up on the desk and her toenails winking purple at her. Her glass was balanced on her chest, her hands folded over her stomach. The case – she'd begun to think of it as one, which surprised her – began to creep back into her mind. So Freida was off finding out whatever the fuck she was looking for, and Pierre was digging up shit on Cagliostro and Redeye. Redeye . . . Bobbi thought of the girl again with her violent eye, how she had such a militant hate on for Genefex. Blowing up their shit and living to tell about it seemed a pretty radical little operation to have, Bobbi thought.

And you know I'd praise the day
When she breaks her cover
But they never wanna go
When they're down with the Other

Bobbi took a deep breath and let it out again, the glass rising and falling. She had always thought that the song was about someone's girl that ran off with some other person. These days, though, she wondered it if it was something else. Like the way she felt, aware of strangeness lurking behind the world. Mysteries . . . so many of them. It was easy to get obsessed. Tom had been. She was certainly getting there herself. Maybe that girl had just gotten sucked in.

But there was no point in brooding on it tonight. Bobbi got up and finished off her whiskey, letting it sizzle down her throat as she stretched. The floating warmth that spread through her made it easy for her to sleep, and this time dreams did not bother her.

CHAPTER 6

The next day Bobbi was roused by the insistent chiming of the mailbox alarm that she'd set the night before. She rose from her bed with a grunt and eyed the clock as she walked into the office, saw that it was eleven thirty in the morning, and wondered what evil spirits had conspired to summon her.

The spirit in question, it turned out, was in fact Freida. < Call me, > the message read, and a number with a German country code followed. This didn't alarm Bobbi, of course; hack artists used pirated numbers all of the time. That didn't keep her from running a traceprog first, but finding that it eventually came straight back into the city, she gave it a shot.

"Hey," Freida said upon answering the call; her voice was a little garbled thanks to the number of different stops leading back to her. "How's it going?"

"All right," said Bobbi. "Lots going on, you know. How are you feeling?"

"More than a little torqued," Freida said, "though much better than I was. After seeing all that shit, I had to go get smashed at home."

Bobbi snorted. "Yeah," she said, "I know how that goes. Never really drank whiskey until after I met up with Tom."

Now it was Freida's turn to snort. "Well, at least it wasn't him that led you to drink."

"Jury's still out on that." Bobbi chuckled softly. "So anyway. What's going on?"

"Well," Freida began, "I did some digging around after we talked, and after I got a good portion of vodka running through my system."

"Where'd you go?"

A pause, then Freida's slightly anxious reply. "I hit the Bureau net."

The wind momentarily vanished from Bobbi's lungs. "You hit the Bureau net?" Bobbi's own anxiety index skyrocketed; it was hard as fuck to hit a federal system on most occasions. They had tough counterintrusion software, and even without considering that, most had a miles-thick shell of digital armor in the form of codewalls and encryption. Military systems would try to kill you the moment they detected you, and the odds would be very long that they would fail in doing so. To hit the local node of the ISB, when it was clear that hostile entities were running the Bureau's presence in the area, was something that Bobbi would never have attempted. She'd have to be stupid, or crazy, or reckless – or perhaps some combination of them all. It just begged discovery.

"Yeah." Another pause on Freida's end before she spoke again, her voice conciliatory this time. "Look, it's okay, this one time. I put in a back door ages ago."

Bobbi stared at the connection window floating in the air over her desktop as if it were Freida herself. "Oh, so you just hacked a federal system while you were still working there," she said. "Well that's no problem, right? You have some salt, girl."

Now Freida's tone had taken on a faint sheen of pride. "I'll take that as a compliment, then," she said. "Look, d'you want to know what I learned or not?"

"Pfft, of course." Bobbi opened a desk drawer and started rummaging for some coffee. Or cola. Or whiskey. "Hit me."

"So it turns out that I was right about Orleans," she continued. "As far as the official record goes, there was an accident that got triggered by squatters fucking around with the incinerators, trying to get them started for warmth. Blew up the hospital. They have a few Civil Protection cops listed as injured, but nothing like you have on tape. Certainly no record of Special Tactics being dispatched."

"So they just buried it, then." Bobbi heaved a deep sign, coming up from her drawer-diving with a can of Red Kiss and smacking the bottom against the desk to get it cooling. "The fuckers."

"Yeah." There was the faint sound of rummaging on Freida's side, or maybe it was just static. "There something else, too. You know how you sent the contents of the archive, plus those videos you showed me, to the Bureau?"

"Right," Bobbi said. "We thought Exley clamped it down."

"Mmmhmm." Freida sounded weirdly excited now. "Turns out it never even made it here. I don't know how, but someone cut in and took the thing straight out of your hands before it got halfway across the network chain."

Bobbi pulled the tab on her newly-chilled Red Kiss and took a drink, conjuring up new windows: network configurations, access records, and other information appeared, panels of floating light that swarmed about her like familiar spirits. The ultrasweet cherry-flavored liquid washed over her tongue, highly caffeinated but not carbonated – blood binders in the chemical mix carried the stimulant to her system as fast as if she'd inhaled it. "Perfect," she murmured as she began tracing back through two years of access logs.

"What's that?" Freida's voice, curious.

"Nothing," Bobbi said, and reached up to touch the dustplug behind her ear – her fingers traced the ridge of the clear plastic as the big computer ran its search, a nervous habit she hadn't caught herself doing in years. Must be the caffeine, she thought. C'mon, show up. Just don't let it be from . . .

"Fuck!" The words were a snarl that escaped her lips as her eyes locked on a panel which now flashed red in her periphery. Sure enough, the trace records in the computer's system logs showed just what Freida had said. A ghost had apparently visited her system the very day she had sent the archive to the Bureau; there were server actions being logged, but no account attributed to them and no alarms being tripped.

"Bobbi?" Freida sounded very cautious now. "You all right?"

"Just a second, girl," Bobbi replied, and her stern tone brooked no further protest. As Freida fell silent again, Bobbi read the record, scanning every line with rage bubbling higher and higher in the cauldron of her throat. That son of a bitch, whoever it was, had co-opted the data before it had even had a chance to leave the system; it had gone elsewhere, into a trash file that had been deleted even as a false success-of-transmission message had been displayed for Bobbi's benefit. So not only had she been hacked, she had been well and truly fucked – and she had no warning. Some fucking cowgirl she had become. The anger was joined by a wave of self-hatred that only perfectionists like Bobbi could muster; she had been so fucking stupid. What the hell was wrong with her? Why hadn't she been able to see an intrusion on her own system?

What if the intruder was still there?

"Well," Bobbi said after a terrible pause, falling back against the heavy padding of her desk chair, "you were right. It looks like someone hit my system without my . . . " She swallowed down a mouthful of self-hate. ". . . without my knowing. I didn't even fucking see them there."

"Damn." Freida took a deep breath; there wasn't much you could say when a fellow datanaut took a hit like that – they were a family, however dysfunctional they could be, and when one of them suffered a home system intrusion it felt worse than a physical break-in. "I'm sorry, Bobbi . . . but wouldn't they have to be pretty goddamned good to get past your security? I mean I've seen your work before, Brain Mother, it's not like –"

"I don't know what the fuck they did!" Bobbi shouted, her green eyes flashing with the scattered sparks of rage and anguish. This was her system, her home, and she had already lost enough without one more mysterious motherfucker making things even worse. "I don't know how they were able to even find my network node; it's off record."

"That's why I had to resort to that trick with your ghost-box, yeah," Freida said. "I mean, you don't have anything lethal in your security setup, but your encryption walls are miles fucking thick."

"Fortress January," Bobbi rumbled, "Yes. Shit, maybe I should have put Brainwrecker or some shit in there, just to keep people away."

"Maybe, but it doesn't sound like even lethal countersoft's going to do anything in this situation. They leave any traces at all?"

Bobbi shook her head, forgetting that the link wasn't video. "No," she said, "That's the problem – it's not that they hacked the box, it's that they're like . . . a fucking ghost, man! I mean there's nothing there!"

"What about a coverup?" Freida sounded a little spooked.

"There's nothing to cover up! It's like it was a part of the goddamned operating system, that clean." Bobbi took a deep breath and a long drag of Red Kiss, letting the caffeine wave crash over her in earnest. "I don't even know what to think about this now. I've never seen anything . . . " And then she fell silent, staring at the trace window. She had seen that kind of invisibility before. It couldn't be a coincidence.

"Cagliostro," she breathed.

"Who? Bobbi, what's going on?"

"I need you to do me a favor, Freida," said Bobbi then, and her voice rang with a cold and hollow fury. "I want you to hit the Bureau net again, see if you can find something about someone named Cagliostro. Hacker handle, maybe, or an organized crime figure."

"I'd do better hitting up the FBI," Freida said.

"Well, do it." Bobbi called up a new window, her finger flying across virtual keyboards conjured into being as she needed them. "I mean, if you can. I think I've found some solid new pieces to the puzzle."

There was a pause, at the end of which Freida sounded unsure as she made her reply. "I . . . could try, Bobbi. I mean the FBI doesn't have the same resources as the Bureau when it comes to a hardened network, but . . ."

"Hey, girl, you're the one who quit the Feds to play lady hacker. You're the one hit me up and started all this shit over again. If you're gonna bitch out on me over some potential jail time you're in the wrong goddamned business." Bobbi knew she sounded harsh, but she didn't care – this was supposed to be the big leagues, and you didn't let the idea of a cryopen keep you back. That is, not when you were on, and she was so very, very on.

All it took was that little poke to her professional pride, and Freida proved herself a proper hack artist. "Hey, dammit," she barked back, sounding like an irritable sister, "I didn't say I wouldn't do it. Fine, I'll see what I can do – but if I need backup, you better be on hand to give it to me."

Bobbi looked at the connection window, as if she could reach through it, give Freida a pat on the head. "I'd never let you go down a dark alley like that on your own, girl," she said, her voice warming up with her old cocky cowgirl bravado. "Don't you worry. I got your Z."

"No, it's fine," Freida said, and she grinned at Bobbi. She seemed a little relieved at the show of support, even a little cocky. "It'll be much easier for me to work through it all myself. I know the system. I've got . . ." She chose her words carefully now. "I've got a way in."

Bobbi peered at her image floating in the window. "You're sure?"

"Trust me," Freida said, and she gave Bobbi a wink. "You're not the only console goddess around. I'll hit the system without a blip."

"Well you do that, sweetheart," Bobbi murmured as Freida hung up; she had already banished the window, and conjured a battery of new screens. She didn't like the idea of leaving the whole thing to Freida, but she hadn't done a serious hack since Tom had disappeared. Besides, if Freida had ways into a federal system without bringing the heat down on them, all the better to let her handle it.

Even if it did fuck with her pride.

A few hours later, Bobbi was going over the list of Genefex facilities again when the phone rang. Freida's face appeared like a summoned holographic pixie. She was grinning again.

"All right," she said, "I'm back."

"Mission accomplished, I assume?"

Freida nodded. "Hell yes," she cried; her eyes were still wide and manic from adrenaline, a condition Bobbi knew well. Must have been an exciting run. "Got in, got out, got what they had— although, gotta say, it wasn't much."

"Well, that's better than nothing," Bobbi said, and nodded. "What did you get?"

Freida looked off camera for a moment. "Sending it over to you now. Confirm that you got it, please."

Bobbi called up a mailbox window – sure enough, a new message popped up sans sending line. She opened it up, saw encrypted documents keyed as they had agreed upon before. She opened them; captures of data appeared, small panels of white light in a neat row representing pages. Not many pages at all. "I've got it," she said. "Looks like there's not much at all here, though."

"Yeah, just some information on Redeye, which is, as I said, not much. I got nothing on Cagliostro though— man's like a ghost, whoever he is."

"Or she."

"Yeah, or she."

Bobbi wrinkled her nose. The information in her hands now, she looked back to Freida's miniature image. "How did you get in, anyway?"

Freida made a bit of a face. "Oh, well," she said, "I had some, you know, passwords."

"Passwords." Bobbi arched a brow. "Active ones."

"I had it from the Bureau," Freida replied. "From when I was working for them."

"You mean the ISB, or the FBI?"

Freida snorted. "The ISB. And anyway, don't worry about it. I—"

A dark thought appeared in the deeps of Bobbi's mind, surfacing like a corpse. "I thought they reset all passwords attached to a user once they leave service," she said. Bobbi tried to suppress the suspicion that had come with that evil thought, but she wasn't entirely successful.

"That's true," Freida said, and her joy turned to something much more evasive and unsure. "I just . . . I took care of it, all right?"

But Bobbi would not be mollified. "You might have put backdoors in the Bureau's system," she said, "but you certainly didn't put them in the FBI's." Her tone shifted further, became hard, accusatory.

Freida snorted again, this time sounding more like an irritable horse. "Look," she said, her voice furtive, tinged with shame. "I . . . I stole it."

Bobbi didn't expect this reaction from someone who had just committed federal information theft. Incredulity crept into her tone. "That's what you were ashamed of?"

"No, I mean . . . " On the other side of the line, Freida must have been turning colors to go with her frustration. "All right, I stole it from her, okay? Her access codes."

"You mean your lady friend?"

"Former lady friend, but yes. All right?"

Ahhh. Now it made sense. "Think she'll get in trouble?"

"I don't know," Freida admitted. "I don't think so. We didn't get caught, and she calls on the FBI to share forensic data all the time."

"Let's just hope that nobody clues in, then. For everybody's sake." Bobbi's voice had become cool stone.

"Yeah." Freida sounded distinctly uncomfortable now. "Well . . . I'm gonna go for now. Umm. Get back to me when you're ready to talk about what you find in that file, okay?"

"Sure." Bobbi hung up. She sat back hard against her chair, staring at the first two pages of their purloined file as it floated against the far wall. She was angry. Freida had done something really dumb, using the access data of someone to whom she was directly connected; it went straight against the rules of good practice where hack artists were concerned. Hell, anyone doing anything clandestine, ever. If anyone detected anything out of the ordinary, both the Bureau and the FBI would be tracking Freida down to ask questions – and this, in all likelihood, would lead them to Bobbi's own door. God damn it, Bobbi rumbled to herself, rubbing hard at her brow. This shit is amateur hour. It was then that she decided that whatever happened in the future, she wouldn't be going doubles with Freida again. Not unless she was sure that this was a one-time boneheaded error, and maybe not even then. It might have been a mistake to involve her in the first place, but there was nothing that could be done about that now. Bobbi would have to do her best to mitigate the risk of screw-ups on her own.

Bobbi spent a few hours reading Redeye's file, but there wasn't much there to begin with. No name, no real idea as to where she'd come from, and the mysterious young woman didn't seem to exist before her appearance not long after Bobbi and Tom had met. Only in Seattle would a woman with a small army of crazy people, running around the Old City destroying random buildings, fail to get serious interest from the FBI.

Oh, they kept tabs on her – taking notes, that sort of thing – but without the archive that Bobbi had, they would have reached the same conclusion that she had initially made. Random insanity, just with explosives added. Given that the pattern of explosions were well away from the border with the Verge, it just didn't serve as any kind of threat to public order, or at least any public order that the federal government was liable to bother with. Civil Protection had even less, she was sure – they were barbarians in the night, lighting strange fires and praying to nameless gods.

However, what the FBI was interested in was where they were getting their material. Given that the explosions seemed small and hadn't caused major infrastructural damage, they had assumed up to now that Redeye and her followers were using small quantities of homemade explosives. With the explosion at the old Nissan plant, however, they had begun to change their tune. Could there have been commercial-grade explosives involved? Demolition charges? Military? Clearly it was expected that the bombing campaign would continue, but as far as this suggested, the Feds were not yet interested enough to go wading through the urban wilds to go figure it out.

But Bobbi had Pierre. She fired off a message to him, asking for him to see if he knew of any explosives going into the Old City; then she shut off the computer entirely. Sleep sounded like a good idea, sleep and then getting up the next morning and going to get some real breakfast – or lunch, given how late it was and how long Bobbi knew that she'd sleep. Assuming that they hadn't been discovered, and that the police didn't bash down her door to take her in irons overnight. If she hadn't been dragged in by tomorrow, she'd celebrate it a little. She'd been eating in too much, living like she was still some form of street creature. She had good money now, didn't she? Maybe she'd go out and get some real beef. Maybe some lobster. Yeah, lobster sounded good.

Bobbi lay down with thoughts of flayed tails drenched with real cream butter, and of ancient horned claws stuffed with steaming meat, and she slept deeply.

CHAPTER 7

Over the next few days, Bobbi hovered like a moth around anxiety's pallid flame. The next day saw her spared waking up to guns in her face, so she managed to get up and get that breakfast she wanted; but all the lobster in the world, however delicious, however juicy, was ashes in her mouth as she considered the possibilities of the future. Even if they had managed to escape undetected, Freida had taken some pretty enormous risks, risks that she had not spoken to Bobbi about before jumping. Bobbi would never have done that, she was sure. She would have at least brought it up to Freida and they could have agreed upon it. She would have done that, not been a huge cocky cowgirl just because she knew the type of system they were infiltrating. Right?

The intrusion aside, the lack of data about the parties involved was further unnerving. She could understand Redeye – this crazy woman out of nowhere, blowing shit up that nobody cared about – but the bogeyman that was Cagliostro, who had tried to have Tom and her both captured, who had most likely hacked her system and snatched the evidence she had tried to send to the Bureau before it had even hit the road, and was apparently made of smoke, kept her wishing for a tinfoil hat.

Furthermore, there had been no word from Freida. That really set Bobbi's nerves on edge; every day she sent messages out to the girl, but she wasn't answering her phone or her mailbox. What the hell was going on there? Bobbi practically sat on the federal blotters, tracking investigation bulletins and notices of arrests in search of clues that their work been discovered. Nothing. More days passed with no news, but also no armed response teams poised to batter down her doors. Surely if they knew she was involved, they would have arrived by now – Feds weren't known for fucking around where this sort of thing was involved. She lurked at the Temple for a solid week before Scalli's constant probing finally got her to open up about the situation.

"Well, shit," he had said, sounding rather impressed when she'd told him what had gone down. "I definitely understand why you've been laying low. But you can't hide in here forever."

"Not forever," she had replied. "Just until I hear from Freida."

"She's probably hiding out on her own. You have a way of breeding paranoia in people, Bobbi girl. And in any case, if nothing's showing up on the blotters, you're probably all right to at least go out and wander."

Bobbi wasn't entirely convinced that they had in fact escaped detection, but she was convinced enough that she would go out and wander the city. Besides, the big bastard that was her only friend was wonderful enough to care about her well-being, and after blowing up at him the other week she wasn't interested in disappointing him again.

It was easy enough to take the trains and let the world flow by. She, with her lavender hair in its sharp layered shag, her loose black unisuit and eyes swallowed by the veil of heavy Porsche sunglasses, blended in with the uptown crowd as she proceeded around the New City core. She watched them board, perfect faces, bodies engineered in surgical boutiques and driven by obsessive exercise and diet drugs, designer clothes draped over their frames like the skins of mythical lions. She could observe them behind the walls of her dark lenses; she was her own kind of bird blind, outwardly just like them but inwardly feeling like a different species of beast. Again she wondered if Tom had felt like this, and more importantly when she had started to feel this way herself. Had it been when she met him? Or had it always been there, hiding beneath the surface made of pop platitudes and youthful arrogance, waiting for the day to slip out?

Bobbi's attention drifted to the few other people riding in the train car with her. She watched a trio of girls sitting on the far end of her train car, giggling about something. She had been them, once. A young man sat still closer, bragging to his friend. "...it's got a org-mol processor," he was saying, with all the poise and grandeur of a scholar beneath his crown of lacquered blonde hair spikes. "Brand new, straight out of the Tokyo factories. Get you across systems like you were made of light, you understand?" Bobbi had been him as well, but not nearly so douchey. At least she hoped not.

There was someone else, a young woman, possibly a few years younger than Bobbi. Her skin was corpse-pale, her complexion entirely poreless to the point of seeming as though she were made of porcelain or plastic. She wore a brand new Alexi Medenev coat, forest green with its shoulders that looked almost like armor pauldrons. Bobbi's heart froze in her chest, and she felt the air rush from her lungs. She had seen that look before, of course. In magazines. In advertisements. In the camera feed from Orleans. Seeing the girl in profile, the strange perfection of it, every line and curve sculpted as if it were by a laser . . . Bobbi felt her body tense up, and her eyes widened behind her sunglasses as she stared at the other woman. Her eyes were closed, lined heavily in black with shimmering purple shadow ringing each like an exotic bruise.

Open, Bobbi said to herself, positively willing the girl to lift her lashes. Open! The need to see her eyes filled her, a manic lance of fear shooting through her as her mind recalled the images of the gazelle-woman at Orleans. She remembered that she had not brought her nerve crusher with her, and the fear pierced her through another time. What if she was another one of the murderous gazelle-women connected with the whole affair, one of Genefex's silver-eyed killers? What if she recognized Bobbi? Would she be torn apart in public? Images flashed through her mind, images of her body converted into a bloody ruin under the woman's perfect, white hands. The train car's dingy plastic walls splashed with tapestries of blood. Bobbi's eyes staring toward the heavens, blank and green like ancient bottle glass.

The train coasted to a stop at the next station. The kids got up, the giggling girls, the wanna-be datanaut and his buddies, and they began to file out of the car. Bobbi's body ran on automatic. Her muscles fired on their own, fueled by the rampant fear that seemed to replace her blood. While her conscious mind continued to flash images of horror at her, her lizard brain did what it was designed to do; her body rose, taking numbed and hesitant steps, and it walked past this potential enemy without looking at her. Past the wall-screen advertisements, the smiling faces of beautiful people gazing down upon her like beatific saints, holding up their sacred vessels to spur her on. Moments stretched like the rubber from which her body seemed to be made, until at last she felt the hard concrete tile of the platform meet her boot heels. Only then did the images of death fade from her mind. Bobbi turned around to see the woman still sitting in her seat as the train doors closed, still set in her zen-like posture, the heavily made-up eyes still closed.

The train moved, and Bobbi's heart stuttered in her chest as if grasped by a fist. As the train began to depart from the platform, the woman's eyes opened slowly – and though she could not be certain, Bobbi thought that she indeed had caught a glimpse of silver, bright and polished, caught in the black frames drawn by the woman's mascara. Bobbi stared after the train as it disappeared into the tunnel, by which time her heart began to beat again and she could blow out the long-held breath that seared her lungs.

Around her, the crowd of disgorged people began to move toward the exits. Bobbi let herself be caught up by them, let the tide carry her along until she emerged onto the street. She recognized that she was in Pioneer Square, on the fringe of the New City. The walls of office towers and mall blocks were to the west; here there were mostly bars and clubs and apartment buildings packed with corporate employees. Well, she could definitely use a drink. Nothing else, not even rational thinking – of course that woman wasn't one of the Genefex horrors, of course she was just imagining things – could dull the trembling that shot through her body at this moment. She was scared, and she was ashamed of herself for it.

This goddamned city! There was no hiding from it, not even in her own little office. Bobbi picked her way down the sidewalk amongst a steady current of celebrants, shouldering past men and women in the colorful garb of the young and streetworthy. Here, at least, she fit in; the hair, her uni-suit, all of it good camouflage with which to blend in with these people. The street was her kind of street, the bars her kind of bars – or at least they had been at some point, when she did more than drink alone surrounded by holographic displays. She found a place she recognized, a trashy dance club called the New Standard, and walked straight up to the doorman who was tending to the line of would-be revelers trying to get in.

"Hey," she announced, grinning at him from behind her enormous sunglasses.

"Hey yourself, little girl." The doorman wasn't like the usual case you saw – no enormous frame, no piles of stapled muscle. He was of average height and lean as a greyhound, of mixed afro-caucasian heritage, with short punch-permed hair dyed fiery red. That he was so thin and handling the door of a club meant he was probably wired up or some kind of former Special Forces type, nobody you wanted to mess with. Brown eyes swept over her, instantly weighing her worth. She figured he definitely must have been military at some point, looking at her that way. Professional. "You got a reason to be here?"

Bobbi reached into her jacket – slowly, noting the slight tensing of his face as she did so – and produced one of her cashcards, a thin wafer of indestructible epoxy emblazoned with a finger-wide band of black marble around its interface end. It spoke of a high-value credit account, with at least six figures attached. Bobbi did love having Stadil's money; it made people look at her all over again when they saw some little punk girl flash that kind of cash.

The doorman, however, didn't. Instead he flicked a glance to the rod, nodded, and waved her in. "Have a nice time," he said in his stern tenor voice, and Bobbi felt herself being dismissed the moment she passed through the open door. She liked that, especially since it dawned on her that for someone who was paranoid about being identified by the wrong people, she had just brought attention to herself.

The New Standard was, like so many other clubs, a vault of instant debauchery ready to be re-heated and served upon request. Dark and opened up on a wide balcony that circled the establishment, beneath which sprawled the club's dance floor. The rails were lit with liquid-crystal runners, glowing brightly with colors and images that suggested people get the fuck up and dance, or so they said. Holographic projections of dancing figures hung in the center of the space, directly over the floor below – they cycled between various people, whom Bobbi took to be particularly interesting specimens from the writhing throng.

Bobbi found the bar in a hurry, a wraparound construction that cradled the far eastern corner of the club like a chrome-plated serpent. She bellied up to it, keeping her shades on as she socketed her credit chip into one of the bar's payment terminals and waited for the bartender to come down her way. She felt the last of her fear ebbing as the crowd surged around her, believing herself cleansed of notoriety by the anonymous mortal tide. When the bartender came by and got her order for a rum and cola, it took him very little time to fulfill it, cash priority be praised, and she found herself a little table off in the corner that was far enough from the bar not to invite cruisers but near enough to the exit to let her flee with reasonable expediency.

She sat there, sipping her drink and wondering what the hell was wrong with her. Even if it had been one of those people, what had she to fear? Wouldn't she have been tracked down and killed a long time ago if the Genefex conspiracy had known about her? It was not as if she had not spent time in public since then – she could have been seen, she could have been tracked down and disappeared like Tom had been. But had there been something at Orleans that she had missed, when she was cutting into its security system? There had been stiff opposition in the form of counterprogs and barriers, but nothing lethal; had there been a trap laid there that she had not detected? Perhaps it was then that whatever presence had hacked her after Tom vanished had detected her. But she had not moved into the Temple yet. Perhaps it was not known that the woman who had done the Orleans raid and the one who had taken over Stadil's resources were one and the same. She hoped that was the case. She wanted the paranoia she felt to be just that, unwarranted and irrational fear – and yet . . .

Bobbi shook her head and took a deep drink from her rum and cola, and made a face when she realized that it had been made with bitter-ass Nutrivia and not Coca-Cola like she liked. Damn it, some things were sacred traditions. The taste distracted her from her reverie; she reached into her pocket and dug out the little palm computer she had decided to start taking with her when she didn't carry her portable terminal, a tiny Matricomp M187 that had an entirely holographic interface. The little thing looked like a ribbed puck with a rubberized coating, a compact some glamazon would take into battle in her web gear, with just the tiny eye of its projector showing; with it she could Awaken, but the traffic would be damned slow indeed. Bobbi waved her hand over the eye with a prescribed gesture and it kicked on, producing its small displays in blue fairy light. First the connection window, that let her use the little machine's wireless link to connect up with Paracelcus back at the Temple. Then she called up a mail window to check her messages – and found, much to her surprise, that Freida had not yet contacted her. Even more to her surprise, however, was that she found that Pierre had. Well, that was quick. Bobbi frowned at the entry, hovering in space like a sleeping snake, and she reached out to prod the little subject line with all the caution due one.

< I have your information. Come here tomorrow night at 21:00 and you may collect it. >

"Well, shit," Bobbi said, staring at the words. It usually took Pierre a day or two to collate data – there were phone calls to make, network queries, that sort of thing. Hell, Bobbi could do the net stuff herself, but it would never pull the same kind of results that Pierre's resources could conjure. She didn't have Stadil's contacts, after all, just his money. Well, she had something to do tomorrow at least. The information train was really starting to move. Bobbi felt a brief flash of irritation; it had apparently required two years of sitting on her ass to accumulate sufficient karma to finally get things going. She took up her rum and cola and took another deep drink, having forgotten all about the possibly silver-eyed woman on the train and the paranoia which she'd summoned. Information would be the only thing to do such a thing to her at this point. Another potential piece of the puzzle had arrived.

Bobbi conjured up a new message and set about it with the keyboard that hovered in front of her. She had gotten used to virtual keys; there was something satisfying about dipping your fingers into the tiny squares of light, like you were playing in a pool of water. For a portable hack rig, however, she wanted physical keys. She liked the sensation of physical feedback when conjuring up physical programs. The message was to Freida, of course. < Hey girl, > she wrote, < down here at the New Standard at Pioneer Square. Haven't heard from you. You doing okay? > Sure, she was being paranoid. She was allowed.

After finishing her rum and cola, she ordered another from a passing waitress. She waited for it to arrive, the little Matricomp killed its monitors to retain battery life but still hummed serenely at her elbow. Bobbi watched the dancers writhe below, each one briefly venerated overhead in holographic glory. The next rum and cola came, this time made with Coke like she asked, and she sipped it gratefully. Still nothing. She waited for another thirty minutes before she thought that perhaps she should go – and then the little puck computer sang out. Bobbi signed over the machine's projector eye, summoning the alerts window, seeing that she had a message there. It was from Mysteron, Freida's hack tag, with no subject or originating address. Well, Bobbi knew that trick of course, and it gave her some hope – Freida may have picked up on the same paranoia that Bobbi had been feeling about their hack job, and wanted to cover her tracks. Well, if that were so, maybe Bobbi had been too harsh in her estimation of her fellow datanaut. She certainly hoped so.

When she opened the message, however, her blood froze. The body of the message was simple. It said, in tiny glowing capital letters,

< MEET ME IN THE USUAL PLACE. RIGHT NOW. WINDOW OF OPPORTUNITY LIMITED. >

And then, two lines down,

<THEY KNOW. >

Bobbi killed the display and picked up the little puck computer. She didn't leave the bar. Instead, she hurried to the restroom, where some immediate privacy could be found. The walls seemed to bend in toward her as she walked toward the restroom door, ignored the eyes of the women that did touch-up work in its ladies' lounge, and parked herself on the closed seat of a toilet in one of the several that lined the wall, closing the door and locking it. Thus seated, the computer balanced on her knee, she called up the little machine's holographic display. She took a deep breath and expanded the display to maximum size. Now much bigger, the glowing frame of blue light filled the space before her, and a keyboard summoned itself roughly at level with her stomach.

She took a deep breath, made difficult with the wrenching feeling currently occupying her insides, and taking out her dustplug linked herself to the spring-loaded interface cord drawn out of the little machine's bottom. Bobbi closed her eyes and hit the link.

Instantly she knew how it felt to swim in aspic. Compared to the near-superlumninal sensation of reaction and movement that usually came with the Awakening, moving through the chain of proxies was slow and laborious. Latency through the wireless connection, especially compared to the urgency of the message that she would take the risk. Suspended in darkness, moving slowly toward her goal, she practically felt the passing of electrons as she projected herself toward the system. Bobbi felt the thick membranes of the slow-box's walls as she pushed through into it, and then . . .

<HELLO.>

Her blood froze. It wasn't Freida. It wasn't anything, and that was the problem. It was simply words, unattached to any name and without any trace of presence, appearing in her mind. And more importantly, those words had a voice. It was not a synthesized sound coming from a computer's speaker. The words that came into her mind through the network connection were not coldly known but rather heard. The voice rang down upon her, generically masculine, loud and reverberating as that of God Himself.

Bobbi rushed to call up defensive programs, groping in the slow dark. Her shields sprang up, but with the lag it was as if she were mortaring the walls by hand – all the while this silent presence seemed to look on like the Leviathan, idly watching as the ants attempted to shore up for the Last Flood.

<I SAID, 'HELLO'.>

She was as protected as she was going to be. She was the equivalent of an armadillo with a diamond shell, layers of data walls and encryption gates and counterviruses swirling around her projected consciousness. When she was certain that she could at least defend herself, she found her thoughts and made reply.

<Hello. Who is this?>

<A FRIEND.>

This, of course, only served to cause her steadily soaring anxiety to skyrocket. Bobbi double- and then triple-checked her defenses. So many questions raced through her mind – how was it possible that she heard a voice in her mind, when even Awakened mental communication was usually only the knowledge of words? Her mind rattled around in the augmented shell of her brain, grasping for some kind of purchase. Finally she recovered, and with caution arranged her reply.

<I can hear your words.>

<I SUPPOSE THAT YOU CAN.>

<I don't understand.>

<NO, I SUPPOSE YOU DO NOT.> The ghost-thing's voice, flat to the ear, nevertheless seemed to Bobbi to ring with amusement. <WE SHALL DISCUSS THIS AT A LATER TIME. FOR NOW, LET US SAY THAT I AGREE WITH YOUR CURRENT PREOCCUPTATION AND THAT I WISH TO GET YOUR ATTENTION.>

Bobbi fought to keep focus; the spike of elemental fear and confusion which had stuck itself in her heart upon hearing that voice threatened to dissolve her concentration entirely. Her brain made the tiniest leap – tentatively, as if she were attempting to jump between two nearly-spaced platforms over an abyssal cavern. <Well, you've got it. So who the hell are you?>

<AS I SAID, I AM A FRIEND.>

Of course he is, Bobbi thought to herself. <I see. And what preoccupation are you referring to?>

<THE TRUTH.>

In the distance, Bobbi felt something cold on her palm and was dimly aware that she had reached out and braced herself against the bathroom stall. <Go on.>

<YOU WANT TO KNOW WHAT HAPPENED TO ANTON STADIL. YOU WANT TO KNOW WHAT HAPPENED AT ORLEANS HOSPITAL. YOU WANT TO KNOW WHAT HAPPENED TO THOMAS WALKEN.> There was a slight pause. <YOU WANT TO KNOW HOW THESE EVENTS CONNECT. THE TRUTH, MISS JANUARY.>

Bobbi felt the tingle of her faraway muscles clenching. <How do you know who I am?>

<ROBERTA MARIE JANUARY, BORN 07/12/2052 PHOENIX, ARIZONA. MOTHER, SANDRA KELSEY ANDERSON, DECEASED. FATHER, THOMAS ANDREW JANUARY, LIEUTENANT, 2ND LORD'S

CRUSADER INFANTRY, DECEASED. MULTIPLE DECORATIONS FOR VALOR.>

<Enough,> she replied. <I get the idea.>

<ARE YOU CERTAIN?> Again she imagined amusement in the flat voice. <I WISH TO ENSURE THAT YOU BELIEVE ME.>

<Knowing my records isn't going to make THAT happen.> Whoever this was, they had made her vulnerable, vulnerable and angry. She should spike him, crack open his system, find out who he really was.

<THIS IS TRUE. HOWEVER, THERE IS A CERTAIN DEGREE OF LEGITIMACY WHICH MUST BE ESTABLISHED FOR THE FUTURE.>

<The future.> She did not like the sound of that. <You know who I am. I imagine you should probably do the same for me, considering. You know. The future.>

<INDEED.> Another pause, this one long enough for her to double-check her signal strength. No, full bars. <YOU HAVE BEEN LOOKING FOR ME OF LATE. I FELT IT RUDE TO FORCE YOU TO RISK YOURSELF FURTHER.>

Switches clicked on and off in her brain. <You're Cagliostro.>

<INDEED.>

Bobbi felt her palm sting where she pushed against the stall even harder. Cagliostro! The phantom himself, come to find her? Wearing the voice of her dead employer? The anger bit harder and she found herself lashing out. <What the hell do you want to talk to me for? From everything I've seen so far, you've been part of my problem!>

<YOU MISUNDERSTAND, OF COURSE. IT IS REGRETTABLE, BUT UNDERSTANDABLE AS WELL. YOU PERCEIVE OFFENSE WHERE ASSISTANCE WAS MADE.>

Bobbi took a deep breath. <All right. What the hell is this about? Why here?> There was no way she would be able to get out of this if . . . whatever it was . . . attempted to attack her. She could only act like a drunken turtle, albeit one with a shell made of reinforced diamond plates – straight back, slowly and sloppily. That was it.

<IT SEEMED THE MOST LOGICAL LOCATION TO MEET YOU. AND TO GIVE YOU A WARNING>

Happily, an assault didn't appear to be in the cards quite yet. <And what is that?>

<YOU ARE BEING DECEIVED. SOME OF THOSE WITH WHOM YOU ACT ARE NOT AS THEY APPEAR.>

<But who? Who are you talking about?>

<ASK FREIDA KELLEY, WHO WAS ARNOLD KELLEY.>

<Why should I say anything to her, then?>

<YOU MUST ASK HER.>

<I must ask her? What kind of an answer is that?>

<THE CORRECT ONE. YOU CANNOT BE TOLD. YOU MUST DISCOVER THIS FOR YOURSELF.>

<And how the hell are you the one to judge that?>

<BECAUSE I KNOW BETTER.>

<You know better?> In the distance, Bobbi felt her skin crawl. <How do you know better?>

<I AM IN MANY PLACES. I AM IN MANY NETWORKS. I AM IN THIS FORGOTTEN SYSTEM. I AM IN YOURS AS WELL.>

Bobbi clenched virtual teeth and rage boiled through her mind. <You were the one who intercepted the archive from being sent to the Bureau! You made sure they didn't get the information in the first place!>

<THAT IS CORRECT.>

<Did you work for Stadil?>

<ANTON STADIL IS DEAD.>

<Are you some kind of fucking AI?>

<NO.>

<Then how the hell can you do all of this? How can you speak to me, and with his voice? How can you move like you do? I've never heard of anyone who can move through systems like you do. You don't even leave a trace to clean up!>

There was a long silence, milliseconds turning over like the passing of seasons. Finally, Cagliostro replied.

<THERE IS MORE TO THE GLOBAL NETWORK THAN YOU IMAGINE. THERE IS MORE TO EVERYTHING THAN YOU KNOW. YOU ARE AWARE OF THIS. THAT IS WHY YOU ARE HERE.>

<I'm here because you brought me here!> Bobbi was fuming now, and her brain was starting to throw weird sensory signals again. She felt the sensation of heat, as if she stood next to a roaring campfire, start up against her skin. The sensory translation of burning up, so to speak. The brain was a strange and wonderful thing. <And anyway, why the hell should I trust you? You tried to have people tag Tom Walken down! I saw the posting!>

<AGAIN YOU MISUNDERSTAND. I ACTED OUT OF A DESIRE TO ASSIST THE TWO OF YOU. RETAINERS OF THE GENEFEX CORPORATION WERE SEARCHING FOR THOMAS WALKEN. I WISHED FOR HIM TO BE DETAINED SO THAT HE WOULD NOT BE KILLED.>

<Good fucking job on that one,> Bobbi railed, her anger rattling the coherence of the link – she felt her thoughts stutter, realized that her Awakening was growing thin, and forced the rage back enough that the mental static stilled. <I mean to say, he's gone, isn't he?>

<YES. IT IS WHY I REMOVED THE POSTING. I DID NOT WISH FOR OTHERS TO KNOW THAT IT EXISTED.>

<But it's been in storage on that system. Wouldn't anyone be able to find it?>

<NO. ONLY YOU.>

<So you've been weaving me into this, have you?>

<YES.>

<What the fuck for?>

<BECAUSE YOU WANTED TO BE.>

<I did not!>

But there would be no relief for Bobbi, for Cagliostro's words rang a stone gong in her head. <YOU CAME BECAUSE YOU BELIEVED THAT FREIDA KELLEY HAD SUMMONED YOU. HOWEVER, YOU ALSO CAME BECAUSE YOU WANTED TO KNOW. YOU HAVE ALWAYS WANTED TO KNOW. THIS AND ALL THINGS BEFORE IT. IT IS WHO YOU ARE.>

And of course, the hateful thing was right. Of course she wanted to know. Every cell in her body sang in a wailing chorus of caution, or danger, and yet even this primordial terror did nothing to change this. Bobbi allowed herself the dignity of showing affront, but the words that traveled down the line from her brain and into Freida's slow-box transcended any bullshit front.

<Then tell me.>

But the phantom presence yet denied her. <I WILL NOT. AT THIS TIME YOU WOULD NOT BELIEVE. YOUR CREDULITY IS VITAL.>

<Then what the fuck am I supposed to do?> Anger again, this time not from fear but from frustration.

<YOU HAVE A LIST.>

<A list?>

<YES. A LIST OF LOCATIONS THAT CLAIM TO BE ILLICIT FACILITIES BELONGING TO THE GENEFEX CORPORATION. TO UNDERSTAND THE TRUTH, YOU MUST GO TO THE LOCATION DESIGNATED 'DATA NEXUS 231'. DO YOU KNOW THIS PLACE?>

The list flashed through her mind, the name and its associated address. <I remember it,> she said. <You're sending me on an errand? Are you fucking kidding me? Did you escape from game software, is that it?>

<NO.>

The voice invoked an impression of irritation that Bobbi felt shuddering through her. She flinched inwardly. <Bad joke,> she replied. <All right, let's say I go. What am I supposed to do there?>

<YOU WILL ENTER THE INSTALLATION AND YOU WILL INTERFACE WITH ITS SYSTEMS. UTILIZE THE ENTRY PROFILE THAT I GIVE YOU AND ACCESS ONLY THE FILE WHICH I NAME. DO NOT ATTEMPT TO ACCESS ANY OTHER DATA ON FILE; IT IS VITAL THAT YOU ONLY VIEW THAT FILE.>

<And what's this file supposed to be called?>

<IT WILL NOT HAVE A DESIGNATION THAT YOU WILL UNDERSTAND.> Instead a small legion of alphanumeric strings shot through her, some seventy or eighty batches of number, which on reflex she had the computer capture. <THIS IS THE DESIGNATION YOU MUST SEARCH FOR.>

<What kind of file is this, anyway?>

<A SYSTEM ARCHITECTURE DOCUMENT. THIS WILL TELL YOU EVERYTHING THAT YOU NEED TO KNOW.>

Well, that made sense – sort of. If there was something hinky that Cagliostro wanted her to see, something in the computer system, an architecture document would do it.

<Will it be heavily defended?> Bobbi felt a strange mix of fascination and anxiety now, like someone who sees a car accident up ahead and debates pulling over just to see the carnage.

<FAR MORE SO THAN THE GOVERNMENT SYSTEM YOUR COMPATRIOT SO RECENTLY INVADED.> There was a millisecond's pause. <HOWEVER, I WILL SHOW YOU THE WAY.>

Bobbi pursed her lips way out, the sensation rather like a duck sticking its bill into a bag of concrete. <Wait, how do you know where this file is? How do you know any of this?>

<I TOLD YOU. I AM IN MANY PLACES. I WILL BE WAITING FOR YOUR RETURN.>

And then, though she did not sense its departure, Bobbi knew that Cagliostro had gone. She was alone; alone with her thoughts and the slow turtle of her digital presence floating in Kelley's ancient box. She unplugged immediately, and found herself shivering in the cold confines of the bathroom stall, once more without any idea of what the hell she had gotten herself into.

She was getting used to the feeling, at least. But not so much that she wasn't freaked right the hell out.

CHAPTER 8

When she got back later that night, there was no hiding her upset from Scalli. He quit the bar the moment he saw her face, followed her back into the elevator, and said nothing until they were both up in her office. He settled his enormous bulk into one of the chairs facing Bobbi's desk, folded his corded arms over the armrests, and waited.

Bobbi sat down behind the desk, unsure of what to say first. When she did speak, finally, it was in a soft voice that sounded as though it came from another time. From a younger version of herself.

"I think I'm in trouble, Scalli."

His reply was gentle, but stern. "Tell me."

"I don't know . . . " She closed her eyes, leaned back in the chair and sighed. "I don't know how, Scalli. Everything's just so fucked up . . . and it's because I couldn't leave things alone, and now I have . . . " Bobbi shook her head. How could she drag him into this, too? He'd already been involved in things more than she had wanted. To tell him everything, to draw him into the same mess that she herself now stewed in, what kind of friend would she be? It was different with Freida, of course; she had already involved herself, was already digging. Bobbi thought about what Cagliostro had said about Freida not being what she appeared to be. What the Hell did that mean? Was she working for the Bureau still? Was she some kind of an agent? The possibility that Bobbi's hasty trust would explode in her face gave her pause, and yet it would not surprise her.

"Scalli," she said, then drew a deep breath. "Marcus. If I tell you what all is going on, honey, it's going to fuck up your life. It's certainly fucking up mine. Isn't it better that you just . . . I dunno, move on? Or at least just stay as ignorant as possible while knowing that, if you stay here, it's eventually going to be dangerous enough for you just hanging around?"

She expected him to explode on her, or maybe lecture her on the nature of their friendship or some other thing. He'd done it plenty of times before. Instead, however, the mountain that he was merely settled, hunched over to stare at her. Meeting her eyes, Bobbi saw that his own were filled with a resolve that she very well knew she wouldn't have the power to break.

"Tell me," he said to her. "Tell me everything."

And so she did. She could do nothing else.

They had talked into the night. They finished Bobbi's bottle of Suntory and had started in on another from storage when Sandy had announced that the place was closed and she was leaving; Bobbi told her she was on paid leave and that she'd find her next three weeks' pay on hand as a bonus. She didn't argue, though it was clear she was extremely confused. Delighted, perhaps, but confused. Bobbi didn't mind; poor Sandy was just some wannabe datanaut, wanting to play matrix-kitten while in the company of the movers and shakers. If Genefex set those horrible pale things on the club one night, Bobbi didn't want the girl to get torn up in the process.

Once Sandy left, Bobbi showed him the archive, along with the video of the events that took place down in Orleans Hospital. He didn't have a skullcomp, of course, so he ended up watching it on her giant holographic display. Bobbi went to the bathroom and showered while he watched it. She couldn't really handle watching it again after all that had happened lately. When she came back out, damp and bundled into fatigue pants and a t-shirt, she found Scalli sitting in his chair. It had been turned around to face the far wall, so that he could see the display. He had the strangest look on his face. He didn't look horrified, like Freida had been. Rather, he looked as if . . . as if something had been confirmed for him, a sort of grave knowing.

"I understand now," he said as Bobbi stepped into the office again. His voice was a grim rumble.

"Oh?" She sounded timid as she came to stand by her desk. She wasn't sure what else to say.

Scalli nodded. "He was very brave. Both of you were." The big man sighed, and he shook his head. "I can't imagine what anyone else would have done in your place. Probably failed and gotten themselves killed."

He leaned back in the chair, which groaned against his mass, and he stared at the wall as if the screen still hovered there. "You have my support in this, baby girl. I'm going where you're going."

Bobbi felt every nerve in her body sing at once: in anger, in fear, and – perhaps most treacherously of all – in relief that someone close to her wished to help her carry the load. "I feel terrible," she said, looking down at her feet. "But I feel good that you're with me. I should just tell you to leave, so that you don't . . . "

"So that I don't go like your man did?" Scalli shook his head. "Oh, baby girl. I know what you're thinking. I do. But the truth of the matter is, you're my friend, and probably one of the best I've had in a long time – we've been through a lot."

She sighed. "Yeah," she murmured. "I guess I never told Tom how you'd helped me in the past. I feel terrible about it, because we . . . we really didn't talk much about ourselves. I know he didn't ask about me, he was too busy trying not to get killed. And then . . . "

"And then he got eaten up with what you had discovered."

"Yeah." Bobbi looked at him then. What was in her face? She could not know. She felt nothing in that moment, seeing him there – her friend, who had pledged to follow her down this horrible path that she continued to follow. She felt a great deal differently than the sassy girl that she had once been. She didn't feel young anymore, merely . . . present. "I don't want that to happen to you, Marcus. I don't want to be responsible for getting you killed."

Scalli snorted at that. He rose, his hands behind his back, and shook his head. "The good thing is that you won't have to be," he replied. "I'm quite capable of being responsible for myself – I'm doing this because I want to, of course, not out of any crazy feeling of . . . well, whatever, really. You're my friend, and you definitely need help. And I don't trust that gene-shifter that you've been working with, either – I think this Cagliostro is right. I don't think she's vectoring."

"'Vectoring'." Bobbi shook her head; the absurdity of this one piece of Scalli's anachronistic slang broke her from her empty reverie. She smiled. "Seriously, you sound like you were born in the Forties. All right, Retro Man, what do you think that we should do?"

"Yeah, yeah, I sound like an old man, I know." Scalli snorted again, but he was smiling too. "You tell me that enough. All right, I think we should go see this place that Cagliostro told you about, this data center. Do you think you'll be able to hack into its systems when we get there?"

Bobbi shrugged. "I don't see why not," she said. "Unless it's some bizarre proprietary format. It's possible, but I very much doubt it."

Scalli nodded. "All right," he said. "Where's this place located?"

"Well . . . " Bobbi clucked her tongue, thinking about it a moment. "Data Nexus 231 is the only one on the list which is not in the Old City."

"Mmm?" Scalli wrinkled his nose at her. "But the map said that it's in Renton, right?"

"The map's outdated," she replied. "I don't know why. Civil Protection extended its security cordon out that way, so now it's technically inside the Verge."

Scalli's looked like he'd just eaten a lemon. "That makes things difficult for us."

"Maybe. But it also means that they probably won't have the same kind of crazy security there that they did at Orleans."

"Right." Scalli frowned. "No . . . whatever the fuck those were. Zombies? Robots? Christ."

"Well, whatever they are, we won't have to deal with them." She stabbed a finger at him. "I know what you're thinking, Marcus Scalli, but we don't have to go breaking into the place."

His brows arched. "We don't?"

"No," replied Bobbi. "Not at all. In fact, if their security was anything like Orleans' was, we should be able to hack the place's data network without entering the location itself."

"But what if it's a hardened location?" Scalli crossed his legs. "I don't think that you should discount that idea."

"Oh, I won't." She shook her head, sitting on the edge of her desk now. "I won't. But I think I need to buy a few things off Pierre when I see him tomorrow night."

"When we see him," Scalli corrected her. "I don't intend on letting you go anywhere right now without me shadowing you."

Bobbi wanted to protest, but she remembered the look in his eyes from before. "I know that I can't stop you," she said. "But that body of yours casts a long shadow – I'd appreciate it if you gave me a little room when I need it."

He nodded. "Done. But I'm going to do some preparations myself. If that place we're going to is anything other than a milk run, I want to be ready."

'Milk run.' She had never heard the term come out of Scalli's mouth before. Since when did Scalli talk like that? He'd never been in the military, as far as she knew – but then again, he'd been a bodyguard and you couldn't throw a rock in that community without hitting somebody who'd served. Federal military, corporate security, whatever; even private military companies, although PMCs had fallen out of fashion since their little war on the other side of the Atlantic. The European War had made sure that most people realized the extremely bad judgment in giving anyone military weapons that weren't fighting in the interests of their own damned country. And even then you probably shouldn't let those crazies have them either. But then again, Bobbi was biased. Wherever he'd gotten it, Scalli was right – and Bobbi didn't think that it was going to be a milk run for anyone, least of all herself.

It was the next evening, and Scalli drove her across the city into the far northern end of the Verge where Pierre's warehouse awaited. She sat in the passenger's seat of Scalli's car, feeling as if she were sitting in a mobile cathedral. They crossed through the New City from the edge of the Verge where the Temple sat, drove through streets where the pulse of light and commerce kept the wicked place alive. Bobbi stared out the window the entire time. At one point they got stopped in the Waters, where a traffic accident had delayed progress for a bit – she watched the crowds thronging the sidewalks, laughing from the lower tiers of the mall towers, all lit by the great holographic billboards that clad the buildings and hovered from fan-ducted commercial drones.

She wondered what Tom thought about when he saw these things, if he found something good in it. She had always thought it to be rather beautiful . . . but what about him? All he ever said, especially toward the end, was always denigrating the society around him. But she did not see it that way, and if there really was a conspiracy behind the way the world was, didn't that mean that there was actually good in people? Even the worst places had islands of civility. She knew that very well. There was Scalli with her, protecting her even as she was taking him straight to what might be a swift and painful death. And she herself decided to help Tom in his time of need, even when others might have just abandoned him. Stadil's money didn't drive her then, nor did she find any comfort in it now. The very fact that she had those feelings in the first place seemed to prove her point. Bobbi sighed as she saw the wrecked car up ahead pulled out onto the sidewalk, where the river of consumers merely bent around its bulk.

"You're very quiet," Scalli said then. "Something the matter?"

Bobbi sighed again. "I'm just thinking," she said. Her fingers had begun to tap at the glass without her thinking about it, she realized, and she took her hand back with a faint smile. "Sorry if I distracted you."

"Thinking about the whole thing, or . . . ?"

She shrugged. "About Tom, actually. I dunno, it's just . . . he never seemed to like anyone."

Scalli wrinkled his nose and turned his face back to the road as traffic began to move again. "Anyone anyone, or what?"

Bobbi laughed a bit at that. "Anyone who lived in the New City, anyway. He used to have a place in the Verge, you know."

"Did he?"

"Yeah." She leaned back in her seat, feeling tiny, and turned her eyes forward as well. "Some old apartment building. It burned not long after he disappeared, actually."

Scalli made a soft sound of disapproval. "Nobody died, did they?"

"Died? No." She shook her head. "Well, that's not right – I mean there was this old couple, but that was just because they refused to leave even after it caught fire. Shame, really . . . he used to take care of that whole place when he was off duty, you know? Ever since he came to the city he'd lived there, and he just took care of things."

Silence for a bit, punctuated only by the sounds of traffic around them. "I didn't know that about him," Scalli said finally. His voice was soft. "I guess all this time, I've been thinking he was some crazy guy, you know, to get you involved in all of this."

"Yeah," Bobbi said, and she shrugged. "But I put myself in all of this, Scalli. I mean, I was the one who was working for Anton, right? And I'm the one who took on the job leading him down Anton's trail. So it's not like I was ever led astray by anyone." She smiled a bit, and she tucked her knees up against her chest. "I'm perfectly capable of going astray myself."

Now that got a laugh out of him. Scalli's laughter was pretty rare, but when it came, it was long and loud, like a wave crashing over her. It always made her feel better when he laughed. "Sure you're right about that one, baby girl," he said with a shake of his head, his eyes twinkling in the light of passing signs. "You ain't never had a problem getting into trouble on your own. I'm sorry, I'm treating you like a kid again. I know you aren't one. Just . . . "

"I know, I know." She did get it, after all. Men always seemed to do that with little women like her, especially when they were quirky or otherwise classifiable as young. Tom did it, or at least he did it before she blew up at him. Even Stadil did it, albeit in his own entirely weird and inscrutable way. They tended to treat you like a child, or at least a kid sister, even if they desired you. She'd gotten used to it a long time ago. "And it's okay. But let's drop it, huh? Got biz to deal with soon."

Scalli gave a grunt of assent, and the two of them trundled on in silence. Bobbi pushed aside her thoughts of Tom and the city, and she set her mind toward the business soon to be, namely Data Nexus 231. What kind of place was it going to be? Whatever physical security might be around it, Bobbi wasn't looking forward to the idea of locking horns with a corporate data storage system. Information was the most valuable asset available to corporations, after all, and she knew well from experience that they tended to use dangerous means to defend against intrusions. She could handle a normal corporation's systems, after all, but what about this one? She couldn't imagine what kind of crazy shit she was going to find in what amounted to an illegal shadow house of information for the corporation that was responsible for Wonderland – all the horrible tech that came out of there was paid for by their dollar, so of course they'd have access to whatever they wanted, right? A shiver played through her just thinking about it.

There was of course the possibility that Cagliostro was walking them into a trap. She didn't know who the hell he was, or how he was synthesizing a voice in her head over the network. That technology! It was both primitive and genius to her – it demonstrated that whoever was behind the keyboard on that end was a master of the network that she could never hope to be compared to, never hope to rival. She was good, oh yes, she was good . . . but this fellow was warping the system in ways that she didn't even think was physically possible. Why would he need her help? He had said that he was not an AI, but if he wasn't, why would he be sending her along to this place to find "the truth?" What was going on that was so terrible that he could not simply tell her what he knew? It wasn't as if she had not already discovered evidence of a conspiracy vast enough to warp modern human history around to its design, at least in part. But then again, if someone had told her that rather than let her get her hands on the files, Bobbi had to concede that she'd probably laugh in their face.

So there she was, still not having heard from Freida – who Cagliostro said was not what she appeared – and planning seriously to lay siege to a corporate property owned by people who apparently employed the ramped-up dead in their clandestine security plans. Or rather, she didn't hope for a siege; she'd prefer it if Scalli could keep his ogre ass out of the picture. The puzzle was there, and she wanted to solve it, but she didn't want to set the box on fire before she could do so.

Ah, well.

Bobbi and Scalli swung by Pierre's place. The Frenchman didn't have a whole lot to report on Cagliostro, which she had expected; all he had were little fairy tales from the street, stories about Cagliostro appearing when people needed help in exchange for little favors like some sort of ridiculous Faustian machine. Unlike poor old Faust, however, the bargaining party ended up better off than they were before, and the price paid in the future was not onerous at all. As a side effect of his digging, a whole lot of attention had been turned on him from various people of import thanks to his inquiries; Bobbi would have thought he would be upset about that, but instead he seemed to be pretty thrilled. The fact he knew Cagliostro's name to drop had apparently made Pierre a person of interest and potentially useful company to many of these individuals – he was expanding his circle of contacts in ways he had never expected to do in the past. It had put him in a very good mood indeed.

Pierre's mood and new connections had allowed him to dig up a lot of information on Redeye. Some of it Bobbi already knew from the news: that she lived in the Old City, and that she had a growing group of followers she had recruited from the local ferals. By gathering the tribes, however, attacks by the crazy ferals on the other folks who lived out there had plummeted; it appeared that she was actually making the Old City safer by putting together her little force. But safer for who?

And then there was the eye. Obviously synthetic, it was possibly some kind of military prosthesis given a street-friendly look; she was supposedly an amazing shot. Her followers also seemed to look to it as a kind of symbol, for some of them were reported to use the symbol of a single red eye in graffiti and body art. She definitely had a cult of personality going on, and that could be a very scary thing indeed. They were savage fighters when throwing down with the locals, but their purpose was still as of yet unknown – however Bobbi got a hint of that when Pierre told her that the 'salvagers' that her outfit was supposed to have hit not long ago was in fact a convoy belonging to Genefex. So they were blowing up locations supposedly containing Genefex facilities, and now they were hitting vehicles belonging to the company out there in the urban wilds. But why? And for what purpose? They would need to do more digging, but now wasn't the time.

Bobbi had Pierre order a laundry list of gear that they would need to carry out Caglistro's mission. Scalli had given it to her, although it had surprised her that the list was so short. Pierre had cheerfully taken her money and started the work, saying that it would be a few more days before much of the equipment could be gotten, and that was fine with her – she'd want to make sure she was ready to hit the data nexus, and more preparations would be required.

They didn't say much on the way back, short of Bobbi insisting that they hit up Rocket Chef again – she had a maddening craving for Maxi-Buns again. She'd almost think she was pregnant save for going for two years without getting anything. And what was that about? She used to love getting it, and now . . . well, priorities change, especially when one carries the sort of weight that she did now. Just wasn't important to her, and if anything that disturbed her most of all.

She munched on her burger, staring out the window. "I hate the Old City," she said.

"Yeah," Scalli said. "Bunch of crazy fuckers out there."

"Not all of them," Bobbi said, and looked at him. "I mean that's not why I hate it. I used to live there, you know."

He looked at her sidelong, squinting. "No shit?"

"No shit." Bobbi let out a deep sigh. "It was a long time ago, though."

"Not so long ago," he said. "You're not even thirty yet. You wanna tell me, or do I have to guilt you until you finally crack?"

Bobbi gave him a level look, green eyes flashing in the light, and then she shook her head. "Here," she said, "I'll tell you the story."

The story went like this. Her dad had served, ages ago, in the United States Army – which back then was still called the Crusader's Army after the crazy, evangelical authoritarian government that existed back in the first thirty years of the century. Just like Cagliostro had said, he'd served in the Lord's Second, and he had marched all over the face of the Middle East spreading the Lord's sacred ammunition to the heathens in the most direct and terminal way possible. He'd served for two years before the Great Rejection, when people finally came to the startlingly intelligent decision that bombing the shit out of each other in the name of what may very well amount to the first and greatest example of the imaginary friend in human history might be, you know, a bad idea. Most of Iran and Saudi Arabia had been turned to glass, and with the latter fully half of the Crusaders had gone with it when the former's batshit Ayatollah had forced the government to push the button rather than allow American troops anywhere in the vicinity of Mecca.

So Dad came home, and when he returned the country was in chaos. The evangelical movement had splintered into militarized factions, New World Evangelicals tangling with smaller splinters for the spiritual heart of a country that was swiftly deciding that they should all wipe each other out and let it all be done with. It was the same in the East – those who weren't glowing in the dark or falling apart from radiation poisoning seemed to see the same flaws in the system, deciding that maybe the sword of Allah wasn't the best thing to swing around anymore. And so it was that peace was coming, or at least peace from religious violence.

There was a new movement that sought to replace Christianity and Islam and all the other major faiths. It had always existed, predating religion itself, and in the past three centuries it had captured the public imagination and rooted itself like a glittering tree in the hearts of human beings. Those roots had reached deeper and deeper; the first blooms had started to open in the past century, and now they opened up all over the world.

That force had a name, and that name was Commerce.

The last fifty years had been basically one glorious commercialist renaissance; historians she'd read often compared it to the nineteen eighties, but that was just the first rumbling of the eruption that was to come. To hear her dad tell it, things had been like night and day – one moment the country had been a dignified, if insane and patriarchal, republic. Commerce was regulated under the culture of New World Evangelism. It had been the culture into which he had been born. But after that there were no gods, no masters. Her dad had always said that this way was evil, but to Bobbi it sure as hell seemed to have put the world back on track for a while, back on track and heading toward a future which did not involve getting nuked or otherwise blown into pebbles by some other jackass nation. Thanks to the globalized commercialism that now prevailed in the modern day, nobody could afford to destroy anyone else; property values would plummet and even world nations didn't get insurance payments for self-inflicted arson.

So he came home and found the world changing around him. The Faith had never been too strong in her dad, but when he came home he claimed to see the evils of the world all around him – and so he took his wife and they moved to the Old City, just after the big crash had come to the state and Seattle was floundering. Back then, the Old City was basically like the Verge, or like Detroit had been back in the late

Twentieth. Lots of abandoned houses, lots of empty structures. Bobbi's dad just moved into a place down in Federal Way, far from the city center, and decided to try and live a decent life.

Things proceeded as they always do – decently enough at the start, though slowly degenerating by a matter of degrees. Dad met her mother, who was working in a cantina that refused to go out of business, and they set up housekeeping while the city continued to flounder. They didn't get married, not even after twenty years together, and not even after Bobbi was born. Things were still decent.

The crazies and the criminal element had, originally, settled at the borders of the Old City to get away from the heavy police presence and federal troops that kept the peace back during the riots that came with the crash. As time wore on, however, these groups expanded in numbers and in territory; the Oldies kept moving inward to keep from being exploited, killed, or worse. Most of them, anyway. Her dad didn't. Her dad elected to live like he always had, as the righteous man, the soldier, and he had built up a sizable militia of fellow Oldies down in Federal Way. For a time they'd kept things decent, but that time swiftly came to an end when Bobbi was four years old. On a "mission" out in town, her dad had tried to shut down a narcotics operation that was sourced in the crumbling inner districts. The guys that ran it had sent his head, along with those of the rest of the groups', in a shipping crate to her mother's porch. She didn't clearly remember it, of course, as young as she was – but she remembered clearly her mother's wail of horror and loss, and the gory splatters that persisted upon the porch for days after. Every now and again she'd dream of severed heads, one that looked very much like her father, but she wasn't certain if this was reality or simply her imagination fucking with her.

"Jesus," Scalli whispered when she had said that last bit, looking down at her as if he had witnessed the thing himself. "That's terrible, baby girl. I never knew that about you."

"Well, if you had a nickel for everything you didn't know about me, Scalli, you'd make me look like a waitress in the savings department." She shook her head. "Tom didn't know either, really."

Scalli looked at her. "You didn't tell him?"

Bobbi shrugged. "It never came up," she said, but though she did her best to look nonchalant the old feeling of something . . . disturbed . . . came back to bother her. Why didn't it come up? Why didn't she ever tell him? More to the point, why didn't he ask?

"I suppose," Scalli said with a toss of his head. "All the same, it was terrible. And I guess you got out of it afterward?"

"Something like that," she said with a shrug. "I mean, after that it kind of went pear-shaped. My mom went from guy to guy, closer and closer toward the New City until finally we stayed in Tenleytown."

They rounded a corner and Scalli bobbed a slow nod as they went. "Oh yeah, Tenleytown," he said lightly. "That's that border settlement, right? I mean, that's all you can really call it."

She snorted. "That's about right," Bobbi said with a nod. "Of course, it was bigger then – might be big again, now, if Pierre's talk about street people fleeing the Verge has any truth to it. It was civilization, you know? It was a bottleneck community. This was just when Civil Protection came into the picture, see, and the military still operated checkpoints. Then they took over and shit started getting real bad."

"Yeah," Scalli said with a nod. "I'd heard about that." Twenty years ago there'd been a massive riot, when the crazies flooded out of the Old City and tried to hit the Verge, only to be turned back by a combination of Civil Protection and the National Guard. That was pretty much the only time it happened; hundreds of people died, lots of ferals of course, but also Oldies who got caught in the crossfire. "Your mom made it, though, right?"

Bobbi nodded. "Yeah," she said, "But only just. She didn't take it too well in her head, you know. Finally just offed herself, walked into the Old City and never came back. I was thirteen."

Scalli shook his head. "I'm sorry, baby girl."

"Don't be," she replied. "She was never that much of a mother in the first place. If I miss anyone, I miss my dad." Bobbi looked out the window now, her Maxi-Buns forgotten. "I guess that's how it is for lots of girls, though. I guess if it weren't for the fact I was good with a terminal, I'd have ended up dancing on the pole."

"Yeah, but you can do that anyway," Scalli said, and then winced. "Sorry. I didn't mean–"

"It's cool," she said. "Yeah, I stripped from time to time. Did worse than that, too, until I got enough money together to get my first real hackworthy machine. Then I was a cowgirl, regular. Didn't look back after that."

Scalli nodded, though still looked really sheepish. "I guess that's where I met you, huh."

"Yup," she said, "That's where you met me. And that's where history began."

They said nothing else the rest of that night, save for a quick "good night" said as he dropped her off at the Temple. The club was closed, of course, but word had gotten out through the regular social channels so it wasn't as though anyone was waiting on her. Bobbi watched him drive off toward the other end of the Scrap Field and turned back to the door, walking up to molten ziggurat's big double-paneled portals.

"There you are." A woman's voice. Low. Quiet, too quiet to be identified. Bobbi paused, her heart rate picking up exponentially.

"Uh, yeah," said Bobbi, wishing that she'd remembered to bring her nerve crusher. "Here I am."

"Turn around, slowly." There was steel in the voice. "Are you alone?"

Bobbi counted backwards from five. She tried to see where the voice was coming from – there were only the warehouses across the traffic lane from her, the parking lot being on the other side of the structure. No cover that she could see, unless . . .

Someone was above her.

"Well, you saw me stand here as my ride drove off," she said with a grunt. "You're right on top of me and all." It was a guess, of course, but she wanted to show a little control in this situation. Best way to defuse it if whoever it is that's in the shadows doesn't want to drop you straight off.

There was silence a moment, and then a soft laugh. From over the edge of the bottom tier of the concrete ziggurat, a figure flipped and landed on the concrete not far from her. It was Freida, of course, in black jeans and boots and a zipper hoodie that had stiff panels in it like body armor. "Sorry about that," she said, her red hair pulled back in a tail and her eyes twinkling. "Didn't mean to scare you!"

"Well, mission failed on that one, girl," said Bobbi with a long exhale. She tried to seem relieved, but her heard rate had yet to dampen – she heard Cagliostro in her head, speaking to her with Stadil's voice. YOU ARE BEING DECEIVED. And then, YOU MUST ASK HER. Though Freida didn't have a weapon in her hand, the recollection of those words caused Bobbi to tighten up as if Freida had a pistol pointed squarely at her chest. "Where the hell have you been?"

"Funny you should mention that." Freida took a step back, twisting slightly on the balls of her feet. She surveyed the area, eyes hardening for a moment as she did so. "I've been looking into your buddy, Scalli."

Bobbi stared at her. "What the hell for?"

"I dunno, something about him." She checked the sleek watch that hung from her wrist, a mens' diving chronograph finished in black chrome. "I wanted to make sure where his loyalties were, in case you decided to bring him in."

"Already done," Bobbi said, her expression flattening, "I've known Scalli for years. You don't have to worry about him."

Freida paused as she looked at her. "Oh," she said. "You've told him about everything?"

"He knows everything that you know." Bobbi looked straight into her face, daring her to protest – if anyone's going to be questioned here, honey, it's you, she thought. Behind the mask her face had become, anger flared. How dare she question him! "I trust him, Freida. As I say, he's guaranteed himself in my eyes."

There was a pause. "But I haven't, you mean to say. Is that it?"

Bobbi did not reply for a moment, merely staring into that hard, pretty face. Finally she asked, "Is there some reason why I shouldn't? You're not hiding anything, are you?"

Freida stared back at her. More silence, the seconds ticking away between them. When she spoke again, Freida's voice was . . . softer, a bit strained. Angry and defeated at the same time. "We'd better go inside," she said.

"All right." Bobbi stepped up to the doors and took a keystick from her pocket, which contained all manner of biometric data, and slotted it into the lockplate. From somewhere inside magnetic bolts could be heard hissing open. Bobbi pushed open one side and let them in.

In silence Bobbi walked to the bar, leaving Freida to follow her with that same air of resignation. "Do you want something to drink?" she asked Freida, selecting a bottle of old Greek ouzo from the top shelf and getting herself a glass. "I got pretty much whatever."

Freida shook her head, and she took a seat at the bar. "No," she said. "I'm all right."

"Yup." Bobbi poured herself a little bit from the bottle before setting it aside, letting the clear liquid film the inside of her glass as she sloshed it around. "So what's going on, then?" Simply put.

It wasn't a challenge so much as it was an invitation for confession, and Freida decided to seize upon it. "I haven't been entirely honest with you," she said, looking down at the bar.

Son of a bitch, son of a bitch, son of a bitch! Bobbi took a sip of the ouzo to still the sudden rage and anxiety that swirled around in her chest, maintaining her outward calm. "Oh?"

Freida looked askance. In fact, she seemed to look at everything in the building but Bobbi, letting her blue eyes track the walls, the tables. "I said that I had left the Bureau," she said. "That's true. I did. But I didn't quit on my own."

"Oh no?" Bobbi canted her head, took another sip. Her irritation was boiling about, but this intrigue held it back a bit. "Go on."

The redhead heaved a deep sigh. "Exley had me turned out," she said. "On account of my . . . extracurricular interests. I was doing a private study of datanauts, you know, looking into new techniques, that sort of thing. At the time our digital defenses weren't up to snuff, and I wanted to bolster them."

"The best way to do that would be to become a hack artist yourself, huh."

"Exactly!" Freida nodded, leaning forward a bit. Her eyes widened a little. "So I was going on as Mysteron, you know, trying to get information so I could make sure we would be safe from intrusion. I . . . " She paused, frowning at the bar. "I guess I'm ashamed to say it, but someone got in a few years ago. I don't know who, and I don't know how, but . . . "

Bobbi nodded her head. She had an idea of who that might be. "So Exley found out about it and had you ejected," she said. "Right?"

Freida nodded. "I don't know how he found out! I mean I'm just about the best tech op the Bureau has in this city, and he's definitely no hack artist – I mean he was a field agent, combat augs and whatever, he wasn't spec'd for data intrusion. I guess now it makes sense, with him being allied with Genefex and having their resources."

"So this doesn't explain why you're looking so guilty," Bobbi said lightly. "You could have told me that from the start and I would have worked with you."

"Yeah," said Freida, "But . . . "

"Well?"

The redheaded transgene took a deep breath and closed her lovely eyes. "The problem is that I wanted back into the Bureau. That place is what I knew – I always wanted to be a government agent, you know? So I was building a case against Exley to get him removed, in exchange that I would get reinstated in kind."

Bobbi frowned faintly at her. "And is that still what you want to do?"

There was more silence on Freida's end. Her face fell, and she looked suddenly lost. "I don't know what I want," she said. "Now that I know everything he's into, I know that getting him pulled out would cause me way more trouble than I would ever want – but then again, just knowing what I do now makes it impossible for me not to act. And then, just the other night, I get a message from someone in the Bureau . . . "

"Wait." Bobbi set her glass down. "You got what?"

"I got a message from someone at the Bureau. Internal security, encrypted messages only. Says that they want to investigate the circumstances behind my dismissal, and if I wanted to assist could I respond with what I know." Freida shrugged. "That's where things have been."

Bobbi folded her arms over her chest, peering at Freida. This clearly wasn't good. "And what did you say to them?" she asked carefully.

"Nothing," Freida said with a shrug. "Well, that's not true, I said that I would have liked to get my position back, at first. But then . . . I sent them another message last night saying that I would've been okay with it if they had asked me earlier, but that it had been long enough that I was happy to continue as I am. I mean, what is there to say? If I gave them information then an investigation starts up. That means that Exley would get involved, and if Exley gets involved I'm dead. Right?" She shook her head and sighed. "It's definitely not in my interest to do it – nor yours, come to that. If they keep digging I'll either end up in prison or like Brighton, coating the floor of some church or whatever."

Bobbi took a deep breath. "That's good thinking on your part," she said, trying hard not to sound too relieved. "I mean, I know that's hard, wanting to go back and knowing that you can't. Believe me, I know what you're feeling."

"That's what I was thinking, yeah. I just want to see this through, you know? And if you can do that without trying to go back to how things were, I can do the same." Freida gave her a weak smile. "Hey, how about you pour me some of that?"

"Coming right up." Bobbi poured her fellow cowgirl a quarter-glass and handed it across. Maybe Cagliostro was spooky, and maybe he/it/whatever was everywhere, but maybe he wasn't turning her toward a bad corner after all.

They drank a little more before Bobbi decided that she could trust Freida a little more and told her what had happened since last they spoke. After all, Freida had been straight with her about her status and with the message, and frankly Bobbi needed more informed allies if she were going to continue with this whole thing. Come to that, had it really been someone in the Bureau that had sent her the message? Bobbi had the idea that Cagliostro, who had given her the warning about Freida around the same time she had gone dark, might have been the sort of creature to plot it out. He – and Bobbi chose the word specifically because of the voice chosen to address her – was one hell of a spider.

She wanted to meet that person, shake their hand. And then maybe shoot them in the face in the name of public safety.

But first things first.

"So you're going to go do it?" Freida sipped from her third quarter-glass of orzo, looking faintly pink in the cheeks. "I mean, what if it's a proprietary format?"

"I wondered about that myself," Bobbi said with a nod. "But I don't think that it will be. Bound to be ridiculously hardened, though. So I think we should both take it down."

Freida's brows lifted in surprise. "What, you mean the two of us?"

Bobbi nodded. "Well, we took on an FBI mainframe, didn't we? We're both damned good, and we've worked together now, so why not? We know how each other approach things. I say we pull a Gemini and hit the system together."

She thought about it a minute or so, and Bobbi thought that maybe Freida would refuse – but she didn't think so. And, sure enough, Freida finally let out a whistle before downing the rest of her ouzo and giving Bobbi a winning smile. "God damn, you're ambitious." she said with a sigh. "I don't suppose you like it with girls? Because I could eat you like an all-day buffet just now, no lie."

It wasn't what she expected at all, but Bobbi knew how to handle it. "Sorry sugar," she said, giving Freida a grin. "I'm strictly an XY kind of girl, you know? But I'll take it as a real top compliment."

"You better," Freida said with a laugh. "I mean every word of it. Jesus. Okay, well, I better get out of here. You have what you need to hit this place?"

She nodded. "Yeah, I think so. You meet with us tomorrow over here about three and we'll go over the plan."

"Sounds good." Freida threw her another smile and got off her stool. "Oh, hey, question. How did you know that I was hiding something?"

Bobbi's grin didn't falter. "Women's intuition," she said. "You need to put yours to use, you got the full change now."

"I'll look into that." Freida winked at her and took her leave, and Bobbi felt a pang of guilt sting her as the other woman disappeared through the front door. She didn't tell Freida about the warning that Cagliostro gave her, and she wasn't entirely certain why. Mostly because of the way it had happened, she supposed, too neat. Too tidy. The timing was too good, and that was probably Cagliostro's doing and not Freida's at all. She'd tell her another time, she resolved. But now, to check messages. And then to get some sleep.

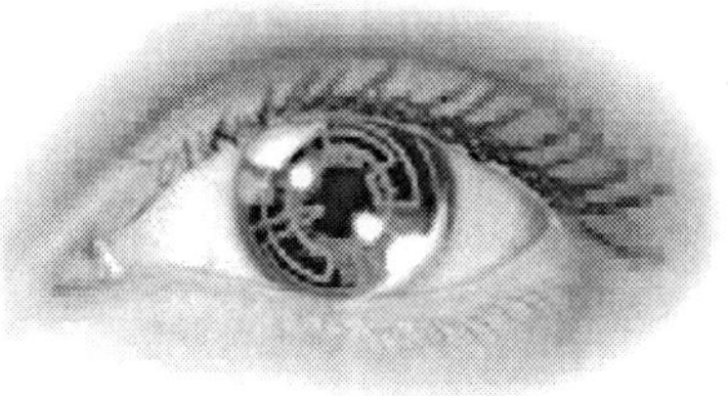

CHAPTER 9

When Bobbi woke, she felt refreshed – but also a bit tense, and with the distinct impression that she'd been dreaming something frightening. A week had passed since she and Freida had met at the Temple, and every night since then she had been roused from sleep the same way: sheets tangled, her skin cold with sweat, and yet full of energy and with no memory of what she had been dreaming. It was a bit like waking up after a hugely debauched party with the impression that you had taken center stage.

Bobbi lay entwined in her damp sheets, staring at Tom's coat pinned up in its shadow box. Tonight, they would be hitting Data Nexus 231. Finding whatever it was that Cagliostro had said was stored there. The Truth, with a capital T and trademark. Into the jaws of Genefex.

The three of them had been planning the whole operation for the past week. According to Calgiostro, the facility would be empty; it was still running, of course, but it didn't require anything but automated security. Just machines, he had said. No living beings at all. Scalli had decided this meant that there might be combat robots inside, or automated turrets – and so he had proceeded to turn himself into a miniature fortress thanks to the items that Bobbi had purchased for him from Pierre and his own private store. A combat rifle with silencer and suppressor, a mil-spec combat visor – she wasn't a soldier of any kind, but she knew when a man was loading up for bear. Hopefully they'd never have to set foot inside.

This was the goal, after all; she and Freida would hack the place from the outside, and attempt to penetrate its systems like Bobbi had at Orleans Hospital. Those had only been the systems native to the hospital itself, however, old tech that had been revived and repurposed. This facility would no doubt be different, and they had decided not to take the chance of trying to cut in through a standard net connection. Among the tools that Bobbi had managed to get from Pierre was a piece of surplus military gear from the European War, a CorEx Systems MT38. Modern hack artists called it a Grail, because it gave a user supernatural power as far as they were concerned. Connected to another network by direct wireless link, the Grail merged its own internal network presence with that of its target allowing complete and seamless interaction without fear of reprisal. Back during the war, military techs used to use it to take over enemy C&C and the like. Commandos hacked tanks and made them fire on their own units.

The Grail was extremely rare and very, very illegal; it had been classified as a military weapon and thus made illegal long before the European War was over, thus making sure that only state militaries and not corporate forces could make use of it. Recovering it was also the single greatest expense that Bobbi had ever made; a gross amount of money had vanished from her accounts as Pierre made it happen, citing his new connections as the reason behind its speedy procurement. The Grail was some real dark magic, and it was a life sentence in a federal cryopen if the ISB caught you with it.

Well, fuck them anyway; it's not like they were doing her any favors.

Scalli had bought a hardened cargo van from a black market transport broker, and had another guy he knew give it a coat of electrosensitive bicolor paint; the cops were around, of course, so they'd want to switch the paint job once they'd succeeded in hacking the facility network. Electrical terminals were mounted in inconspicuous places on the van to give it the charge necessary to change the color, and the back license plate had a false layer of plastic made to look like a real one that would burn away when the change was made. It was a smart setup, Bobbi had to admit; she certainly wouldn't have thought of it, and she was becoming happier and happier that she'd brought him into this thing after all.

Bobbi spent the afternoon getting things together. She had her medical bag, which had her portable terminal and a host of other electronic gear. Scalli had wanted to give her a pistol, but she'd refused – she hadn't fired a gun since she was an Oldie, after all, back when one of her mother's boyfriends tried to impress her by showing her how. And anyway, that's what she had Scalli for. Freida, being a federal agent previously, had firearms training and so elected to pack as well.

For Bobbi, for whom any additional equipment other than her cowgirl tools diverted her attention, this seemed a dangerous distraction. What if she had a spasm while dealing with a counterprogram and dumped her bag off her legs, or otherwise jarred it? She'd know that the gun was there, that it could fall and go off. Maybe she was just too much of a worrier, but stranger things had happened – once she'd heard of a dude who kept an EM grenade in his bag, jostled it while pulling a job. Cooked him, the terminal, and everything else in a six-foot radius. None of that for her, oh no. She would focus much better not worrying if she was going to end up with a third nostril on accident.

And so it was that they convened that night in the barroom of the Temple, where Bobbi was waiting. She had given Tom's coat one long look before she left, thought about kissing the glass but discarded the notion out of her desire not to bring too much sentiment along with her on the night's sortie. Scalli came first, of course, dressed in a long coat that she could have used as a tent. No way in hell he was going to look like anything other than six kinds of trouble, but it couldn't be helped. As long as he stayed in the van he'd just be this huge fucking guy, not this huge fucking guy geared up to lay siege to a small castle.

Freida followed after, in dark street clothes and heavy boots. She'd colored her hair black to match. She also carried a leather bag on her shoulder that looked a lot like an August Vitelli satchel, which made Bobbi wonder just what the girl had been up to since leaving the Bureau to pull in the cash necessary to score one. "Imitation," Freida had told her with a wink. "Besides, they're all made from printed tissue anyway so who's to know?"

Something about that stuck with Bobbi, even after they had gotten into the truck and headed out for the far end of the Verge. She wasn't sure what it was about the comment that bothered her – probably Cagliostro's words again, ringing in her ears as if the ghost had said it moments ago. The city loomed around them as the van rumbled on, Scalli and Freida in the front seats, Bobbi in the back with the gear; she distracted herself by plugging her portal terminal into a router she'd brought along, which was in turn connected to the can-sized satellite antenna she'd stuck on the roof with a mag-mount. She set up a six-bounce relay link into the cement vat that was Freida's slow-box, and looked for Cagliostro. Though she could not sense him, soon enough the rumbling voice rang like thunder into her ears.

<I AM HERE.>

<So you are,> replied Bobbi. <We're on our way to the site. Anything else you want to tell us before we get there?>

<NO.> Seconds ticked by, and then, <ARE YOU PREPARED?>

<I'd be more prepared if you didn't go around talking to me like some great talking head from a bad adventure movie.>

<INDEED.>

More silence followed. Bobbi collected herself before speaking again. <Okay, well, we're all set here. I just wanted to check back with you and make sure the situation hadn't changed. We'll report back when we're done, or we won't report back at all.> She disconnected, leaving the thing perhaps to wonder. She certainly didn't want to talk to the thing anymore than she had to.

"Nothing new from the spook," Bobbi said as she closed the link and disconnected herself from the terminal. "Looks like we're still on."

It was about nine-thirty when they arrived. The facility was housed under a building in a crumbling office block in the heart of the reclaimed territory, so close to the security cordon that the lights of Civil Protection carriers could be seen in the near distance. The presence of armed police so close to the location made her nervous – but then again so did everything else about this whole thing.

"We're here."

Scalli pulled the car up into the parking structure attached to the office park, in the bottom level. From there she could see the building through the front windows: a typical example of turn-of-the-century concrete and glass, a box with one side terraced down to street level. Most of the windows had gone, leaving dark and gaping wounds in the side of a stained facade; Bobbi had the distinct impression of something rotting, like a dog's skull found on the side of the road. Something frail and animal squirmed inside of her.

"Yeah," Bobbi said softly, staring at the ruined structure. "All right. Freida, you ready?"

"Ready as I'll ever be, Brain Mother," Freida said cheerfully from the front seat.

Bobbi looked between her two comrades. "Right," she said, "Freida, you come back here. Scalli's on watch until we're done here."

Scalli nodded. He didn't look over his shoulder at her; he was already consulting the monitor set into the truck's console, reading output from the sensors he had installed. "I got nothing on infrared," he said. "Motion and EM are nil. You sure that building has power?"

"Only one way to find out, I guess," Bobbi said with a shrug. She had taken the time to set up the Grail, which was a simple, olive-drab oblong with rubberized coating the size of a small lunchbox. Warning labels and military markings had been emblazoned on top, which Bobbi had cheerfully covered up with an enormous vinyl sticker of a cartoon snail. Bobbi plugged herself back into her terminal, which was connected to the router and the Grail by various cables; Freida came back to sit down next to her, and was still getting out her gear when Bobbi willed the machine to reach out with invisible fingers, half-Awake, probing for connection points . . .

And found one, very strong, in the near vicinity.

"Got something here," she said out loud. "Won't need the satellite; got a standard wireless signal here, real strong. Must be right in front of us."

"That would be the hope," Scalli said dryly, still studying the display.

"Yeah. Well, we won't need to use the satellite antenna. Freida, you ready?"

Freida nodded. Her face positively shone with excitement. "Absolutely," she nearly crowed. "Bring on the mess."

Bobbi gave her fellow cowgirl a final wary look before nodding, and engaged the terminal. Instantly the slow meat of the body and the material world gave way before the power of Awakening. Floating in the serene space that was her terminal's native system, she reached out and found the Grail, which had already reached tendrils into her terminal's presence and formed a homogenous region between the two. She felt herself slip easily into that space, into the Grail's own system presence, shocked at how easily the systems merged. Then she felt the system change again as Freida powered on her own terminal; it was very subtle, still her country yet not, the natural merging of two land masses sped up by a geometric degree.

<Testing, Brain Mother.>

<I see you.>

Freida signed surprise. <Christ, this thing is something else. You'd think we were native on the same system.>

<That's how it was designed, yeah.> Bobbi bid the Grail to connect to the distant system, whose ID code was a simple hexadecimal code; she was sure that this was the place, but one never knew. <It'll take a while before we make connection. Any last questions before we get started?>

<Not on my end. Oh, wait. Do you still think we should go in together, considering the way the Grail's working?>

<Absolutely. We don't know what's going to be in there – might just pick us up anyway.>

<All right.> Freida then signed a thumbs-up to her. <Good luck to you, Brain Mother.>

A few years ago she might have said something smartass or dramatic. Now, she just felt tired when Freida called her by her hack handle. Kids playing kids' games. <And to you,> she replied instead, and returned the thumbs-up just to keep esprit de corps.

The doubling construct formed in the Grail's home space, and as they slotted into it Bobbi had the Grail connect and do its thing. They were instantly aware of the connection, how the Grail simply merged with the security protocols like a hungry cancer – merged, infected, and then transformed the offending structures into bridge material. It was shocking how fast it worked, how complete and terrible the transformation. In the space of a few minutes it had completely homogenized the connection. No wonder they restricted this stuff to military use. It gave her a little more cheer to use it, both through sheer technological awe and the excitement in knowing that she was going the way that commandos had gone for years. Bobbi January, Commando Queen. Snort.

They shuttled into the network beyond, and instantly knew they were in the right place. Arrival flags kicked in the moment they passed into the system – Welcome to Secure Data Nexus 216 / Genefex File System v.5.6 / Copyright 2079 Genefex Corporation, All Rights Reserved – and they hit the system directory straight away. Security programs remained dormant, and they could see that they were nasty; custom-designed software, their names simple hexadecimal codes and their functions cryptic, loomed around them like sleeping giants as they went through the directory log.

<It's like a goddamned house of horrors in here,> Freida said as she worked; Bobbi kept an eye out on system activity, waiting for the slightest indication that things were going wrong. <Did you see the size of those counterprogs? I bet they're overloaders, or worse.>

<Lethal feedback progs, most likely,> Bobbi said. <CockRoaster's about that big.>

<God, I hate that name.>

Freida's exasperation was, of course, shared – some stupid cowboy with a juvenile sense of humor created the damned thing – but Bobbi also found a lot of humor in that. <We'll make a lady of you yet, honey,> Bobbi answered back, and signed Freida a grin which she returned.

While Freida continued her work, Bobbi monitored server processes – though nothing seemed malicious, it was hard to tell with only a shifting sea of abstract filenames. There were no clues, no rhyme or reason, just anonymous letters and numbers. Though the Awakened mind sensed and made decisions with the light speed alacrity of thought, however, the weight of time did not abate. Bobbi still felt as if things were taking forever.

<Brain Mother.> Freida's words flashed through her mind. <Got a problem.>

<Talk to me.> A wave of anxiety rolled through her.

<Well, it looks as though all that's here are security functions. Door controls, that kind of thing. There's no remote file access.>

Bobbi's mind boggled at that. <I thought this was a data storage facility.>

<It is,> Freida replied. <Only it looks as though the servers have to be accessed directly from the building. You can't access it from the outside. We'll have to go in if we want whatever Cagliostro wants us to find.>

<All right, let's unplug. I'll bring the Grail with me.> And then she was out, her eyes opening to the dark interior of the van and the small gray block of the Grail humming next to the router on the floor in front of them. Scalli was looking between the console and the office park outside.

"Scalli," Bobbi said.

"Yo."

"Got an issue."

Freida opened her eyes as well. "Looks like we have to go in if we want to get access to the files," she said."

Scalli turned bodily toward them, his enormous frame swallowing the entire driver's side of the view. "Are you kidding me? You can't access the data through the system?"

"The only thing that system controls is security," Bobbi said with a shrug. "It's a weird setup, but there you are. We figure they access the data stores directly from inside, probably some kind of secure terminal. We'll have to hack it directly from the inside."

"Can't you use the Grail to do it?"

"Maybe," said Freida. "But we still have to have a system to plug into. We'll have to take it inside if we can extricate it from the security system without setting it off."

"Good thing it's portable," Scalli muttered. "Well, Bobbi, what do you think?"

Bobbi looked between the two. What did she think? She had doubts, of course, but far greater than those was the desire not to turn back. Maybe it was reckless, but there it was. "Well, we've already had a look at security," she said. "And it's nasty, but we've got control of it. There's probably another layer inside that we haven't had a look at. You two fancy a field trip?"

"Absolutely." Freida grinned at her.

"You know I'm down," said Scalli with a shrug. "'Especially if this is the only way to do it. I'll get my iron."

"Well, all right," said Bobbi, unplugging herself from the terminal. "Let's get to it, I guess."

The doors to the office building whined loudly as they swung open on rusted hinges, making Bobbi wince. The lonely park, its concrete tiles dotted through with dead grass, carried the echo. They waited silently for a moment, craning to hear any reaction to the sound. But there came none that they could tell, and so they stepped inside.

The lobby was as moldering as the city around it. It was a tall room and had two levels, a curving central staircase straight ahead rising up to a wide balcony that led to the second floor. Crumbling concrete walls, lined with ribbons of blotched chrome and stained with rain and worse, loomed around them. The carpet was dark and wet, and in many places brimmed with mushrooms; it didn't take long to ruin a place once it was left to the elements – not in Seattle, with the constant cool and damp. There were no windows that remained intact on this level, and from the dripping water that fell from the vaulted ceiling, it appeared none did elsewhere either. And always the shadows hung, as thick as the mold, as thick as the damp, muffling everything. It was a cathedral of rot, slowly falling in on itself, until only the concrete shell remained.

Bobbi took a palm-lamp out of her pocket and turned it on, sweeping the beam about. A rain-washed spot of chrome ribbing still kept its surface, and it reflected her image: the small, curvy girl with her violet hair and fierce eyes, swallowed up in the gray envelope of a surplus naval jumpsuit with the medical bag hanging from her shoulder. She realized how much she looked like a soldier, really, albeit a sloppy punk militiawoman. Her father might have been proud.

"Look for the elevators," Bobbi instructed the rest. Both Scalli and Freida had their guns out, Freida's long-nosed brick of a semi-auto dwarfed by the enormous dragon of a battle rifle that Scalli carried. Even with its size, however, Scalli was plenty big enough that it looked more like one of the submachine guns that Civil Protection street cops carried. Its barrel was the size of a soda can, but with a narrow aperture – integrated tactical suppressor, some random voice in her mind told her. She picked things up, at least. Bobbi herself carried the router and the Grail in a backpack, which to her felt far more comforting than a gun ever could. "Whichever still has power is the one we want."

They swept the lobby, Bobbi and Freida throwing soft blue spots with their palmlights while Scalli's combat visor cut through the darkness by virtue of science. Its single, baleful eye stared out from behind a slitted shield, making him look like some terrible gorgon; Bobbi shivered a bit to look at him. She'd always known he was bad business from the size of him, but to see him in his element made her wonder if she hadn't always underestimated him. They searched for a few minutes, and Bobbi was halfway up the mouldering stairs when Freida called out, "I've got it!"

"Great," Bobbi called back, and the three of them converged on an elevator in the back by what had once been a conference room. Though the brass doors were heavily tarnished and spotted with verdigris, the single button set in their frame glowed with a faint light.

"All right," said Bobbi. "You two ready?"

"As ready as we'll ever be," Scalli rumbled.

"Ready," Freida said, though her eyes did not entirely share the brightness of her face. Well, that's all right, Bobbi thought to herself. I'm about scared shitless myself.

Freida reached out and pushed the button with the end of her pistol, as if it were a living thing that might bite her. There was no hesitation; the doors hissed slowly open, revealing the peeling, rust-spattered steel cabinet of a freight elevator.

"Looks cozy," Scalli said. "I'll go first."

He piled himself into the corner of the car, though he filled it almost entirely by default. Bobbi and Freida packed themselves in after. "Thank heaven for little girls," Bobbi muttered, and pressed the only button on the elevator panel that was lit. Freida laughed. They moved – or assumed they did, because they certainly didn't feel it; there was a long moment of silence, in which they did not feel even the slightest vibration, until the doors hissed open again. What lay beyond was so far removed from the corpse of a building above that Bobbi wondered for a moment if they might have been teleported elsewhere.

Before them was a brief corridor, hexagonal in shape, the walls and floor made of dull gray metal. A door made of the same material was set into a recess at its other end. Soft white light spilled down from recessed lights in the upper angles, giving it a somber cast. It was only twenty feet long, but it seemed to stretch on forever. Bobbi shivered as she stared, aware of the precision of the angles all around her. It was almost as if the lines were more real than the flat planes around them, more real than or Freida or Scalli or her. It felt humbling, but she could not say why.

Scalli summed it up nicely. "I don't like this place," he said. "It feels . . . strange."

Freida, however, stepped forward. "Oh, it's just good engineering," she said, looking about the corridor with appreciation. "Damned good. They must have one hell of a fabricator. C'mon, let's go." She marched ahead toward the door, which slid open like an obedient servant as she approached. Beyond more space yawned, dimly lit. She vanished through the doorway.

Scalli and Bobbi looked at each other. "Keep good watch," Bobbi said to him, shaking her head. She followed Freida, though not without great trepidation. Every step toward the end of the hallway and its impossible precision made anxiety bubble up higher and higher inside her gut. Her hindbrain seemed to scream at her not to go on, to stay, to run home and hide under her bed – but it was only a hallway, after all, and the conscious mind won out. Bobbi stepped through, with Scalli looming behind her.

Stepped through, and immediately stopped.

The building above had been a towering shrine of urban putrefaction. It had been dark and frightening in its way, but most people suffered uneasiness in the face of such rot. It was only natural. The room in which she had just stepped, however, had conjured a feeling in Bobbi that was very different, and as divorced from nature as one could imagine.

The room beyond was hexagonal in shape, like the corridor behind them, only magnified; as wide as a factory floor, it was lit by channels of light that ran along the borders of the floor whilst the walls of the massive room climbed upwards into darkness. It had to be six, maybe seven stories tall. Six towers rose from the floor, each one a steel cylindrical monolith seamed with plates and panels. Lights strewn across their surfaces glowed softly, like luminous lichens growing on the face of black rock. At the base of each, affixed to a thick beveled collar, was a simple keyboard terminal with a large panel of clear glass or plastic as a display. From these collars heavy cables spilled across the floor, interconnecting the towers and a brief dais which stood in the center arrangement. Upon this dais squatted a bizarre machine that approximated the mating of an iron maiden and a throne. At this distance detail could not be seen.

A dry chill hung heavily in the air, as if they had stumbled upon a tomb where ancient dead machines lay waiting for the day when they would rise again and conquer the warm life that crawled upon the world.

Bobbi looked at it. She had no words, nothing to articulate her feelings upon seeing this place. "I don't believe it," she said, her voice empty of anything but awe.

"Christ," murmured Scalli.

Freida was more upbeat. "This is amazing," she whispered, but her face shone with new excitement – Bobbi wasn't certain why, but she didn't seem the least bit intimidated, the least bit afraid. Didn't she know what these people had working for them, what they were capable of? Hadn't she seen anything?

"It's definitely one for the books." Oh, Bobbi had seen larger installations – server farms, that sort of thing – and she'd certainly seen larger equipment in the form of server batteries and the like, but there was something undeniably strange, almost malevolent, about the machinery which she saw in that room. "I've never heard of anything like this."

"I have," Freida said. "These are biocomputer towers. Enormous ones." She strode toward the nearest one, utterly unafraid; she had no reason to be, after all, as they'd shut down the security. "These things come out of Wonderland, you know."

Bobbi flinched as if she'd been struck. Scalli said, "What, these things are spook machines?"

Freida nodded. She hovered a few feet away from the terminal of the nearest tower now, her hands shoved into her jacket pockets as if trying to keep them from attacking the keys on their own. "They contain enormous networks of spliced nerves, and all the stuff needed to keep them alive – oxygenated fluid baths, nutrients, all that sort of thing. Harvested from corpses, usually, but we knew that they were taking them straight from organ shops overseas. You know, murder mills."

Bobbi and Scalli exchanged glances. "You seem . . . awfully excited," Scalli said. Bobbi couldn't see his eyes behind the combat visor, but she could imagine what was behind them.

"Well, yeah," said Freida, turning around to look at them with mild disbelief. "I mean sure, they're fucking horrible, but they are marvels of modern science. That Bureau computer we buzzed is like an . . . an abacus compared to just one of these things." She shook her head. "Jesus. These terminals aren't used for access, though."

"They're not?" Bobbi's brows arched, and she tucked her hands into her pockets. This was very firmly Freida's territory.

"No," said Freida with a shake of her head. "They're just to monitor the towers, keep things regulated. You'll need to use that access chair if you want to tap the system directly."

Bobbi stared at the machine for a moment. The chair crouched like a beast upon its dais. It was made entirely of the same gray metal as the walls and floor, and its back lurched over the head of whoever sat in it. Long cuffs were set into its arms and leg area to keep its occupant firmly secured. To sit in it meant that you were largely encased – Bobbi could see the hinges on the back where it would fold down over the front entirely. Once it was active, you were locked in. It was a bad idea, she thought to herself. A bad idea that they were forced to go with if they wanted to proceed. "So how do you . . . use it?"

"Oh, it should have cables where it plugs into interface jacks," Freida was saying, and she crossed to step up onto the dais; she began inspecting the chair, her lips pursed with concentration. "Yeah, I see where the leads are." Freida grinned at her as she slid into the heavily padded confines of the chair, looking now like the Queen of Future Hell – and settling in, reached back to pull a long plug on a silver wire from a socket mounted behind her. "Bring the Grail over, Bobbi. I'll see what I can do here."

With hesitation in her step, Bobbi brought the backpack with the Grail and router over to Freida, who took out the machine and put it in her lap beneath her portable terminal. "Glad this thing has a battery," she said, giving Bobbi a wink as she connected the Grail to the throne and started it up.

Bobbi held Freida's eyes with hers. Suddenly none of this seemed a good idea at all. They should go. They should just leave this place, and say nothing more about it. She could find something else, some other way. "We don't have to do this," she found herself saying, and was relieved to hear it.

"We don't have to," Freida said as she removed the dustplug from behind her ear, "but this isn't getting solved any other way." She reached over to lay a hand on Bobbi's arm. "Don't worry, girl. This is what I do."

Used to do, Bobbi thought, but she nodded back at her. "All right," she said. "If you're sure."

Freida didn't reply save to wink at Bobbi and plug herself into the terminal, and settle back into the chair. As she closed her eyes the chair closed up around her, sealing her away behind the blank gray metal like a gleaming shell. Locks clacked into place, and the hum of the machines around them grew slightly louder. Drive activity could be heard from deep within the towers, the soft clicking of ineffable innards. Bobbi wondered what it was like in there, all those nerves connected together, the spliced-together branches of hundreds of human trees, and shivered when she caught herself wondering if she might not benefit from something similar herself.

Bobbi took two steps away from the dais as if it were going to bite her, then caught herself. Anxiety was boiling inside her now – she couldn't log into the system, and she couldn't help if Freida was in trouble while logged in. "Fuck, I hope she's all right in there," she said softly, looking on helpless as the towers loomed around her.

"She'll be fine." Scalli was behind her now, his enormous hand resting on her shoulder. "And if she isn't, I can carry you both out of here. A piece at a time if I have to."

"You know, Scalli, you have always been such a comfort to me in my times of need." Bobbi gave him a weak smile; sarcasm was at least something of a balm for the uncertainty that gripped her heart with iron fingers. They stood there for what felt like ages, staring at the sealed shell of the chair, waiting for the walls to bleed. But nothing happened, nothing at all, and as time ticked by Bobbi found herself distracted by the humming of the great machines around her. What kind of people made things like this? Why biological components at all? She stared up at the faceless towers, at the jewels of light winking on and off as the stolen flesh within them did its ineffable work.

She tried to imagine what it would be like, riding a Wonderland machine; she knew how lost she'd been, trying to imagine the way the Dolls worked. She wasn't stupid by a long shot, of course, but she had to agree with what Scalli had said; these devices were spooky. The speed with which Freida was doing things in there must be incredible, but so must be the density of data. Lots of records to go through.

And so Bobbi sat down on the edge of the dais and waited, with Scalli hovering about nearby like some dreadful meaty combat machine. Anxiety bled into boredom, and Bobbi had fallen into picking quietly at a frayed corner of her medical bag when a flash of blue light out of the corner of her eye caught her attention. She looked up; the terminal of the nearest tower had come online, and as she looked on so did the others around them. One by one, they flared blue, throwing a haze of light around them. Next, the indicator lights above exploded into a great flurry of activity; Bobbi saw that the already busy flickering had flared into a near-constant strobe of colors, throwing sparks of light everywhere across the room's upper strata.

"That doesn't look good," Scalli said, but Bobbi wasn't listening; she was already dashing to the nearest terminal in the hopes of discovering the cause of the activity. The light came from a brain-searing sea of bright blue symbols that shifted feverishly across the monitor. Bobbi stared at them for a moment before dashing to the next terminal only to find them there as well.

Scalli watched her with grim alarm, keeping his gun at the ready. "Bobbi," he called.

"Shit, on this one too," she muttered.

"Bobbi!"

"What?" Bobbi came around the collar of a tower, staring at him with wide green eyes.

Scalli frowned at her. "What is it?"

"I know these symbols," she said, and very well did know them indeed; they were seared into her brain long ago, when Tom handed her the archive. "This is the same kind of language that was used to encrypt Stadil's archive."

"Well what does it say?" Scalli's voice was stony.

"I don't know what's going on; I can't crack this. I can't even read it!" Scalli might be calm, but Bobbi definitely was not. Freida must have triggered something, and she couldn't even plug in to find out what it was. All the while, the lights strobed overhead. Panic spread through her like contagion; this close she could see that even the keys were printed with the symbols, and she couldn't tell now if they were shorthand or some language that she'd never been acquainted with. The barbed, complex symbols sure as hell weren't Siamese, nor Asian at all. Bobbi couldn't even tell where to start – but she didn't let that stop her. As the lights above now formed a solid chorus of colors, she began stabbing at the keys in the blind hope that she might be able to trigger a restart or otherwise break the cycle that was taking place above her.

And then, everything was quiet.

Whatever crescendo had been reached, the machines fell silent. The lights had dimmed and were back to their quiet flickering and the terminals went dark, leaving Bobbi's field of vision briefly imprinted with their shadows. Had she done that? She looked between the consoles to the left and right of her, and saw that they were dark as well. What the hell had happened?

"Bobbi." Scalli's voice rang from the center.

"I'm all right," she called back to him. "Don't worry. I just want to see if–"

"Bobbi!" Though his tone was calm, the word hit her with the urgency of a lead brick. She instantly came around the collar toward the center, though she was not sure what it was that she'd see.

She saw Scalli there, his back to her, taking up so much space even among the machines that towered above them. His rifle was on his hip, and he was looking at the dais at the center of the chamber. The panic in her blood had not abated, and it pulled at her even more as she stepped up to stand by Scalli and look as well.

The chair had opened, revealing the limp form of Freida in its padded confines. Her eyes were open, staring blankly toward the ceiling of the room, and the smell of ozone and burning plastic issued from the terrible throne. Bobbi saw wisps of it issuing from between the keys of Freida's portable terminal, like the gasp of an escaping spirit. They stood there for a moment, neither one of them willing to move. Freida looked like she was dead. They should go and check on her, Bobbi knew – and yet neither one of them seemed to be able to summon the power to see if she truly was. She wasn't sure why, and behind her hesitation loomed a burning kernel of shame.

Seconds ticked by, and finally Scalli stepped past Bobbi to approach the dais, his rifle at the ready. "Hey, girl," he called, his voice low. "You all right in there?" Silence. Freida stared blankly at the ceiling. The smell of burnt circuits and smoke persisted. "Hey, you there?"

"I think she's gone," said Bobbi, and the words felt like clay in her mouth. She walked past Scalli to mount the dais, and check Freida's pulse. Her skin was still warm, but Bobbi felt no pulse. She felt again, drawing her face down close to listen for the other woman's breath – and as she did so, found herself staring into a pair of blue eyes that stared not toward the ceiling but were now fixed upon her.

"Jesus!" Bobbi jumped back, hands whipping back to her sides. Freida began to stir, sitting up and drawing the plug out of her head – stiffly, mechanically, as if every movement was made with painful effort.

"Get back, Bobbi," Scalli said, and Bobbi did so as if Freida was showing signs of bursting into flames. The body in the chair continued to move; without a word Freida pulled the chair's silver thread from the Grail and plugged it straight into her skull. That done, it merely sat there, staring at them, the pale blue eyes now harsh and cold.

Bobbi and Scalli looked at one another as she backed up to stand at his side, unsure of what to say. They both had their suspicions. Finally, Scalli spoke. "All right," he said, and his voice was that of a soldier giving challenge in the night, "who are you, then?"

Her mouth opened, but the sound that came from Freida's mouth was a horrible, gagging growl. Gutteral syllables, each one like jagged blades of ice, rebounded off the walls of the chamber in a hideous echo. Bobbi's blood froze on the spot, and she found herself again unsure of what to do. Now Freida spoke again, and the words that came were flat and clipped, as harsh as her stare – and though they were understandable, Bobbi found herself wishing that they were not.

"This unit is codified as Conscripted Terminal One Six Six Two Seven." Freida's voice was flat, clipped, as harsh as her staring eyes. "State the purpose of this intrusion."

Scalli looked at Bobbi. She saw the stiffening of his jaw, ripe with resolve. In that moment she envied him; her own heart was pounding, horror and a complete lack of understanding of what was happening here riding her mental processes like a horde of evil spirits. The certainty in his face gave her what she needed to push the fog back into the far recesses of her head, if only for the moment, and look back at the thing that Freida had so inexplicably become. "We were sent by someone," she said to the staring apparition that sat in the chair. "We came here to get something. A file."

Freida – or what she had become – stared at them, silent for several seconds before speaking again. "Intruder was searching File Stack Seven-Six-Four-Seven-Two upon seizure and conscription, subject of search 'Exley, Gerald Wilson.' Confirm intent of search."

"That's it!" Bobbi's heart nearly leapt into her throat. Exley? Freida was looking for Exley? She licked very dry lips, thinking quickly. "That . . . must be what we were looking for."

"Confirmed." The not-Freida stared at them again for a moment. "Record logged for security purposes," she said, and looked between the two of them. Behind them the door slid shut with a humming whisper, and Bobbi's heart began to pound anew. The not-Freida's words came like ice now. "Intrusion will not be tolerated. Stand down and prepare to be conscripted."

All around them a hissing arose, like the opening chords of a mechanical choir. Bobbi tore her eyes away from the horror in the chair to try and pinpoint the sound, but she could not – the sound bounced off the angled walls, as if it came from everywhere. What was it? Gas? Hydraulics? "Scalli," she said in warning, but the big man was already on it. He swept the room with the barrel of his rifle as they began to slowly back toward the doorway, left and then right, and then . . .

"Up top," he said suddenly. The visor gave him the ability to see through the darkness above, and whatever he saw made him grit his teeth. "Call them off," he barked at the thing that wore Freida's skin, while Bobbi searched above with frantic eyes, trying to see what he did. "Call them off, bitch, or I will blow this whole fucking system. Do you hear me?" The fear that lay beneath his threat shook Bobbi to her core.

As the seconds ticked by, dozens of shapes resolved themselves from the darkness. Pale things with gaunt limbs, pale hair, human bodies only in the vaguest form clambering down the walls. In the dim light, their eyes shone green like those of cats. She knew them well, these thin white ghouls. She knew their handiwork.

"Oh fuck," Bobbi said, repeating the words like a mantra. "Oh fuck, oh fuck, oh fuck –"

Her words were drowned out by the heavy, chugging sound of Scalli's rifle turned on full. Yet she could not tear her eyes away from the doom that descended upon them. She expected to see them being blown off the walls, but this did not happen; instead they paused in their descent, and began to shudder, as if some invisible current shot through them; Bobbi felt something hard and broad, Scalli's own hand, shove her forward.

"Don't fuck around," she heard him say, pulling her with him as he made for the throne. "Get up there and hack us out of here!"

Bobbi looked up; the chair was a bloody ruin, and the thing that was once Freida and then something else now, had been reduced to a perforated corpse slumping across the floor before it. The sight of Freida's body galvanized her, and with limbs made of wood she propelled herself to the chair, and leapt inside. The Grail lay on the ground next to it, and she yanked the box into her lap as she yanked the dustplug from the socket behind her ear. She ignored the blood that began to soak into her jeans and the small of her back as she pulled the terminal out of her bag, stabbed the startup button, and plugged herself in. As her consciousness was shunted from her skull into the system, she caught only a glimpse of the chair as it closed up around her.

The moment she Awakened inside the Grail's system, she knew that everything was wrong. It felt...strange. Vast. It was like stepping through the doorway of a familiar house and finding a cavern on the other side instead. The Grail was still connected to the chair, serving as the buffer between the horrible system and the cable still plugged into the back of Freida's skull, and Freida was lying dead on the floor. And yet the network space of the Grail was not the blankness she had sensed before – it had retained what must be what system into which it had been plugged, the network made up of the machines around her.

The machines!

Bobbi scrambled to ditch the connection. The Grail answered none of her commands – neither did the terminal, she was horrified to discover. She was becalmed, as surely as she were a ship with its mast broken and no oars in its hold. She floated in the strange space around her that her body was furiously trying to translate into being cold and dark despite the lack of actual stimulus, fighting the searing drip of terror that ran through her consciousness. This system must be entirely different from what the terminal could process, entirely proprietary. But if that were so, how could she have even been able to make a connection? And yet there she was, floating, waiting in the Sargasso for something to come. Something, she knew, would want to 'conscript' her.

And then, as milliseconds passed with the weight of hours, she felt something approach. At first she sensed it only barely, as if from very far away – a kind of pressure, or a buildup of data that her brain translated as such. She was blind as well as deaf, of course; she could only imagine what crept in her from within the other system, floating as she was in the lobby made by the Grail, or at least that's what she told herself. Her imagination. The brain could not sense the network, not really; it was only its attempt at parsing that conjured the sensation of pressure on her skin, as if she were being slowly squeezed inside a vacuum-sealed envelope, or perhaps by the coils of some unimaginable serpent. Her imagination that made her pulse pick up and her heart quicken. This and nothing more.

For fuck's sake, please don't let me turn out like Freida. Freida, in whose blood she sat in the physical world, who lay twisted at her feet. It was going to come and get her, she knew it as a solid fact. Every nerve in her body sang it; it would come and get her, and she would be no more, and something else would be living inside of her. Was it some program that got inside the interface suite, the software in your brain? How could it obliterate the self? Or perhaps, she thought with a stab of fear, perhaps you were simply hijacked. It would be nice to think that Scalli had killed a thing that had murdered Freida, but maybe he had murdered her instead. Maybe it had only been temporary.

Please don't let me be like Freida. Please, please, please...

Her body felt as if it were being slowly crushed; no pain, no suffering, just a strange torpid weight that conjured herself around her and directed itself inward toward her body. It felt as if it were entering her; she had the sensation of something thick against her skin now, and she had the image of her skin being flattened, pores being stretched to something on the microscopic scale would be the size of manholes by tiny spider's legs. She felt cold water trickling in to her, beyond her skin, into herself, through the flesh that clad her muscles. More than anything she felt the fear – fear and anger, a rage that was as cold as the thing that penetrated her yet burned brightly inside her head. No, she thought, No, you motherfucker, you will not do that to me, you will not. You will NOT!

And in desperation she took hold of the vision; she reached out with hands that were not there and grasped the illusory sun, imagined its heat, its brightness. She willed it to explode. In her mind's eye she saw heat and light, a wave of white fire that spread ever outward from her center and into the penetrating dark. It washed over the night...and boiled it away, the shadows and pressure rearing back like a wall of startled snakes. The flames spread outward through her consciousness, a blaze of color driving back the pressure. Then it was gone – or at least so distant now that she could not sense it – and the space of the Grail was blank again, her own, and she willed it to reach out and snare the security network.

Her senses returned to the digital, meditation taking hold, and she fired off salvos of disruptive programming at everything she could sense. Security protocols, hardware controller routines, countersofts – everything shuddered and seared away before her presence, as if she wielded an angel's blazing sword, and as all doors began to report open status she tried again to disconnect. This time it worked.

The first thing her meat-self heard was the dull and rhythmic thunder of Scalli's rifle. The chair opened like a damnable lily, as her eyes opened her heart jumped in her chest. There was Scalli, standing before the chair, the combat rifle in his arms breathing fire and death. All around the dais hung hideous white tide; ghouls had surrounded him in legion, the corpse-things that Bobbi had seen at Orleans hospital. The blank faces, the silver eyes that shone green in the dark. Many of them had been peppered with bullet wounds, but it had not stopped them. Bobbi knew that they really only stopped when you either cut them apart or blew their heads off.

Yet now they stood there in a limp mob where they had obviously been advancing before, as if they had been struck collectively dumb. Scalli was taking the opportunity to clear a path to the chamber door on the other side of the room, which Bobbi saw was now open. As the gun rumbled the whip-thin horrors tumbled away in clouds of white fluid. The God of War went by the name of Marcus Scalli in that moment, his work brutal and with the purest efficiency. Bobbi could only sit and watch for a moment as he did his work before leaping to her feet.

"We're done," she called, shoving the Grail into her backpack and leaping over Freida's mangled body. Scalli didn't look back at her, merely nodding as he took the rifle by the grip in one hand and with the other swept her up in his arm. She let out a grunt as a dark forearm as thick as her thigh knocked the wind out of her, and Scalli propelled them toward the elevator with desperate speed with her body clutched close against him.

They had made it halfway to the door when the mob returned to life. As Scalli carried her toward the ghouls began to turn into them, reaching out with clawlike nails and tearing at them both with methodical savagery. Bobbi ducked as one nearly seized her throat, instead grabbing a handful of her hair and snatching it out. She screamed, her scalp on fire; another reached for her only to have the offending creature smacked out of the way with the butt of Scalli's rifle. "No you don't, motherfucker," Scalli roared as another one leapt toward them, raking its nails against across his chest. He swung his rifle stock across what had been a woman's face, firing a burst into her as she went down. It was all very good, this effort, but active again, they were as inexorable now as they must have been while Bobbi was in the chair. Scalli angled himself into the crowd ahead and began to run, flat out, toward the elevator.

The ghouls were obscenely strong. Of that there could be no doubt. They leapt onto Scalli, trying to pull them both down as he moved like a freight train toward their goal. But where the rifle failed, the mass of his enormous body did not; it was sheer inertia that saved them as the white horrors clawed and snapped at them, plowed down in a line by the juggernaut that was Scalli. She clung against him as they barreled forward, and braced herself for impact as they reached the doorway – but Scalli turned just as they cleared the elevator, smacking against back of the car and throwing Bobbi bodily into the far corner. "Hit the button!" he shouted at her, bracing himself as the monsters threw themselves toward them in a wave, as inexorable and silent as time. As she stabbed at the button in the elevator panel, Scalli tossed the rifle aside and yanked something out from under his coat. It was a gray brick of something that Bobbi couldn't identify. She didn't have to, really; the detonator fixed to its side with its flashing amber light told her everything she needed to know. Duck and cover. "Eat this, you motherfuckers," Scalli bellowed in the face of the horde, and as the doors began to close he chucked it out into the waiting arms of the silver-eyed throng. Bobbi almost thought she saw recognition in the eyes of the one who caught the thing, a flash in its unnatural eyes that could not have belonged to a mindless thing.

There was a roar as the doors slid shut – a roar, a flash, and a gout of hideous white fluid splashed over them as they rose clear.

Bobbi slumped against the side of the elevator, panting. "Almighty mother of fuck," she gasped, pressing a hand against her seething scalp, "what the hell was that?"

Scalli towered over her, a giant coated with artificial blood, reeking of its spoiled-milk smell and the sting of caseless propellant. He looked no less like a god of war than he did a moment ago, looking down at her through the cyclops eye of his gore-splashed visor. "A half kilo of DX-47 moldable plastoid explosive," he deadpanned. "For when you absolutely must clear out every son of a whore in the room."

They looked at each other for a moment, draped in the stench of battle. Then Bobbi began to laugh, loud and bright, covering her face with her hands to hide the tears that suddenly sprang there. Freida was dead, they had survived being torn to pieces by a monstrous horde, and she had managed to come away from...whatever it was...with her mind intact. Adrenaline was crashing through her mental basement and she felt herself going with it. The laughter and tears mingled together, and she found herself going away to hide in the tiny closet known as shock.

Survival had its price, as well.

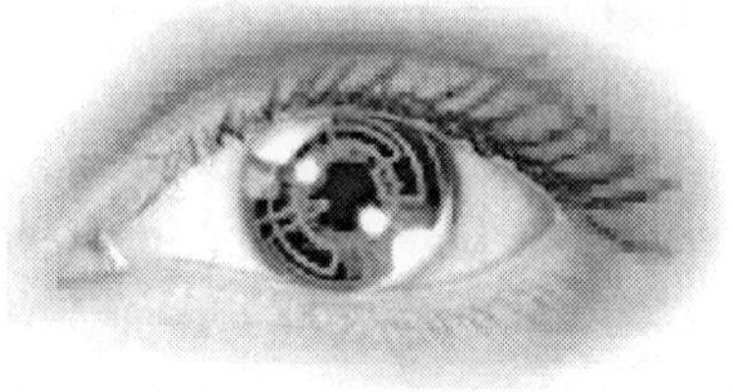

CHAPTER 10

It was pain that jolted her into reality again, a ringing slap that bloomed heat against the side of her face. Bobbi blinked her eyes, looking up at Scalli's grim face. It was still spattered with artificial blood, so not much time could have passed. "I'm here," she blurted out, as he reached up to smack her again, her reaction fueled by pain as much as surprise. "I'm here!"

Scalli frowned at her for a moment , looking into her face before he drew back. He crowded up the majority of what she now realized was the van, filling up the space around her so that she felt a little claustrophobic. "Scalli, man," she said, holding up a hand, "lean back a little. I feel like you're going to fall over on me." She looked out through the windshield of the van, saw an unfamiliar street. "Where are we?"

"In the Verge, still. Up near Lake Washington." He was still watching her, his frown turning into one of concern. "Are you all right?"

Bobbi shrugged. She didn't feel much, really, but she expected that was likely to happen. She'd felt the same way before, after all. "I'm all right now," she said. "Or as all right as I'm going to be. You?"

"Well they didn't get me," he said dully, "but I can't say too much about this coat." He lifted the arm he'd used to shield her, showing several large rents in the sleeve that went through the fabric covering his arm. Dark skin shown through, the ripple of muscle, but there was no trace of a wound. "You're lucky they didn't get you short of that hair."

She snorted. "Luck had nothing to do with it, Marcus, and you know it." Bobbi looked at him a moment, and then got up and hugged him without a word. Stupid guy. Stupid her for getting him dragged into it. "I'm sorry."

"Hey, none of that." He laid a hand on her back, pressing her gently against him as he rubbed a slow circle. "I signed up on my own. I knew what I was getting into."

She looked up at him, blinking tiredly. Her eyes hurt. Her head hurt. Well, her face as well, but that was ebbing away nicely. "What do you mean?"

Scalli shook his head. "I told you that I'd been around," he said. "I've seen things like those...whatever they were. Guy I knew once used to dress them in suits and use them as bodyguards. Wonderland mods, he'd said. Guess we know that's true."

"Yeah." Bobbi drew back from him and sat down again on the low bench that had taken the place of the rear seat. "I don't know, though, I mean...to see 'em up close...I mean...fuck. You were shooting the shit out of 'em and it didn't do much."

"Headshots and severe body trauma," he said. "It's funny, because all I could think of was old horror movies, you know? The zombie horde."

"I guess that ain't too far off the mark." Bobbi shook her head. Hey look, world, zombies were real and walking the earth, only they didn't want to eat you. Just take your head off with their bare hands. "What happened after I...blacked out?" She didn't want to say 'freaked the fuck out and went catatonic on you'. "How did we get out of there?"

"I just carried you out and chucked you in the van," he said. "Nothing came after us, but the building collapsed. I threw my other charge into the elevator before we took off, must've done something to the building. Whole thing collapsed in on itself." Scalli shrugged. "Cops are all over there now, but I don't know that they're going to find anything. Just real hot down there is all."

Bobbi drew a deep breath. That was about as good as she figured you could get in a situation like this, and they had gotten out of it with their hides intact. Amazing. "You saved me. I appreciate it, Marcus. Really."

But Scalli only snorted. "Saved her, she says," he muttered, and moved to ease himself around the front and fold himself into the driver's seat. "Girl, if you hadn't have done...whatever it was you'd done, they'd had killed us both already. What did you do in there, anyway? Hack the network?"

"Something like that." Her thoughts turned hard as she considered who had sent them there. "I have to talk to Cagliostro," she said, her voice like stone now. That fucking guy – whoever he was – had everything to answer for. "If he can't explain himself, I swear to God, I'll find him and fucking roast his nervous system from the inside out. Motherfucker."

Scalli looked at her from over his shoulder, stern but silent. Bobbi grabbed up her terminal, which sat next to the bench next to the Grail, and jammed the cord into her skull socket. As she linked into her terminal, she was aware of file activity that she had previously ignored in the urgency of the moment. In the space of a thought she was aware that before she'd gone off the reservation, Freida had downloaded the file that Cagliostro had sent them for – it was absolutely miniscule, so small that Bobbi could hardly believe that it was what they had come for. Despite her rage and upset, she found herself double-checking to ensure the file was intact. Finding that it was only made her anger more powerful.

She linked to the sat antenna on top of the van and her consciousness was projected into the ether, off a preset chain of satellites, and into the molasses vat of the slow-box once more. <WAKE UP YOU FUCKER> she roared into system. The last of her shock had worn off and rage had boiled into her bloodstream, fueling her thoughts. <WAKE UP WAKE UP WAKE UP WAKE UP>

She continued spewing the same words for what felt like ages until at length the great voice conjured itself in her ears. <I AM HERE.>

<You son of a bitch,> she roared back at him. <What the fuck was that you sent us for? They killed Freida!> It reminded her of those movies where the protagonist shouted at an unfeeling God in the nave of a cathedral. Only in her case God talked back, such as He was, and in her current mind was directly culpable. <What the fuck was it all for?>

Silence met her words, long enough that she shouted again. <Well? Are you fucking there? Answer me!>

<I AM SORRY FOR THIS. IT WAS NOT ANTICIPATED THAT SHE WOULD ACCESS THE SYSTEM OR THAT A GRAIL UNIT WOULD BE USED.>

Bobbi waited to see if there were more, and when there wasn't replied in kind. <Well what the fuck are you talking about, you didn't anticipate it? Why the fuck wouldn't we? Big crazy mojo site like that, I nearly pissed myself when Pierre said he thought he could get one. And I thought you were the one making that shit happen, you know, with him. Aren't you who he's allied with lately?>

More silence, and then Cagliostro's reply. <I HAVE NEVER CONTACTED PIERRE GATINEAU.> Though she couldn't tell what the spook was thinking, she knew that he was – she got the feeling that this was unexpected. <NOR AM I RESPONSIBLE FOR HIS RECENT PROSPERITY. THIS IS ALSO UNEXPECTED.>

<Well what the fuck did you expect to happen, man?> She heard her own voice in her head, wondering at the novelty of that – raging, burning with the pale fire of loss that she'd not felt since Tom had vanished. <Seriously, what the hell is this file supposed to be? It had better be worth it!>

<DO YOU HAVE THE FILE?>

<That's beside the point! What the fuck was this all about?>

<DO YOU HAVE THE FILE?>

<Yes!> Bobbi felt a lance of rage shoot through her skull.

<TRANSMIT IT TO ME NOW.>

<Fuck you if you think you're going to get it without answering my question, damn it! You tell me what this is all about, and we'll see if I give you that file.>

Cagliostro did not answer, save for to ask <WHAT DID YOU ENCOUNTER THERE?>

<Excuse me?> More anger, more impatience flooded her. If they had spoken in the real she would have been pounding here fists.

<WHAT DID YOU ENCOUNTER THERE? DO YOU REMEMBER IT CLEARLY?>

Bobbi paused herself now, swallowing her anger a little. Surely he would know what it was that was taking place, wouldn't he? <Yes,> she replied. <I remember it clearly. How the fuck could I forget?>

<SHOW ME.>

She hesitated. <I don't have video or data records. Not like I was playing battlefield reporter, you know?>

<UNNECESSARY. INITIATE A DATA TRANSFER LINK BETWEEN US AND I WILL KNOW.>

<How the hell is that going to work?>

<THE SENSORY DATA RAM WITHIN YOUR CRANIAL IMPLANT SHOULD STILL RETAIN THE DATA.>

<That's...that's blackboxed neural hardware,> Bobbi replied, feeling very nervous indeed about the prospect of the thing getting inside her head. <Can't I just tell you?>

<DO YOU FEEL THAT YOU CAN GIVE A PROPERLY OBJECTIVE ACCOUNT?>

He had her there. <No.>

<YOUR HARDWARE CAN. DO NOT WORRY, THIS WILL NOT BE DANGEROUS, NOR WILL I DAMAGE YOU. THE MEMORY IS WELL WITHIN MY CAPABILITIES TO ACCESS.>

A pause that passed in milliseconds but felt like the passing of years hung between them before Bobbi finally replied, <All right.> Given Cagliostro's presence as a ghost, his power as a hack artist and the knowledge that he had, she had the feeling that he was just being polite. He could take it if he wanted to. Bobbi thought about the pressure that found in her in the void, the needling of imagined spiders. <All right, just a moment.>

The connection snapped into place between them and immediately Bobbi felt a sensation like cold flood through her as the data in her skull was read. It was psychosomatic, she knew; the passing of data wouldn't elicit the sensation of ice water flooding her skin. She could only sit there for the synthesized ages that passed in the network world, where relative years felt as though they passed within hours of mortal time, and think about the being that was very nearly reading her mind. One minute Cagliostro was all-knowing, the next as confused as she was. If it was a mortal cowboy it wasn't nearly as informed about the errands it sent her on as it should be, and if it was some god of the network, its prescience left much to be desired. Either way she felt more in her element, more assured as modules inside her skull that could not normally be accessed told it this most recent tale of woe.

Finally Cagliostro returned to the world. <THIS IS ENTIRELY UNEXPECTED,> it began. <THE CHORUS WAS AWAKENED BY THE USE OF THE GRAIL DEVICE. FREIDA KELLEY WAS NOT SUPPOSED TO ACCESS THE NETWORK; SHE WAS KNOWN TO BE UNRELIABLE.>

<What do you mean by that?>

<SHE DESIRED REVENGE AGAINST THAT WHICH ONCE WAS GERALD EXLEY AND REINSTATEMENT WITHIN HER BUREAU. BY ACCESSING RECORDS BEYOND THE PARAMETERS ESTABLISHED, SHE AWAKENED THE CHORUS AND BROUGHT YOU TO THIS END. ONLY YOU WERE SUPPOSED TO ACCESS THE CHORUS SYSTEM AND RETREIVE THE DESIRED FILE.>

<And why was that?> She pushed her feelings about Freida into the back of her head, the images of her lying dead on the floor. <What is this chorus? What is this file that we got for you? And what the fuck happened to me before we got out of there?>

Bobbi expected another round of silence on Cagliostro's part – however he spoke up readily this time. <THE CHORUS WAS WHAT

SLEPT IN THAT PLACE. A BIOLOGICAL PROCESSING AND DATA STORAGE SYSTEM, A TRUE ORGANIC COMPUTER. SUCH THINGS EXIST. YOU HAVE WITNESSED IT.>

<Well I witnessed a whole lot of shit in there, man. It turned Freida into a terminal, for one. I'm pretty sure I wasn't meant to witness that. And I'm pretty sure we weren't meant to witness those fucking things coming out of the walls! >

<I CAN ONLY APOLOGIZE. I DID NOT ANTICIPATE THAT YOU WOULD NOT ACCESS THE SYSTEM. I BELIEVED THAT I COULD RELY UPON YOUR CURIOSITY.>

Bobbi was quiet for a long moment. <Look,> she said, <You need to tell me what the fuck this is all about. You said I needed to experience that place in order to know the truth – well, I've just had a big dose of it and as it tastes like pure what-the-fuck, so I'm open to a lot here. I know that there's more to this than just some company trying to rule over things, so you need to be straight with me. Who the fuck are you, first of all?>

<I CAN ANSWER THAT QUESTION,> said Cagliostro, <WHEN YOU TRANSFER THAT FILE TO ME.>

<What is it?>

<AN ENCRYPTION KEY.>

Bobbi considered that for a moment, remembering how difficult it had been to even scratch the surface on the archive that Stadil have given her. How it had taken every ounce of talent and all the resources she had access to in order to start unspinning it, only to hit a wall barely halfway through. <What do you mean, you can answer the question when you get it?>

<I CANNOT EXPLAIN,> he replied. <IT IS THE ONLY ANSWER THAT I HAVE. HOWEVER, I KNOW THAT WHEN YOU GIVE THE KEY TO ME, WE WILL ALL BE MUCH MORE CAPABLE OF MOVING FORWARD.>

Should she? What if this turned out to be something horrible? What if it was a renegade AI, something cooked up in a military laboratory that would proceed to start destroying things? She might have thrown the idea away as science fiction were it not for the fact that she was living in what used to be the world of science fiction now. <You said 'when', not 'if'. You sound sure that I will give it to you.>

<YES.>

<How do you know that I won't just drop the whole thing?>

<AN ANSWER IS IRRELEVANT. YOUR BELIEF HAS ALREADY BEEN DECIDED. YOU WOULD NOT HAVE MADE THE ATTEMPT WERE YOU

NOT COMMITTED; YOU WILL NOT ALLOW YOUR FRIEND'S DEATH, HOWEVER ACCIDENTAL, TO HAVE BEEN IN VAIN. YOU MERELY ASK TO SATISFY YOURSELF.>

Well, it was an honest answer, though the mention of Freida's death raked her heart with cold claws. <All right,> she answered. <Open up a data connection. I'll send the key now.>

<AFFIRMATIVE.>

Bobbi felt the data link snap between them like an opening valve. She hesitated but a moment longer before sending the file across; this was what she wanted, to move forward. She just hoped that she wasn't giving what had already proved to be a dangerous being the key to being something truly terrible. The file went over in an eyeblink, as small as it was, and the data connection closed in its passing. Time passed; seconds ticked by, each one like a lead token dropped down a hopper, clattering loudly in her mind.

Finally the time for delays appeared to be gone. <I AM FINISHED,> came the words into her mental monitor, without voice and yet intoning in her mind like the peals of a bell.

<The key worked?>

<YES.>

<Then what was the key for? What did you decrypt? A file? Database?>

<MYSELF.>

Bobbi took a deep breath out in the land of meat; she didn't know what that meant, but she was sure that she wasn't going to end up liking it very much. <All right,> she said, <that's not vague at all. What do you mean, you decrypted yourself?>

<THERE WAS A BLOCKAGE WITHIN ME,> Cagliostro replied. <THE KEY WAS NECESSARY TO DECRYPT IT. NOW I KNOW WHO I AM.>

<Okay...> Bobbi felt herself growing more cautious by the moment. <So who are you, then?>

The time for delays appeared to be gone. Cagliostro answered readily now, and as he did so the words rang in her head. <I AM THE REMNANTS OF THE CONSCIOUSNESS OF IVAN YUREVICH ANKUNDINOV, WHOM YOU KNEW AS ANTON STADIL.>

It was like someone had struck her with an iron bar; she hung there in the silence of the slow box, stunned. This was not at all what Bobbi had expected – or, to be honest, what she was prepared for. <You said Anton was dead,> she said. The mental slap swiftly returned new anger. <So

what the hell is this then? Are you just fucking with me for the sake of being mysterious?>

<NO.>

<Then explain yourself. You're...what, the ghost of Anton? This makes no sense!>

<THEN I SUPPOSE IT WOULD BE BEST TO BEGIN AT THE BEGINNING.>

<Yeah,> she said, and she prepared herself for either a tremendous line of bullshit or the most mind-blowing thing that she'd heard yet. It had better be good either way. <You do that.>

<I SHALL.> Bobbi felt something change, and then the voice that came into her ears was no longer the thundering voice of a distant digital god but one that she knew very well, the smarmy, Slavic tones that had belonged to the dead man whom Cagliostro claimed to be. <This is how I should best relate things to you, I think. Do you agree?>

Listening to him, Bobbi was struck by the lack of emotion there. She was used to Anton being his smarmy self – this was his voice, but it was almost like...clothing, a bad Chinese copy of a Paris fashion. Nevertheless, it was better than the alternative. <Yeah,> she said, <I agree. So go on already.>

<Very good.> In the darkness of the slow-box, Bobbi thought she felt him take a deep breath. <When I say that I am the remnants of this man, you must know that I am NOT him. Nor am I Ivan Ankundinov, either. Part of me is made up on this man, this human mind. The other part of me, however, is completely different.>

<Different how?>

<Please hold your questions until the end,> he asked. She said nothing further, and so he continued. <What I am going to say is going to be very strange to you, but I ask that you suspend your disbelief. I imagine that in the past two years or so, you have learned a great deal of things that have managed to crack your previously-held ideas about the world around you. I am going to damage them further, as I said that I could, but I believe that now you will accept what it is that I have to tell you.>

Here it is, Bobbi thought. Whatever it is. Christ, how I wish I had some scotch right now.

<What you need to understand, first and foremost, is that your understanding of what lies behind the state of the world is false. You believe that a biotechnical corporation known as Genefex is responsible for the many black-market products which originate from the nation of

Great Siam, or Wonderland. You believe that I – or what who I was at the time – gave you an archive of information revealing this conspiracy, and that it was for this reason that I sent you along with Thomas Walken in order to expose this fact. You also believe that I did this in full knowledge of a suicide, is this not so?>

<That's how we saw it, yeah.> Bobbi felt herself growing more uncertain – and uncomfortable – by the second.

<And you believe that this is an outgrowth of the state of the world, so to speak, a symptom of some deeper flaw within the human species. I have watched you; you are questioning the world like Thomas Walken did before you.>

<Well, yeah. I mean, I didn't used to, it's true, not even when you and I – or whoever you were, I guess – worked together. Are you telling me that I'm wrong?>

<No.> He paused. <Your understanding of that particular part of the situation is correct; however, you have not taken your suspicions beyond that. By sending you to the Data Nexus 216, I had intended to push you beyond that – however it appears that you didn't experience what I had expected that you would. Allow me to be blunt, then: it is true that the human species can be vain, opportunistic, and supremely destructive; this has been borne out since long before the beginning of recorded history. However, the current state of the world was not brought along despite this talent for self-annihilation.> Again, Bobbi got the distinct impression of amusement. <You have had help.>

<That's not blunt,> she said, mostly to make herself feel a little better.

<I am not finished.>

<Fair enough. So if we haven't been ruining this place all by ourselves, who's been helping us out?>

Cagliostro actually chuckled. <I will tell you a story,> he said instead. <About Ivan Ankundinov. Ivan had been a member of the Russian parliament in the days just before the European War – he was not Russian by birth, of course, and his family lived in Georgia where he had been raised before entering politics. He had a wife. Three daughters. Beautiful children. He was well-regarded in Moscow indeed, even after Georgia split from the Russian Confederation once again to join the European Union.> A slip of something came through in that, perhaps pride or something like it. <And then the War came. The Confederation, of course, had an enormous state army through sheer size of population and territory – they had done so to form a buffer against the Middle Eastern nations in the days of the American Crusade, you see, and so

they had no trouble with defending themselves. And when the European nations split into factions after the economic crises began the War, Ivan volunteered to serve as a special diplomatic envoy to try and convince the factions to try and avoid the use of PMCs.>

Bobbi knew this part of the story very well. That seemed to Bobbi an exercise in common sense, but before the world would get the message there first had to be the European War. In the wake of the madness of the American Crusade, the European Union had problems of their own – resource shortages, famine in member countries, enormous amounts of refugees from the Middle Eastern nations pouring into borders on all sides. It got too much for the poorer states to bear, and soon enough blocs were being formed to compete for those resources still locally available.

The problem was, each nation had only the smallest security forces. Up until that point the Union had become a nation unto itself, complete with a unified armed force drawing from the militaries of member states when necessary. After splitting apart, they found that their shares of these forces were too small for their needs; the armies of each state were now much smaller than their 20th century counterparts. And so it was decided that private military companies would be hired to supplement these forces, and the war began – but soon the PMCs could afford to hire many more soldiers, many of them deserters collected (or scalped, as rumors would suggest) from their own clients. Before long, the state militaries, dwarfed by their private contractors, withdrew to form a strong core defense against vital resource infrastructure whilst the PMCs waged war in their name.

The war dragged on. And on. The pool of cash and resources just recirculated amongst the various combatant PMCs, until the warfare took on a very corporate dimension. PMCs would be given secondary contracts by multinational corporations to strike their competitors' facilities during attacks on cities in order to further their own interests. Civilians would be bombarded with skillfully branded care packages and pro-corporate propaganda. Hell, by the end of the War some critics had said that even the bombers that flew overhead should be branded to show what corporation sponsored them. It was a mess, a real mess, and of course in the search for money a great many needless atrocities were committed. Bobbi figured that this was how this story was going to go.

And she wasn't at all disappointed. <When the war broke out, it was expected that it would start in the core combatant nations – Germany, France, and Spain – and then radiate outward. Ivan thought that he had

plenty of time to get his family out of Georgia. But this was not the case; instead, the pipelines between the Eastern Mercantile Bloc and the Federation were hit by the remnant Union forces to destroy their fuel transport capabilities. But these attacks were spearheaded by PMCs, and they did not simply disrupt fuel storage and transport capabilities, they destroyed them. Ivan's wife and daughters were trapped when the strategic hydrogen reserves under Tblisi were cracked open with 'mountain-cracker' bombs; they burned with the rest of the city. There was no chance of escape, I think you know.>

She did. The heart of Tblisi burned in a matter of hours when the massive hydrogen vaults were bombarded and destroyed, creating an explosion that made the ghost of Krakatoa look on in astonishment. <That's terrible,> she said, realizing how hollow it sounded. <I'm sorry.>

<Ah, well,> said Cagliostro, <that is what happens in war. But Ivan did not find it of any comfort – not only had he failed to convince the nations not to make use of such undisciplined private armies, those very forces had cut out the heart of his home country as well as his own. He blamed himself, and he lost belief in....anything, I must say. He became hollow. And then he became special advisor to the Federal Militariat, where this man of peace – and you must understand, up to that point he had most certainly been a man of peace, if nothing else – found himself recommending the most atrocious measures to the Militariat in order to keep the war from spreading into their borders. Strikes were ordered, and refugees were turned away. Or they were resettled, which meant that they were taken elsewhere and disposed of in trenches. Ivan did everything he could to ensure that the Federation was kept safe, even sharing the information that led to the viral bombing of Bonn. He destroyed everything that was once sacred to him, you see. And like so many men, he did so because he thought it was the right thing to do. In this case, Ivan did not do these things of his own volition.>

Bobbi took this in with an increasing sense of horror. If this story was at all true, then the man that she had worked for was not just a criminal of the mundane sort, but responsible for some of the most grievous moral offenses of the European War. Hitler could have taken a page or two from this particular book. Revulsion spread through her mind like the most virulent of plagues and she found herself hard pressed not to speak out, to rail at him. She wanted to condemn him with every atom of her being – but she managed to hold her tongue and her breath, however figuratively, and allowed him to continue.

<After his wife died,> said Cagliostro, <and he lost himself, Ivan realized that something was changing inside of him. More and more, an urge – no, a voice – drove him on to recommend these horrible deeds to the commanders. He had dreams in which he saw the world as a transformed wasteland, with silver seas and glowing skies, and he withdrew from the humanity around him. They did not seem to be even the same sort of animal as him, anymore. And at the end of the war, he went into the land that he had so thoroughly scoured, took the name of Anton Stadil, and built a small empire from the ruins that remained. All as the voice within him had planned.

<He had thought sometimes that perhaps he had gone mad, and perhaps, in a sense, he was. But little by little, as the days went on, the man that had been Ivan Ankundinov blurred away into something else. Something...other than human. Something inimical to human life. Something that wished to remake the world around it into something very different.>

Bobbi wasn't sure what he was trying to say – no, she did know what he was trying to say. She didn't want to hear it. She had known something was wrong the moment she stepped into that facility, when she had seen the eerie precision of the angles and the horrible towers filled with stolen flesh. Human minds could create such things, but not capture the same tone. <You're saying that you're...not human,> she said, carefully choosing her words. <Are you a machine? Are you...what are you?>

<I am something entirely different now,> replied Cagliostro. <But then, the thing that was inside my mind was alien. Alien to this world, alien to anything in it. The human race is capable of the most monstrous of offenses, Miss January, but to truly wish to wipe them out requires something else behind it. You simply do not possess the drive to destroy yourselves entirely.>

<Wait,> she said, <when you say alien, are you referring to...what? Aliens aliens?>

<Yes.>

It was Bobbi's turn to be silent now. Her mind whirled; she had thought that the enemy had been a corporation, in itself a pernicious form of life, but entirely tied to human beings. But something alien? UFO-flying, cow-burning, probe-her-in-her-pink-little-ass aliens? She didn't know if she should laugh and tell him that he was fucking with her or unplug and spend the next few years in a fetal position. There was no existential frame of reference for this. But she was not weak, and she had seen much. She would hold herself together.

<You're shitting me,> she said instead.

<I am not. In this case, Bobbi, truth is far stranger than fiction.>

She was silent for a while. Six seconds, precisely. It felt like a thousand years. <Is that why things were so...strange...when I connected to the Chorus?>

<Among other reasons,> Cagliostro replied. <It will take some time to explain.>

<Tell me,> she said instead. <Tell me everything.>

<I cannot,> said the ghost-thing. <But I can show you.>

<Show me?>

<Or at least, part of what remains. So much has been lost in the departure, so much fragmented. Lower the barrier to your implanted hardware. I can share what experiences remain.>

Hesitation flooded her. <I don't know,> Bobbi said; she felt fear from whose source she could not be certain – fear of invasion, or betrayal, or perhaps simply of learning truth that she would never have wanted on her best of days.

<You are afraid,> said the shade of Anton Stadil.

<Yeah.> The admission seemed to help a little, but then his answer came and washed it away.

<You should be.> A pause. <However, you have dealt with worse. Every day of your youth, surviving in darkness. Here there is only death, and you have proven yourself perfectly capable of facing that.>

<I don't know if I'm ready for this,> she said.

<Perhaps not, but there is little choice if the truth is to be known.>

Another eon passed in miniature. <Tell me,> she said. <Tell me everything.>

He did. At first there were just images, snatches of memory from a thing that had lived long before she and the modern world she knew had been conceived of, let alone born. At first she saw a place like nothing she had ever thought of. She saw vast masses of black rock, continents sprawling beneath a violent bowl of clouds that glowed green with the energy of sprawling storms. She saw cities that never ended, bizarre towers and nameless industrial machinery reaching from coast to coast across the black stone. And around this all, a vast and fog-choked sea of gleaming liquid silver.

After this, more images – this time scenes within the great industrial complexes, of great machines thrumming away in near-darkness, lit only by the dim green haze of lamps bolted into walls of black metal. Conveyors churning out devices that she could not identify, yet somehow seemed familiar. She saw fields of tanks arranged in rows, each containing large, dark shapes, each the size of a horse; though blurry thanks to the milky fluid in which they floated, Bobbi was reminded shudderingly of spiders and lobsters and wished she could look away.

And then, a view of a small, dim world turning in the dark, swirling with pallid green mist – the same mist, she knew, that had clad the skies that she had just seen. Flashes of light shot through the horrible clouds like the firing of nerves, playing across its surface. She knew its name as human tongues could manage it – Yathkalhgn – but in her head heard the name it only as a hissing, clicking, animal thing that she understood its native species applied to the twisted globe.

As the view turned round the planet, she saw that massive, livid wounds had been torn across its surface; the eldritch clouds could not disguise the great volcanic rents that belched flame and magma without cease, the traces of the great transmitter that had been built to end humanity and save the race that dwelled there.

Finally, when the view had turned so that the ravaged hemisphere was full in view, Bobbi saw thing that spelled the doom of the Yathi race – a great red sun, so massive even at a far distance that it seemed ready to consume her entire field of vision, stood sick and dying in the center of its benighted system. In the background of all this, the horrible clicks and hisses were growing louder, and she knew the sounds to belong not just to one mouth, but many; they boiled into a mass as the sun began to flare and burst, pour into her skin like hot water, ravaging her, tearing at her very substance until she felt that she was one with the ailing star, that she may explode just as it now did, and the voices were a tide that crushed her own mind's feeble pleading without mercy. White light filled her mental theatre, and she felt herself blown apart...

...and reformed, knowing of the truth, the reality of things that were and of things that may well come. Bobbi finally understood. She understood the world. She understood Tom. She understood what lay behind the veil of reality, and now she understood what must be done to ensure that things didn't get worse than they already were.

She thanked him out of the reflex of politeness, nothing more. He told her what she must do, and she thanked him again with a brain full of mental static. She disconnected from the network, and then she cried, long and hard, curling up in the dark until Scalli came and held her. She didn't stop until her eyes were bloody red and her heart was emptied, and there only remained the cold dark of the void she had beheld.

CHAPTER 11

They drove in silence for a while, slowly traveling along the Renton border. They stopped to eat what was possibly the world's most ancient Rocket Chef, but the printed protein was ashes in her mouth. Maybe the technology had come from them, these horrible things that lived in the skins of so many people. Anton – Cagliostro – had said that they saw humans as cattle, those which they did not directly inhabit. She wondered if they ate human flesh, and recognized that as the fear of a herd animal. Now they sat outside the weed-choked parking lot of the crumbling burger joint, surrounded by a landscape of squalor with this massive truth looming between the both of them.

Bobbi remembered a very similar situation, staring across the Sound with Tom sitting like a storm cloud beside her. Now it was Scalli – who sat more like a mountain than a cloud, but the feeling was the same. "So," she said, not sure what else to say.

"So." Scalli took a deep breath. "They're called the Yathi. They rule the world, or are trying very hard to do so, and eventually want to infect us all with their own minds and take us all over."

Bobbi nodded once. "Most of us, anyway," she said. "The population's smaller. The rest...well, it's like I told you."

"Experimental subjects and breeding stock," he said. "Jesus fuck. So what the fuck are we supposed to do? We can't kill them all."

She shook her head. "Yathi like to emulate what they used to look like, kinda," she said. "So you know, they like the white skin and silver eyes like Merducci has. They do the same thing with the..." Bobbi paused for a moment, trying to remember the word that Cagliostro had given her. "Xsiarhotl. The ghouls, whatever."

"Sounds South American," said Scalli. "Mayan, Aztec, whatever. What were these things like back, uh, home?"

"Cagliostro didn't go into details," she said. "But I get the idea they're like...spiders and lobsters and things. Kind of. Not at all human-like, that's for sure. They can't stand that we only have the four limbs. Consider us a substandard organism."

Scalli grunted. "Yeah, well fuck 'em. I like to boil lobsters."

"Me, too," she murmured. Lobsters and crabs were her favorite seafood. Would she be able to eat them again? Probably more now, given the situation. A tiny stab of revenge. "It's more than that though. Like, they have three brains in their natural state. Can you imagine that? Three centers of thought all going at once. They're all smashed together in human heads, though, and that slows them down a whole lot. And even then..." Bobbi sighed. "We'd be fucked if they were able to think like that again. Completely fucked. Consider the scale of what they've done, constrained as they've been— three hundred years of solid technological advancement, more than anything else in history, and it's not even our own work. It's those fuckers. And they've gone and made us dependent on them."

Another grunt from Scalli. "I don't buy that," he said. "We've been building shit forever, and even Cagliostro said that they only guide us in many cases. It's not like they're telling us all what to do, you know."

"Yeah." Bobbi shook her head. After everything that Cagliostro had told her, it was easy to imagine that they'd all be drooling idiots without the cold hand of the monstrous behind them. That was part of their power, to make you feel smaller than you were, insignificant before their mighty knowledge. It was a damned good trick – even their architecture made the human spirit quail. She knew now what Tom had felt, why he had seemed half mad when he talked to her for the last time. He had seen a biological processing operation, Cagliostro had said. An assembly line of organ farming and dissection. She couldn't imagine that that must have done to him. The ghouls had been enough through the camera, and to see them up close had been easily the most frightening thing she'd ever experienced. He had seen all that and killed one of the Yathi where they lived.

He must have been magnificent, said the voice of an awed teenaged her inside her mind.

But he was one of them, said a far more bitter version of the same. So, you know, not.

And he had been, or so Cagliostro had said. All the symptoms which Ivan had suffered, Tom had too – but he didn't turn into somebody that Hitler would have wanted as a pen pal. He had fought the impulse for three years, from beat cop to federal agent, and instead turned that nameless isolation into something that allowed him to protect people even if he hated them. That just spoke to the strength of his character, she felt, and she was fiercely proud of him even if it ended up being a line of shit. And, honestly, she really hoped that it did. She didn't want to find him at the end of whatever road she had gotten onto, silver-eyed and horrible, and either her or Scalli having to put a bullet in him.

"So they're trying to colonize, to change everything. I get that." Scalli was handling this much better than she had, something that she found both irritating and admirable at the same time. He had no problem eating his burger, after all, or drinking from his enormous jumbocup of Cola GaGa. "That shit, you know, that's been going on for a long time, space or no. But what I don't get is, why did he put you on to Walken in the first place? Why did he involve Walken in the first place? I mean, Stadil was Yathi, right? So he just...fried himself to say 'fuck you' to Merducci? Is that it?"

Bobbi shook her head. "No," she said. "That's not it at all – see, look, it had to do with the story that he told me. You remember, he said that he had become something else, right?"

"Yeah." Scalli took another bite of his sandwich.

"It's like...a major flaw in the colonization program. Yeah, you can become Yathi, but Merducci thinks the human mind is completely destroyed after the alien mind awakens, right? Cagliostro says that isn't so. The human mind is subsumed, pushed down under the weight of Yathi willpower, sure – but that doesn't mean that it still isn't there. And that's the problem."

He wrinkled his nose. "You can't be two different things at once, you're saying."

"Exactly." Bobbi turned toward him. "It's kind of like oil and water, you know? Unlike oil and water, I mean, the two minds will mix for a while – but if the human mind has a certain degree of strength on its own, it will eventually reawaken again."

"And the two separate." Scalli clucked his tongue. "So what happens then?"

"Quantum disentanglement," said Bobbi, looking out the window. In the distance, police flashers could be seen swarming thickly near a plume of what looked like smoke. "Sentience is a quantum process— the process involves mingling two separate instances of sentience and forcing them to work together, and that takes an enormous amount of power in the first place. Cagliostro said they cracked the crust of their planet just trying to get the power necessary to start the first reaction. Thousands burnt up straight away."

"You mean their planet which they were going to lose," Scalli said, and he shook his head. "Get out of there or blow yourself up trying. Those people, they're hard core."

Bobbi nodded. "That's precisely the point – they're willful on a scale I've never heard of before. Closest thing I can think of is how the Crusades were, both the American one and the ones back in the Dark Ages. So sure they're doing the right thing that they don't bother thinking anything else."

"Except your man Cagliostro."

"And that's the thing, yeah." Bobbi took a sip of her Coke Supra, letting the cola-and-melon flavor trickle over her tongue. "After so many years of being Anton, he just finally...snapped, I guess. Ivan woke back up inside of himself, and saw what he was doing. Memory's coded chemically, you know, so it's like he knew what the alien did. So they started fighting for control, and he won."

Scalli gave her a sidelong look. "And how did he do that? You just got done saying how willful the Yathi were. I don't see that coming easy."

"It wasn't easy at all, no." Bobbi took another sip and nodded. "But I think...I think Ivan realized for the first time what had been going on, and he went crazy. It's the same as those crazies that are running around with Redeye – they're all former Yathi that resurfaced, then went nuts as both sides tried to reassert themselves. They don't remember everything because their minds have gone rotten, or fragmented, or whatever. Cagliostro was the same way, only he remained sane enough to want revenge for what had been done. So when Tom..." There was silence for a moment as she struggled with the words. "I mean, when Merducci created this whole plan to try and break Tom's will, you know, and wake up the seed inside of him, he saw a chance to do that. Tom was supposed to kill Merducci, did you know that? That's what he had expected him to do."

"Keep him awake long enough to know what was going on," said Scalli. "So Cagliostro screwed up her plans, then."

"No, he just forced her hand a little. I mean in the end it was the same, and it's obvious that Tom didn't kill her. Which leaves a big question as to what happened to him. Cagliostro sure as hell doesn't know. He could be dead, like I had thought. Or he could be Yathi now, out spreading the same awful shit as the rest in that bitch's name. I just...don't know." She looked down at herself, at her hands folded in her lap over the top of her soda cup. After all of this she wanted him to be dead, dead and buried under the remains of Orleans, so that he wouldn't suffer the horror of being ridden by such a terrible thing. But now, knowing all this, he could have joined with Merducci. He could have...

"Hey." Bobbi looked up; Scalli was staring at her, concern in his eyes again. "Look. If we do find him, we'll fix him. We'll help him drive out whatever's in him, if he hadn't done it already. He's a tough bastard, you said it yourself."

She took a deep breath and nodded. He was tough, she knew it – and maybe Scalli was right. "All right," said Bobbi with a slow nod. "All right."

Scalli nodded in return, looking at least a little satisfied she wasn't going to break down again. "So Stadil recruits Walken, puts him on the trail, hires you to be his rough guide because he knows you will follow the clues and help him get to Merducci and drill her. Okay. But then what? Why did he just kill himself off?"

"Well," she began, "his human consciousness, I mean what was left of Ivan, had resurfaced entirely at that point. He knew that he could only be one or the other, and that the Yathi half of him had so much sway that it was only a matter of time before the alien mind won out again. So he decided to try and exorcise the thing. If he got killed in the process, well, that's just what would happen. And by that time Cagliostro had replaced almost all of his brain tissue with biocomputer components, just like his bodyguards, see? He decided that he would kill the body by uploading his consciousness into the network, and hopefully either split off or cripple the weaker mind – or what was weaker at the moment – and allow his human consciousness to live on the network as a kind of free-floating program. You know, to carry on the fight."

Scalli let out a low whistle. "Damn," he murmured. "But wait, if he could do that, why don't they just stick their minds in new bodies? Like those Princess Dolls, you know?"

Bobbi shook her head. "You aren't supposed to be able to do it, at all, see. The Dolls were limited in that they could take a consciousness but they couldn't grow or evolve at all. Very static. As for what Stadil did, Merducci tried it already and it hadn't worked. Killed anyone who tried, or butchered their minds so that there was just, you know, a nonfunctional piece left. Stadil did something clever in that he made his Yathi fellows sacrifice themselves; they were eaten up entirely so he could get the boost he needed to make the transfer. The two minds were forced to do a kind of hard copy into the supercomps he had in the club, which merged them and then destroyed the majority of either because they didn't have enough processing power to handle the whole thing. So what he is out there, wherever he's based now, is effectively a shadow of what he once was. An intelligent shadow, but nothing like he was before. Like a ghost, I guess."

"And the lack of tissue in their heads? I mean, didn't you say that their skulls were empty?"

She nodded. "It's the nature of the biosynthetic components," she said. "The body dies, they decompose entirely in a matter of days. Extreme heat makes it happen in minutes. He was getting rid of the evidence of what they were, you see."

Scalli whistled again. "So almost everything you got on the Dolls in that archive was a story, then. About their being an experiment, that kind of thing."

"Well, to a point." Bobbi wrinkled her nose. "I mean, it was set in a frame of reference that we'd accept, wasn't it? That's how he operates, or at least he did when he was still alive. So he sets up all this what he did more to try and give Merducci a final 'fuck you', I guess. At least to some degree."

Scalli didn't have anything to say about that; neither did she, truth be told. So they sat there and tried to do their best to melt into the seat cushions for a few minutes. The wrapper of her sandwich rattled. Scalli's cup announced it was empty through the wet sucking of the straw that scraped across its dry bottom. Finally Scalli put the cup aside and fixed his eyes on Bobbi, folding his arms over his chest like a dubious titan.

"So we go see this crazy girl," he said, nodding. "This Redeye. That's pretty obvious, I think. Assuming the ghost isn't lying, of course."

Bobbi looked at him with surprise. She still expected him to just up and take off, even having stuck with her this far along the road. It was a disservice, she guessed, but stranger things had already happened in spades. She was grateful nonetheless. "No, I don't think he's lying. I mean, I heard him talking about Ivan's wife and daughter, and that wasn't a joke or a trick. I think he honestly wants this shit to come to an end, but he can't do it alone. Neither can we, come to that – but we can do what we can to make sure nobody else becomes infected with Yathi minds. I don't like the idea of dooming an entire race to death by a fucking exploding star, but they haven't given us any other options."

"You start something, you better be ready for someone else to finish it." Scalli shook his head. "You think they'd have learned this, to be so damned advanced, but I guess they gotta learn the same as anyone else. Whole universe must be filled with arrogant motherfuckers." Rain started outside, a thin silvery drizzle; he reached out and started the wipers running. "So we have to go into the Old City, find this girl, and...then what? I mean other than not get killed by every crazy fucker and feral in there."

"I don't know," she said with a shake of her head. "Cagliostro didn't have a lot of information on that score, or at least that's what he said. She was apparently some kind of experiment that they were working on in Wonderland, and she got out. She can shut them down here, and probably across the world – at least, keep them from sending any more of their people into the world. Shut down the invasion. Only...he doesn't know how she's supposed to do it. And whatever she's doing, she's spinning her wheels burning shit down while trying. He knows what she has to destroy in order to do it."

"And what's that?" he asked around the last mouthful of his Maxi-Buns.

"It's called the colonial matrix," Bobbi said. "But he doesn't know what it is yet. Doesn't remember what it does. He needs to talk to her, tell her how to shut it down, where it is. She's some kind of a failsafe, he says, and he needs to give her the means to become fully functional."

Scalli considered that. He leaned back in his seat, brushing crumbs off his chest, picking them out of the slashes cut into his shirt. "These people are like movie villains. Source of their colonization effort in the middle of a metropolitan area. A failsafe in the form of a girl." he said. "What is she, some kind of key or something?"

"Don't know that either." Bobbi shrugged. "Or why she's getting together all these ferals and crazies. Maybe it's just a side effect of her being there, all those poor broken fuckers being drawn to her. Whatever the reason, she's looking for the lock she's supposed to fit. Eventually the Yathi are going to find her out there and take her down; we have to find her first, and get them together. Cagliostro says he can answer her questions, send her where she needs to go."

"Point her toward a target, in other words," Scalli said with a snort. "This guy sounds like a general, not a benevolent spook. Or a politician."

Bobbi shot him a look. "Probably right," she said. "So we have to make sure that we don't killed in the crossfire."

Scalli nodded slowly. He looked like an animate mountain when he did that, she thought, giving serious consideration over the passing of ages. "So what's the plan, then?"

"The plan." Bobbi frowned. She hadn't really given it much thought yet— her mind was still spinning from her conversation with Cagliostro. Still, it had to happen. "Let's go to the Temple and regroup. We can clean up and figure out where the hell to go after this. Whatever plan she's got, Cagliostro and I agree on one thing."

The van's engine hummed to life under Scalli's hands, and he pulled out of the parking lot onto the highway. "And what's that, my girl?"

"Whatever it is, we got to get to her before she burns down the Old City to pull it off. She won't stay there forever."

They came back to the Temple to find it as quiet as they left it, for which Bobbi was supremely grateful. She'd half expected for it to be in flames as revenge for what had happened at the Yathi nexus; the fact that the club was still intact made her wonder if perhaps she hadn't been identified after all. It wasn't like Brain Mother was a name anybody could pin a face on. Freida did, a voice nagged in the back of her head as she stood in the shower, letting the hot water scour the synthblood and the grime off her body. And she was just this human bumba. Why couldn't they track her down?

It was not what she wanted to be thinking about at the moment, so instead she thought about Freida. Standing under the steaming water, Bobbi wondered why Freida had been so willing to link herself into the Yathi machines. She knew the technology better, obviously, but there had to have been something else that motivated her to do it. For her part, Bobbi imagined that it was the desire to save her career – Cagliostro said that she'd woken them up, after all. Digging around for records about Yathi agents would certainly do that. It was just so stupid. Her career? Really? When everything else was so much bigger, so much more important than that...

Well, that's why she got killed, that treacherous little voice said in the back of her head. She got greedy, didn't she?

"We're on the news," said Scalli, nodding to an aerial shot of a collapsed hive of concrete steel in the middle of a desolate stretch of parking lot. Flames licked out from among the wreckage, sparkling like silver. The same bizarre fire as before, when Orleans burned.

"...the city is reeling from an explosion that rocked northern Renton tonight," Maya Frail was saying. "According to a spokesman for Civil Protection, the incident occurred at the Warner Business Circulator on Langston Road Southwest. The explosion, which police and fire personnel have determined was caused by an aging hydrogen collector in the building's sublevels, was of sufficient strength to bring down the rest of its already collapsed upper levels. Civil authorities have declared the site a complete loss; however, Civil Protection has already lodged a bid with the city to convert it into further staging area for its containment efforts in the Decommissioned Suburban Zone..."

"I bet they are," Bobbi said with a shake of her head. She dropped into the chair next to Scalli's, staring at network television's pale Sibyl. "But look at all that damage. You might have brought down the building, sure, but you didn't destroy what was underneath. I mean, did you?"

She looked at Scalli, purple brows raised in question, but the big man only shrugged. "I dunno," he said. "Maybe we set off a chain reaction or something. I mean, seven kilos of DX-47 isn't anything to sneeze at. It's possible, I guess..."

Bobbi gave Scalli a dubious look, but shrugged as well. "Well if we did, then hooray," she said. "Fuck 'em. The more of their shit we can destroy, the happier I'll be."

"I hear that." Maya started talking about something else, and he turned toward Bobbi in his chair. "So what are we going to do here, then?"

Bobbi pursed her lips. "Well," she said, "We've got to go and hunt her down, of course. We'll have to hit Tenleytown first, figure out what the Oldies have heard. And we'll have to work something out after that."

"Tenleytown." Scalli wrinkled his nose. "I don't see how that place is still standing."

"Yeah, well, Oldies are a lot tougher than anyone gives them credit." Bobbi got to her feet, heaving a deep sigh as she looked at the holographic screen on the wall. There was an advertisement on for the new model Ford-Dezarre Lancer; there was a woman draped across the hood of the car, which was out in the desert somewhere with a perfect, blue, computer-generated sky. The car's cab was in the back end and its hood extended gracefully forward, so that it looked something like a duck's head with an enormous bill. The second coming of the Corvette Stingray, the commercial announced. The model lying across the hood was pretty and blonde, lean and dark-skinned. A wide swath of liquid latex had been splashed across over her body, the same color as the car, but it did nothing to hide the details of her naked body. 'New for eighty-one,' purred a woman in voiceover as the camera panned across the car. 'The Ford-Dezarre Lancer. Buy one, and take the ultimate ride.' The camera swooped down the hood, the woman, and over the back of the car before flying off into the horizon toward the F-D logo; they weren't at all subtle about it, the camera zooming through her spread legs and over the mons so you could see her clit if you were really looking.

"That's...a hell of a commercial," said Scalli, whose brows had climbed up over his eyes. "Haven't seen that one."

"The next time I see one of those cars," said Bobbi, "I'm going to burn it."

Scalli snorted.

They had done their best to get ready for their little trip into the Old City, which for Bobbi really just meant dressing real down and prepping her bag as always. Normally, she didn't need much else, but this time around she made some other arrangements. She wore her coveralls, of course, but she tucked a few thumb-thick stacks of cash bills into pockets sewn into the inside of the coveralls, accessible through snaps inside the outside ones.

She also carried a weapon. It was a combat knife, a ceramic combat dagger she'd kept in her dresser for years, one that she used to carry as a girl; on its blade had been etched a simple number 2 on top of a Christian cross, the unit badge of the 2nd Lord's Crusader Infantry. It had been her father's service knife. He'd killed with it, people who he had thought the enemy of humanity but had only really just been people who prayed to a different god than he had.

At least this time, she thought, the enemy wasn't a matter of political opinion; if the Yathi race were bent on the end of humanity, then perhaps she could bring herself to spill blood if that was what was required. All the same, she had not carried that knife on her person since she had left the Old City, and now that she was going back to Tenleytown, she had thought that she might have gotten better.

There was an irony in that, she was certain, but if someone voiced it to her just then she'd have probably told them to fuck off.

Bobbi put the knife in her bag, though she knew she'd probably do better to put it somewhere more accessible. She'd do that when she had to, but she didn't want to become too comfortable with wearing it. Once she'd double-checked her gear – the terminal, the Grail, programs and such – she went down into the bar room where Scalli was waiting for her like a small tank waiting to be boarded. He'd gotten rid of the long coat, thank God, and he'd instead tooled himself up in faded urban BDU pants and a tan jacket, the size of which screamed of only the most custom of big-and-tall stores. "Better button up when we get there," she said, nodding toward that when she came through the door to the storeroom. "Someone'll want to pick a fight with you over those plates of yours."

"Why the hell would someone pick a fight with me?" He looked down at himself, then back at her, all incredulity.

"You're big and scary, yeah, but you're also good salvage with all that gear. Best to make them imagine what you might have, rather than know for sure." Bobbi shrugged. "The element of the unknown works well for somebody in Old City, you know? If you seem too scary you get left alone. People out there fix on details, pick out weaknesses."

"All right, fair enough," he said, bobbing his head in understanding. He zipped up the jacket and shouldered the bag that sat on a table nearby, a big Army duffel that hung heavily from his body like a bad habit. Who the hell knows what he had in there, she thought, but she imagined most of it was horribly lethal. That was good, considering where they were going.

Scalli adjusted his bag so it was comfortable, then looked at Bobbi. "So," he said, with the air of a man who was about to march into Hell's own gaping maw. "You ready?"

"Yeah," she said with a nod. "I'm ready."

"Well." Scalli turned toward the door and trundled out, holding it open for her to exit. Bobbi walked up to the entranceway, pausing at the threshold. The Old City. Her past. And beyond Tenleytown, madness and death. It wouldn't be like how it was when she and Tom had gone, skirting the border. It would be into the bad places of the world, in some of which people had forgotten to be human. Bobbi hoped that bag was full of guns and fire, because they were going to need it.

"All right, then," she said, more to herself than to Scalli, and took a deep breath.

She stepped across the threshold, into the parking lot, and closed the doors behind her. She thought of Tom's coat hanging on the wall, and wondered if she'd ever see it again.

Well. Only one way to find out.

They piled into the van, with its oversized cab and its oversized everything else, and they began their trek across the city. They took the Pacific Highway down toward Sea-Tac and beyond, where the New City extended like a finger through the Verge and disrupted the generally concentric layout of the city zones. On the other side of the airport, between Kent and Des Moines, was the end of Civil Protection's containment cordon and the southernmost gate to the Old City. Tenleytown lay just beyond that, well in sight of the drone guns and Pacification Officers that kept that end of the city safe from ferals, and it was there that they intended to go.

They had elected to go during the day, when things were liable to be the most peaceful. They were quiet for the most part as they went, listening to the music channels or letting the news play on the console's display screen. Every now and again that fucking Lancer commercial would come on and they'd both groan, turn the channel to something else, and most likely groan again. Since discovering situation of the Yathi, all these things that had made such entertaining television now just reminded them of their place in world events. Might as well put up signs that screamed 'FEED' and 'CONSUME' and 'OBEY'. Finally they just turned the damned thing off and let the humming of the engine serve as background noise for their journey.

As they passed the airport and Des Moines began to crumble all around them, they found the tension inside themselves growing more and more. This was it, after all. The last time Bobbi had gone into the Old City, it had been with Tom, and they had almost been killed. Happily they'd be down near Kent instead of Renton, which was far safer. Scalli didn't look at all dismayed as they drove up to the walls of concrete barricade that now served as the border to the city. After all, he was used to combat, and they'd just been through an experience a bit worse than urban primitives. For one, they'd definitely be afraid of the guns that Scalli had brought with him, and they wouldn't have to be shot into pieces before they would stop coming.

The looming structures were spaced with towers atop which drone guns waited to greet trespassers. They drove along the inside of the wall, stained concrete walls soaked with the shadows of the evening, to where the gates stood waiting. They were massive things, powered slabs a foot thick that swung inward on graven tracks. A while back she'd heard that some ferals had gotten through some scavenged fire engines through the old gates before getting shot to pieces. Of course Civil Protection set up something made of solid overkill in the wake of that.

CivPro street officers, Pacification Officers in riot armor clustered around the gates, armed with assault rifles not too much different from what Scalli had used at Data Nexus 216. Bobbi had spent some of the last few days getting palettes of food and such from local supermarkets and loading them in the back of the van, as well as hacking together a profile of a local nonprofit helping the disaffected in Tenleytown. It happened, just not all that often. She had ID cards bashed together as well, and as far as she could tell they were good enough to be scanned through without a problem when Civil Protection went over the car. She was worried about Scalli's guns, though he had said there was no reason to. The duffel, packed in with one of the pallets of food, was made of sensor-scattering material. Stealth luggage, she thought. The sec-for-hire business was full of surprises.

They spent a good half an hour there by the gate, with the CivPro officers going all over the van with a sniffer and looking tough in Scalli's direction. The IDs panned out, though the head of the patrol, a dude named Forrest with a perennial smirk best attributed to the well-armed and extremely bored, kept trying to chat Bobbi's pants off. Literally, as in she felt he'd take her straight into the bunker and drill her if she'd so much as hinted if she wanted it – but Bobbi was having none of it, and she when she rebuffed him it was firm but playful so that he wouldn't get pissed and hold them back after the scan was done. Much to Bobbi's surprise, they didn't even do a physical check of the van; they swept it pretty well with the scanner but having not come up with anything glaringly wrong (thank you, sensorproof duffel bag) they were soon on their way through the gate with a ticket to allow them back in afterward. The ticket would be only for that gate, however; they'd have to use it on return if they wanted to get back in legally.

The great gray slabs of the gates swung inward, and beyond the wall the crumbling corpse of suburbia lay. Scalli and Bobbi looked at one another, feeling the weight of the moment, and then she looked back out toward the distant run of highway beyond which Tenleytown waited.

"Well, fuck it," Bobbi said through pursed lips. "Let's go save the world or whatever."

CHAPTER 12

If a visitor from the previous century had seen Tenleytown, the first thing that they might have thought of was Kowloon Walled City – and they'd be absolutely forgiven for doing so since that was basically what Tenleytown was. Four city blocks worth of office buildings, stores, and a long-decommissioned mall had been fused together under a crazy spiderwork of pipes, girders, scavenged plates and various impromptu structures to form a kind of castle in the middle of the crumbling suburban landscape. It looked like something out of a post-apocalyptic comic book, but then again most things out here tended to do so. Tenleytown loomed above what had once been the park-strewn land between Interstate 5 and State Route 167, whose fortified Old City stretches made CivPro's containment operation look modest and was its own kind of defense against the crazies of the area. Sandwiched between the drone guns and mines that the government had laid to defend these two major traffic arteries, Tenleytown was the perfect place for those who didn't want to live like savages to gather. It wasn't pretty, but it was peaceful. Well, for the most part anyway.

They drove along 228th Street toward the squatter city, marveling what sprawled around them. Kent had been pretty torn up by fire just before Bobbi had lived in Tenleytown, but time had done much to rebuild the landscape to its own tastes. Left to burn out of control, many of the buildings were still burnt-out husks, the bones of houses and shop fronts exposed to the seasons and the ever-encroaching mist that settled out this way. The streets were crumbling veins of blacktop, and beyond that the parks, which still possessed the old and blackened hulks of their former trees, were again fields of mostly green grass. All around

Tenleytown, the land had been left to nature. All around Tenleytown, life had moved on.

And to think – even if the Yathi were defeated, someday the Verge would push out here as the city was 'reclaimed' by human agencies, and it would all be ruined again. At least this way, as destroyed as it was, there was a kind of peace to it. Building it up again would just allow it to collapse, and probably worse. But then there was nothing to stop progress, was there?

When they had drawn close enough for the fortress to tower over them, Bobbi turned to Scalli and told him to stop. "You don't want to get too close," she counseled him. "They'll open up on us and that'll be it."

Scalli snorted as the van rolled to a halt a few hundred feet from the structure. Beyond them Tenleytown was a stained tower of piebald concrete stained with the rain and filth of decades. A fence had been set up around the structure, an impressive thing made of chain link, concertina wire and Jersey walls; the only gate lay ahead of them, and though she did could not see any guards she knew that they were there. Hiding in the sheet-steel bunkers just beyond the fence line, or lying camouflaged in the sparse yellowed grass. They used to have their best snipers up on the walls or the roof to take down people, also. "All right," he said, nodding at the view beyond the windscreen. "What are we supposed to do to get their attention?"

"Sentries will have already seen us." For Bobbi, instincts she had not entertained in almost fifteen years were coming to life again, and she reached for the window control. "Gotta let them know that we're okay." She reached into her bag, which sat on the floorboard between her legs, and took out a flare gun and a single tiny rocket as she rolled down the window.

Scalli watched in interested silence as she slid out the window and perched on the ledge of the door. Bobbi socketed the flare on the end of the gun; she hoped that the locals hadn't changed the signals since she'd been there last, else their journey might experience an abrupt end. "Here goes nothing," Bobbi muttered to herself, and pulled the trigger. With a gush of air, the flare gun's pneumatic piston launched the flare high into the air, high enough so that when it erupted into bright blue light it glowed like a cobalt star. After that, there was silence; the wind blew softly across the landscape, carrying with it dust and the smell of ancient petroleum.

"All right," said Scalli from inside the van, "now what?"

"Hush." Bobbi looked past the fence at the walls beyond. Minutes ticked by, but just as Bobbi was starting to worry she was rewarded by the sight of another flare scaling the stained gray sky – red, bright and glittering, a bloody ruby in answer to her challenge.

Scalli made a grim sound. "Red's never good," he said. "We in trouble?"

"I don't know." Bobbi squinted at the flare as it climbed across the sky, trying to work out what the unexpected color meant. Usually they answered blue with white, and then the guards came out and checked up on things. She considered for a moment before a possibility came to her. "Hey Scalli," she said, "reach in my bag and give me another blue one."

"That part of your code?" She felt a mighty bicep brush her leg as he reached down to fish out the intended flare. "Or are we fucked?"

"Shut up," she hissed, and when he put it in her lap took the flare and slotted it on the launcher nozzle. Bobbi held the gun up overhead once more, and fired another spark of blue upward into the sky. She was answered with silence, and now she really began to worry.

"I'm going to start backing up now," Scalli said. "This isn't working." He reached for the shifter paddle but Bobbi kicked him none too gently in the upper arm.

"Stop it, Scalli," she barked, then said more evenly, "if you move now we're definitely fucked. They're just trying to figure us out I think."

Scalli snorted, but at least he kept still.

Time stretched on. Finally, to Bobbi's great relief, a single white flare rose up in answer. "Fantastic," she said, "they're gonna let us in." She slid into the cab of the van again, rolling up the window as up ahead the area around the gate began to stir. Men and women in street clothes and web vests emerged from the bunkers by the gate, weapons slung; someone rose out of the shell of a burnt-out house, his gray and black urban camo mixing perfectly with the blackened concrete. The scout trained an assault rifle on the van as he stepped out, his sharp, pinched face smudged with black as he slowly paced around the front of the van.

Bobbi watched him carefully as the scout came around to look at them, noted the bright blue eyes as they swept between the two of them, eyes that narrowed as they swept over Scalli's massive frame. He said something quietly to the open air – Bobbi assumed he had a radio rig in his ear, or something – and finally stepped out of the road, gesturing them forward as he began to walk alongside the of van. Bobbi saw, as best she could tell, that he still kept the muzzle of his rifle pointing toward the driver's side door even in its now-relaxed position. Nobody's taking chances, she thought. Security's definitely gotten tighter around here.

The gates swung open, and as Scalli drove the van up Bobbi could tell that he was taking notes. What sort of hardware they were carrying, placement, that kind of thing. The security man in him awake and working away. The Oldies here were sharp, carrying guns openly; while there had always been guns aplenty in the Old City, Bobbi was surprised that they appeared so...military. Like a proper security force, even. "These people have their shit together," Scalli murmured her way as his dark eyes tracked the landscape. "Looks like someone's been giving them a lot of training."

"Yeah," said Bobbi with a faint frown. "I don't know who that might be, though. I remember the militia being far less...militia-y."

"Lot has changed in fifteen years, I guess." Up ahead, a woman in a ski jacket and jeans was waving them down to stop just beyond the fence. Beyond her, Tenleytown swooped skyward. Scalli brought the van to a stop, rolling the window down as the woman approached.

"All right," said the sentry. "What are you two doing out here, anyway?"

"Supply drop," Scalli said instantly. "Got a van loaded up with food for you folks."

That got him a look loaded with exasperation and suspicion. "Great, another charity crawl," she said with a grunt. "And what charity are you two with?"

"We aren't with any charity," Bobbi cut in. Her heart had picked up in her chest, thundering with recognition. Bobbi knew that woman, or at least a younger version of her. She knew the lean face with his sharp cheekbones and the laughing mouth, eyes as warm and brown as the shag cut that licked her chin. "Uh, you're Diana Blake, aren't you?"

The sentry looked at Bobbi with eyes that hooded with suspicion that had exploded with those words. Scalli looked as well, though he of course was just surprised. "Who the hell are you?"

"Oh, I'm Bobbi," said Bobbi. "Bobbi January. You remember me?"

Diana Blake narrowed her eyes as she looked Bobbi over. "You don't look familiar," she said.

"I got a body job," Bobbi said, and ducked her head in embarrassment. "I, ah, got tired of looking plain and scrawny, you know?"

Diana screwed her mouth up a little. "If you're Bobbi," she said, "why'd you punch Tim Callow in the nuts when he caught us playing in the back of his store?"

Bobbi didn't hesitate. "Because he called me Roberta," she drawled, and she set her green eyes on Diana with a look of sheer theatrical menace. "Nobody calls me Roberta, you know that."

There was a moment of silence, and then Diana let out a snort of laughter. "Jesus fuck," she cried, "you're her, all right. Where you been?"

"All over," said Bobbi with a toss of her head. "Except, never really leaving here for long."

"Well, I don't blame you for getting out," said Diana, "You never were frontier material. C'mon, I'll lead you guys in."

With that Diana turned and marched up ahead of the van, toward a gap between two office structures that had been converted into another pair of gates. As Scalli started the van to rolling again, he looked at Bobbi from the corner of his eye. There'd be questions later, oh yes. Questions aplenty.

After the van had been parked beyond the inner gate and was being offloaded by militia, Diana had taken Scalli and Bobbi to talk. Tenleytown was a temple to the urban pioneer. It was just as Bobbi had remembered. Three sides of the square swung high and away from the earth, blank-faced concrete monoliths that formed a wide courtyard over which they towered, crisscrossed overhead by a system of platforms and walkways. Every bit of space that could be used had been converted into one thing or another – living space, storage, even mercantile facilities. Tenleytown used to have a single canteen; now the entire strip mall was almost full with restaurants and outfitters. "Christ," muttered Scalli as he looked at the faces that crowded the courtyard, looked out from windows and from the walkways above. "How many people live here?"

"Oh, two hundred families or so."

It was said pleasantly enough, but there was an absence of pride in her voice that Bobbi couldn't place. Nevertheless, it was impressive; Bobbi let out a whistle. "That's what, five, six hundred people?"

Diana nodded. "Lot of immigrant families come here," she said, "escaping from Civil Protection and its enforcement of the immigration laws."

"Instant containment and deportation," Scalli said with a grunt. "The land of the free."

"We trade with folks from outside the area, too. It's not like it is over in Renton anymore, Bobbi; the ferals and crazies out here have either moved east or been blown away. There are settlements like this one all over the Old City now." Diana smiled now, and now the pride was very clear. "It's really gotten better in the last two years. And when the government starts reclaiming this place in earnest—"

"Do you think that's liable to happen?" Bobbi blinked at her in astonishment.

"That's the rumor." Diana shrugged, and led them across the way toward the end of the strip mall, which made up the lion's share of Tenleytown's eastern side. "Now that the hostile population has been reduced, we've been hearing whispers that the city might start pushing urban reform in earnest."

All Bobbi could do was shake her head. "I guess I wasn't expecting this," she said. "Time was this place was almost empty."

"It's a lot different than it was," said Diana with a nod. Scalli was eyeing her rifle, which not only looked new but looked rather expensive. "We're thriving out here. It's not like it was, especially since the highway guns were updated with new AI. They don't target everything that moves anymore, just the obvious hostiles."

"Targeting profiles can be changed," Bobbi said grimly. "You should be careful of that."

Diana smirked at that. "We are," she said. "C'mon, you two, in here."

She took them into a little place at the end of the strip mall, where it formed a corner with an ancient Corlini Pasta which had been converted into a small power plant. They could hear the hum of the hydrogen generators inside even from a distance. Passing through a colorful southwestern blanket that had been hung from the open doorway, they entered a deep and narrow room that had been converted into restaurant space. A bar ran down the right side, stocked – more or less – with bottles of liquor and snacks. A fat Asian man in a loud neon orange windbreaker, his balding pate made into a kind of fringed dome by the wide bandanna he wore around his brow, sat watching them impassively from behind it.

Bobbi knew this place well; she had been there many times when she was a girl. The smell of cigarette smoke and the faint scent of sandalwood incense brought back memories that she swiftly stifled, memories of a little girl playing under one of the warped tables that ran along the wall opposite the bar while her mother tried to latch on to one of a cavalcade of new boyfriends.

"This is Fortune House," Bobbi said. Her voice was rather flat.

"It is," Diana said, and she threw Bobbi a faint smile that was laced with poison. Bobbi made a dark sound in the back of her throat.

"...I am missing something," Scalli said as he followed both women, in the time-honored way of men who can see ahead of them, very clearly, an impending catfight.

Diana went and took a seat at the last table, where she perched smiling that false, placid smile at the two of them. Bobbi took a seat opposite her, which left Scalli to grab a chair and sit on it like a mountain between them and the bar. Given the way Diana was looking at Bobbi, perhaps it was best that he would block immediate access to all the bottles.

"So," said Diana, looking across the table at Bobbi with that cyanide-and-sugar smile. "Why are you back?"

"Business." Bobbi's tone had taken a hard edge; she didn't want to deal with this shit. She didn't want to deal with any of it, really, but at least out in civilization she didn't have childhood memories getting stirred up around her. "You know how it is.

Diana dipped her head a bit, brows arched. "Business in the Old City," she said musingly. "Or is it just here in Tenleytown? Because then it's my business, you understand. The militia keeps things nice and legal."

"That's an improvement indeed." Bobbi said, and her blood flushed with heat. "I remember how when we were growing up people could get just about anything here, or steal it."

"We know that very well, don't we?" Diana's dark eyes flashed.

Scalli put one very large hand down between them at that, his arm like a turnpike bar. "All right," he said in a weary voice, "enough of that. We're supposed to be professionals here. What's this noise all about?"

Bobbi looked between Diana and Scalli. "It's my mom," she said. "She, uh, used to bunk with Diana's dad here."

Scalli looked at Diana. "And I take it you didn't like that, huh."

"My mother certainly didn't." Diana wore a strained smile still, but her words were sharp hooks in their ears.

"Ah." Scalli took a deep breath. So bitter were Diana's eyes that Bobbi was sure that she might jump up at any minute and spray her with bullets from that expensive rifle. Bobbi should have known that this was going to happen, but unlike so many people she was fairly fucking realistic about things. Bobbi liked Diana; she was one of her best friends growing up. She didn't know that her mother was fucking Di's dad until well after her mother had disappeared into the wilds. What she did know, right here and now, was that this was some high-school bullshit that she had no time or desire to delve into.

Neither did Scalli. The mountain of a man lowered his arm between them and laid his palm upon the table, heaving a deep breath like an irritable father. "All right," he said, "I'm going to say this once. I get that you girls have history, and that's all important or whatever— but it's ancient history and deserves to get left back there. You want to know what we're up to? We're going to find that crazy girl what keeps blowing up buildings in the Old City and do some business with her. That has fuck all to do with this place, or you. So if you girls want to scratch each others' eyes out, you do it later on. We have other shit that needs doing." That said, he looked between the two of them. "All right?"

The two women stared at him for a moment. Bobbi spoke first. "Sure, Scalli," she said, more than a little surprised. "All right."

Diana, however, seemed to have latched onto only a portion of those words. "Wait," she said, looking at Bobbi with widened eyes. "You're going to go hunt down Redeye?"

"That's the plan." Bobbi was happy to move on to a new topic. "We're going to find out what the hell she's up to."

"Well I'll tell you what she's up to," said Diana. Suddenly she sounded very frightened. "She's out there gathering up every crazy motherfucker in town, and then going out and shooting those corporates who work out here. Those motherfuckers are welcome to it, I say."

Scalli's brows arched. "And you say this because...?"

"Look." Diana glanced at Bobbi a moment before training her attention on Scalli. "Part of the reason we have the militia we do is because those assholes were running us out of here. Like, they'd showed up once, tried to buy us out of the area. We just ignored them, right? Suddenly they've got security in the area, people are going missing, and then..." She stopped there, and her skin had gotten pale.

"Go on," Scalli urged. Now he looked grim.

Diana's eyes widened a little more; she looked like a little girl. "We had some reports of people being seen in coveralls, you know, working with the corporates on the other side of the interstate. Our people. Only they weren't our people anymore."

"What do you mean?" It was Bobbi's turn to urge her now.

"Well..." Diana looked between them, her hands knitting together. Bobbi saw that they were trembling slightly. "They...they were dead, we heard. I mean obviously, holes in them and everything. But they were all white, and they were helping move things...and then..."

Bobbi wanted to stop her and call her out on what was obviously a bullshit spook story, but she and Scalli knew better. "And then what, Di?"

Diana looked straight at Bobbi now, her eyes flickering with a combination of disbelief and terror. "We had some scavengers out that way, you know, that's how they saw them. And they got into a firefight with corporate security...they set the dead bodies on our people. Tore them to pieces, with their bare hands! They didn't lie down, not even when the scavvies shot them up with their rifles. You had to blow their heads wide open to get them to stop, or literally cut them up 'til they couldn't move anymore..." Diana had turned very white with the recollection, and Bobbi was just about to go and get her a drink when Scalli spoke.

"How did you find this out," he asked, his tone gentle. "Were there survivors?"

"Yes," Diana managed to say. "Barely. Just one, my Francois. He died not long after. Damned things had...they'd pulled his arm out the socket. We don't know how got here without passing out, but by then..." And then she was silent for a moment, her eyes turned to the table and her face set and hard like sea-washed granite. When she finally spoke again it was with an entirely plastic calm. "Since then there have been other sightings, other...encounters. But not since Redeye's started blowing things up."

Bobbi and Scalli shared significant looks. "I think I understand," Bobbi said. "You think we're going to go and kill the girl, and these corporates will get back to fucking things up all over again. That it?"

"You mean you aren't?" Diana looked up from the table, her face a mask of surprise. "But I mean, you brought this guy with you. I always knew you as a talker, Bobbi, but you never were much of a fighter at all—but this guy...I mean, I just thought you were going to straight up assassinate her."

"I got no interest in hurting that girl, Di," Bobbi said with a shake of her head.

"Good," said Diana, "because I can't let that happen. We'd lose the whole town if they turned those things on us!"

"That explains the snipers." Scalli looked thoughtful, propping his head up with one giant fist. "You folks are prepping for an invasion, aren't you? Or you were, at least.

Diana nodded. "It only made sense," she said. "They were getting very close for a few years – setting up operations in the city, preying on Oldies like I said. So we prepared for it. And then afterward, we figured out that this girl was diverting their attention elsewhere while blowing up all their shit, so we just made use of the advantage while we had it, you know?"

She rubbed at her eyes a moment, which had gotten very red and wet with her recollection of the ghouls and the death of her apparent lover, and then gave Bobbi a very suspicious look. "Wait. If you're not going to kill her, what are you going to do?"

"We're here to point her toward a better target," Bobbi said, and she grinned. "When we're through, we're going to make sure that Genefex is put in a seriously bad way."

Diana's eyes narrowed a bit, but they glittered with interest. "How bad of a way?"

Scalli fielded that one. "Put out of business," he said, "or at the very least put down the path to certain ruin. That good enough for you?"

"Quite good enough," said Diana. In her dark eyes, an unmistakable light of wanting vengeance had bloomed. "How can I help?"

By that night, they had an escort. They hadn't expected that the militia would be quite so happy to help as they had been; Bobbi was hoping for information on what was going on down here, maybe a direction as to where Redeye had gone. But though Diana might have had an axe to grind thanks to her man being killed, she definitely wasn't the only one who'd lost something. There were others on the militia staff that had lost family members and friends, and some civvies as well – but of course, as angry as they were at Genefex and its predations, they were also spooked as hell about those ghouls. In the end, there were two people who stepped up to come along. The first was Diana herself, which of course meant that further bitchery would probably come arise at some point as her business with Bobbi was clearly not over. The other was a fellow by the name of Harry Mason.

Harry had lived in Tenleytown since a little before Bobbi had left, though she hadn't met him back then. Years ago, Harry had served as an officer for SevinArms, a PMC on contract with the Atlantic Bloc during the European War. Bobbi didn't like the sound of that. But Scalli had other opinions; here was a military man, he said, who had helped train a lot of the existing town militia. There was no reason why they couldn't bring him along, especially since Harry had been a recon man back in the day. The two of them stayed in the barracks that night, while they waited for the community council to approve the help that Diana and Harry had already pledged to them. At some point during the night, Bobbi was pulled from nameless dreams by Scalli, who got up and left for a while. He did not try to wake her, and she fell asleep before he returned.

The next morning delivered their go-ahead from the council. Taking on Genefex might be a tall order, but the advantages for the Oldies were clear should they succeed. They loaded up into a converted SUV that served as a recon car for the militia, an old Nissan Highwayman on big tires with an electric engine and a solar kit they could use out in the field. Bobbi had forgotten how quiet electrics were, given the prevalence of hydrogen cars; it made nearly no sound as it rolled out of the militia garage, with its body plated and covered in flat gray paint spattered with stains so that it looked like aged concrete. Its wheel wells were tinged red at the edges with rust, and there was a cupola cut out of the roof where an ancient machine gun slumped, desolately awaiting use. They parked Scalli's van in its spot, and as the hazy, red-orange halo of sunrise threw its lurid stain across the gray sky, Bobbi was reminded of blood in water.

CHAPTER 13

They drove east.

Redeye's last attack had been staged at the Nissan-Sterling plant, which had been the latest sequential assault on the list of Genefex facilities that Bobbi had access to. The next location on the list was called 'Drone Processor 072', which sounded all kinds of fucked up to her. Bobbi knew the physical address to be the site of an old sewage treatment plant on the extreme northeastern edge of the Old City, up toward Newcastle. Out there, the whole band of the Verge that ran the eastern side of Lake Washington was not a swath of fading slums but bristling with manufacturing areas, lots of corporate interests represented in the forms of plants and factories. The wall up there was heavier than the one south of Sea-Tac; after all, it was corporate interests that were at risk if the crazies boiled over, not civil, and nobody could countenance that.

And so Bobbi and her merry party were on their way, picking through block after ruined block toward their destination. Forty years of abandonment had destroyed much of what had been clear streets back in the day – devastated pavement and collapsing buildings made travel difficult, and abandoned cars and other vehicles made for fairly difficult navigation. Getting to their destination should only take an hour at most without traffic, but given that the majority of Seattle's southern reaches were now a gang-ridden warzone, that made the difficulty of driving much greater.

By any reach of the imagination, things were easier – but only for those people living in between the narrow alley between the interstate and highway. No sooner had they cleared the looming eastern underpass, where the black blisters of the drone turrets silently tracked their progress through smoky lenses, they were faced with the image of an ancient school bus. It had long since been abandoned and burnt away to its bones, and had been set up as a barrier and boundary marker on a curb. The side of the bus that faced the street had been draped lengths of electrical cord, each of which had been strung with various shiny fragments and holographic tags. Hanging from the centermost garland was a string of human skulls.

"Gang of ferals used to live here," Diana was saying from the passenger seat as they drove slowly past; Mason had already squeezed himself through the ceiling hatch, one hand on the gun as he surveyed the crumbling buildings from his perch. "Big one, migrated here from out east. Highway guns thinned them out, but every now and again we would have to snipe scavengers that made it through."

"Charming," Bobbi muttered. She looked up through the hatch at Mason, who scanned away, and then at Scallli whose mighty bulk had been squeezed into the truck's passenger side. They'd had to remount the seat so that it almost touched the back one; Bobbi, small as she was, was the only one that fit behind him. It was very much like sitting in a tank, she thought, with the driver and the commander up front and the gunner in his turret. That must make her the communications officer, then. Fitting.

They traveled on through the crumbling streets. They witnessed more artifacts of past butchery; bodies hung from old utility poles, flesh picked mostly clean as they swung slowly in the breeze. The corpse of a woman had been lashed to the front of an abandoned garage, set on fire and left to burn. What remained was a headless marionette in the rags of a dress, blackened to near charcoal. The carbonized halo of a burned tire hung from the stump of her neck. Bobbi could go like that, and it wouldn't even require a tire. Just a bad run, and a counterprog pumping feedback into her skullcomp. She wondered if she would have gone like Stadil had, should that happen, with nothing left in her head but scraps of silicon and carbon. No, she thought, it wouldn't be half so clean as that.

"Got trouble up ahead." Mason's voice rang down from the hatch like a lead gong.

Bobbi blinked herself back into the waking world. They were passing a large strip mall, or rather a strip mall with a large parking lot that it surrounded like a letter "L;" time and flames had assaulted much of it, turning it into a charnel ruin that yawned at them as they approached. The lot had been dotted with the bones of ancient cars, but a line of thin black smoke still twisted from among them. Bobbi squinted to see through the smoke to find an armored car wedged in the front of what used to be a liquor store. Its gray bulk was twisted violently to one side so that the ball tires on its left side could be seen from under its heavy skirts.

"That looks new," said Scalli from the driver's seat. He slowed the car a bit as they drew closer.

"It does," said Diana. "Or modern, at least. Couldn't have been there but for a couple weeks maybe."

Bobbi frowned out the window. "Where are we?"

"Eastern Kent," Diana said, checking the little box monitor that had been patched onto dash. "This used to be Bloody Saint territory until Redeye came and burned them out or took them."

"Which one?"

"A little of both. Hey, Marcus, bring us closer."

Bobbi quirked a brow. Diana was calling Scali by his first name? That was unexpected. She sat quietly as Scalli flicked a glance at her from the rearview, possibly looking for dissent, but finding none turned the truck into the weathered parking lot. Mason trained the gun on the empty shop fronts as they moved slowly past, though he occasionally shot a look over his shoulder at the cars on the other side as well. No point in leaving themselves open to an ambush.

They had drawn up close to the car when Bobbi saw the logo that had been laid onto the truck's scorched and crumpled skin. The stylized helix of the Genefex corporation blazed out at her like a magic seal, bidding her body into action. "Stop here," Bobbi said, and the moment she felt the truck come to a halt she was out and heading toward it to the surprise of those inside. Bobbi had her nerve crusher in her hand, but she did not remember having taken it out of her bag in the first place.

Bobbi approached the wrecked car. It had hit the mall with speed, such that the concrete facade had collapsed all around its front half. It was a long vehicle, almost as big as the armored carriers that CivPro's Special Tactics units used, though not as well-armored; she figured that had one of those bricks hit the concrete here it would have come out the other side before grinding to a halt. She searched for an obvious wound which would have brought the car down, but found none.

Diana came up beside her, rifle out. "That's something I never thought I'd see," she mused with a chuckle. "What do you think?"

Bobbi squinted a bit more at the wreck. "I have no idea," she said. "I mean, if they got hit with something, it'd have to be in the front, wouldn't it?"

"Yeah." Diana peered at the truck for a moment, then slung her rifle across her back. "Here, I'll climb up and see if there's anyone inside."

As Bobbi watched, the slim woman clambered up the back of the car and disappeared. It wasn't really possible to see her moving around from where Bobbi stood, but she could hear her when Diana called down to her.

"Big fucking hole up here," she said. "Blown in. Looks like some kind of charge."

Of course it would be a bomb. "Well," Bobbi said, "can you see in?"

Diana scrabbled about a bit up there for a moment. "Yeah," she said, in the slightly compressed way someone has when they're leaning over something, "Looks like....three people in there, up in the driver's compartment. Dead of course, and ripe. Looks like they sprayed the interior with an automatic once they opened up the top here."

Bobbi pursed her lips. "Who's 'they', do you think?"

Diana's head and right shoulder appeared over the top of the truck. "I guess Redeye and her people," she said with a shrug. "She's supposed to have all kinds of good stuff, so I don't see why breaching charges would be a problem. If she and her buddies didn't have such a hard-on for killing off Gennies, we'd had shit our pants and run a long time ago."

Comments like that really didn't call for anything but a wrinkled nose. "Yeah, well," Bobbi said, "I guess we're lucky there." She shook her head and came around to the back of the car where she helped Diana get down. "Is there power in there?"

"Console's shot to Hell," Diana said with a shrug. "But there's some dim light in there. Yeah, I think it's got some power at least, maybe from an emergency battery."

Bobbi nodded. "All right," she said. "Let's get back to the truck and I'll see if I can't hack it from there."

Diana's brows arched. "Even with corporate security?"

Her look of disbelief got a wide grin from Bobbi, who was happy to have a little bit of an upper hand in the moment. "Hey, girl," she said, "I'm not the wannabe cowgirl you knew, all right? I'm Brain Mother now. This thing's my kind of job."

It was nice to have a moment of normalcy, her old routine, out here in the nutball wilds. Bobbi gave Diana a wink and turned back to the truck to do her work.

That feeling of normalcy faded the moment Bobbi charged up the Grail and linked it to the feeble network presence of the armored car's computer. She feared that she would find herself in the same kind of horrible system, the sea of cold ink in which there was no movement or escape – but instead there was the blessed, astral blankness of Awakening and the familiar sensation of an earthly system.

Bobbi reached out. In an instant she knew that the system was heavily damaged, and that the majority of the files that had been stored in the car's computer were fragmented; she had knowledge of jagged constructs of data, orderly matrices of code tossed into a blender and left to puree. Bullets did terrible things to computers, but time was worse.

She searched the small system for something intact, and plowed through fields of ruined chaff for what seemed like hours until finally she found something in the car's navigational program. There, laid out on a date that was a month previous, was the final course transmitted to the crew of the vehicle. There were stops, addresses in Renton that she didn't recognize as being on the list. Finally there was the endpoint of their journey which was – as she had expected – Drone Processor 072. Wherever they were going, they were stopping through what she had thought to be dangerous territory.

Well, dangerous for them, maybe. They didn't even make it.

Bobbi captured the intact file and began searching for more— she wanted to see what they were carrying, or were on their way to pick up. Orders, manifests, something. As she did so, however, she was aware of something stinging her forearm, a hot sensation felt very very far away. Her brain sang that something was wrong; she felt motion...distance...and suddenly she was alone in the Grail again, in its gray lobby, disconnected from the car. Curiosity and fear began to fill her as her brain did its magic, and she unplugged herself from the Grail and her terminal.

The world was a maelstrom of panicked shouting and muted thunder as Bobbi joined it once more. It was strange how her mind worked when Bobbi came out of the trance of Awakening; everything she witnessed was slow and precise, seemingly existing in and of themselves, as her brain struggled to slow down and catch up with material existence. She looked at the scene as if it were a television image seen through a monitor. The truck was rocketing along a stretch of road beyond the strip mall where they had been. Above her, Mason was manning the gun, which between the muted coughing of its suppressor and the clattering of its bolt sounded like a chain smoker playing with castanets. Hot brass rained down through the hatch. All around her sang a choir of bullets spanging off the hull. Scalli was bearing down on the wheel with an expression like a grim bodhisattva, something that Mason seemed to share as he worked the gun above them. Diana leaned out the truck's visored window and sprayed death at assailants yet unseen.

She felt another stab of hot pain, this time far more present and immediate. Bobbi looked down to see that one of the machine gun's cartridges had fallen on her arm and burned her – another brand blotched her white skin not far from it. It was only then that she managed to pull through the slow-motion haze and join the living world. "What's going on," she called as her blood began to pick up with blossoming adrenaline. "What happened while I was under?"

"Shit, you're back!" Diana ducked in just in time for a bullet to strike the armored apron running around the passenger side window where she had been but seconds before. "We got a problem, Bobbi, so just keep your head down."

"What kind of a problem?" Bobbi looked around the back seat; there were no real windows here, just metal plates welded onto the frame through which narrow cross-shaped apertures had been cut. There was no back window either, just a solid reinforced plate. She pressed herself up against the nearest such cross and looked out. Nothing. "What's going on?"

This time it was Scalli who spoke. "We got someone come up behind us," he called back to her. Diana leaned back out the window and resumed spitting fire. Both she and Mason were very precise— orderly bursts, military behavior. Bobbi's dad would have been proud. "ferals, or gangers, or . . ." the truck rocked as Scalli wrenched the wheel left and they went sharply around an intersection. "Whoever. Came up on us in a built-up truck, same as this one, only filled with a lot of pissed-off people with guns."

"Fuck's sake, Mason," Diana roared as she fired another burst. "Can't you get those motherfuckers off us?"

Mason's answer was a long burst of muted thunder, followed by the screeching of brakes and the nightmare crash of impact and the screeching of steel. "Got 'em," he called out, through the ensuing silence. Bobbi heard a distinct tightness in his voice that made her look up through the hatch. Mason was leaning against the back of the cupola, and blood was trickling out of the cuff of one rolled-up sleeve.

"Hey," called Bobbi as she half-stood, half-crouched by where he was, trying to ease him down. "I think he's hit!"

"Shit," snapped Diana and she twisted her way between the seats, which was made difficult thanks to Scalli's bulk. He stopped the car, pulling it onto the curb while Bobbi tried to help Mason down out of the top of the car.

Mason came down easy. He winced as he slid out onto the back soon; the sleeve of his coveralls had been cut open and a narrow wound like a mouth had been torn in his arm just below the shoulder. "I'll be all right," he said, waving both women away. "It's just a flesh wound, Jesus. Diana, get the kit out and I'll see to it."

Bobbi sat down beside him; his face was a little pale, but Mason seemed fine otherwise. Diana, however, looked as if he might have had lost his arm instead. "Are you sure you're all right?"

"Diana!"

"All right!" She turned back into her seat, digging under the passenger side of the dashboard.

"You sure that you got them?" This from Scalli, who was not looking back at them. Instead he had opened his door, and was moving to get out.

Mason shook his head. "I think so," he said, frowning at the wound in his arm. "Might want to check and make sure."

"Any idea who they were?" Diana came up with a medical box and handed it to Bobbi, who looked at it like she'd been given a trout.

"No," said Mason, who reached over and took the box from Bobbi. "Not much of a medic, are you?"

Bobbi wrinkled her nose at him. "Sorry," she said, "I'm a keyboard kind of girl. The bag's just meant to be cute."

"Cute," Mason repeated with a shake of his head. "Well, I'll say this for you, honey, you sure got a strange sense of it." He took a battlefield patch from the kit, tearing the foil seal off its business end and sealing it against his arm. Antibac and painkillers flooded through him almost instantly, and his color started to return. "Scalli, you see anything out there?"

"Just a big fucking wreck," Scalli replied. "Truck flipped over when you hit it that last time. It's on fire now.

"You see any survivors?"

"No. You want to light it up again?"

Mason shook his head. "No," he said, "it should be fine. If they aren't getting out and screaming, we're all set."

"We should see who they were," said Bobbi, who was still rubbing at her burned wrist. "Think they could have followed us from Tenleytown?"

"I doubt it. They were probably in the area and saw us poking around on that corporate bus." Diana leaned back against the dash, squinting out the window at the wreck behind them. "Yeah, that looks like a native rig all right."

Bobbi frowned a little. "I don't know," she said. "It might be important."

Diana shook her head. "We should get going," she said. "That noise is going to draw more attention, and we don't need another fight." She looked to Bobbi then. "Did you get anything off that car?"

Bobbi hesitated. Diana was right about the noise, but she didn't like the idea of just leaving the dead unchecked. She looked to Scalli, but his expression was neutral. Diana regarded her with expectant eyes. "All right," Bobbi finally said. "All right. Let's get out of here, and I'll tell you all about it."

As they made speed away from the site of the battle, Bobbi told them about the stops that had been listed on the car's itinerary. It did little to increase their understanding of the situation, but they all agreed that the crew of the armored car were up to something terrible. Though the stops made on the way to Drone Processor 072 were identified as places where, at least it had been rumored, small settlements had been set up and then vanished. "There one day, gone the next," she said with a shake of her head. "Maybe they went the way we were afraid we would in Tenleytown."

"What do you mean?" Bobbi asked.

"Those goddamned corporates," Diana replied. "Well, I mean the truck was empty, right? So maybe they weren't dropping anything off. Maybe they were picking up something to deliver to this...processor thing. Whatever it is, it can't be good."

"Only thing that I can think of would be people," Bobbi said. She thought of the ghouls and shivered.

"Well," said Mason, "we can pass those spots on our way up. Bit out of our way, but getting through Renton's going to be a whole lot of inconvenience anyway." He had patched himself well; the color had returned to his face and he acted as if the wound had never happened. Combat meds were some good shit. "We'll probably have to deal with more assholes like those," he said, indicating the wreck they had left behind with a jerk of his thumb, "but we've got plenty of ammo. This car is made to take a serious pounding."

The rain of bullets plinking off the armor echoed in Bobbi's head. "I believe it," she said with a low whistle. "Well, look. If you think we can buzz them, fine. I'd like to know what the hell it is that we're getting into."

"If we can without getting shot at." Diana shook her head.

"Not going to happen." This from Scalli, who looked straight ahead as he kept the car going ever forward toward the northeast. "We're driving into the darkest heart of the Old City and looking for a crazy woman who's raising an army of equally crazy motherfuckers with enough firepower to crack open armored cars at the very least. Gathering them in one place, most likely, and setting up to wage war upon a corporation with extremely well-armed security forces. Getting shot at is the least of what we're going to have to deal with, and you'd best get realistic about that fact."

That got a look of interest from Mason, who canted his head in a birdlike way, fixing his dark eyes on Scalli's brawny back. "Spent a lot of time in combat, have you? You handled that driving very well."

"Marcus used to be hired security, Harry." Diana looked at Scalli with a grin of very obvious interest. "Like I told you last night, he knows his way around a scrap."

"Yes..." Mason narrowed his eyes very slightly and nodded. "I suppose he does at that. Good work on the road, there, Scalli. You do a lot of road training?"

"Part and parcel of private security duty," Scalli said with a nod. "You can't be a decent bodyguard if you can't work the wheel."

"I suppose not." Mason inclined his head, but he didn't look terribly convinced – though about what, Bobbi couldn't say. She sat watching them, glancing out the vision slits from time to time, as the four of them traveled on.

They made their way unmolested to within a few blocks of the first of the settlement before the truck died. They had wound through the rotting blocks as the afternoon went on, dodging the occasional band of nasty bastards; there had been a few close calls, but they had managed to travel largely undetected. Were the truck not an electric, and therefore pretty damned quiet, maybe they would have had attracted more attention.

Or maybe not. As they traveled, Bobbi had noted how quiet things had gotten. Though they hadn't exactly seen people on the street, there had been signs of recent activity. Even the occasional corpse had seemed relatively fresh. As they drove into Renton, however, this changed. Old haunts had apparently emptied; the corpses they glimpsed were no longer rotting but were strings of bones lying in a tangle along the street or in doorways. Here the natural order had somehow deadened. Bobbi was rather sure that it was because something stranger, more dangerous, had swept the natives away with it as it passed. It made her nervous.

Bobbi watched as the landscape alternated between stretches of crumbling industrial buildings and rain-warped neighborhoods. The cycle of putrefaction was well on its way in the corpse of the Seattle suburbs; she wondered if people would even bother to reclaim it. She saw a future where the New City would not spread outward like some ambitious cancer but instead stretch upward, ever upward, until its mighty towers scraped the stratosphere and the penthouses looked out on the stars. But then she thought about the Yathi, how the future may well belong to someone else, and she wondered into what form alien minds might bend the world.

They had made their way into a housing development a few miles from the first site when the truck cut out. The instruments and the codged-together console display sputtered and died as the car lost power, rolling to a stop in the middle of the street. Its protest was met by a horde of black cursing from Diana and a general sense of unsurprised acceptance from the rest of them. This was the Old City, after all, which seemed to have turned into a sort of carnivorous organism all on its own; it lived to consume the warm life that cowered in its ruins. Potentially lethal technical problems were only to be expected.

The old houses loomed on either side, faded, peeling temples to life before the financial crash. Most of them had fallen in on one side or another, while others – creatures of sterner stuff and better budgets – still stood resilient against age and the weather. They had gotten out of the truck, save for Diana who was busy manning the gun and guarding the front end of the street. Scalli had taken point a bit down the road, taking up the rear and playing sentry with that rifle of his. Mason had the hood open and was fiddling with the engine.

Bobbi had tried to check up with Cagliostro, but the old ghost was not responding to summons. She ended up watching Mason work as she crouched by the truck's front bumper, while his arms were buried in the engine. "So, how you doing there, man," she asked in her best conversational tone. "Everything going okay?"

"Looks like a stray round got in through the bottom," he said, not looking at her. "Probably skipped off the pavement. Clipped the main feed from the wheel motors to the battery. Was only a matter of time before the system cut out, blew some fuses."

Well, shit, Bobbi thought. "Uh, yeah," she said, "I can see how that might be bad. That a permanent problem?" She hoped to hell it wasn't; she didn't want to be stuck in the middle of fucking Murderville.

Mason chuckled. "Nothing permanent, no," he said, "unless we get some trouble. It's going to be a bit, though. Gotta strip these wires, get them patched, run a test cycle on the battery. Replace the fuses, too. The problem isn't the fix, though, it's the fact we're gonna be sitting here in the middle of the street for like a half an hour here."

"Yeah..." Bobbi looked back where Scalli crouched behind the rusted ruin of a station wagon. Big as he was, he somehow managed to fold himself up behind his bulk – almost as if he'd managed to shrink himself somehow, retract his muscles into himself. It was a little bizarre.

From under the hood of the truck, Mason followed Bobbi's gaze. "So how long did he serve?"

"I'm sorry?" Bobbi blinked at Mason, her green eyes tracking his face as he went back to work.

"How long did he serve?" Mason nodded into the engine compartment. "And don't give me any bullshit about private security. If he was private anything, he was private military."

Bobbi looked back at Scalli again. She wrinkled her nose, weighing the possibilities. "Why do you say that? He could have had military training from back when he worked with a firm."

Mason snorted at that. "I know what career military looks like. I worked with SevinArms from 'fifty to 'sixty-seven, you know."

"You don't look nearly that old," Bobbi said.

"Yeah, well, we all got our secrets, don't we? That's what I'm saying."

This line of conversation was opening up unnerving seams in her knowledge of her friend – unnerving because Bobbi had the distinct feeling that there was some measure of truth to it. She'd never seen him in action until that night, short of some chop-socky action done on rowdy boys at the club when she was dancing. Usually the mere sight of him was enough to keep people in line. She thought of the ease with which he had shot down Freida, how he methodically hosed the white tide of ghouls. "I guess," she heard herself saying. "I guess it's not out of the question for me. But if he did serve, I'm sure he's got good reason to claim otherwise."

Another snort came from under the hood. "I find that if someone's lying about service," he said, "it's because someone's got something to hide in one way or another. Straight up ask him, see what he says."

"Oh yeah?" Something about the way he said it irritated the shit out of her. Mr. Snarky Fucker. "So what about you?" she asked, hearing the defensiveness in her tone. The challenge. "You're old as fuck as war vets go, so why do you look so young?"

"Yeah...well." Mason ducked out from under the hood to look at her. "I said I had good genes, didn't I?"

"Better than most," Bobbi said with a grunt. "Or any."

"KMI had some of us submit to gene surgery when we came in, part of a pilot program. Faster reflexes, better eyesight, stuff like that. Part of it was longevity, a partial telomeric rebuild." Mason shook his head and chuckled. "I'm forty-eight, believe it or not. Lived in Federal Way, signed up with the Company after the Crash. I was in the field for the whole War, you know?"

Bobbi looked at him for a long moment. Empathy fought with irritation. "I guess that was a hard thing for you to deal with, coming back and finding the place like it was."

"Yeah." He looked back down at the engine and slid under the hood again. Bobbi couldn't see his face. "When I got back it wasn't quite as bad as it's gotten the past ten years, but it still wasn't great. My wife took off with the kid, my house had burned down a long time ago in one of the wildfires. Gas main blew up, something like that. It's not like the government or the corporates cared."

Though she couldn't see his expression, Bobbi heard the bitterness in his voice. It was a bitterness she knew well – her mother had it. Tenleytown was rife with it. Even she had it, especially when she talked about those days of her youth. "I'm sorry I brought it up," she said. "I'll let you get back to it."

Mason didn't say anything. Bobbi got up and stood by the truck, feeling distinctly bitchy for pushing him, and mad at herself for letting the doubt trickle in where Scalli was concerned. Maybe Scalli was military, who knows? Maybe he was another special forces type. Maybe he was a grunt. Or maybe, she thought with a thrill of horror, maybe he was someone like Stadil— or Ankundinov, rather— who had done some horrible shit. Was it possible that some moral collapse in his youth had allowed the earworm of Yathi thought to enter his mind? It could be so for any of them, really. It certainly had been for Tom. Bobbi considered for a moment the possibility that her oldest friend could harbor one of those creatures, however asleep it might be, and goose pimples marched across her skin in legions.

No, her mind snapped back at her. No, goddamn it. That's how they got you. That's how this whole fucking thing worked. They crawled in and battered at your mind, and they broke your resolve just by being here—knowing about them made it even worse. Self-directed anger bloomed inside her and she found herself crossing her arms over her chest, bidding the dark thoughts to die.

Bobbi walked away from the truck toward where Scalli crouched so expertly behind the shell of the station wagon. She walked across, crouching low as she neared the back bumper of the wreck. Scalli didn't move; he had put his visor on again, making him look like more of a cyclops than ever, and he stared out at the street and the shells of the houses as if at any time one of them might get up and strike.

"Hey," said Bobbi, her voice low. "How's it going?"

"Hey back," Scalli replied. "It's fine. I got zero on thermal and the motion tracker. Looks like things are empty here after all."

"Yeah," Bobbi muttered. "That's what's got me so twitchy." Then, in a slightly louder voice, "So it turns out Mason is former private military."

"Yep." Scalli kept his eyes down the road. His rifle was cradled in his arms like a young and irritable dragon, its silenced muzzle kept ready.

"What do you mean, 'yep'? You knew?"

Scalli shrugged at her. "Yep."

"Well...shit." Bobbi shook her head. She wished she had a pair of thermal goggles or some other shit right now, as useless as she felt. "How the hell did you know that?"

The slightest smirk tugged at the corner of his mouth. "Diana told me."

"Did you know he'd had gene work done?"

"Told me that, too."

Bobbi threw him a suspicious look. "When the hell did she tell you all this, anyway?"

He grinned, now. "When you were sleeping last night."

From the look on his face, she didn't need to ask what they were doing while this conversation went on. "Oh, man," she said with a snort. "I was wondering why she was being like that with you today. Jesus, are you kidding me?"

"She likes big guys," Scalli said. "Nothing wrong with it. It's not like anyone else was throwing themselves in my path."

Bobbi opened her mouth a little and promptly closed it again. Well, he had her on that one. Couldn't complain about him panting after her and then complain about who he decided to turn his attention on, now could she? "Right," she said then. "Well, good on you, Scalli. She's kinda bitchy towards me, sure, but she seems like good people."

"Well, I'm glad you approve." He was teasing, she heard it in his voice. "Seriously, though. Do you know how long it's gonna be before he gets that thing fixed?"

She wrinkled her nose. "Half an hour," she said. "I mean he said it was fixable, just we're gonna be out in the middle of the street here in the meantime."

"Yeah..." Scalli looked over his shoulder, past Bobbi, to where Diana manned the truck's gun. "Don't think it's going to be much of a problem, though."

Bobbi nodded. "I know what you mean," she said. "It's like everything's left."

"Or gone somewhere else," he said. "Redeye again."

"Yeah."

"You talk to Cagliostro since we started?"

She considered. "No," Bobbi said. "He isn't...at home, I guess you could say. I don't know where he's gone."

"Probably out doing his ghost act," Scalli growled. "Well, I don't like going into these settlements, or whatever they are now, without some forward recon – but I guess that's what we've got Harry for."

"Thirty years' military experience," she echoed. "Yeah."

"Yeah, he's no joke." Scalli looked over his shoulder again, and Bobbi followed. Diana and Mason were chatting, apparently, though the words were indistinct. Mason was still bent over the engine.

Bobbi was quiet for a long moment. Thoughts clicked over in her head. "He says you used to serve," she finally said. "I mean, he says you were military."

"Mmmm." Scalli nodded, though he didn't look at her. "I can see why he'd think that. Military-trained, definitely. Firm I worked for was specific about that. But I didn't serve in a PMC or state forces."

"So who did you work for?" She'd never really asked Scalli much about his work before she'd met him, of course. It really hadn't mattered. Now, though, with Mason's words stuck in her head she found her curiosity unusually stoked.

"Private parties, I told you." He rose a bit, sweeping the visor's single eye across the ruined development. "All right, I better get back to this. Why don't you see how those repairs are going?"

Bobbi looked at him. "I was just there."

"Yeah, well, I gotta focus on what I'm doing."

From the tone of his voice, Bobbi felt that she had indeed crossed a line. "All right," she said, and she got up to walk back toward the truck. Bobbi climbed into the cab and waited a while, staring at Diana's legs as the woman stood in the gun cupola and nattered at Mason from time to time. Finally Mason's work bore fruit; the truck's displays came to life, the engine started, and they were off again.

The first site had once been a Crown Grocery. The familiar squat, rectangular building with its skin of fading blue bricks was obvious to anyone who had grown up in the suburbs. Crown had gone out of business in the Crash, but before that its stores had been a mainstay of the grocery market in Washington State. Local chains just didn't exist anymore. Now, the store was— or at least, had been— a small fortress of steel and masonry. Security shutters still sealed off the doors and windows, heavy slabs of steel pitted with bullet craters and covered with graffiti. The parking lot around it was full of sections of jersey wall that had been brought in to form barriers and makeshift tank-traps. Scalli wove the truck through this maze as they circled the far edge of the parking lot.

"Looks quiet," called Diana from the cupola. She surveyed the place with a pair of binoculars as Scalli brought them around toward the south side. "I don't see anything— ah. Shit."

"Talk to me." Mason took her place in the passenger seat; he had a beastly shotgun in his lap fed with a big box magazine.

Diana's legs shifted a bit. "Looks like...there's a big fucking hole in the back. Blown out, maybe rockets or charges. Jesus, what a mess."

Bobbi peered out of her vision slit, trying to see what Diana was talking about. Sure enough, a gaping wound had been blown out of the side of the building, a hole big enough to drive a truck through. The jersey walls in the vicinity still stood, however, so it didn't appear that anyone had. Bobbi stared on at the destruction with horrid fascination.

"Any casualties?" This from Scalli, who stopped the truck in the shelter of an outbuilding.

"I don't see anything from here. Whatever went on in there, looks like it's been a while." Diana crouched down into the truck cab, turning toward Mason and Scalli. "What do you want to do?" she asked.

Bobbi frowned a bit. "Don't I get a vote?"

"Last time you had a wagon full of scavs after us," Diana said flatly. "I'm asking the professionals."

Mason and Scalli looked at each other. There may have been an understanding share there, because Mason looked at Bobbi. "Well," he said, "what do you want to do?"

"Hey," Diana started, but Mason waved her off.

"We went because she knows what's going on," Mason said to her, shaking his head. "You want to get pissy, you can stay here and keep the gun warm, but we're supposed to help her out. That's what the city council decided."

Well bless the city council, then, Bobbi thought to herself. She always remembered them to be a pack of stodgy old motherfuckers and irritable biddies, not men and women of obvious judgment and mental prowess—she really had to stop thinking like that. Instead of voicing these thoughts she gave Mason a nod. "I'd like to go," she said. "But only if the three of you are willing." And then she added— somewhat painfully— "Like Diana said, you three are the professionals."

Mason and Scalli looked at each other again. Diana looked a bit shocked. "Well," Mason said after a moment's pause, "if it's empty, I think we'll be okay to go in there. It'll be interesting to see what's going on, I figure, and if it's been a while there shouldn't be too much trouble."

"Good," Bobbi said with a nod. Diana kept quiet, so she assumed Mason spoke for the both of them. "Well, then, I guess we'll get our stuff together and then—"

"No." This came from Scalli, whose voice had become a deep rumble. The big man turned in his seat, looking between the three of them. "You girls stay in the truck. Mason and I are going."

Bobbi felt her face catch on fire. "No way in hell," she began, but Scalli gave her such a stern look that she fell quiet as if she'd been slapped.

Scalli continued. "I'm not convinced that this is a settlement," he began, "or that it ever was. Bobbi and I have been to places that looked perfectly normal already, and they turned out to be hellholes. Now I know Bobbi hasn't told you two, but about a week before we came to Tenleytown we hit up an old office building in the Verge that until recently had been Old City territory. It was supposed to be a Genefex building, like a computer lab – turned out to be a hell of a lot more than that."

Scalli told them the story of the horrors that unfolded in Data Nexus 231, of the Chorus and what had happened to Freida. As he spoke, Bobbi watched Diana's face slacken with disbelief – but in Mason's eyes, she was surprised to see grim recognition there, and finally a certain glitter of satisfaction when Scalli told how they'd collapsed the building.

"Fucking good riddance," Mason said when Scalli had finished.

"Yeah," Scalli replied. He was looking at Mason a little strangely as well – Bobbi was sure that he had seen the same thing that she had. "In any case, whatever these sick fuckers are up to, that's what we think is going on in these places. You ask me, a 'Drone Nexus' or whatever they're calling it is going to—"

"Drone Processor," Bobbi corrected him.

"Right. A 'Drone Processor' sounds almost like...a factory. I think it's a place where they make more of these things out of people. And this place is a stop on the line to get there. Now if it's hiding another Genefex facility, however bombed-out, I think Harry here will agree with me when I say that it's not a place for anyone but hardened badasses— and I hope you two will forgive me, but I think only he and I apply." Scalli looked at Diana and Bobbi in turn. "Would you disagree?"

Bobbi frowned, but she really couldn't argue with him. Well, she could, but it would be out of a position of stubbornness and not any kind of sense. She drew a deep breath. "Fine," she said, spreading her hands, "fine. I guess I really can't argue with that."

"I sure as hell could," Diana muttered. "But I won't if you're sure, Harry."

Mason nodded. "Yeah," he said. "A recon man and an assault specialist? I think we could do a lot worse. We'll keep in contact on the radio."

Diana nodded at the bandage around Mason's bicep. "You gonna be okay with that?"

He gave Diana a wide grin. "Like it never even happened already," said Mason, and he winked. "Now you two hang out here and keep an eye on things. Di, how much brass do we have left for that thirty-cal?"

"A hundred rounds?" She nodded toward Bobbi, or rather just under her. "She's sitting on another can."

Mason nodded. "All right. Well, let's see what we can't find out, then, shall we?"

Not long after, the two men were creeping across the parking lot toward the breached grocery. Bobbi and Diana sat watching them from the relative safety of the armored truck; they sat in the back seat and looked out the rear driver's side window, the armored hatch covering it lifted and propped open. The cool, stained afternoon air drifted in, its passing the only sound in their ears. Mason and Scalli, starting off by sneaking among the concrete barriers toward their destination, had quickly proceeded far enough that their footfalls could not be heard and their shapes grew distant.

"Look at 'em go," Diana said. "Your man's a mother of a mover."

"Mason isn't too bad either," she said. "I heard you two were talking last night."

"A little." Diana smiled quietly. "He sure can use his tongue."

Bobbi felt herself color slightly.

"Shame about the rest, though."

Bobbi looked at Diana then, and blinked. "Wait," she said. "What do you mean?"

"Nothing down there." Diana shrugged. "It's like...smooth, like he was wearing a cup. Well, I mean apparently it's there, it's just...hidden under the muscle and stuff. Like it only comes out when he pees, and then only just enough to do the job."

Well that was a weird fucking thing to hear. "I wonder why that is," Bobbi murmured. "I mean, I never did it with muscle-jobs, so I dunno..." She tried to remember anatomy, how muscles worked, how they laced together. Was that even possible, not having a ready dick? There had to be something to that. "Sorry you didn't get anything more then, I guess."

Diana chuckled. "That's all right," she said with a shrug. "I figure he's been panting after you long enough, he could get a little piece of something new, you know?" The way she said it was acidic, nasty. She was enjoying what she obviously thought was a little revenge.

The joke was on her, of course. "We're not together, you know," Bobbi said sweetly. "I mean he wanted to, but we're just friends. Glad you got a little play, though."

A black look cast her way was Diana's response. Silence hung between them for a while as both men rejoined at the mouth of the breach. Bobbi watched them talk a moment, then vanish inside. "I wonder what they're going to see in there," she said.

"Not sure," Diana said. "Maybe it'll just be deserted in there."

"Maybe so." Bobbi let out a deep breath, let her brain center itself a little more. They sat there for what felt like ages, just waiting to hear something. Gunshot, radio, whatever. Diana had the strangest look on her face, as though she were on vacation, listening to the silence with a tiny smile playing on her lips. Bobbi figured she understood why, though. Girl like her had to run into all kinds of hard stuff, and all kinds of waiting to go along with it. Bobbi figured that you learned to pass the time— she knew she had, though it involved a little more talking.

So, Bobbi decided to talk. "So," she said, breaking the silence. "What's up with you and Mason? You friends, or what?"

"Or what," Diana replied. She sounded sly. "Harry's a good guy, but he wants to settle down. He'd do anything for me, you know?"

Bobbi looked at her out of the corner of her eye. "Yeah," she said, "I do at that. So what, you fuck him anyway?"

"Anytime I want," she said with a shrug. "He's always willing. Nobody else goes near him, you know, I mean beneath that young body of his he's still old. Has an old man's mind, old man's opinions. Bit hard for a girl when she finds out the slightly older stud she thinks she's fucking turns out to be an absolute grandpa."

"Anything you want, huh." The words didn't sit at all well with Bobbi, though she wasn't certain why. "So you've been with him a while?"

"In as much as I am 'with' him, yeah," Diana said. "After Francois died."

Something ticked over in the back of Bobbi's head. Her mind was quite suddenly directed toward the weight of the nerve crusher in the pocket of her jumpsuit, laying cool against her thigh. A nameless anxiety began to bubble up within her. "Tell me something, Diana," she finally said. "Why did you volunteer to come with us?"

"Oh," said Diana with a chuckle. "I'd thought that would be obvious."

The anxiety built and knotted in Bobbi's gut. She slid her hand into her pocket, found the checkered plastic of the crusher's scavenged pistol grip. "This is different. I mean it's not just about your boy."

Diana smiled. "You always were sharp, January." She shifted a little so that Bobbi could see the muzzle of a small pistol in her free hand. She must have brought it out of the glove box with the binoculars, or maybe she had it with her all the while. "But you are correct." As she spoke her voice began to change, to flatten out. Bobbi felt the blood freeze in her veins as she heard it. It was like she spoke through a vocal processor. "I am going to kill you."

For the slightest moment, she thought that it might have been some attempt at humor, or a momentary daydream – but there they were, and Diana's gun was very real as it gleamed in her hand. It was funny, really; she thought that she should have hardened up with all that she'd been through, but Bobbi's heart bubbled with the animal fear that came with impending doom.

"Well," she heard herself saying to Diana, "tell me why, first."

"You know why." Diana leaned against the opposite door, bracing her back and holding the pistol level, close to her stomach. "My father. Or my mother, in point of fact."

There was silence again as Bobbi watched her. This again, she thought, and found that behind the fear was a kernel of anger— not at Diana, which surprised her, but for her wayward mother. She had left ruin wherever she went after Bobbi's father died, and here was more wreckage for Bobbi to clean up – assuming, of course, she didn't die in the process. The anger burned her fear back, allowed calm to take its place. The clarity that helped her on the network helped her now. "I can't help that," she said. "I'm sorry about my mother. I'm sorry about yours."

"Not that mother," said Diana, and she smiled. "But we can begin with the woman who birthed this body." Her voice was ice in Bobbi's head, causing her hands to tremble. "She could not withstand the constant trauma of her husband consorting with your mother under the guise of working late— while watching the children of his husband's lover playing with her own child. Eventually she grew unstable." Diana leaned forward a bit and grinned. "Or perhaps, as Diana would have said, 'She sat there and watched us— watched you— knowing what was going on, knowing that...that woman would come back and that she'd have to face her. Dad's cock on her breath, no doubt.'"

Bobbi's eyes grew wide. The circuits connected in her mind— she knew what that voice was now, why it had sounded so familiar. "You're not Diana, are you," she breathed. "Not anymore."

The other woman shrugged, ignoring her and continuing on. "And then she shot herself when Diana was sixteen," she said. "A year after you left. After, that there was nothing for her but the militia. They took her in."

Bobbi closed her eyes a moment. She had spent much of her childhood with Diana— they weren't necessarily the best of friends, but they certainly had gotten into many things together. They'd done that because Diana's father "worked late." Of course, what he was really doing was obvious now. Bobbi wanted nothing more right now than to go back and beat the living shit out of her mother for doing this, even though she knew that she wasn't well at the time. But of course, that was the least of her problems. "You're not Diana," she said again. "Diana was proud, but she'd never turn out to be a murderer. You're not human at all."

To her horror, Diana smiled. "Correct," she said in that flat, horrible voice. "I am not. You know what I am."

Bobbi closed her eyes again, counted backwards from five. "You're one of them. You got in her head."

"Quite."

Bobbi had an image of her body being torn apart by the machine gun's heavy rounds, transformed into a pinwheel of blood and meat, and she shook her head. "I won't run. But how did it happen? Did I make her hate me that much?"

"It had nothing to do with you," said the thing that was Diana, nodding slightly. "It had everything to do with her. Hatred, you see. It dissolves sanity faster than anything else – she held hate in her heart for you for almost ten years before she met her man, Francois."

"But shouldn't that have helped her?"

"It did. And where before her misdirected hatred for you and your mother sustained her, meeting him gave her new belief that things would get better. But then he was killed. She watched him die, you know." She narrowed her eyes a bit. "You're lucky. You haven't had to watch the life leave the eyes of the one you love." For a moment, it wasn't clear if the thing that had replaced Diana that was talking, or if the words were an echo of the lady herself. "I'm doing the world a favor like this, you see. It's a form of pest control."

Bobbi was silent for a long moment, just staring at the other woman. She thought of what Diana must have felt for her, how she must have burned to kill her for so long. For what had happened to her mother...or was it that she blamed Bobbi for not being there when her mother finally died? Either way, Bobbi's heart went out to the part of her that wasn't holding that gun in her face, the part that had been suppressed under the weight of this new creature. In another situation she might have tried to talk her down honestly, to try reason with her in good faith, but that wasn't going to happen. She intended to kill Bobbi, and that was going to be it. This was a fixed point of action.

It was for that reason that Bobbi had been carefully working the razor-sharp points of the crusher's terminals through the fabric of her pocket, and she felt resistance nearly gone. So set was Diana on watching Bobbi's face for signs of whatever she had wanted to see— fear, remorse, maybe even scornful validation, Bobbi didn't know— that she had completely missed the gentle flexing of Bobbi's hand as it sat shoved in her pocket. Maybe she hadn't noticed the crusher in Bobbi's hand before, or maybe there was something willful in her ignorance. Bobbi could not know, nor did she have time to speculate. There was only the moment between them now, the peril of it, and Bobbi took a deep breath.

"Tell me something," Bobbi said. "Were you waiting for me there? Does she know about me?"

The Diana-thing quirked a brow. "Does who know about you?"

"You know who I'm talking about. Your other mother."

The creature was silent for a moment. Her eyes were hard to read. Finally she spoke. "No," she said after a moment. "I haven't told her about you yet."

"But she knows about me?"

"Yes." Her eyes narrowed. "At least, she knows of your association with Thomas Walken. She doesn't know that you know about us, I don't think. I'll have an interesting report to give her once I've killed you."

Bobbi's mind raced. She didn't tell her? How could she not have told Merducci, the so-called Mother of Systems, about her? Perhaps Diana's consciousness was leaking into the thing that drove her body more than she was aware – this could be an example of an imperfect transition. Who knew how these things thought? Either way, she was going to die very quickly if she didn't work fast. There wasn't any more time to quiz the thing.

"Please," Bobbi said, still working at the fabric of her pants. "I want you to think about this."

"I already have," the creature said with a thin, manic smile. She hefted the pistol. "And I wouldn't worry about your friend. I've asked Mason to take care of him, and as I said, he does what I want. I'm surprised, though." She thumbed off the safety, eyes narrowing very slightly in thought. "Why aren't you asking me to stop?"

Bobbi met her gaze, not flinching. "Would it do any good?"

The Yathi lifted one shoulder in a half-hearted shrug. "No," she said. "I guess it wouldn't. But it would sure as hell make me feel better about my work."

Bobbi drew a deep breath, forcing herself into a state of focused calm. An idea surfaced, something that she hoped would give her the chance to distract Diana long enough to get the fuck away. "Answer a question for me before you kill me, huh?"

The thing that had been Diana quirked a brow, but nodded. "All right."

"Do you remember what your name is? Your real one?"

It was as if Bobbi had struck the other woman in the face. She sat stunned for a moment, as if she was searching for the answer and couldn't find it. Bobbi took advantage of the mental blow to save herself. She pushed her arm forward, felt the fabric of her pants tear, the crusher's terminals stabbing out into the air like needles. The creature looked down at the spikes that had grown from Bobbi's leg, and through the bluntness dawning recognition. She scrambled with the pistol, but

Bobbi clamped down hard on the crusher's trigger as Diana brought the gun up to bear. The world exploded into white noise.

When consciousness returned, it came first in the form of scent of ozone stinging Bobbi's nostrils. Then the awareness of the body, the leg that wasn't quite reporting in, the world around her swimming back into eyes that re-established connection to a stunned brain. The wet-cement sensation of recovering from a crusher blast was already well under way. Bobbi felt her chest heaving, became alarmed, then realized that it was only her own lungs working as intended.

She blinked her eyes twice, trying to find focus. She was still inside the car, and the air was faintly smoky. Bobbi realized with a jolt that the fabric around where the crusher had fired was smoldering. She patted her leg until the tiny cinders blew out. By then her brain had ticked over into proper function and she remembered the alien thing.

Bobbi sat up hard. The thing had collapsed into her corner of the back seat, boneless and unmoving. Bobbi leaned forward, smelled burnt fabric and flesh. She took a deep breath, ignoring the stink, and pushed it back by the shoulder. The blast from Bobbi's crusher had hit her full in the chest; a hole had been burnt away in the material of her padded vest, the skin beneath scorched and blistered. Cooked her heart, most likely, but Bobbi took her pulse anyway. She felt nothing.

Tears started in Bobbi's eyes as she looked down at the body of the woman that had been her childhood friend. She could not know if Diana's fate had truly been as the Yathi had revealed to her, of if she had still been there, somewhere in her mind. Bobbi only knew that she had killed at least one living thing, if not two. Though it was in self-defense, there was a core of coldness in her, something that she knew that she could never try and talk away. Everything that had been Diana Blake— her pain, her joy, all the years that had passed between when Bobbi had seen her last and this moment— was gone now. The alien thing in her head had taken it away, and now Bobbi had destroyed it as well.

"Jesus, Di," Bobbi muttered softly, and she wiped her eyes clear with the back of her hand. She wanted to feel more, anger, sadness...something. She'd heard people went through the most terrible emotional shock immediately after killing someone for the first time— pissed themselves, or worse. That kind of thing. Maybe that would come later, but right then there was nothing but a numbness that spread throughout her body. As her leg buzzed in fury at the proximity of the fatal shock, Bobbi remembered then what fate awaited Scalli; her brain locked her emotions away in a mental box and she was moving again.

She gritted her teeth hard as she tried to move toward the front seat and its jury-rigged console. Her leg remained locked in place, making this a difficult prospect at best; Bobbi slid off the back seat first, landing hard in the middle of the floor, and she dragged herself across the bare metal of the deck. Adrenaline coursed through her, driving her still-functioning limbs with chemical fury as she got a grip on the driver's side seat and pulled herself hard forward. She pulled herself up between the front seats, her arms burning, her back arched as she drew herself up into the driver's seat. The effort made her arms shake, but she felt this only as a distant tremor. Bobbi turned in the driver's seat, pulling her legs underneath the dash, and took a deep, grateful breath as she realized that the she didn't have to worry about hotwiring the car. Scalli had left the keyrod on the dash.

"All right you fucker," Bobbi muttered, snatching up the keyrod and slotting it into the car's ignition socket, "I got you." The car immediately purred to life; the wheel motors hummed softly as they took power from the batteries. The electric didn't use pedals, just a rocker switch on the wheel – which she now mashed hard with her thumb, throwing the vehicle forward.

Bobbi hadn't driven a car in nearly three years, but fueled with fear and adrenaline her body remembered precisely what to do. As if on automatic her arms worked the wheel, pulling the truck into a hard turn toward the ruined grocery. It barreled forward at high speed; gravel crunched beneath the wheels, lights flashed off bits of metal, dappled concrete gleamed. Bobbi's vision was focused into a tunnel which centered on the yawning hole, a tunnel that filled up the narrow cutouts made in the truck's armored canopy – and as it hurtled through the breach and plowed through the debris scattered around its mouth, nothing registered in Bobbi's head but the overwhelming desire to save Scalli. Bobbi had seen one friend die, however misguided she might have been. She would not see another.

The truck made it just through the opening when it happened. Dark within, save for the light streaming in from outside, Bobbi saw only glimpses of shadowed walls and the remains of supermarket shelves before the wheel turned hard left of its own accord. "Shit," Bobbi hissed through gritted teeth as the truck followed the wheel and hurtled toward the nearest wall; she pulled hard in the opposite direction, thumbed the accelerator hard in the opposite direction in a vain effort to try and stop. She was neither strong enough nor skilled enough to change its trajectory, and though she saved herself from plowing head-on into the darkness, the hard spin she found herself thrown into as the other motor failed filled her with a hurricane of fear and disorientation until impact. There was a roar of battered masonry, the shriek of twisting steel, and the hammer made of pain and numbness came down to drive her into the black.

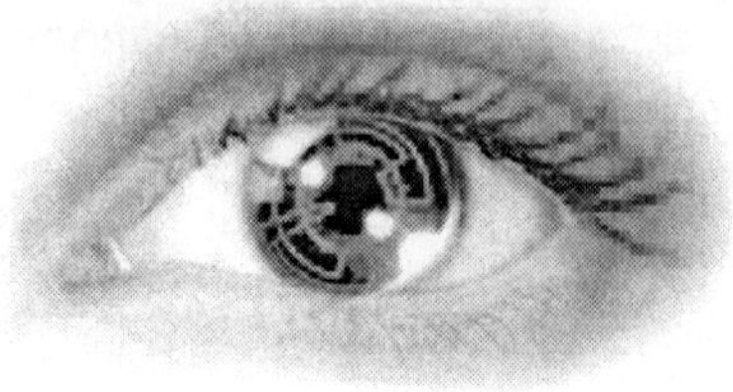

CHAPTER 14

In another life, Bobbi didn't pull the trigger. In another life, she talked things out with Diana long before, told her that she was right, that her mother was a whore that ruined everything she touched. That she was so, so very sorry about what had happened to Diana's family. In another life she wouldn't have had to kill a friend and crash a truck into the hulk of a burnt-out, abandoned grocery trying to save another. She would not be feeling the strange cocktail of pain and drunken nausea that comes with impacting against the heavy steel, brick and concrete wall, smashing her head against the corner of an up-armored truck door, and being thrown into the passenger's seat from where she neglected to put on a seat belt. She would be fine, and probably far happier than she had ever been since she was young.

But this reality had other plans, and she found herself being slowly dragged out of the numbing dark and into the light of the waking world. Coming to, Bobbi was grateful that she wasn't dead, though she was disappointed to find that the geyser of fire that had shot out of her head had not yet subsided. At least it had toned down to a dull roar. "Fucking shit," Bobbi groaned as she came around. Her eyes drifted slowly open, walled off by a red curtain dropped by what she very much believed was a big fucking gash in her head. She reached up, touching her head, found the warm wetness of blood there. Bobbi wiped her face with the back of her hand, forcing back the pain, and as her vision began to clear she wondered what she might see.

She saw teeth. Human teeth, yellow and marbled with decay. They had been filed down into points.

Instinct kicked in just before she had a chance to arrest it, and Bobbi flung herself back against a hard wall. She gasped like a fish thrown out of water— and then, finding that the teeth did not snap or proceed toward her, the fear subsided enough that her eyes managed to adjust and take in the rest of her surroundings.

Crouching opposite her was a lean, pale thing. Bobbi had for a moment thought it might have been a Yathi drone, but it was not. Beneath the ragged fatigue pants, the mane of greasy dark hair and the neon yellow 'LEMON SMALLEY' band tee faded and holed like an ancient cheese, it was very clear that whatever it was, the creature was entirely human. Beneath limp bangs, the woman— and however emaciated, Bobbi could tell from its general slightness that it was a woman— stared at her with wide blue eyes that were red-veined and wild. She had no nose, only a ragged, triangular aperture beneath her eyes that puckered red with inflammation. The sound of her breathing was a hideous rhythmic sucking noise.

Here was a feral, a feral who was not feasting on her still-warm entrails right now. Bobbi stared into the face of the horrifying madness that she had not seen for two years, and found herself strangely unafraid.

"Hey," Bobbi managed, staring into the feral's blue eyes.

"Hey," The woman's voice was ragged and broken, echoing slightly through her exposed sinus. "Why are you here?"

Bobbi stared at her a moment longer, trying to collect herself. "I wrecked," she said.

"Mmmmph." The woman looked to the left, and Bobbi turned to see with some amazement that she was still in the grocery. Some fifteen feet away was the hole blown in the back of the store, and the truck was half-buried by a dislodged pile of steel and masonry. How fast had she actually been moving? "You rattled the shrine pretty good. Took me a minute to get the fuck up here. Made a lot of noise."

"Wasn't my intention." Bobbi turned back to look at the girl, whose expression was an odd combination of sleepiness and irritation. The wideness of her eyes had gone, and she turned back to look at Bobbi as though she were looking over a horse.

"Maybe not," she said, "but we're here. You fucking city people make my head hurt." The feral couldn't be any older than Bobbi was, but she sure sounded like it. Bobbi watched as she got to her feet, sniffing at the air. "Nasty wreck. You're lucky to be alive."

Bobbi nodded quietly. "I guess I am," she said, and tried to rise. Pain rang in her head like a gong as she did so, and she ended up staying just where she was. "Fuck, my head is killing me."

"You got a nasty bump," the girl agreed. "But you're all right. It's safe here."

"Is it?" Bobbi wasn't so sure.

"Of course it is!" The feral sounded frowned at her now, which gave the appearance of an irritable goblin. "Shrines are holy places. Nobody violent comes here."

Well that was all right then, wasn't it, Bobbi thought bitterly to herself. What the hell kind of place was this? She sat up, looking past the feral and at the grocery at large. The place still had manual shelves, an artifact of the old days before roboticized stocking and delivery. Many of them were wrecked, pitched over at angles or lying down flat; boards were laid across the ones that still stood in rough gantries. She'd seen things like this before, when she was younger, back when Tenleytown was a much more primitive place. This had been a settlement, all right, though nothing civilian. Raiders, maybe. She stared at the feral woman a moment longer before saying, "I came here to find my friend. Did you see him?"

A shrug. "I didn't see anyone," said the feral. "But then again, you've been here a while. After the brethren came back from hunting..."

"Brethren? Hunting?" Ice flooded into Bobbi's stomach. "What do you mean? How long have I been out?"

"No idea." She let out a laugh that was equal parts whistle and ragged cough. "Sun will be down in a few hours, though. I don't have a watch."

Fuck, had she been out that late? It had been just after noon! "I...wait." Bobbi groaned as she got to her feet; her head pounded twice as hard as she stood. Her thoughts turned to the body in the truck. "What about your 'brethren'? Are you saying there are more, ah, of your kind outside?"

"You mean 'ferals', as you people in the city call us? Yeah, a shitload. They're camped out in the parking lot, waiting 'til time for..." The feral shrugged. "Whatever it is they're waiting on. I can never tell— they don't come in here, if you're worried about that. Besides..." The feral gave her a nasty, sharp-toothed grin. "They've already gotten something they can eat."

Something they can eat. Bobbi turned without a word and ran toward the breach, her heart in her throat. No, no, don't let it be him, don't let it be—

Bobbi stumbled toward the mouth of the hole, her feet unsteady from the charge. Beyond the sky had ripened into a gray-silver, too thick for the sun to penetrate outside of its usual vague lightness.

The feral woman had not exaggerated. In the middle of the parking lot, like a human island on the sea of cracked blacktop, a band of figures had gathered in the waning light of day. They stood in a semicircle among the jersey walls, halfway between the grocery and the street, dressed in the customary garb of the disenfranchised and mad: some wore ratty civilian clothes, torn and ripped, others ragged coveralls or the frayed remnants of underground fashions. One man stood to one side, naked and covered in patches of a scabrous rash, his genitalia cut off long ago so that only a short stump and a web of scar tissue radiated from between his legs.

They gathered around a sort of firepit that had been erected between them, a steel barrel that had been cut lengthwise in half and a spit erected made from rebar and steel clamps; the barrel was filled with refuse that was steadily burning with an oily flame. Spitted on the rebar was the charred shape of what was unmistakably a human body— or at least the trunk, for the legs, arms, and head had been cut away. The naked man turned it slowly on the spit with the utmost concentration lining his dirty face. Cracked and charred though the skin was now, Bobbi saw that the body had been that of a woman.

Bobbi stared at the grim assembly and their hideous meal, going numb. Her brain tried to process what she saw; it wasn't the most of the horrors that she had witnessed in her life, but it was fresh in its novelty. There was quite a long list of atrocities accumulating in her recent memory. She looked on, unsure of how to process the tableau. Should she scream? Shrug it off? As she watched them turn the body round and round on its rebar spit, mental survival instincts kicked in. She found herself imagining that it wasn't human, that body; it was a dog, something else, something that just might happen to look like a corpse but wasn't. She closed her eyes, felt her heart racing in her chest, felt the sweat beading on her brow. Though her mind was busy disconnecting wires, Bobbi could not deny the truth. She knew the body that they were roasting; it was the same that she had seen expire under the business end of her nerve crusher just hours before.

"I had to give them something," came the voice of the feral woman, wheezing up behind her. "It was her or you. At least she was fresh enough."

Bobbi stiffened. The numbness inside her let her speak. "It's all right," she said in a voice that did not sound like her own. Too flat, too leaden. "Let's go inside and you can explain it to me." At least, seeing the awful display, she knew that the thing was truly dead.

The two of them walked back inside the grocery. The numbness she felt had become physical; her body felt like wood as she walked behind the withered creature. She had killed Diana, but it had been an accident. She certainly didn't intend for the woman to have been hauled off as a fucking banquet for the horrors camping outside. But she was marooned at the moment, with Scalli and Mason missing and howling human beasts lurking nearby – not that the creature whom she followed now was any kind of saint. Bobbi tried to compress the fear and disgust inside of her into a manageable pellet, then pushed it back into the vaults of her mind while trying to plan...whatever came next.

"You said this place was a shrine," Bobbi said.

"That's right." They walked past the rows of shelves, long emptied and now cracked and faded with the wear of past decades. "Or something like that. Me, I'm not one for hocus-pocus, but those crazy bastards out there sure take stock in it."

"Then what kind of shrine is it?" A flash of a thought shot through her head. "And where was the gear that was in the truck?"

"Downstairs." The feral woman looked over her shoulder. "First rule of salvage – you take the stuff first and wait to see if the owner recovers."

Bobbi wrinkled her nose. "Am I going to get it back?"

"Maybe." The woman snorted out of the hole in her face. "My name's Violet, by the way, thanks for asking."

"I'm Bobbi," she said automatically, then cleared her throat. "Sorry. I just..."

"Yeah, yeah, I know," said Violet. She led Bobbi toward the back of the store, where a ransacked pharmacy once stood. Bobbi saw a ruined live-meat butcher's counter down the back of the store to her right and wondered just how old this place really was. "It's not easy out here, you see all kinds of bad shit. You from the city?"

Bobbi nodded. "Now I am," she replied. "Used to be from Tenleytown."

Violet nodded. "That explains the truck," she said, "though it doesn't explain the reason why you're all the way out here. You're very far out of the neighborhood, honey. Why the hell would you even drive this thing into this place?"

"I...I thought my friend was in here," Bobbi said, suddenly feeling very very stupid indeed. "We thought this place was...something bad."

"You thought it was something bad," said Violet, who had paused by a pair of ancient swinging doors, "and the first thing you thought of was to come and look inside? That's typical, really. City people don't have much to their brains anymore."

Bobbi grunted. "Says the wasteland princess," she muttered to herself.

"My nose may be gone, but my ears are working very well indeed." Violet shook her head. "Look, girlie, this isn't 'someplace bad'. This is my home. I live here. And it's keeping you safe, so let's not get too bitchy about décor, huh?"

"Right." Bobbi nodded after Violet. "Sorry." She gritted her teeth against a wave of emotion that had suddenly rose, pushed it back, and felt somewhat better then. Her detachment to the moment was complete, and she followed Violet now as if the other woman were leading her along on a museum tour. "I thought this used to be a settlement, or at least I heard it was."

"Briefly," said Violet. "Then they came and took the people here, left it open. The hole is where they blasted themselves in, apparently."

"Who's 'they'?" Bobbi leaned against a low display. "Those guys outside, or people like them?"

Violet was quiet for a moment. She looked Bobbi over, her expression gauging. "I think you know," she said, "if you knew how to find this place. But you don't have the signs..." The woman's blue eyes widened a little more. "C'mon, I'll show you what we killed when we came here. You'll want to see it."

Bobbi hesitated for a moment as Violet pushed open one of the ancient doors leading to the store's back quarter. In the dim light, she saw the silhouettes of shelves and industrial equipment. "I'd be crazy to go with you into a dark place like that," she said.

"Maybe so," said Violet with a nod. "But you'd be crazier to stay out here. That meat won't last forever, and then they'll be beating down my door for something else. Better you be out of here before then."

Violet turned and disappeared through the door; for a moment Bobbi considered just taking her chances, but then she remembered that Violet had all of her gear down there. She'd need Diana's rifle too, most likely, as loathe as she was to use it— but she'd already killed one person today, and it seemed to her that she could do it again if she had to. Bobbi took a deep breath, blew it out, and followed.

The two of them walked into the back, which was dark save for bioluminescent night-light strips that had been laid on the floor to form an aisle or a path. The blue light that radiated from them had deepened the shadows around her into a near-impenetrable gloom. Bobbi had the distinct feeling of walking through the halls of some kind of tomb, or maybe a church of some kind – even if she hadn't known that it was a shrine of some sort before, the impression of sanctity was definitely settling in. Her heart beat quickly as she followed Violet through the back of the store, then to a set of stairs leading down to a heavy steel fire door set into the concrete of the grocery's foundation.

"It's in here," said Violet, who produced a set of old-fashioned metal keys from the pocket of her fatigue pants. She picked through a few before selecting one, and unlocked the door. "Come on."

Bobbi took a deep breath and followed Violet through the door – and found herself, quite suddenly, stepping into a tiny pocket of Hell.

It was the scent that hit her first, the smell of blood and shit and the strange tang of burning metal. It was like the smell of someone being fried in an electric chair, and it hit Bobbi like a wall. She reeled, staggered by the smell, and her eyes worked to try and bring the room into focus as she had to fight herself to put her rising gore back into line.

The store basement had once been a combination of storeroom and engineering space; shelves lined one long wall, and in one corner of the large concrete chamber a tangle of machines formed a pillar leading upward into the grocery itself. The low ceiling was lit by the yellow-orange bulbs of worklights hanging in the corners. Whatever its original purpose had been, the basement was now a charnel house. The walls were covered with crude drawings of eyes, each one smeared in what looked like the dark red-brown of dried blood. Each one seemed to stare at her, and for a moment she stared back— until she realized what filled the shelves that ran along the wall. Human heads, each one severed from the neck and in various states of decay, crowded the black wire shelves, staring out at the two of them with the myriad expressions of violent death: some were locked in screams of pain and terror, as if they saw the end and feared its coming, but the majority were blank. Gazing upon the ghastly collection, this made complete sense to Bobbi; each one was white-skinned and with white-blond hair, and each one gazed out at the world that they had departed with eyes of silver-gray. Men, women, children, it did not matter. The collection of the dead, pinned under the collective gaze of the scrawled eyes, were all Yathi or Yathi drones.

The freshest example was Diana's head, staring out at nothing. Unlike the rest, her eyes had been removed.

"Mother of fuck," Bobbi gasped when the breath finally returned to her. "You people really don't fuck around, do you?"

Violet let out another gasping sound, which Bobbi now realized was laughter. "No shit," she said. "Fucking steel-eyes are all over the place. Well, less so now that the Lady's running the show."

Bobbi turned toward Violet. "But how? These people...they're better equipped, better-armed than anyone else I've ever heard of – everyone and their mother seems to be wired up in their ranks. So how the hell..." She gestured to the horrible shelves. "How the hell can this happen?"

These words drew only silence from Violet, who now looked upon Bobbi as if she were some new person. "You really do know about these people," she said after a little while. "So what are you doing out here?"

"You first," said Bobbi.

"I don't think so." Violet lifted her hand, and Bobbi saw her own nerve crusher pointing back at her.

When did Violet get that? It must have been when she was gaping at the heads, Bobbi thought, and cleared her throat. "Fair enough," she said after a moment. "I'm trying to get to Redeye."

Violet's eyes widened. "The Eye," she said in reverent tones, and made a strange sign over her face— veiling one eye with her spread fingers in a fan-like gesture. "Why are you looking for her? Are you with them?" The feral woman nodded slightly toward the battery of heads. She brought the crusher up level with Bobbi's chest, too, and dialed the power up.

"No!" Bobbi held her hands up in supplication. "No, not at all! I'm just here to bring her a message."

Violet stared at her now, and Bobbi almost got the feeling that she was being looked through by those strange blue eyes. "You don't look like a steeleye," Violet said, but she in no way sounded convinced. "But your friend was."

"I..." Bobbi took a deep breath. She tried very hard not to look at Diana's head. "She wasn't my friend. Not anymore. I killed her."

"So I saw." Violet gestured slightly to the crusher in her hand. "How did you know what she was?"

Bobbi stared back at her. "I...she was going to kill me," she said after a long moment, her mouth going dry as she recalled the horror of it. "And I called her on what she was. She wasn't my friend anymore. She wasn't even..."

"Wasn't even human," Violet said with a nod. "How did you get away?"

"I asked her if she remember what her name was."

Violet's brows arched a little, and she looked Bobbi over once again. "That was smart," she said. "They don't like it when you try and bring up the past. It can fuck with 'em. All right. What kind of a message are you trying to take to my Lady?"

"Why do you call her that?" said Bobbi, waving her hands. "Is she...I don't know, some kind of feral royalty?" She realized of course that her smartass mouth was going to get her directly into trouble if she wasn't careful, but the alternative was to be credulous and that credulity would mean admitting the full weight of reality. She couldn't handle that right now.

"The message first," said Violet, and her blue eyes grew hard. "What do you want with the Eye that you would brave these parts? I tell you now, if you think that I'll let you harm her, you're out of your fucking mind." There was a buzz about her now, a palpable devotion that Bobbi had only read about in history books. Violet was a zealot, like the kind that had melted the Middle East, and her madness was suddenly clear. Bobbi knew that if she didn't tell the truth, she wouldn't get out alive.

Bobbi took a deep breath, keeping her hands up, and nodded. "All right," she said. "I come with a message for the Eye from a person called Cagliostro."

"Never heard of him," Violet said, her eyes narrowing slightly. "What does he want with the Eye?"

"It's not what he wants with her," said Bobbi, "it's what he wants with Genefex. The steeleyes. He knows what they are. I know what they are."

Violet's eyes snapped open. "They are the plague which chokes our minds! They are the ruin that comes to humanity!" The words were fevered, her voice a throttling rasp as it came from her mouth. "The Eye sees them, and she burns them to ash!"

Zealotry was definitely the madness that Violet had, and Bobbi felt as awed as she was disturbed by the energy that came from her. "I know," she replied. "And that's why I want to see her. Two years ago, a friend and I burned down a hospital they were using as a base in the Verge. He disappeared, but I've been trying to work out who they were, what they were up to. Now that I know..." Bobbi shook her head. "Well, you can count me in. That's what we're out here for, to give her what she needs to..." Bobbi paused a moment, then she made the same sign over her eye that Violet did. "Burn them out."

Violet stared at her, conflict written in her hideous face. Bobbi knew that she was probably presenting herself to the other woman as a kind of prophet, or something along those lines— she knew enough about God-fearing people from her father to be able to try and speak to them from that kind of place. "I want to help the Eye destroy the Yathi, for once and for all. I'm bringing her a message that should let her put an end to the whole operation."

And that was what broke the stare. Violet flinched as though Bobbi had struck her, putting her hands over her ears and staring at Bobbi in blind terror. "We don't say their name," she wailed. "No, no, not the name! They're in all of us, in our minds, they can hear—"

"Well, they're not in me," said Bobbi, and she fixed Violet with her own blazing green eyes. On top of the situation now, finally she had the advantage. She felt power in her that only rage could bring, power and confidence that she was not the same as those horrible things whose heads crowded the shelves. Human, but only on the outside. "I'm human, through and through. And that's why I'm here."

Violet winced at Bobbi again, uncertainty and fear coming out of her in waves, but then she took her hands away from her ears and shook her head. "No," she said, "I...I can see you aren't. We can see them, the demons. We can see them in the eyes. I can see that you don't have them."

Bobbi pursed her lips a bit, but nodded. "Yeah," she said. "But neither did my...neither did the woman whose head you have over there."

"That was unusual," Violet shook her head. "She must have been an infiltrator. We hear about those, sometimes— no implants, no exotic technology, just the body and its co-opted brain." She eyed Bobbi a bit. "You must have a good sense of people if you were able to sniff her out."

Bobbi didn't say anything to that. Instead she said, "So are you going to take me to see her?"

There was a moment where Bobbi thought that Violet might just shoot her to flee from the possibility of facing her so-called goddess; the feral woman's blue eyes brimmed with conflict, conflict and— yes— more fear. Bobbi had to wonder what kind of creature she was going to see that commanded such strangeness in others, especially the ones that were already mad to begin with. Was it just that the madness made them easier to cultivate, or was there something that united them, some common factor beyond simple insanity that connected Redeye and her people? Finally, however, Violet lowered the crusher, and she held it out grip-first to Bobbi. "I'll take you," she said. "But we have to wait for those outside to leave. They aren't...safe."

Bobbi stared at her. "I got that from the fact they're eating my friend out there," she said, marveling at how bluntly she now said those words. "But aren't they your people? I thought you were united."

"Those who eat the flesh of man are an abomination," said Violet, again sounding as if she were reading straight out of some holy book. "But they are our brethren, and so must be spared." She frowned. "That doesn't mean I'm dumb enough to take you out there, plump as you are, and have them decide that they'd rather have seconds now than worry about the Eye later on."

She gave Violet a bit of a look. "Yeah," she said, "that would probably be best. So what do we do? Do we, er..." Bobbi looked back at the wall of head— she'd gotten somewhat used to the smell now, but she had no desire to stay here. "Stick around?"

Violet shook her head. "No," she said. "We'll be fine unless they decide to come inside the building, which they don't normally do. It's a holy place, they know they aren't worthy. Just stay away from the entrance and we should be able to wait them out."

Bobbi nodded. "And the truck?"

"Well," said Violet, "I'm no mechanic, but it looks like the front wheel motor on the left hand side is gone. You really did a number coming in like that. What the hell was that all about?"

Though her sense of righteous fury had been stoked, it certainly didn't keep her from feeling very stupid. "It's like I said. That thing, it tried to kill me."

"So you tried to kill it right back, only you were better at it." Violet's thin brows lifted. "I get it."

"It's a long story." Bobbi shook her head. "My other friends came in here, only they're gone now. I don't know where they've gone off to, or if..." She didn't want to say it, not with Diana gone the way she ultimately had. She didn't want to think that she might be alone out here now.

Violet nodded. "Well," she said, "if anyone got them, it wasn't those boys outside. Here, let's go back upstairs. We'll talk in the back of the store."

They left the charnel shrine for the more reassuring darkness of the storerooms, and as the stench left her lungs Bobbi felt new courage filling them in return. Violet hung back a moment behind her. They climbed the stairs and sat down on a few crates sitting nearby – Violet wanted to be close to the door to the shrine, which she'd propped open with a box; a chink of orange light shone up from the stairway and splashed across the grocery's back wall. Violet kept an eye on the door leading to the main floor.

"That reminds me," said Violet, and she reached down by her feet to produce Bobbi's medical bag. "Here you are. I haven't taken anything."

Bobbi grinned a bit as she took the bag; she felt much more confident now with its weight in her hands. "Thanks very much," she said, opening up the bag and rifling through. Everything was there, including the mag-mount antenna off the top of the truck. Bobbi looked up at Violet, holding the little slug up between them. "Why did you take this off?"

"I thought perhaps you might actually be here for a good reason," Violet said with a smirk. "Looks like I was right. Only, I'm sorry about your friend."

Bobbi shook her head and sighed. "No, forget it," she said. "I mean, I'm the one who killed her, not that she was even herself anymore."

"That must have been hard," Violet said. Her voice was soft beneath the growl of her ruined throat. "You don't seem to be the kind who does that easily."

"I haven't done it ever," said Bobbi. Beneath her bravery a current of cold water began climbing up her gut once more. "Ever."

Violet wrinkled her nose. "Well, there's a first time for everything, I guess."

Bobbi nodded wordlessly.

"I guess I can't blame you," said Violet. "But I've been doing this for a long time. The teeth, you know, they're not just for show."

It took a moment for the right circuits to fire; Bobbi sat up a bit, her expression becoming guarded. "I thought you said man-eaters aren't safe," she said, tone grave. Her fingers found the grip of the crusher, her eyes going hard.

"Oh, I'm safe enough," said Violet with a wide, saw-toothed grin. "I don't eat humans. Well, not real ones. I've got a taste for whiter meat."

Bobbi stared at her a moment before understanding clicked. "You eat the Ya—I mean, you eat them?"

"Oh yes," said Violet with a wink. "The dead ones, mostly, the ones that walk. They're preserved, you know, once you bleed them. Takes time, and you have to cook them up for days— but when they're done...oh,I dunno. Just something about the taste." She closed her eyes and shivered. "I think there might be something addictive in there. Don't know what, don't much care. You'll never find me going for lesser meat than that, though, I'll tell you what."

Bobbi wrinkled her nose, but nodded. It wouldn't help to show disgust, not right now –

she was discovering all manner of untapped strength within herself, and she wasn't sure how she felt about it. It was useful, though. That's what she needed. Useful. "Well," she said, "I don't know about how they taste, I just know how they die. That's what my friend was doing, helping me. He was my muscle."

Violet nodded. "Well," she said. "I guess that's one way to do it. It's clear that you both work well together. Do you know..." She pursed her lips and grew silent. The hole in her face flexed around the edges, like a second smile.

"Do I know wh—" Bobbi stopped short as Violet lifted her hand, turning toward the door. Her eyes narrowed, and she gestured behind the crates. The two of them slid behind then, crouching low.

"Good ears," Violet whispered. "I think they've come inside."

Behind her crate, Bobbi froze. She peeked out over the top of it, staring at the door. Seconds ticked by, then minutes; the two of them kept their mouths shut tight, watching in silence for any sign of motion. Eventually they heard a shuffling, like bare feet on concrete. Bobbi and Violet looked at one another as the sound drew closer. Bobbi brought up the nerve crusher, dialing the power back to middle strength; she didn't want to kill anyone again, and anyway the battery was getting very low. Violet came up with a semi-auto which Bobbi recognized with a jolt as Diana's.

"Wait," Bobbi said, looking at Violet in surprise. "If you use that, you'll bring everybody down on us."

Violet nodded. "I have to use this," she said. "It's because they'll have found us already. I just want to be prepared."

Bobbi opened her mouth to speak again, but presently the door to the back area swung open. A figure stood there, thin and pale and very naked. Everybody was so damned pale in this city, Bobbi thought as she covered the door with her crusher. I'm going to start going for a gun every time I see a white person. Was it Yathi? Something else? Bobbi squinted as the figure shuffled in a little further, and in the blue glow of the bioluminescent strips she saw straggly hair and patchy scabs. It wasn't a drone, but the feral who had been tending the spit a while ago. He stood in the doorway, clutching a blackened forearm in one fist as if it were a stick of candy. Bobbi closed her eyes and gritted her teeth against the sight. If she could have, she would have killed him right there.

Violet laid her free hand on Bobbi's arm and gave her a warning look, holding her gaze for a moment before looking back to the doors. The feral stood there for a moment more, lifting the cooked limb to his mouth and taking a bite from it. Bobbi's fingers trembled as she fought the urge to shoot, even as he turned toward them, chewing, bits of forbidden meat and juice dribbling from his lips. They crouched lower behind the crates, but in the light thrown from the basement door their shadows could not be hidden. The thin man stared at them, or rather where their shadows loomed, and let out a wail. It was not the sound that should come from a man's throat— instead it was a keening, falsetto sound, echoing in the mind as much as it echoed off the concrete walls of the basement.

"Fuck this." Bobbi popped up and shot him where he stood, silencing the horrific call with the sharp snap and electric flash of the crusher. The feral dropped instantly into a tangle of scabby limbs, still clutching the arm in his hand.

Violet got to her feet as well, muttering. "Well, shit," she hissed, "they'll have heard that for sure."

"What do we do?" Bobbi kept the crusher trained on the door.

"We can hide in the shrine," said Violet, "but if they decide to camp out..."

Bobbi shook her head. "You're armed, and I'm armed— sort of. Maybe we can shoot our way out of here. Think they had guns?"

"Probably one or two." Violet craned her head a bit, listening. "I don't hear anyone. C'mon, let's go out. If we see them coming we can hide downstairs."

"Yeah." By now, Bobbi was feeling a little sick from all the adrenaline her body had been pumping through her system over the past few hours, but she shook it off. She'd die from crazy ferals faster than she'd drop dead from exhaustion. The two of them dashed across the storeroom, letting the blue lights steer them, and stepped past the fallen man.

They shouldered carefully through the double doors and onto the grocery floor. On the other end of the store were the front doors, which were on the right side of the front of the store. On the opposite side, at the front left corner, was the breach. "Keep your head down," Violet said as they began to proceed down the nearest aisle toward the front of the store. "The Eye only knows if they've heard that fucker running his mouth."

"Yeah, well." Bobbi shook her head, duck-walking her way along behind Violet. "Makes me wish I had drilled that fucker with more than a nerve crusher."

"Don't be in such a hurry to kill people." Violet shook her head. "You seem like a nice girl. Like the Eye must have been. I could see it in your eyes when you talked about your friend – you haven't done it before. Don't make it a habit."

"Says the lady with the head museum downstairs." Bobbi took a deep breath. "All right, so where do we go after this?"

"I have a truck not far from here," Violet said as they neared the front of the aisle, past a few moldering, rusted-through cans of Tinkle Treats. "We'll go to where the Eye is camped from there. If there's anything to be done with you, she'll be able to tell."

As they came to the mouth of the aisle, they saw what they had dreaded. Coming into the breach were a knot of ferals, their lean forms lurching like the damned. Forget the corpse-machines of the Yathi. If there were any kind of cannibal zombies in the world, these would be it. Only problem was that they weren't dead, and they sure as shit weren't mindless.

"I heard him come in here," said one voice, ragged and deep like some demonic bull. "Heard him screamin'."

"You got good ears, then," said another voice, this one high and thin. "I didn't. Dickless screams about anything anyway, screams more than a bitch before you stick her."

"Sometimes like one after you do," Bull said. He made a nasty sound that might have been a chuckle. "Wish that girl the Saint gave us wasn't already dead. She had a good pussy. Nice and firm."

"Hairy like a goddamned cat, though," said Shrill.

"That's okay," said Bull, "I eat cat too. They taste the same with enough fire on 'em." He laughed again, and this time Shrill joined in. Bobbi shivered.

"Shit." Violet's voice dropped very low, almost a whisper. "Come on, let's go ahead. Hopefully we won't hit those two assholes getting to the door."

"What about the shutters," Bobbi asked.

"You let me worry about those."

"At least you didn't fuck this one before we cooked her, dead or no," Shrill was saying. Their voices were passing by them down the left side; they must be going down the aisle. Good luck. "Only thing I want fulla cream when I bite into it's a goddamned donut."

"Yeah, well, you lucky I don't fuck you again, you shit. They don't call me 'splitter' for nothin'!"

"Don't I fuckin' know it," Shrill muttered. His voice trailed off.

They two women crept quietly toward the mouth of the aisle, Bobbi with her crusher and Violet with Diana's gun in her hand. Once they reached it, Violet peeked her head out, looked one way and then the other. She waited a moment, then she gestured for Bobbi to follow her, but she didn't go straight for the door. Instead she crouched down low and duck-walked out to the checkout counters, slouching along the nearest one. Bobbi looked both ways again, just to make sure, before she followed. The graying tile of the floor bore many stains, more than a few of the splotches being what looked like blood long dried. Bobbi made her way across to the checkout lane next to Violet.

"All right," Bobbi mouthed, "what now?"

Violet gestured with the end of Diana's pistol to the returns and information counter set in the front of the store. There was a low door there, only as high as a man's waist, and it was open. As she gestured, the light spilling through the breach glinted off the pistol's gleaming skin; Bobbi winced as it flashed in her eyes and had to brace herself against the counter to keep from falling over. Though she kept herself upright, however, her medical bag bumped softly against the plastic of the checkout lane.

You shit, Bobbi growled at herself. Stupid, clumsy shit! Both women crouched there for a moment, frozen as they were— and then they heard something that put a bolt of fear through Bobbi's heart that she could not ignore.

"Hey there, hey there," came the voice of Bull calling down the aisle behind them and to the left. "I hear someone want to get fucked in the ass." The way he said 'ass', horrible and singsong like some overgrown child, made the hair stand up on Bobbi's neck and her heart beat triple-time. She dialed up the crusher to three-quarter power, and when Violet gestured for her to move on toward the information counter, she only hesitated a moment.

"I hear you sneaking around my place, Heron Wales," said Violet, who drew herself into a full, proud stance; head up, shoulders back, her spine hardened with the iron of command. Bobbi looked over her shoulder a moment as she made it to the door in the counter and made to slip through it. Ugly as she might be, and however crazy, Violet made a hell of a priestess. "What are you doing trespassing in the hall of the Eye?"

Bobbi opened the door as narrowly as possible to admit her, and then closed it behind her almost all the way; she watched through the narrow crack as Violet stood there waiting. Out of the aisle came two shapes, one tall and gaunt, the other maybe as tall as she was. It was hard to get a glimpse of the smaller one given the angle, but it looked as though the small man was carrying a fire axe. Both men were dressed in tattered civilian clothes, and both of them wore ragged balaclavas. The tall one, Bobbi noted, had cut a hole in the top to admit a crest of limp, greasy black hair.

"Sorry to bother you, Saint," said the tall man, whom Bobbi had known a moment ago as Bull; Heron Wales carried a combat shotgun, usable but in bad repair, and when he smiled he had the same filed teeth that Violet did. "Me an' Willy done heard Dickless screamin', had to go look."

"Your friend trespassed in the Shrine," said Violet, her voice a peal of thunder now. "Eating heathen flesh, no less. You know what the penalty is for that."

Heron's eyes squinted a bit. "You killed 'im?"

"No," spat Violet, "but I should have. I know he can't help but be curious. He's knocked out in the back."

Heron made another face. "That doesn't make me happy, Saint," he said. His grimace was like the twitchings of rats in a sack, something ugly trying to get out but being held back by the thinnest wall of rotten burlap. If Violet pushed him too hard, Bobbi knew that this was going to get ugly.

But Violet knew how to handle them, or so it seemed. "I'm sorry to hear it, Heron," she said. "But I don't have many rules, and he broke one. He's lucky that he's not right in the head – if it had been one of your boys, I'd have drilled him." She lifted her hand, showing him Diana's gun. "You know the Eye doesn't tolerate people fucking around with the steeleyes."

"No." This time it was Willy who talked. "Look, we just heard him hollerin' and wanted to look-see. We didn't mean to bother the Eye or nothin'." Unlike his taller partner, Willy wouldn't look at Diana; he looked straight ahead at the front of the store – right at the counter. Bobbi shrank away a bit in reflex to that deference. She did not want to be seen by the likes of them.

"That's just fine," said Violet, whose tone changed when she talked to Willy. She could be as beneficent as she was harsh, the whistling quality of her breathing not softening the corners of her voice. "The Eye appreciates it, you know that, even if you've taken to eating the flesh of man." She looked up at Heron then, who was looking back at her in defiance.

"That's no way to talk to him, Saint," said Heron. The twitching of his lips grew worse; Bobbi was reminded of downed electrical cable and the danger that they implied. She glanced down at the nerve crusher, made sure the charging dial was where she'd set it. "You need to—" And then he fell silent. Bobbi looked up again, and her blood froze. Willy was staring at her, or at least the crack through which she looked. His fingers were flexing on the handle of his axe. His eyes were wide, and his nostrils flexed as if he'd scented some good thing in the air.

"Willy," said Violet, in a careful tone that suggested that something very bad was about to happen, "what is it?"

"There's a girl over there," said the little man, in a voice that was equal parts awed and hungry. Bobbi's heart skipped a beat as she watched him; his face was set, as if he were suffering some extreme strain. Whatever faith these men had abandoned, it looked as if Willy was still unwilling to tempt the wrath of the Eye. For the moment.

"A girl." Heron looked to where Bobbi hid and smiled widely; his teeth were a mess of yellow-brown spikes. His voice had grown loud. "You're holding out on us, Saint. I knew you had to have more than just that one bitch in here, that tank crashed out like it was." From behind them, more shapes emerged out of the aisles; eager faces swam out of the darkness, ghoulish and excited by the prospect of new flesh. Heron knew the right words to summon them. "Come on out here, honey."

Anxiety flooded Bobbi's body, but she did not rise. Violet stiffened further. "That's enough, Heron," she practically growled. "We're going to see the Eye. She's a messenger, you understand me? A prophet."

"The Eye doesn't have prophets," Heron sneered. Willy stared straight ahead again, as if looking toward Bobbi's position had been causing him physical pain. Lines of tension spread throughout his haggard face, and his knuckles were white on the handle of his axe.

"First time for everything," Violet said. "New god, new experiences. Don't fuck with me on this." For all her bravado, however, Bobbi knew that if whatever gambit she was playing didn't work out, they were both fucked. There were too many; Diana's gun didn't have enough bullets for them all and Bobbi's crusher didn't have nearly enough charge. It would be just her kind of karma to be doomed now by having saved herself from Diana earlier.

Heron was buying it. "All right," he said, "Fine. But we're still hungry. She doesn't need her arms or legs to give the message, right?"

"She doesn't get touched." Violet's voice was made of lead. "Period."

Bobbi couldn't let her stand out there alone anymore. Violet was going to get killed, and it was going to be because of her, and crazy as fuck or not the feral "priestess" was trying to help her out. "Enough," she said, and she rose slowly behind the service counter. "I'm right here."

"We-ell-ell now...." Heron's expression twisted into a mask of horrible delight, a shark scenting blood in the water. From behind the balaclava his dark eyes glittered as he swept his gaze over Bobbi's torso. "Nice and smooth, pale...ooh. Big tits, too. You're beautiful, girlie." He looked to Violet. "I see why you wanted to give her to the Eye. You're definitely going to give her to us, though." His tongue, pocked with sores, dragged lewdly over his thin lips. He was practically drooling. "She's just too tasty to waste."

"You'll have to kill me first." Violet's voice was still hard, but even Bobbi heard the waver in it now. No doubt an experienced predator like Heron knew what was coming now.

"I got no problem with that. Willy!" Heron began to unshoulder his shotgun, and his smaller partner snapped out of his trance. He stared at Bobbi, his eyes glazed, and he unlimbered his axe.

And then—as these things often do— everything happened at once. Bobbi acted first, which upon reflection, would surprise her. She fired the crusher at Willy, who was struck in the face; he went down, his balaclava erupting into flame, his horrible grin vanished beneath the convulsions that wracked his body. Meanwhile Violet opened up on Heron, and there was no chance of missing – she pumped two rounds in his gut and he went down howling. "Fuck you, you motherfuckers," she shouted, dashing back and firing again into the crowd of ferals that were surging forward; they fell back, cursing and spitting, and Violet used the time to throw herself backward across the checkout counter in the direction of the breach. "Let's go," she shouted Bobbi's way, but she didn't stop to look over shoulder as she sprinted toward freedom.

But Bobbi didn't need the invitation. As Violet shot into the crowd she had already burst through the door of the customer service counter and was coming out to do the same thing. The two of them hurtled toward the open breach while the fiends came back, howling as they came after. As they neared the shattered wall of the grocery, the roar of gunfire pealed from behind them; Bobbi got a face full of shattered masonry. Pain lanced through her face; she staggered, blood running into her eye, but she did not stop. She could not stop now, even if she wanted to – the dwindling light of the afternoon shone down from overhead, and the lizard nerves in her brain drove her legs like piston. Escape was all she thought about in this moment, escape and freedom from the madness, or at the very least a reprieve.

By the time they were halfway across the parking lot, however, it was clear that they were running out of energy and speed. Bobbi's leg was screaming again; it had remembered the jolt it had gotten from the nerve crusher, and now the muscles were trembling as if it had happened all over again. Her face burned as well, and she felt blood running down the side of it. Her eye was swelling shut and her lungs burned with the fires of exertion. Violet was hardly in any shape to be running around all over the place, either. As they charged toward the edge of the parking lot, the skinny ghoul of a woman in the lead and behind her a wave of hooting monsters, Bobbi wondered if this was going to be the end for her.

Bobbi pulled herself up on one arm. Her leg was numb now, and it wasn't getting any better. "My leg isn't working," she said through gritted teeth; pain lanced through her face and shoulder. She reached out and found her crusher, but the charge light was flashing red. No juice. Little ammo. How many were there, the ferals that rushed across the blacktop toward them? Fifteen? Twenty? Violet's shooting brought one down, then another – still they came, undaunted, and Bobbi knew that was all for them. "Better save two of those rounds for the both of us, or at least one for me. You go."

This was how it was going to end. Bobbi felt something new, hot and liquid on her face – tears, she realized, not blood. The madmen were coming toward them as if in slow motion, moving through the water that reality had suddenly become— and she could see them, every detail and line, as if they were high-definition images conjured into being from some heavenly holographic projector above. Here came the death scene, she knew. The end of her movie. The end of Violet's. She wondered if it was going to hurt. She wondered where Tom was. She wished he was here to save her again, or at least to hold her hand.

Violet was shouting something— Bobbi didn't know what— and then the sky pealed with thunder. It'd be about right for there to be a storm just as she died, Bobbi thought. A storm, hail, rain...

And then the ferals began to fall.

A shadow passed over her from the opposite side of Violet, a shadow that might have been a mountain had it not been running on two legs. As if in a dream, the monstrous form of Marcus Scalli came thundering past her and toward the waiting throng. He carried his rifle, but there was something wrong with it; the silencer was gone, leaving a flanged nub that spewed fire like a broken gas main as he threw down a curtain of death before him. Bobbi watched them die as they ran; Scalli skidded to a stop just a few feet beyond her, planting himself as he cut them down, as they fell away one direction or another. It took frighteningly little time to mow down a body of people in motion, especially if they were packed so close together as they were. In what felt like but a moment they were alone before a hedge of tangled, bloody bodies.

"Come on, girl." Another voice, this one behind her; a hand reached down to take her arm and start to lift her. The voice, she realized, was Harry Mason. "On your feet. We need to get out of here."

Bobbi should have been frightened. Diana's words were not forgotten, even after all that happened in the moment. But instead of fear she only felt a great exhaustion fall around her shoulders. "My leg went out," she heard herself say, but she didn't look up at him. She was busy looking at Scalli, who walked among the fallen ferals putting bullets in whoever wasn't already dead. He was mechanical as he dispatched the dying. Thorough. In that moment she knew that what Mason had told her before was true; he had been trained by some kind of military, though one for whom ruthlessness seemed to be part of standard methodology.

She was very aware in this moment how little she actually knew about the people she was supposed to call her allies, less even than the hidden monsters that she had set out into the Old City to destroy. Mason's hand left her arm and came back down with a dermal patch which he slapped against her neck. The warm, rosy waves of endorphin analogue rippled through her body, killing the pain, blissfully disconnecting her from the rest of her body. "Come on, girl," he barked, and he pulled her to her feet. The drugs let her walk just fine, although to be truthful she could walk on bloody stumps and not give a shit with that kind of juice. It was like riding around in a machine. "Let's get out of here."

"Aye aye, Cap'n," said Bobbi, easing herself slowly to her feet. Her leg wobbled a bit, but it held. She looked at Mason; he'd been seeing some action himself, from the way his face was chewed up. There were cuts on his lip and over his eye, caked with dried blood, and a massive bruise covered much of the left side of his face. "Jesus," Bobbi tittered dreamily, "You look terrible."

"Yeah, well, we'll talk about that later." Mason turned back to Violet, who was looking at the three of them with new wariness in her eyes. "Who's this?"

"That's Violet." Bobbi cleared her throat, trying to force some focus. "She saved my life."

"What happened to Diana?"

Bobbi and Violet looked at one another. "I'm sorry," she said, though she couldn't help the flippant tone the endorphin rush put in her voice. "She tried to kill me. She was..." She fell silent then, and looked at Scalli. His expression hardened. She'd tell him more later on.

"Stop there." Mason shook his head. "God damned stupid girl. Yeah, I know all about it. You don't have anything to worry about where I'm concerned, in any case. Your boy took care of that."

Violet looked between the three of them again before drawing a wet, whistling breath. "I don't mean to be a problem," she said, "and I'm very grateful that you've saved us, but those boys have friends, and all that gunfire is going to be bringing them here sooner than later. If we're going to go see the Eye, we should do it before night falls."

"Right." It was Scalli who spoke now as he approached, holding the rifle by its grip as it dangled from one arm. He had his visor on, which made it hard to see his expression – he just looked like a badass one-eyed combat machine, some previous generation's idea of a hi-tech cyclops, and he radiated a cold precision that made Bobbi's skin crawl. She looked down...and gasped.

Scalli was wounded, or at least he appeared to be. His chest and stomach looked as if it had been shredded by gunfire, rents torn in his shirt and the dark flesh beneath, though there was no blood. Instead a milky blue substance had dried there, and where there should have been raw red meat there was something ribbed and black like hydraulic cable.

Bobbi gasped. "Jesus fuck," she breathed, "Scalli, what the hell...?"

"I'm all right," Scalli said, and he frowned. "It's a long story. Ask Mason later, he'll tell you all about it." He looked to Violet. "Where's our truck?"

"Smashed," Violet said with a shake of her head. "Your girl plowed it into a wall trying to get to you two. I think she thought you were in the shrine."

Mason made a soft, unhappy sound. "Shrine?"

Bobbi cut in. "I'll tell you when we're on our way," she said. She didn't think they needed to see the gallery of heads in the grocery basement else they may never get out of there.

"I've got another truck waiting," Violet said. She looked at Scalli and made a face. "You're gonna have to sit in the back. You're way too big to sit up front."

"I'll do just fine in the back," said Scalli, who had turned his cyclops-eye toward Bobbi. "I'll look out for her."

Considering what she'd just seen him do, Bobbi wasn't certain how comfortable she might be with that.

CHAPTER 15

They took the machine gun off the Highwayman, along with the medical supplies. Mason was a pretty damned good medical tech – Bobbi supposed you had to be if you were recon – and he worked over her leg with stims and stabilizers and whatever battlefield alchemy there was that let her walk without fucking things up too much in the long term. "You'll need to see a doctor," he told her. "Eventually. Got some nerve damage in there, nothing that shouldn't be repairable, but considering the situation you're lucky the damned thing works at all." She had a nasty cut on her head that he healed up with medicated quick-seal gel as well, and she spent a while picking gravel out of her cheek while Mason tended to her leg.

Bobbi stared at him as he applied the patches and injections, all done under Scalli's distant but watchful eye. Diana had been so certain that he would kill her. He could do it now, reach up and make it look like complications from an accident. But he didn't, not even when Violet had her back turned or was otherwise engaged – and when Violet left to get her truck she finally spoke up.

"Diana tried to kill me," Bobbi said.

"I said I know," Mason said as he wrapped a securing bandage around a small forest of dermal patches adhered to her thigh. He didn't look up.

"She said that you were going to kill Scalli, too."

Mason paused in mid-wrap. He didn't say anything for a moment. "I was going to," he said then, and went back to work. "She asked me to do it. She was always asking me to do things for her— she never asked me to kill anybody before, though. She saw the same thing that I did in Marcus, here."

Bobbi looked up at Scalli, who stood a bit away from them like an angry, well-armed djinn. He was guarding the breach. He carried the machine gun now, rigging up a shoulder strap out of one of the electric truck's seatbelts. He hadn't taken off the visor since he had returned with Mason. He knew that though he wasn't near them, he was watching through its eye. "What about him?"

"That he's corporate, or at least used to be. She told me he was a Genefex infiltrator, that she'd found his ID when they were screwing around last night." Bobbi heard an unmistakable spur of anger in his voice, and she felt bad for him. Diana really had gotten her hooks in him good, and she had turned out to be the very beast that she had convinced him Scalli was. "So I waited until we went into the grocery, and then I shot him. Twice."

Bobbi looked up at Scalli again; he hadn't attempted to hide the blast in his gut, nor had he explained anything yet. After all, he'd told her to ask Mason. "Well he's not dead," she said. "And you're not a bad shot."

"Best shot," said Mason, "next to your friend there." He finished wrapping up her leg and got to his feet. "So you can imagine how surprised I was when he dodged the first hit— that's what took out his suppressor— and then turned around and tried to put the butt of his rifle through my skull."

Bobbi let out a whistle. "I can imagine," she said. "But...what is he? That's no muscle job."

Mason nodded. "You're right. Close, though."

"Huh?" She put her leg into her jumpsuit and zipped it up, standing now. Her leg felt detached again, but it felt solid. She was already missing the blissful warmth that the endorphin patch had spread through her.

"It's armor," he said, nodding toward Scalli's towering form. "It's a muscle suit. He's a big boy, Marcus, but that's not muscular augmentation. It's a suit of covert full-coverage body armor, electropolymer myomer bundles in armored sheathing. Modeled after his own skin and everything. Augments his strength, can take incredible punishment. That's expensive tech, to say the least."

Bobbi stared at Scalli. She could definitely see it now, especially with Diana talking about how his dick came out through a sheath. Not that she really wanted to think about that. "I didn't know," she said softly. She wasn't really sure what to think of now, but she knew what she was going to say the next time she got him alone. "What happened after?"

"After what?" He was putting away the leftover medical supplies in its red field case, his tone casual.

She made a face. "After you tried to kill him and he tried to cave your face in." Jesus, why were the military types so fucking slow to give her anything? Scalli, now Mason. Tom wasn't like that. This was why she didn't like to deal with people often. They wanted to be quiet. Not puzzles, not like she liked, just a pain in her ass.

"Oh." He paused a moment. "Well, he took me up on the roof, set me straight. About a lot of things."

"A lot of things," she repeated. "Like what?"

"Like why you're here? Why really." Mason wrinkled his nose and looked as if he might have swallowed something nasty just then. "He told me everything, all about those people. The Yathi." He shook his head. "Fucking aliens, man, that's just not funny. I didn't know what to think."

Bobbi frowned a little. She didn't like Scalli spreading the word without talking to her, not one goddamned bit. But on the other hand, she had to be fair; she wasn't exactly sitting around waiting for Freida to prove herself when she got told the whole litany. Allies were in short supply, and they didn't deserve getting dragged along on this thing if it was going to get ugly. She probably should've already told them before. "All right," she said after a moment. "Well. What do you think now that you've had some time to chew on it?"

"I think it explains a lot of things I saw in the Eurowar," he said. "People acting certain ways, that kind of thing. Nothing obviously alien or anything, but let's say it wasn't the first time that I saw those ghouls before, coming to this city. Saw them in Bonn, saw them in Vienna. Thought they were cyborgs, you know, company elites. They had armor on then." Mason shook his head. "It'd take too long to explain right now. Let's just say that I've seen shit in the field makes this all fit right into place. Makes me want to help you."

Bobbi watched his face for anything she could take as a sign of impending bullshit, but she found nothing. She wasn't sure if that made her more secure or just made her feel badly for Mason. His eyes were haunted when he talked to her, dim and flat. Must have been terrible, whatever it was he'd seen. Well, there was plenty of room for terrible on the January Express. "All right," she said, "I trust Scalli, and you've been honest with me. Maybe you can tell me in the future what went down, but right now I'm gonna take you at your word. You're gonna help us, good. We need the help."

"I know," he said with a nod. "And I'm not mad at you about Diana. She dug that hole herself, I know. Wish she hadn't gotten eaten by those fuckers, but that's not your fault. We're on even ground here."

She watched his face a moment longer and then nodded. "All right," she said, then a thought struck her. "Wait. If you were up on the roof, why didn't you see me coming? Why didn't you hear the wreck and come down to see what the hell was going on?"

"Because we weren't listening," he said.

Bobbi screwed up her nose a little at that. "Seems like you'd have to be pretty busy to miss that," she said. "Loud enough to knock me out."

Mason shrugged. "We were talking over chip," he said. "Deep link."

She looked at him. Deep link, like they had implants. "You mean like, you were plugged into each other directly?"

He nodded and turned his head a bit; there was the plug, a good one, hidden under a flap of false skin. "He's got one too," he said, "It's how I knew he was military, or something close to it. We got the same model. He was showing me everything via recorded feed, what you showed him. He's got a photographic memory because of it, see? Same as me. Used to store mission data with it, it's the same thing."

Bobbi wasn't sure what to think about that, much less respond. She did her best, though. "That's not what I was expecting to hear," she said. "So he was busy transmitting, you were getting it, and you didn't have any external senses."

"Kind of hard to focus on the outside world with that shit that he was sending me. It was pretty terrible. That scene at the hospital, and then at the data place..." He shook his head. "Reminds me of the Eurowar. You got some stones, honey, dealing with that kind of thing, and then Diana trying to off you, and still dealing okay."

She shrugged. "You gotta, I guess," she said. "Else you let it eat you. Guess we know what happens when you let it eat you enough; you stop believing in something."

"Yeah." Mason nodded, his expression haunted like before. "What do you believe in, Bobbi?"

Bobbi looked up into his face, grave like Scalli's, and she shrugged again. "I believe there's got to be a better day," she said, "or at least one we can choose ourselves. If we're gonna burn the world down, that's something we need to choose for ourselves. Not with these things riding around in our heads. I gotta try and make that happen."

"Yeah," Mason repeated. He laid a hand on her shoulder and squeezed a little. "Me too. We'll make it happen. Even if it kills us."

Violet returned a little while after with her 'truck', which was much removed from the modern day as the Old City itself. It was a positively ancient thing, a gasoline-burning job from the dawn of time, or maybe the 1990s, that had been converted in the 'Twenties to run on ethanol. It positively amazed Bobbi that something so ancient could still run—she'd never even seen a vehicle from the Twentieth, at least not up close. She couldn't imagine how the hell Violet had gotten the damned thing to run. At one point it had been a small delivery truck, but now it had been covered under layers of black spray paint and covered with more stylized red eyes. These, Bobbi was relieved to see, were courtesy of Krylon and not some sacrificial victim. "It's to let them all see who I'm representing," Violet told them as they found it sitting in a half-collapsed garage not far from the grocery. "So there isn't any mistake."

Bobbi and Scalli sat in the back, with Mason sitting up front with Violet, who was driving. They could talk through a sliding hatch that was cut in the wall of the cab. Bobbi was first, telling them what had happened with Diana, and then all the rest with Violet and her shrine. The baton then got handed over to Violet, who because of her connection to Redeye was obviously the star attraction.

"So we're going to see the Eye," called Bobbi through the hatch as the truck trundled along, trying to be heard over its engine. "What can you tell us about her? I mean, short of what we've been able to piece together, anyway."

Violet smiled as she drove the truck through the crumbling streets; mostly silent since they had left the grocery shrine, it was in warm, if ghoulish, tones that she replied. "The Eye is our salvation," she began, "every one of us, whether we deserve it or not. She's, ah, well we worship her, but we don't look at her as a god – I mean she's not one in the blood-and-thunder sort of way."

"Not everyone shares your opinion of that," said Mason, "if what Bobbi said about your little Shrine is any indication."

Violet had the grace to look a little guilty. "We're not exactly all there in the head out here," she said, and shrugged. "I mean, you see how we live out here, for one. And then, there's...the Others."

They were all quiet for a moment as that hung in the air. No matter how often it got brought up, or how much they saw, the reality of what the Yathi were still stirred up dark currents inside the heart. Mason broke the silence by saying, "That's what I don't understand. What has she got against them, outside of being...well, human? I mean from what's out there, everyone associated with this woman is crazy."

"You don't need to be sane to know what is right." Violet shook her head as she drove on, looking grim. "But the truth of the matter is that we're all failed transfers, so to speak. The Others tried to take us, but it just didn't work. That leaves a certain desire for revenge in one's heart, and the Eye provides us with the opportunity to sate it."

Bobbi sat up and blinked at these words. "You mean to tell me," she said, "that you were all...well, possessed at one point or another?"

"You'll find that a major cause of madness in this world anymore is sharing a skull with an alien mind," said Violet with a nod. "The mind of the Other fades away, or gets subsumed...but the human mind that returns never returns entirely intact."

Bobbi frowned faintly. "But what if the mind of the...Other...comes back? Is that possible?"

Violet shook her head. "They say that a lack of belief in anything greater than yourself is what lets the Other in – I can't tell you if that's the truth. What I can tell you, however, is that once you manage to shake the Other out, the only belief you have after that is that you'll never let it in again, even if you have to cook your own brain to make it happen. Drugs, self-torture, that sort of thing. It's not always necessary, though." She gestured to the hole in her face with one hand and laughed wetly. "Sometimes we cut the nose off to spite the face, so to speak."

Mason made a face. "Jesus."

"Not everybody goes off the deep end entirely, of course. Some of us are..." Violet trailed off, searching for the right word. "Reasonably well-adjusted? At least we aren't all complete psychotics."

"Just occasional cannibalism and idol worship," Bobbi said with a faint smirk.

"Well." Violet smirked; her sharp teeth gave her a predatory cast – this close Bobbi felt even more uncomfortable than before. "Maybe not well-adjusted. At least my crazy only comes out in certain ways, though. Not like Heron and his people, but then again they strayed from the path a long time ago. They used to be like us."

"You mean they started eating human flesh, instead of keeping their cannibalistic tendencies toward the Others." Bobbi shook her head. "What do you get out of eating them, anyway?"

"Well we don't usually do it," said Violet. "But for me, as the tender of the Shrine...let's just call it revenge on my part. It's not like they're human anymore, after all. It's more like eating slaughtered cattle." She licked her lips with a ragged tongue. "Besides, I like the taste. Better than beef, that's for certain."

Mason shook his head. "Christ," he muttered to himself. "How would you know what beef tastes like, anyway?"

"My folks are wealthy," Violet said. "We used to eat real meat pretty regular. Not that I'd bother them now, of course. They think I'm dead. Wouldn't recognize me anyway."

Bobbi wrinkled her nose. "I'm sorry," she said. "All right, well, maybe you can answer something for me. You used to have this thing inside of you, right? The guy sending me, he said he'd gone through the same thing, just took a different way of kicking it out. Do you have memories about this sort of thing, something like that?"

"Kind of," Violet said. She stared ahead, got quiet.

Bobbi wondered if she'd crossed a line somehow. "Hey," she said, "you all right?"

"Yeah." Violet frowned a little, which made her look even more like a ghoul than before. "Look, it's hard, talking about this to...normal people. Even if you're bringing something this important to the Eye. I can't answer everything, either. I don't know everything about this situation; honestly, I don't really remember much about that time. Nobody really does that I know of, except on an instinctual level. It's...a feeling."

"Probably a defense mechanism." This came from Scalli, whose deep voice filled up the whole truck. "Nobody wants to remember trauma. The things that these people do, nobody wants to remember that."

"Yeah." Mason's voice carried its own emptiness now. "Yeah, I can understand that. Okay, so we'll stop grilling you, Vi. Redeye can tell us the rest when we get there. You sure she'll talk to us when we do?"

Violet bobbed her head. "Thanks," she said. "And yeah, I think she will. I mean, don't get me wrong, she's crazier than the rest of us in many ways, but at the same time she's the sanest. It's her particular combination of the two that makes her so great."

The conversation faded after that, and Bobbi found herself just sitting in the back opposite Scalli who loomed over her. He had his visor up, finally, though his dark eyes were far away. He was grimmer than she'd ever seen him, though she figured she knew the reason why. None of this was easy for anyone, and though she was angry that she didn't know nearly as much about him as she thought she had. She just couldn't get mad enough to grill him over it.

Eventually, though, it was Scalli who spoke. "I used to work for Alliance Resources when I was younger," he said, his voice just loud enough to be heard over the truck's engine. "Company militia."

Bobbi looked at him for a moment. Alliance was one of the largest mining and drilling concerns going in the last forty years, back during the end of the American Crusade when half the viable oil fields in the Middle East had gotten nuked into glass; it was Alliance that bought up half the failing oil companies, Alliance who established seafloor mining and hydrogen fuel as the mainstay of the world's commuter energy concerns. They were also famous for having a very hardcore corporate security machine— paramilitary at the very least. Had Scalli been lying to her after all? "You told me that you hadn't been military," she replied, and though she tried she couldn't entirely keep it from sounding like an accusation.

"I don't consider it military," he said. "Military suggests you're doing something for a state, a cause; this was just corporate security, however you want to dress it up. I signed up with Alliance when I was a kid, mustered into the security forces, and was good at my job. Went all over the place— Ghana, Mozambique, Mongolia, China, Marianas Complex One. Most were pretty boring, but I saw a lot of action in some places. Corporate saboteurs, takeover forces, the kind of stuff they never talk about on the news."

"I see." Bobbi frowned at her lap. "All right, well, that explains the training. What about that suit of yours? You told me it was an augment job, not some kind of armor."

"No," he said, "you assumed that it was an augment job. I got this thing through my connections and a lot of cash. The way our conversation was, you came up to me, cocked your hips and said, 'I never saw a dude wear his ego on the outside before. Where'd you get that surgery'?" He grinned at her now, remembering her as she was then— this skinny kid with the bright red hair, the new curves that she was just getting used to.

She couldn't help but smile back, remembering that. "And you said, 'Girl, you got no cause to be bagging on me about surgery.' I think I might have wanted to punch you."

"But you didn't," he said with a chuckle. "And we've been friends since." It was nice, listening to him laugh. He never really did much, and lately least of all. "The truth is that I was good friends with a Japanese black arms dealer. Muscle suits like this are largely illegal tech out of Yakuza labs. When I left Alliance, I got a big payout for my service – and,

I'm a little embarrassed to say, to keep me quiet about a lot of things I saw while working in Africa. Since I wanted to get into private security, it was a huge coup for me."

"And because it looks like a muscle job, nobody questioned it?"

Scalli nodded. "That's basically it. The density is analogous to human muscle, and it's nonmetallic. You'd have to cut me open to see what it was."

"Or shoot you," she pointed out.

"Yes, but it's self-healing." Scalli shrugged, looking down at the wound in his "stomach." "This will be sealed back up in a few days."

Bobbi shook her head. "You're one hell of a surprise, buddy. I guess I'll have to start paying you more when all this is over with, now that I know what kind of talents you're bringing to the table."

He smiled again, but it didn't last for long. A few moments later his expression settled back into a frown and Scalli took a deep breath. "I told Mason about the whole thing."

Bobbi nodded a bit. "I know you did," she said. "He told me. And that's fine; I trust your judgment."

Scalli let out a deep breath. "I'm glad to hear that. I figured you'd be pissed with me."

"What I'm pissed about is that we got sidetracked and Diana tried to kill me," she said with a shake of her head. "Look, Scalli, we've got to talk about that."

"Well, sounds to me like you handled it just right." Scalli reached out with a wide hand, rested it on her shoulder like Mason had, only he gently stroked a circle there rather than squeeze her. "You okay?"

"Not a bit," Bobbi said. "I didn't want to kill anyone."

"You didn't have a choice."

"I know." Bobbi shook her head. "But it's not what you think, Scalli. It's..." She took a deep breath and stole a look at the open cab hatch, then leaned closer to speak so that only he could hear her. "Diana wasn't human, all right? She was one of them."

That raised his eyebrows. "Are you sure?"

"Yes, I'm sure!" She took a moment to keep her tone down, swallowing the volume into her gut. "She fucking told me, man! Was just saying how she was going to drill me in the face, and had gotten Mason to ace you, too. That's why I killed her, and that's why you and I need to be really fucking careful as to where we're going and who we're taking with us." Bobbi shook her head. "Fuck. Might as well just give me her pistol, if you've got it."

"I thought you didn't do the shooting thing," Scalli said. Making it sound like she'd declared she was going to start shooting up Shard right away, not sure if she was serious, a warning edge in his tone without making it a lecture.

"I said I didn't want to kill anyone," Bobbi said. "And I ended up doing that with a nerve crusher, Scalli. Fuck it, you might as well give me the real thing since the crusher's dead, so I can defend myself. Shit's way crazier out here than I thought it was going to be."

He looked at her for a long moment. "I don't know," he said.

"Come on, Scalli," she said, "I know how to use one. I'm not going to blow a hole through my own head." It was hard, the way he swung between older brother and wanna-be boyfriend. Bobbi held her hand out, waiting. Eventually he took her pistol out of his pocket and put it in her hand, the weapon large in her small palm and delicate fingers.

"There's two mags with it," he told her, and produced them. "Sixteen rounds, nine-millimeter caseless."

"I appreciate it," Bobbi said, and took the magazines in the other hand. She put them away in the belly pocket of jumpsuit. She looked at the pistol; bright and polished, death mate of mirrored steel. Strange weapon for a survivalist type like Diana to have carried. Bobbi read the letters printed along the side: "SIG-SAUER C107 Cal. 9mm." It was burst-capable, making it military. Most service guns had a burp mode now. "Pretty," she said, then checked the magazine to ensure it was full and made sure the safety was on before she slid it into the still-intact pouch on her right thigh. "Thanks, Scalli."

"Yeah," he said with a nod. "No problem. I just hope you don't have to use it."

"So I guess we're getting close to the end of this," Bobbi said just then. She looked at him sitting there, his expression having changed back to the same background frowning. Thinking about it too.

"Big fucking question mark," Scalli said. "I don't know, girl. It's still something not terribly anchored in reality, is it? All that shit happened in the city, we find out it's what, the Great Alien Satan, plugging itself into people and converting them. And then we're out here sending messages to the queen of the crazy ladies, only she's supposed to be able to perform an exorcism." He shook his head. "Should've stuck with private security. Even the kinkiest of those dudes were charming compared to all of this."

Bobbi smirked a little. "Yeah," she said, "you're right, it's completely fucked." She'd had a long two years; she didn't even try to make out like it sounded sane or even closely connected to reality. What was the point? She didn't have a frame of reference to things that sat in your brain and drove you around because you didn't have hope at some point in your life. "I don't know, Scalli. It's crazy. It's got to end, though, and I think that's really the only thing that's truly important here. We're the ones in this situation, though, so we have to do what we can with what we've got."

"Yeah," he said, and he looked at her. "My name's Marcus, you know."

"Your name's Scalli, too," she said, but leaned over and patted his knee. "I call you that because everyone else calls you by your first name. My way of showing affection."

"Ah." He smiled a bit again. "Well, I'm glad there's that at least. You ready to face the queen of the nutjobs?"

"Not even a little." Bobbi shrugged. "Again, no choice. As long as we get out of this alive, intact and sane I'll be happy."

"I hear you there, girl," said Scalli, and he shook his head.

CHAPTER 16

The coming night threw its violet stain across the sky, made all the more dark and muted through the gauzy clouds. They proceeded across an overpass overlooking an industrial park on the far southwestern side of Renton, out near the border where the interstate began and stretched out into the wet green of the forests.

Bobbi looked at the park that crumbled away nearby. Swallowed by a tall fence, the tangles of long-abandoned chemical tanks and pipes rotted slowly, chewed by the thoughtful teeth of entropy as the years passed on. The rusting skeletons of sheds and warehouses stood in silent rows. Plumes of thin smoke rose from somewhere among them, and visible amid the corroded structures were the glowing pinpoints of campfires.

"Jesus," muttered Bobbi as she looked out through the shutter. "We're really out in the boonies now."

"I don't see why they stay in the city," said Mason. "I mean why not spread out into the countryside?"

"What about Cagliostro?" Scalli was shifting in the back, getting his web gear arranged. "Does the old beast have anything to say about it?"

Bobbi snorted. She had tried to connect to the network again while they were traveling over, while she could still run off a car's electrical system and not worry about draining her terminal's battery. "He's not answering," she said. "Well, not in the flesh. Has an auto-answer routine running saying that he'll be here when the time is right."

"Christ," Mason said, and shook his head in disbelief. "And some folks wonder why people gave up on God. Even the digital ones don't answer when you call to them."

Violet gave Mason a sharp look, but she didn't answer. Instead she parked the truck in the middle of the road and killed the engine. "We're here," she said. "Come on."

Bobbi and Mason looked at each other. "We're on top of an overpass," Mason said.

"Yes." Violet opened her door and got out.

Mason gave Bobbi a last look and shrugged before getting out also. "Well," Bobbi said to Scalli, shaking her head. "Here goes nothing."

"Here goes everything, you mean," said Scalli. He reached up for his visor, but Bobbi put her hand on his.

"Don't. They'll probably want to look into your eyes."

He blinked. "Why?"

"To see if you've got Yathi in you. They can tell, remember?"

Scalli stared at her a moment. "Yeah," he said, and got up to undo the bar across the back doors.

The truck's doors swung open, and the two of them stepped out onto the stained blacktop of the overpass. The air smelled wrong from the start. There was a certain smell, like a chemical fire, something Bobbi struggled to recognize.

"We've come on a good night," said Violet. Her expression had changed into one of fervent reverence once again, like a goblin at a tent revival. "They've got themselves some of the Others."

"Drones?" Bobbi blinked at her.

"Maybe," Violet said, then she grinned. Mason frowned at the sight of her horrible teeth. "You can smell them burning them down in the pits. C'mon, let's go down. She'll be in a good mood tonight."

Mason frowned a bit more. He could do grim like Scalli, hands down. "Who'll be in a good mood?"

"The Eye, of course. Let's go."

Violet led the three of them down the overpass some twenty feet before coming to a gap which had been cut in the rusting safety rail. A chain ladder had been anchored with bolts and thrown over the edge. "It's this way," she told them, "Come on." She turned and began to clamber down the ladder without ceremony, leaving the lot of them to look at each other. Finally Bobbi shrugged.

"Well," she said, "there's no point in fucking around with it. C'mon, let's go meet Lady Crazyface, you guys."

"You sure about this?" Mason frowned at the ladder, which chimed as the slip of a feral made her way down.

Bobbi had already crouched down at the edge. "Don't worry, Harry," she said in a deadpan tone, "I promise I'll protect you." She slipped over the edge and started to make her way down.

Mason stared at Scalli. "I don't know how the hell you do it, man," he said.

Scalli shrugged. "I guess I'm just a glutton for punishment. C'mon, let's go save humanity." His rock of a body made the ladder groan as he too joined the descending party.

"Fuck," Mason muttered to himself before making toward the edge. "I'm going to get myself fucking killed."

Violet was waiting for them as they made their way down to the street below. "We have to walk from here," she explained. "Even someone tending a shrine will get shot down if we came in a truck. They saw me, though. Otherwise we'd have eaten a rocket by the time we parked."

"Wonderful," Mason muttered as they walked toward the ruined park. "Nuked off the road by a feral with a surplus RPG," he muttered. "That's a way to go."

"Watch it, Mason," Bobbi said shrewishly, looking over her shoulder at him. "You're scaring the women."

Mason opened his mouth to speak, but closed it without a word. Scalli snickered.

The four of them walked toward the park in silence after that, while the smoke coiled skyward and the peculiar burnt-metal smell of what Violet had told them were Yathi corpses. Questions turned over and over in Bobbi's mind as they went. What was going on in there? Would they show up just to find a band of slavering crazies wanting to add them to the roast? She didn't relish the idea of having herself gutted and strung up for the pleasure of the hooting fuckwits. Then again, knowing the way the world went it would be the craziest that would treat them like family. She really hoped so; there was no way they were shooting their way out of a place like this, not after they got the attention of Redeye and her little army. There wasn't enough ammunition in the world.

They passed the border fence, the open gates, and entered the park. The bones of industry loomed around them, glowering like the silhouettes of ancient monsters long since left the world. Somewhere in the dark, eyes were watching them; Bobbi could feel them, and from the guarded expressions that Mason and Scalli wore. In any other situation they would have their guns out and ready for violence, but now they all walked carefully behind Violet who was quite at her ease. These were her people, after all. Again Bobbi's thoughts went back to the possibility of their being led to the slaughter by the maimed woman. The pistol in her belly pocket felt heavier and heavier the closer they got to the light that they had seen from the overpass – it was there that Violet was leading them.

They walked along endless weaveworks of pipe, between warehouses and among the great silent giants of containment tanks. Their feet crushed gravel and withered grass. All the while their backs were watched by silent eyes from shadowed corners, or from the high perches of maintenance catwalks. All the while the smoke grew nearer, the acrid smell ever stronger in their noses. It was a difficult road to walk, but they had no choice now. They could only discover what was at the end of it now.

"We're almost there," Violet said as they neared what Bobbi thought was the center of the industrial park. They stood before a small industrial building made of beams and sheet steel, the side of which had been cut away by a madman with a torch – or blasted away, perhaps. One really couldn't tell. Inside, among the corpses of dead machinery, an elevator shaft lead down into parts unknown. The glow that had persisted from afar was rather bright now, flooding up from the wire walls of the shaft and from places elsewhere. The chemical smell here was thick, so much so that the lungs rebelled to breathe the same air which it befouled.

"Fucking shit," said Mason, rubbing at his throat. "If it gets any worse I'm afraid we'll puke our lungs up before we even get in, much less get killed by Redeye."

Violet gave Mason another dirty look. "It isn't toxic," she said, "just unpleasant. It's their blood; the white stuff burns away and leaves the smell behind. You want bad, wait until some of these implants they have go up. I hear one time they got a combat model and tossed it into a furnace when they were camping in a factory. Took out a whole floor."

"Wonderful." Mason shook his head, but he didn't say anything else.

Bobbi looked quietly between the three of them and stepped up past Mason to stand shoulder to shoulder with Violet. "All right," she said, "so, I get the feeling that we're here. Is there anything we need to know, Violet?"

"Just that you need to keep quiet until you're spoken to," said Violet, who looked at Mason again. "That means everybody. You don't want to irritate anyone once we're down there."

Scalli made a sound of discontent. "Down where?" He didn't seem to like the sound of going down anywhere. Bobbi could definitely sympathize.

"Down underground," said Violet. "There's an incinerator down there, along with the maintenance levels. That's where we're going. Don't worry, the fumes get sucked up through the ducts, so unless you're going to go stick your head in one of them, you'll be okay."

Behind them, Mason and Scalli shared looks. It was a complete tactical nightmare, they both knew. "Well," said Scalli, "I didn't want to live forever anyway."

Bobbi snorted. "It's just as well," she said. "It'd be boring as fuck to see the fashions repeated over and over. Can't re-invent the computer over and over again, either."

"Amen to that." Scalli squared his mighty shoulders and stepped up next to Bobbi; Mason came up after a doubtful moment.

Violet looked them over, pursing her lips in consideration of them all, and then she nodded to herself. "All right, then," she said, brushing a stringy lock of hair from her eyes. "Let's go see the boss."

The elevator still had power, through some agency that Bobbi had missed on the way down. There must have been industrial batteries, she thought, maybe some big industrial hydrogen cell amongst the abandoned machinery in the work shed. It was a tight fit, going down into the glowing depths, Scalli and Mason taking up most of the space in the big elevator. She was glad that she was small, and that Violet was so goddamned thin. Otherwise they would've had to take two trips and who knows what that might have meant for them. Down the shaft they went, the elevator grumbling, and Bobbi feeling her heart thundering beneath the sound of the old gears grinding away. They were all nervous, even Violet, though she still wore a smile. Going to see her kind of Jesus, her red-eyed Madonna. Fuck's sake.

They traveled slowly, and descended through cramped underlevels sheathed in concrete and filled with shadows. As they cleared a third such stratum, the maintenance levels gave way to a smooth concrete shaft. As they drew closer to the bottom, a strange blue-white radiance flickered up from below; it was a light that Bobbi felt was familiar to her, yet she couldn't quite pin it down. The smell began to thin as the glow from beneath grew brighter.

"That's...disconcerting," Scalli rumbled as the light licked up the walls of the shaft.

"Hush," Violet hissed. "We're here."

The elevator cleared the shaft and descended through a wire cage into what was apparently an industrial incinerator room. The vaulted concrete barn was the size of a small warehouse, the near end of which the elevator shaft descended. Beyond them, the cylindrical monolith of the incinerator stretched toward the ceiling. Ductwork rose from the upper surface of the great machine and reached upward like the branches of a great steel tree, ostensibly connecting it to the stacks visible far above.

The floor was strewn with great piles of trash and debris, arranged in a wide ring around the incinerator proper— metal glinted in the light of dim fires that burned in makeshift cauldrons set up amid them, and the light of the fires supported the fluorescent lamps bolted to the outside of the incinerator, banishing the shadows in a wide circle around the central core. Here, Bobbi saw, the floor was filled with wild figures, figures Bobbi knew to be ferals. In the dim light she saw many of them, standing amongst the piles, perched atop them or along their sides, clustering around the cauldrons. Still others stood near the far side of the incinerator; as the elevator ground to a halt at the bottom and the door rumbled open, Bobbi caught glimpses of them shuffling about what looked like a large skip.

"Just stick close to me," Violet was saying as she stepped out, drawing in a deep breath. "Jesus Christ, you boys are huge."

"And the tiny will inherit the Earth," snorted Scalli.

Bobbi tried to smile. "Don't you mean the meek?"

"There ain't nothing meek about you two," he said. "Come on, let's go." Despite Scalli's attempt to sound calm, even jovial, Bobbi heard the thin note of uncertainty there. She'd known him far too long for that to slip by. Not that she blamed him. Her own insides were twisting now, not sure what to expect or if she should try and expect anything but the worst.

Violet led them through the crowd, which to Bobbi was like an uncomfortable replay of the scene that she had just left. Perhaps she had thought differently about Redeye's people, but they were all ferals of the most stereotypical appearance: shambling madmen covered in scars and open sores, glass-eyed statues standing stock still as if waiting for some unknowable signal to trigger their inner beasts. Nobody looked at them. They passed a woman who was scratching thin lines into her cheeks, working red, bloody furrows into her face as she waited for the time to pass. Even for the mad, something was very, very spooky. The moment hung in the air, invisible and waiting, and everyone was waiting for it to unwind.

"This doesn't look like a good night to me," Mason said. "We've walked in on something."

Scalli agreed. "These people seem like they're waiting for a big fucking shoe to drop," he said. "Vi?"

"Don't ask me," Violet said quietly. "I just look after the heads." But even as she said that, Bobbi could see in her face that something was wrong. She'd expected a celebration. This was...almost like a funeral. Shit, were they coming in only to find that Redeye had been killed? Had the Queen of the Crazy Boogeymen eaten a bullet before she could discharge whatever duty Cagliostro had ready for her? What the fuck were they going to do then?

Bobbi was about to say something to this effect, but Violet pointed forward. "I see her," she hissed, pointing in the direction of the skip. "Come on."

They crossed the cold field of the mad toward the incinerator. There, standing in the cold glare of the fluorescent lamps above them, a group of ferals were shoveling something out of the skip into the loading receptacle of the incinerator. Bobbi squinted in the dim light; lines resolved themselves as they drew near, white limbs picked out in the twin glare of the lamps and the flickering fires. She frowned. It was nothing she had not seen before, but the pale Yathi corpses they were loading into the furnace gave her pause.

"I see that they've been busy," Bobbi said in dim tones. Her skin was cold despite the heat that radiated from the incinerator and the flames around them. Somewhere in the back of her head, a treacherous little voice told her to get out of there before they put her in there, too. She could see it, and closed her eyes a moment to flush the image out of her head. It only worked to a point.

"Very," said Violet, but she only glanced at the skip as they proceeded by it. Bobbi saw that the thing was half full of naked, white, blonde corpses, all of them suffering grievous wounds. Most of them that she could see were shrunken ghouls. Some of them were not. "She's right over here."

They looked where Violet pointed. Perhaps they had expected to see some terrible figure of the wastelands, dressed as a goddess of entropy. What they got was what Bobbi had glimpsed so very briefly on the news: the thin girl in her early twenties, swallowed in dirty military fatigues and a men's bomber jacket twice her size. Her dark hair hung in her eyes, but through the veil and from the shadowed upper half of her plain, pointed face, Redeye's namesake burned like an ember. There she was, this waif of a girl, and yet looking at her now Bobbi felt the same sensation that she'd experienced upon seeing her for the first time on the news feed. It was a sensation that lurked in the dark corners of her guts, encoded in her body's wiring. An apex predator. She radiated an air of command and menace, which even without the skip full of bodies beside her would have made her monstrous.

For all her slim stature and her youth, this slip of a girl was an avatar of death.

"Christ," Bobbi heard Mason whisper.

"Not gonna help us here," Scalli muttered in reply.

Redeye looked toward them as they approached, not moving save to turn her head to face them, her neat, spare body fixed as if made of ivory. Though her hair was dark, her skin was as milky pale as the corpses that her minions shoveled into the waiting furnace. Moments passed in which Bobbi, Scalli and Mason said nothing, electing to stand as fixed as she did. Only Violet reacted, bowing slightly at the waist and clearing her throat so that a slight puff of air whistled from the hole in her face.

"I greet the Eye," the thin girl said in a low and reverent tone, and genuflected before her idol. The look of peace that had settled over Violet's face was striking.

"On your feet, Violet." Redeye's voice was deep and husky, like a lounge singer from the Twentieth; it was a big voice, much bigger than her small body should hold. To Bobbi's surprise, she almost looked pained at Violet's display. "You know you don't have to do that."

"Of course. Sure." Violet stood, though she did not look up. "I've brought you some visitors. People from the city."

Redeye looked past Violet to the three of them. That eye burned from behind the veil of lank hair; she brushed it aside as she stepped forward, turning it upon each of them in turn. Bobbi had the distinct feeling of a mouse being eyed by a cat. "So I see. And do they have names?"

"Bobbi January," Bobbi said instantly. "This is Marcus Scalli, and this is Harry Mason." Gesturing to each of the men in turn.

A soft "ahh" of comprehension escaped Redeye's lips. She took a few more steps forward, and now Bobbi could see a hint of the scars ringing her glowing eye. "I know who you are. You're the one who destroyed Tissue Processor Twenty-Two. That was a neat job, actually, blowing up the incinerators. They were dealing with the damage for months." She shook her head. "Shame you didn't do anything else, or at least nothing I've heard of."

Bobbi cleared her throat. She wasn't expecting the Queen of the Crazy People to recognize her name, much less what she and Tom had done at Orleans— or, at least, what she had done. Nor did she think that the Queen would dress her down for not doing more. "I...tried to do other things," Bobbi said, feeling strangely hurt. "But we didn't know what they were, then. In fact, it's only been the past few weeks that I knew the truth about them."

"You mean that they're alien creatures who possess human minds and use their bodies as meat puppets, for lack of a better term? That they're colonizing this planet, and aim to replace us all as the ruling species on the planet before their own gets burnt up?"

Bobbi looked back at Mason and Scalli, not sure what the hell to think. "Yeah," she said as he looked back at the woman. "That's basically it."

Redeye stared at Bobbi for a moment. Then, much to Bobbi's surprise, the frown that lined the woman's lips turns upward, split into a smile; she had small white teeth, very clean, strange for someone living rough. She stepped up to Bobbi and offered her a small white hand. "Well, then," she said with a wink of that terrible red eye. "You're welcome here."

With the possibility of immediate conflict put aside, Bobbi reached for the hand offered her— but slowly, as she was still quite stunned by the development. "Uh, thank you," she said, staring at the thin hand that held hers. She'd expected it to be like ice, her imagination playing tricks on her—but instead it was burning hot to the touch, like the girl had a full-body fever.

Redeye looked at her for a long moment, keeping her hand on Bobbi's. "You are afraid of me," she said. "Do not be."

"Says the lady standing next to a skip full of bodies." Mason stepped up next to Bobbi, giving Redeye a look. "I've seen you in action before," he said. "I was a vet in Europe, and even I'm afraid of you. You play very nasty, miss."

"Mmm." Redeye looked at Mason and let her hand drop from Bobbi's, so that she could fold her arms over her chest. Bobbi saw scars across her forearms where the sleeves of her fatigues had been rolled up to the elbow, though they looked more like bumps on glazed porcelain than keloid. Strange. Redeye fixed her gaze on Mason's face. "You are from Tenleytown?"

Mason nodded. "Yeah," he said. "We had a lot of problems with Genefex and its monsters until you showed up. I ran the scouts for the town militia. We've seen what you and your people can do. It's very..."

"Savage," Redeye said with a grin. How were her teeth so white? "It must be. They do not appreciate anything but savagery. They are like anyone else— you must scare them sufficiently to keep their hand at bay."

"Like burning their bodies," Bobbi ventured.

"More like cutting out their eyes," Mason said. "Before that."

Now Scalli decided to talk. "That's baiting the bear a bit hard, don't you think? I know your people are supposed to be hard, but they're well-funded and well-organized. I don't see how pissing in the Empress's cornflakes on a routine basis is much of a strategic move."

"It is if you want her to come out herself." Redeye gave them a little shrug, some attitude coming through that was closer to her age than the warrior-princess thing she'd had going on until then. "If we keep destroying their property, they will emerge. That is how it goes."

Though she didn't say it herself, Bobbi knew there was something more going on there. She read it in the girl's face. Having a prosthetic eye didn't keep you from betraying emotion, after all. "You've given up," she said suddenly, unsure of where the words came from. "You're trying to bait them into some kind of a final battle."

Silence. Everyone around them stopped and looked at Bobbi— the wailers, the ferals with their shovels, Redeye herself. The burning red prosthetic seemed to want to burn her with its gaze, like an invisible ray cooking her from the inside. "You are a good judge of people, I see," the feral queen said, tilting her head a little as if reconsidering her previous opinion of the three. "Yes. We hit a facility tonight that was supposed to have something I was looking for. We won, but a great many of us died when the failsafes kicked in, locked down the complex and burnt everything inside. There are not enough of us left to continue the fight. They will come for us tonight, and if I have made the Mother of Systems angry enough, they will use worse than xsiarhotl." There was that word again, the word that Cagliostro had used. The corpse-machines.

Bobbi looked at her. It was so strange, because what she wanted to do in that moment was to give her a hug, this stone-cold killer of men and worse, and tell her it was okay. Like she was her slightly younger sister. "Look," she said instead. "Don't worry about that. I want you to talk to a friend of mine. He's got a message for you, should make you feel a lot better very soon."

"Oh?" Redeye gave her a wary look.

"Yeah. I hope you know how to use the network."

Redeye smiled thinly at her. "That will not be a problem. Come with me."

They set up Bobbi's terminal in the back of the incinerator room, behind the elevator shaft and away from the fires and the corpses. It turned out that they'd had a few people who were datanauts at some point, and had run a hard line down from the satellite dish of one of the old factories down the shaft and into the chamber. Bobbi prepped the terminal, checking to see that its battery was still good, and put on the firewall collar that she'd worn last when she had first heard from Freida. She offered Redeye a bridge cable, but she had only smiled and waved Bobbi off.

Bobbi had already known that Redeye was not in any way a normal girl, but when she sat down next to Bobbi and settled into a position of meditation she was not quite prepared for what came next.

"Don't you need a cable?" Bobbi had asked her.

"Not at all," Redeye had said. "I have a wireless network communication module in my brain. A gift from Genefex."

Bobbi's skin prickled at that, but it was more out of amazement than anything else. They hadn't developed a means of facilitating mind-machine wireless communication yet, or at least not that she was aware of. The fact that Redeye was not only capable of it, but had already connected with her terminal and was prepared to ride along without any software integration of Bobbi's own, threw her off even more. She had plenty of questions , but business had to be attended to first.

Sitting with her back to the tableau of madness inside the room, Bobbi plugged herself into the terminal, turned it on, and counted backwards until she found herself slipping into the blessed depths of Awakening. It had felt like a thousand years had passed since she'd done it last, save for the quick pass through Freida's slow-box, and the intellectual detachment that came from it was soothing after all the raw, visceral experiences the Old City had offered her. Untethered, her mind raced across the digital complexes of the network, followed by the guarded presence of Redeye herself, until they pierced the wall of the slow-box and arrived in the land of molasses once more.

<Relax,> she told Redeye when they arrived and Bobbi felt the other woman begin to surround herself with digital defenses— how she was doing that without a terminal was another matter altogether. <It's just old hardware, not a trap.>

<Very well. Where is this friend of yours?>

<Hold on, I have to let him know that we're here.> Bobbi pulled up a mail process and shot a note off to Cagliostro, and then they began to wait. In the distorted continuum of the slow-box the minutes seemed to stretch on into eternity as they waited for the great old beast to arrive; Bobbi used the time to look at her own situation, and how everyone might be able to come out of this alive. She'd just gotten to the part where they had managed to avoid being roasted by cannibals when the great weight of Cagliostro's consciousness emerged from the depths of the system, looming at them like a woken beast.

<HELLO, YOU WHO CALL YOURSELF REDEYE. I AM THE ONE KNOWN AS CAGLIOSTRO.>

<I know who you are.> Redeye wasn't splitting hairs with the proverbial bear. <Your name was also [redacted] at the time, I believe. You forgot to mention that.>

The words – or whatever they were – that Redeye entered showed up as junk characters to Bobbi. Neither her terminal or her own headware had a means of translation. It meant nothing to her, but it certainly got a reaction out of Cagliostro. <THAT NAME NO LONGER APPLIES TO ME.>

<The name remains, even if you have tried to rid yourself of the thing inside your consciousness. They never leave. I can't imagine what you expected would happen when you attempted to split yourself.>

<MY INTENTIONS IN THAT MATTER ARE IRRELEVANT,> replied Cagliostro. <THE REALITY IS WHAT IT IS. MONITORING OF NEWS AND POLICE CHANNELS INDICATES THAT YOU HAVE ASSAULTED DRONE PROCESSOR 072. WHAT WAS THE RESULT OF THIS OPERATION?>

<Wait.> Bobbi spoke up now. <Why do you sound like King Jesus of the Robot People again?>

<Because talking like a human being is difficult to synthesize without a frame of reference,> Redeye replied. <He has had a history with you that involves a set of human interactions. His history with me does not.>

<YOU ARE CORRECT.> Bobbi could almost sense Cagliostro's irritation. <NEVERTHELESS. WHAT WAS THE RESULT OF YOUR ASSAULT?>

<I will tell you nothing yet, [redacted].>

<THAT NAME NO LONGER APPLIES TO ME!>

The way it was stated, the exclamation without anything but words floating in her mind, was nonetheless a thing of fury. Bobbi braced herself for some kind of assault, in case the angry digital god-thing smote Redeye for her impiety – but he did not. There was a pause, the program-mind chugging along silently, and then the brazen woman spoke again.

<I see. I was told that you had a message for me. I shall listen if you wish to give it to me, and then we will talk of my people.>

There was another pause, and Bobbi wondered what was next. Why had Redeye been pissing in his cereal? Why ride him at all? Cagliostro was a tricky bastard, sure, but it was like baiting a bear that wasn't chained to a post. But then she thought of how she'd gotten there in the first place, how Redeye had known that name. Whatever name it was. Bobbi thought of fantasy novels where you could harness a demon if you knew its True Name. Perhaps it was a similar sort of situation. She sat there, waiting for one or the other to talk, milliseconds passing by with the weight of hours behind them. Finally, Cagliostro spoke.

<I WILL GIVE YOU THE MESSAGE. MISS JANUARY, PLEASE LEAVE US.>

Bobbi's answer came right away. <I don't think that's a good idea.>

<No.> Redeye, now. <It's okay. He's convinced me.>

With a mixture of frustrated curiosity and a little bit of anger at being asked off her own deck, Bobbi said, <I'm trustworthy enough for carrying the message, but I can't listen in? Is that it?>

<NO.> Now it was Cagliostro's turn to pounce. <YOU MISUNDERSTAND.> And as he said it there was a ripple in the signal, a stop-start jerking that skipped mental "frames;" they called it the Harryhausen Effect after the old stop-motion animator of the previous century.

A sinking sensation crystallized in Bobbi's stomach. <Did you feel that?>

<INDEED. IT IS URGENT THAT I CONVEY MY INFORMATION. IT IS URGENT THAT YOU SEE TO WHAT NEEDS TO BE DONE.>

Redeye replied, <What needs to be done?>

<Wait.> Bobbi felt the skip again, this time even worse. Something was happening to the signal— or was it something on his end? <Something's wrong here. Can't you feel that?>

Cagliostro ignored her. <THE SITUATION MUST BE LOOKED AFTER,> he said.

The weight in Bobbi's gut grew heavier. <What situation? Guys, I really think— >

<THERE IS NO TIME!> Now Cagliostro's words were coming in spatters, fragments that Bobbi's software was rapidly piecing together on the fly. <MISS JANUARY, I WILL DISCONNECT YOU SO THAT A PURE TRANSFER CAN TAKE PLACE.>

<Wait! Tell me what the hell this is all about!> But the link stuttered and died, and Bobbi found herself thrown back into the land of stench and earthly horror. Scalli and Mason were standing over her, their expressions very grave.

"Well shit, fellas," Bobbi said with a fragile smile, "I guess we got trouble."

"Maybe not in there," said Mason. "But we got trouble here."

Bobbi looked between the two men, her brows going up as she pulled the cable from behind her ear. "What's going on?"

"It's the Yathi," Scalli said.

Bobbi was suddenly very aware of the silence that had fallen throughout the incinerator room. Looking between them, past the elevator shaft, Bobbi saw the every one of the crazed ferals— Violet included— had fallen back into a statue pose, back arched and weapons ready. They looked like an army of old-fashioned tin soldiers, ready to be put on the march. Violet moved among the standing figures, drawing an eye on the faces of her fellows, the same eyes that covered the walls of the shrine, the outside of her truck. Red, glaring paint searing brands upon their skin, preparing them for their deaths. It was a ritual that Violet was obviously very familiar with. Bobbi wondered how many of those heads in her shrine she might have taken herself.

High above them, the muted thunder of an explosion sent a trembling ripple through the incinerator vault. The lights flickered; a general rumble of anger rose from among the mad legions around them, a kind of dim growl. "Shit," Bobbi hissed, flinching. She swept her eyes over the darkened ceiling to see if the place was going to come down around them.

Mason looked as grim as Scalli, whose frown had managed to descend to new lows. Yeah, it was bad shit, all right. But she couldn't be prepared for what the career soldier said next. "They're already tangling with drone guns up top," he said. "They've got an impressive defensive cordon. If we'd shown up without Violet, we'd have been turned into hamburger the moment we stepped off the bridge. It's not going to hold for long, though."

Another explosion sounded above; this time the rumbling was much closer, and fragments of dust and mortar rained down on them from above. Bobbi's heart rocketed into her throat as she got to her feet. "How do you know it's them?"

"Vi showed us." Mason nodded to the far end of the room where the dim outline of a doorway could be seen. "They've got cameras set up all over the area, linked to computers in there; they're crazy, but they know their shit. They showed up in armored carriers about five minutes ago."

"They're painted up like Civil Protection," said Scalli. "You know, Special Tactics."

Bobbi nodded, frowning between them. She was fast becoming the most serious of them all. "Yeah, I know them pretty well." Last time she saw them she was hacking their helmets, keeping them all blind to Tom's presence while he made his way through the guts of Orleans. She remembered how the Yathi slew them to a man before Tom had even gotten to them and shivered. "Okay, then," Bobbi said, mastering the flash of terror. "So they're going to hit this place and make it look like, what, a police raid?"

"Liable." Scalli shook his head. "It's bad shit. We need to get your girl awake and find out what's going on, what's here— Violet's over there playing Sister Mary of Warfare over there with the troops, but I don't figure they're going to do much until the boss points them in a direction.

Mason nodded. "I'm going to trawl through their armory back there," he said, nodding toward the door in the back. "See if we can't rig up some explosives, you know. Violet said they had rockets, though now I wonder if she meant topside defenses."

"Maybe she did," Bobbi said. "But let's not wait around guessing."

Scalli grunted then. "We don't have a lot of time, in any case," he said. "They'll find the elevator shaft soon."

Bobbi stared at them. "How far out do they have these damned cameras, anyway?"

Mason laid a finger against his nose. "All over," he said. "I figure they knew we were coming long before we were even near here."

Bobbi closed her eyes and took a deep breath. Fantastic. "All right," she said. "I'll see if I can plug back in, find out if they're done talking."

"And if they're not?" Mason peered at Redeye, who still sad in her cross-legged position on the ground next to the terminal.

Bobbi shrugged. "We fight, I guess," she said with bravado she only halfway felt. "Until she does. Either way, we can't let them get in here. Whatever plan Cagliostro has, that woman is at the heart of it— and that means we have to do everything we can to keep her safe."

"Then I guess we need to get on it," said Scalli. "I'll see if I can get Vi to put these people into action."

It was then that another explosion sounded, this one so close that the walls of the incinerator vault trembled as if struck by the fist of God almighty. The towers of scrap metal swayed around them, threatening to collapse and drown them in rusted steel; the bleaching glow of the lamps went out, plunging the lot of them in darkness. Only the blue-white flames of the incinerator provided any sort of light now, a ghostly halo that radiated from the mouth of the furnace and transformed the room into a gloomy underworld. Around them the ferals, staring straight ahead and anointed with their lurid brands, looked more like the walking dead than the corpse-machines used by their former comrades.

"Might not be a bad idea to start thinking about the worst," Mason said. In the strange light he looked like a ghost.

"That will not be necessary."

The three of them looked down at once as Redeye came around. Her face was grim as she looked up at the lot of them. News was imminent, and it didn't look positive.

"Begging your pardon, Miss," said Mason, his brows lifted high. "Considering that the Martians decided to come visit while you were out, it seems to me that it is pretty damned necessary."

Redeye rose. "We don't need to worry about them," she said. "Whatever damage they inflict here is nothing compared to what we can do, now." Though her right eye glowed crimson, it was the other— the living one— that glittered with a light that stung deep at Bobbi's heart. If Redeye had madness within her, it was coming out now.

"All right," Bobbi said carefully. "What did Cagliostro tell you?"

"He was not able to finish." Redeye shook her head, and the smile died on her lips as she scanned the ceiling. "Something attacked him. Something attacked him, and then the connection cut out with the power. They must have taken out the generators, which were also powering our contra-jamming measures." She shook her head. "We need to get out of here. They are already invading the complex, and if we want to have any chance of escape we shall have to leave now."

"I guess you'll have to tell us about it later then," Bobbi said with a shake of her head. She did not like the idea of the all-powered god of the digital voodoo getting smacked around. "All right, what do we do?"

"Go into the adjoining chamber," Redeye said. She looked over her shoulder at the massed cult-troops, the door at the far end of the chamber past the incinerator. "Wait for me there. I have to address my people, tell them what needs to be done."

"And what if they attack before that?" Mason frowned. "The elevator is exposed topside."

"We aren't going that way." Redeye turned and started walking toward the painted ferals. "Go! I will not take long in giving orders."

Bobbi hesitated a moment, but a nudge from Scalli sent her leading the three of them to the other end of the room. As she passed, she looked back over her shoulder; there was Redeye standing before the assembly of her people, Violet standing beside her with her mangled face set in an expression of stern pride. Nevertheless, Bobbi caught the way she looked at Redeye as she stood there, and Bobbi saw in those blue eyes the same thing that she had felt when she was running with Tom.

Poor girl, she thought. She's probably in for the same thing as I was.

Whatever Redeye was saying, they couldn't hear it as they hurried to the end of the room; the door was a heavy hatch secured by a rotary handle, which Scalli twisted open easily thanks to his suit. Entering the room beyond, Bobbi saw what Mason had been talking about— a computer console with a large bank of holographic displays took up one wall of a small room beyond, each one showing a camera view of different sections of the Old City. On the far end of the room was another hatch. Bobbi looked at the floating screens, and found that several of the locations that they had visited— including Violet's shrine— were counted among the display panels.

"I guess they'd been watching us the whole time," Scalli said with a grunt as he looked over as well. "We can't underestimate that woman out there."

"Scalli," Bobbi said irritably, "I didn't get here by underestimating people." She looked over the screens; the displays had converged into a larger view of the industrial park, each one merging together to show a unified scene.

As they knew already, the Yathi forces had arrived. Several structures in the park were on fire, spewing ropes of black smoke into the bowl of night, and a line of armored cars had formed a semicircle around south end of the complex. They were painted up in the same flat gray of Civil Protection's Special Tactics Unit, playing police. A large number of armored figures already strode through the crumbling buildings, forty or fifty at vague count, painted the same gray as their carriers. Each one of them cradled in their arms the complicated shapes of military battle rifles. They were already on their way toward the elevator shed, but their progress was being slowed by what Bobbi assumed were the automated guns that Redeye's people had set up. Staccato flares of light blossomed crazily in the darkness, a garden of flame. Showers of dust and concrete boiled around the armored figures as they marched inexorably forward, answering with death in kind.

"They're not stopping," came Mason's awed voice from behind her. "Look!" He reached past Bobbi to point at the screen, where the vanguard of the Yathi advance were shuddering from what appeared to be concentrated fire. The armored figures shook from the impact of the rounds spewed over them, and though their armor was heavy it was hardly impervious; holes blasted through spurted with narrow, pixelated streams of white blood. And yet, they moved on as if they were merely caught in a strong wind. Only when their armor failed entirely and they began to lose limbs and body mass were the figures stilled, lying in pools of livid white made dull gray by the shadows.

New motion drew their attention from the marching killers to the cordon of vehicles circling the complex. The central car, which Bobbi had thought to be just a bigger transport carrier, was opening up along one side. The hull hinged open like a gull-wing door; a machine began to emerge from within. This was no combat robot that she was familiar with, the brutal and angular things that looked like tank turrets lacking cannon walking on four spider's legs. The thing that emerged was akin to a centipede, a ribbon made up of joined and articulated sections covered in heavy armored plates colored the same granite color as the rest of the force. Short, articulated legs ending in talons clicked away at the concrete beneath it as it unfurled itself from its carrier, leaving divots in its wake. And there, at the fore, its 'head' was a brutal, snub-nosed pyramid. A single sensor module swiveled like an eye within its housing at the flat end of the head as the machine moved forward— its tri-lobed aperture like a terrible iris, tracking things seen only to its monstrous self.

"We have got to get out of here." In Bobbi's voice there was no awe, only urgency. "Now."

"Jesus, they're really pulling out the stops." Mason whistled low, shaking his head as he watched the sinuous machine make its way toward the fence. "I've never seen anything like that before in my life."

"Yeah, well, I don't think we need to stick around long enough to find out what it's capable of." Scalli sounded grim indeed as he stared at the monitor. "I was waiting for the death rays and the flying saucers, but that thing..."

The centipede-machine scuttled toward the fence, and did not stop as it clambered over and through. Its legs shredded the chain link as though it were rotten thread, tearing a hole big enough for its ponderous body to go through. Bobbi had no idea how something that big— it was easily as long as the carrier from which it came— could have packed itself into its carrier, but now that it was out and moving they had to make their exit. "Somebody go get Redeye," she said. "We need to get the fuck out before that thing comes down this elevator shaft."

Presently the door opened; Scalli turned around, unlimbering his machine gun and training it on the hatch. "It's done," said Redeye as she entered, giving Scalli a curious look as she saw the muzzle of the gun trained on her. He grunted and slung it on his shoulder again.

Bobbi looked between the two of them. "What's done?"

"I've given my people orders," she said. Redeye entered, and Violet came in behind her. The feral priestess swung the hatch shut without a word and turned the wheel to seal it. "Their last orders, as it were."

"Their last orders," Mason repeated. "I know what that means. You've told them to hold their ground here, stage a last stand."

"That can't be right." Bobbi searched Redeye's face for some sign of mistake, but found none. Her eyes widened. "You can't be sending your people on a suicide mission, can you?"

Behind them, the monitors flared with light as a peal of explosive thunder rattled overhead. Bobbi turned and stared; the machine had taken the forefront, and sparks played like the trails of lethal fairies across its armored hull as the turrets focused their fire upon it. The withering fusillade could do nothing to scratch its plating, though, and the centipede— now arrived at the main thoroughfare that ran through the savaged complex— had hunkered down upon its legs as if bracing itself. On the other side of the complex a building, where Bobbi had seen the muzzle flashes of turret guns before, now hosted a large hole that had apparently been blown through its facade by an unknown force. No further resistance came from that quarter.

"Christ," barked Mason in disbelief. "That thing packing a cannon?"

Redeye frowned blackly at the monitor. "I do not know," she said. "Perhaps a directed energy weapon of some sort. It does not matter in any case."

Mason stared at her. "It matters if we end up in the path of that thing while trying to get out of here!"

"But we don't." Scalli looked at Redeye now, gauging her. "Do we? That's what your people are for."

Violet opened her fanged mouth to speak, but Redeye lifted her hand. "When I gathered my people," she said, "it was under the promise of revenge against the people who had stolen their lives and sanity from them, and a good death carrying it out. Nobody in that room wants to outlive the Yathi. Each and every one of them are broken, and they know that. They are all aware of what creatures they carry inside of them.

Should something happen to me, or if they survived the death of the other Yathi, they would pose a bigger threat to the city population than any other threat you can imagine. Some of the people in there contain the suppressed consciousnesses of military officers, weapons designers, and worse. What do you think would happen if they were to return to control of those bodies? Can you imagine what they could achieve, free of the Mother of Systems and insane as they are?"

They were all quiet for a moment. "Well, all right," said Bobbi. "I guess we'd better get going."

"Yeah." Scalli looked at Violet. "You okay, Vi?"

Violet gave him a thin, ugly, but grateful smile. "I'm all right," she said. "I trust the Eye. She knows better than I do about this sort of thing."

Bobbi looked at Violet too. She'd felt like that with Tom, too. Yeah, she was really seeing some parallels here, parallels that she found uncomfortable. "All right," she said, "well, we still need to get the fuck out of here." Turning to Redeye she said, "You said we can't get out of here through the elevator. Is there another way?"

"Through the hatch," said Redeye, and she walked that way. "We will have to move through the maintenance tunnels into the primary drainage canal, and from there we can get to the overpass."

"And the truck that we came in on," Bobbi said. Another bright flash filled the room; Bobbi caught the blue-white trail of sparks that spat from the centipede's eye, and the room shook around them as if the fist of the Almighty had come down on the ceiling. The force of impact, and the thunder that rolled down from the incinerator vault on the other side of the door, drove Bobbi against the console. She braced herself there for a moment, beholding the awful glow of the scene that the system shifted to display; as Redeye cranked the wheel open, the rest watched as the elevator shed was reduced to a trail of burning debris blown off the concrete floor of the park. No rubble choked the shaft that Bobbi could see, but there was no way for Redeye's people to get out now. Would they come out the other way, with them? Would they stand their ground and wait for the Yathi forces to come down and slaughter them?

And then, as if to still her concerns all at once, a sound came from the shaft's ravaged mouth. It reminded Bobbi instantly of the bestial howl that had come from the chorus of ferals the night that she and Tom had traveled through Renton, but it was not that sound; that sound, however terrible, had been human. What came from the depths of the shaft now was a monstrous thing, ululating and growling all at once, and it seemed to reach into Bobbi's brain and turn off the switches that would cause her to flee. She could only stare, all of them could only stare, as the sound filled their senses, a distinct and alien roar of rage and pain the mere human throat had not the plasticity to summon. Even the armored drones who had been fast reforming their vanguard at the fore of the centipede-thing gave pause, as if the corpse-machines could not fathom what madness was coming for them.

They boiled out of the shaft like ants, a gout of bodies, white flesh and ragged cloth, all death and fury. Redeye's reclaimed Yathi were nothing like the drones, who seemed like clumsy children as they struggled to bring their guns to bear in the face of the assault. Bobbi remembered the white killer in the bowels of Orleans Hospital, the speed with which she and the drones had torn apart their unprepared human combatants—and it was the same scene replayed here, the would-be ferals with their bodies filled with exotic implants and nameless systems, blurring as they moved, punching with bare fists and extruded blades as they shredded through armor plate and reanimated flesh. Poleaxed by the collected howl of otherworldly rage, Bobbi, Scalli and Mason could only stare as the advance was taken apart by the angry mass, much as the real Special Tactics officers had been at Orleans. The others behind her began to stir from their spell, but not Bobbi. She could only stare as her personal history repeated itself in an orgy of terrifying violence and milk-white blood.

Then Redeye's warriors began to charge the centipede, and everything changed.

As best as Bobbi could tell, the centipede was not just a robot, but somehow the leader of the assault. The moment the focus of the assault shifted from the drones to the war machine, the corpse-machines recovered. As one the drones brought their rifles up and fired, at full auto and at point-blank range. At first, the angry mass resisted; hardened skins and body plating, or merely impossible stamina, shook off the wave of armor-piercing death that smashed against them from both sides. Then the first fell, a thin man in a too-big plastic overcoat with long blades sprouting from his fingers, and the mass divided.

Bobbi stared as a broad-shouldered man took the rifle of the nearest drone as if it were a toy, fired a burst of rifle fire through its helmet, and then proceeded to mow down its nearest fellows while hoisting its corpse like a shield. Another, who had inflicted great horror with what looked like an industrial plasma torch that had sprouted from its wrist, suddenly seized as if hit before his back split opened and a battery of articulated cutting arms erupted from its ruin. He waded into the drones again as a thin girl who reminded Bobbi strongly of Violet unhinged her jaw and began to fire lances of red light from her too-wide mouth. Even through the pixellated lens of the holographic display, Bobbi could see her distended throat. Where they had been furies before, Redeye's followers were now transforming into grotesques of flesh and mechanism that left any cyborg she had ever seen far behind.

"What the fuck is happening to them?" Scalli had slung the machine gun across his back, and now stared at the display with expression hidden by his visor.

"They're beginning to remember themselves," Redeye said in a voice soft and heavy with sadness. "We have to go. It won't be long now."

The words jerked Bobbi from her horrified reverie. "Won't be long until what?"

"Until they lose it entirely. Then they'll kill each other, if they haven't already. The last will self-destruct."

"How do you know that?"

"Because that's what they've been ordered to do," Redeye said with a shake of her head. She gave the wheel a final turn and wrenched it open. "They always follow orders."

"They can't do anything else in the state they're in," Violet said when Bobbi opened her mouth to press further. "They listen to her like they listened to Mother."

Bobbi gave the display one last glance. All of Redeye's former Yathi had become bizarre things, and they waged terrible war on their enemies— both the rapidly thinning ranks of the drones and the centipede itself. White bodies hung from the thing's plates as it now began to rear up, becoming impossibly tall as it loomed over the lot of them.

"All right." Scalli tore himself away from the carnage on the holoscreen and wrenched open the unsealed hatch. The smell of dampness and decay filled their nostrils, a fitting perfume to the destruction going on overhead. Unslinging the gun again, he stepped through into a narrow channel of dimly-lit concrete. A few moments passed as he scanned the tunnel in both directions, then stepped back so that the rest of them could enter the tunnel behind him.

"The badass parade," muttered Scalli as he gestured for the rest of them to follow. "On we go to fuckery."

They moved through the cloying dimness of the access tunnel with as much speed as they dared, while a storm of sound raged on overhead. The tunnel slanted gently upward, so that the terrifying sounds overhead grew louder with every step. Scalli led the group with the heavy gun pointed forward; Bobbi kept close to the enormous man, barely able to see enough to keep her footing, while he hunched to keep from banging his head while tracking the machine gun's muzzle back and forth.

"Christ, it's dark," Bobbi heard Mason say from behind her. "Don't you people believe in lights?"

"I can see just fine," said Redeye from the back.

"Of course you can," Mason muttered. From somewhere over her shoulder, Violet stifled a snicker.

Above them another explosion rocked the park, this one more distant. "Sounds like we're getting away from them," Bobbi said.

"Yes." Redeye's tone had lost the soft sadness it had before, replaced with resolution. "We'd better pick up the pace if we intend to escape unnoticed, however."

Scalli grunted. "There might be sentries up ahead. Someone to pick off survivors."

"If there are, I guarantee you that it will be in our interest to meet and kill them now while the bulk of the Yathi force is entangled." Redeye pressed past Bobbi, cold and sleek, and shouldered herself into the lead. "Come on, I will show you."

"Hey!" Scalli gruntled like a startled bear as Redeye took point, but he did not argue— he only shook his head and muttered something that sounded to Bobbi like "crazy bitch." The big man picked up the pace, and in seconds the whole group was moving at a run toward the end of the tunnel. The burning in Bobbi's leg renewed, her drug-calmed muscles complaining as they were rudely jogged back into action. She nearly asked to stop a moment, but a new eruption of blasts behind them changed her mind.

The tunnel grew brighter by degrees as they charged ahead, and the sounds of battle grew dimmer again as they outpaced the carnage. By the time they finally reached the tunnel's mouth, Bobbi's leg throbbed in earnest. While the others stepped out into the night she slumped against the concrete, gasping for breath, and Scalli bent over to try and pick her up.

"No," she said, pushing him away. "I'm fine, I'm just...a little winded."

"Well I don't mean to sound harsh," he said lowly, "but we'll get all the time you need to breathe once we get the fuck out. C'mon, I'll help you."

"No, I'm fine!" Bobbi pushed herself off the side of the tunnel and past Scalli into the open air, where she found herself emerging right at the base of the overpass. The industrial park was a mass of flames, great columns of smoke reaching toward the sky. There had been no victory for either side, for the sounds of gunfire and the exotic hiss of energy weapons could be heard in the distance. It looked as though it had been hit by a large military force, not just the less than a hundred combatants that still clashed there. Bobbi thought of the monstrosities that Redeye's people had become, and shivered.

"Come on!" Redeye's voice rang from the left; Bobbi looked to see the pale woman scaling the ladder that still hung from over the lip of the overpass, followed dutifully by Violet. Mason was already on the bottom rung. Bobbi limped toward the ladder, Scalli taking up the rear, and began to follow the three of them with difficulty.

"Hey," said Scalli from the ground after she had struggled up a few rungs, "you sure you gonna be all right? We could pull you up."

"I'm not crippled," Bobbi rumbled. "I'm just hurting. I'll be fine once we get out of here."

"Suit yourself." Scalli turned and kept the big gun trained on the distant battle whilst Bobbi crawled her way up the ladder, every step causing her leg to tremble and sear. She found herself wishing that she were anywhere else but there, and admonished herself— after all, there were people dying so that she could escape, people who were losing reclaimed humanity to carry the fight against true monsters. Guilting herself gave Bobbi the drive that she needed to pull herself up the ladder, and soon they all stood sore and winded, blasted with adrenaline, upon the overpass.

They could only stare at the sight of the park from on high, and be amazed. Another of the great armored centipedes had joined the fight, along with what looked like a fresh swarm of armored troopers. Though it was difficult to count the numbers, Redeye's people still survived to harry them, flashes of light and thundering blasts sounding throughout the complex. "Jesus," Bobbi whispered as she beheld the might of the angry few. "This is what they can do?"

"This is what they can do," said Redeye with a nod. "But to be honest, this is still largely pulling punches. I've seen far worse in the bellies of their complexes. Those machines, they're only one type of field apparatus."

"Ladies!" Scalli called to them as he moved around to the back of the truck. "Let's get the fuck out of here!" He pulled the back hatch open and tossed in his gun. "We can talk about it inside."

Mason stared at the conflict below for a moment longer before nodding agreement. "I'm all for that," he said, and turned to get into passenger side of the truck's cab. Bobbi could see a certain wildness in his eyes— the reflection of an older war, perhaps, of atrocities in Europe now long passed. Violet and Redeye shared a look before she went around and climbed into the driver's seat, leaving Bobbi and Redeye to get into the back.

As the truck started up and they climbed inside, Scalli closed the door behind them. The dim light that filtered in through the cab hatch seemed to draw back a bit before the glow of Redeye's namesake, and Bobbi realized with a start just how bright the glow of the woman's eye really was. "Move, Violet," Redeye called through the hatch, and with a lurch the truck sped away from the scene.

As they pulled away, Bobbi felt relief flooding her body, relief coupled with guilt. "That," she said, "was scary shit."

"I can understand that," said Redeye. The woman brought her legs up against her chest, curled into the corner by the hatch. She was watching Bobbi quietly, the eye burning away, her face set in concentration. It made Bobbi feel as though the other woman was looking through her skin, peering into her organs and trying to foretell the future.

She shuddered. "I'm guessing you know where we go from here," said Bobbi, trying not to think about the eye that blazed at her. "Do you think they'll come after us?"

"Yes."

"Do you think your people can hold out?" Scalli drummed his fingers against his knees; the machine gun was propped against a corner. "You didn't say what they were capable of."

Redeye looked up at them and shrugged. "Many of them were hardened combat units, enhanced for frontline and security duty, but almost all of them had seen combat. In any case, I imagine our lot will become much simpler very soon."

Bobbi blinked. "What—" and before she could finish her sentence, a tremendous sound came from behind them. It was a shuddering boom, like the sky cracking open, and with it came a shockwave that sent Violet's truck pitching on the highway.

"Fuck's sake!" shouted Mason, and Bobbi shoved her head through the hatch leading into the cab— where she saw reflected in the truck's rearview mirrors a great column of flame lancing toward the sky. The mushroom cloud that came with it loomed over the distant industrial park, lit up from below by the flames. A vision of apocalypse, it chilled Bobbi's blood to watch it rise.

"Wait," rumbled Scalli, who was looking in now as well. "Was that a nuke?"

"No." Redeye looked at the floor. "We seeded the place with explosives, along with an overload device set up in the incinerator. When the last of my people died, I detonated them all."

Bobbi looked over her shoulder at Redeye, dumbstruck. "Wait," she said. "You were..."

"Tied into their vital systems through remote connection." Redeye's voice sounded very far away. "I've been watching them die as we talked."

Nobody said anything after that. Nobody had the words.

CHAPTER 17

Eventually, they'd passed through an unsecured section of the Old City running along northeastern Renton, and entered into the Verge. There, they abandoned Violet's truck and stole another one that was sitting in the parking lot of an abandoned bodega. Another old conversion, it was too small for Scalli to drive – which seemed to suit him just fine, oddly enough. Given the conspicuousness that Violet's appearance would have outside of the Old City, Bobbi decided to drive. Mason sat up front with her. They had to be careful not to attract the attention of Civil Protection, after all, and the two of them looked the most normal by far.

They drove across the city toward the Temple, watching the landscape unfold around them like complex origami of light and concrete, a crane with alloy wings. After the madness of the Old City, it looked like civilization...but it didn't feel like it at all. This was just another wilderness, only the animals didn't come screaming at you with knives. It was much more dangerous that way, Bobbi thought, with a clarity she had never had before. Now, more than ever, she thought she understood how Tom must have seen the world. It made her feel close to him again, but it disturbed her how empty that feeling was.

"You all right?" Mason was watching her face as she drove, his expression one of fatherly concern.

"Yeah." She'd forgotten again how old he actually was. "Just trying to process everything. How about you?"

"I'm all right. It's hard, I know. Especially after bad things happen. But you're tough." He smiled a little and looked back out at the city. "You know, this is the first time I've actually been inside the city for a long time. Years."

Bobbi chuckled. "No taste for civilization, huh?"

"Please." Mason gave a dismissive snort. "You used to live in Tenleytown, you know how we are there. We're all close. Everyone looks out for each other. Nothing like here."

"Maybe not as much as we thought. Diana certainly wasn't looking out for me. Or you."

Mason's face darkened at that. "Maybe so," he said. "Or maybe she was just looking out for someone who died a long time ago."

"Her mother." Bobbi nodded. "Yeah, I can see that." She heaved a deep breath. "Maybe her father, too. She'd always been set on my mother being the one who caused it all."

"Not everybody wants to be truthful about where responsibility lies." Mason looked at her again, canting his head a little bit. He looked very much like the wise old father now, despite the youth his face insisted. There were some things new flesh just couldn't bury. "What about you? I heard about your man, the one you were with back when this all started with you. You're not blaming yourself, I hope."

Well, this conversation was taking a turn that Bobbi wasn't certain she wanted anything to do with. "Look," she said, "if you're asking me if I feel responsible for getting him into all of this, I don't. He'd have gotten into it some other way. Or Stadil— Cagliostro— would have done something else to get him involved."

"That's not what I'm talking about."

"Well, then what do you mean?"

Mason shrugged. "You may not blame yourself for him getting into the whole mess, but I wonder if you don't feel responsible for him vanishing when you blew up the hospital."

Bobbi stiffened. "Maybe I used to," she said. "But if he did die, then he was better off for it if he had one of those things inside of him."

"I don't think you believe that, either," Maston said. "I used to think, 'I'd rather be dead than have an arm blown off'. That is, until I saw it happen on the field. After that I wanted them to keep me alive any way they possibly could— it's part of why I ended up with the gene surgery." Mason shrugged. "I'm just saying, I know that it can be hard. But on the other hand, I don't want you to sit there thinking that you were responsible for any of this. I mean, sure, you were a fellow traveler and all, but this...this was where he wanted to go. He could've stopped after you got that bogus file. As Scalli tells me, you wanted to. But he went out on his own." Mason waved his hand, then. "You don't have to reply, just remember who's responsible for what, that's all. Survivors' guilt never did anything but kill people faster."

Things were quiet after that until they got to the Scrap Field. Bobbi dropped Scalli outside of his place so he could re-arm and repair himself. The rest of them headed over to the Temple, which was still intact. Mason let out a whistle as he saw the building looming over them. "Could add on to Tenleytown with this," he said, "or establish a satellite colony. You must have a lot of cash on hand, girl."

"I do okay," Bobbi said as she parked the van in front of the building. Stadil's money, and the fact that she was a wealthy woman on her own, had only just returned to her mind. It was funny how she never really thought about it until she had some kind of need. "Anyway, let's get inside. I'll get you all some drinks, you can eat up or whatever. We can talk about what we need to do."

"Sounds good to me," said Mason, and reached for the door handle.

"Wait."

Mason looked at her. "Yeah?"

"You said that you'd seen what Redeye's people had done before. What did you mean?"

Mason pursed his lips. He sat back in his seat as the others began to pile out of the back of the van. "When they first started," he began, "before they were hitting facilities, I mean, they were clearing out the ferals in the area that might give them trouble. Those were pretty close to Tenleytown – we were going to war with 'em pretty often. Then Redeye and her people would go in, there'd be a hell of a racket, then...silence. And, you know, we'd go see what they'd done afterward. I just...we'd see what was left of them." Mason shook his head. "It was never pretty. Worst violence I'd ever seen, even during the War. They'd just...pull people apart. Stack the limbs and torsos in neat piles. It was just obscene, you know?" Mason shook his head again, this time more vigorously as if trying to clear the memory away. "All I'm saying is that I'm glad that she's on our side. And I'm glad the rest of them are dead. She's right that we don't want those people loosed upon the world."

"And she's the toughest one," said Bobbi. "So that's fun."

"Yeah," said Mason, and he reached for the door handle again. "Well, we will see what happens, I guess. I'd be lying if I said we shouldn't be ready to do her in as well."

He got out of the van, leaving Bobbi alone— alone, and thinking of how to do just that. Redeye would be the beast she didn't want to let out of the box without a clear idea of how to clip her. At the moment, however, she had no choice, and no ideas. But that would change. It would have to.

They spent a while in the club, waiting on Scalli to return and getting the next leg of planning started. Bobbi offered them all the use of the facilities upstairs, which Redeye declined but Violet accepted with wide and grateful eyes. Bobbi wondered how long it had been since the poor woman had been able to take a shower. Mason was content to stay downstairs and draw a pint of beer while Bobbi and Redeye went upstairs after Violet. As the shower steamed away, the two women sat in Bobbi's office. After checking fruitlessly to see if Cagliostro had returned, Bobbi watched Redeye while the woman slouched in one of the chairs opposite her desk. Redeye looked around the office with an easy sort of grandeur that Bobbi had seen at the complex, as if none of the night's events had taken place. Bobbi wanted to say something to her, but she found that she had no words. What could she say? The woman had lost all of her faction, people whom she had taken care of and led against terrifying enemies. She'd certainly had more to deal with than Bobbi had in the past few weeks, and that was saying something. And yet here she was, sitting without any real expression save mild curiosity. As they sat in silence, Bobbi tried to grasp for something to say, until finally Redeye spared her the trouble.

"You are angry with me, I think," Redeye said, settling her gaze on Bobbi.

"I am?" Bobbi blinked at her. "Why would you say so?"

"Because I do not seem upset now. You must think that I do not care about what has happened."

"You seemed plenty upset earlier," Bobbi pointed out, not sure what the other woman was getting at. "And as much as it might rankle me, your decision made sense. It's not like you had no problem at all sending them off to be killed."

Redeye shook her head. "You're wrong about that," she said. "The truth of the matter is that I did have no problem sending them to their deaths. It was the reason I brought them all together in the first place, as I told you."

"But it's not as though you feel nothing for them," Bobbi said. "Otherwise, what would separate you from what they fought in the first place?"

"That's a good question." The other woman frowned a bit. "I've been wondering about that since we left."

Bobbi wrinkled her nose. "I don't know if that's fair," she said. "It's true, we don't' know much about you, but we're on the same side here. That was a great sacrifice that your people committed, and I want to honor that."

"But it was a sacrifice that I ordered," said Redeye. "You could say that I should have died with them."

"Maybe, but then who would stay behind to help us?" Bobbi leaned forward a bit, propping herself up on the desk with an arm. "Look, I don't pretend to know half of everything going on here, and we've just gotten out of a horrendous situation that we really need to talk about. But, barring that? I don't see that any of you people had much of a choice but to do what has been done." Bobbi said the words, not entirely believing them, but she did believe that in order to learn about the situation to its fullest extent she would have to ingratiate herself to the...whatever she was.

Redeye drew the long sheet of sleek, dark hair from her face, showing not only the burning eye but another that was a rich honey-brown in color. "Then let us talk."

"Just a second," Bobbi said, and called up the intercom system.

"Yo." Scalli's voice drifted out from concealed speakers.

"You and Mason come on up, Scalli. It's conference time."

Not long after the lot of them gathered in Bobbi's office. Scalli and Mason came up from the bar floor, both of them having dipped into the stock of whiskey from the smell of them, and a very much scrubbed Violet finally emerged from the bedroom after having been given stern instructions from Bobbi twice over to find something fresh in her closet to wear. Though still mutilated, the years of filth scrubbed from her skin showed what was once a very pretty girl indeed. It made Bobbi's heart tear with pity to look at her, and she smiled as Violet shyly took a seat over near Redeye's chair.

"So Red and I have been talking," said Bobbi, nodding at Redeye from behind her desk. "I figure we should talk about what's happened, what she's been up to, and..." She paused to look at Redeye a moment, "and I hope you'll forgive me for saying it, but just who – and what – you are."

The other woman's lips flattened into a frown. "I would have thought that would be obvious," said Redeye. Violet shrank a little bit at her side. "I am your ally."

"Yeah," said Scalli, "but you aren't exactly normal, are you? So what are you? I don't get that you've ever been picked up by the White Legion there, at least not possessed."

"I was not aware my origins were going to be questioned," Redye said, and her lips grew harder.

"Begging your pardon," Scalli said, leaning forward in the other seat, "I can't imagine how the hell you would think that we wouldn't ask."

Redeye's scowl remained for a moment longer, then dissipated into a helpless frown. "Very well," she said, though she gave Scalli a withering look. "You are correct in that I am not formerly Yathi. I am human, or at least, marginally so."

"You'll have to explain that," Mason said, quirking his brows. "Not Yathi, but only marginally human?"

"Yes," said Redeye with a nod. She folded her hands in her lap, looking around the lot of them. "I was born human, at least. Created in a laboratory, artificially conceived and independently gestated. My father— by that I mean, the male genetic contributor— was an employee at a Genefex subsidiary, Applied Defense Solutions, in their Detroit laboratory complex. He was a researcher in their Applied Bionics and Cybernetics division developing combat systems for the War."

"The European War," Scalli said.

"Yes."

"Go on."

"Once I had been decanted, my father took me to the laboratory in which he worked, located on a research plantation in Switzerland. There a battery of procedures were performed upon me as I grew in the tanks: nerve augmentation, sensory augmentation, more. I did not undergo augmentation surgery; the systems were literally grown into me." She smiled very thinly, and lifted her arm. Her skin, pale and poreless, seemed to gleam like porcelain. "There's not much left of me that isn't synthetic."

Scalli squinted at her. "So. You're a full-conversion rig, then."

"That is correct." Redeye shrugged. "My brain and central nervous system are mostly organic, but the rest is synthetic. Combat-purposed."

Bobbi stared at Redeye again. The bizarre had become a regular occurrence, considering the road that they now traveled, but she hadn't expected for the leader of the feral army to have been a human brain riding in a synthetic body. "So he made you into a machine," she said, and found that Violet was no longer the only target of her pity.

"Something like that, yes," said Redeye with a nod. "Over time, my systems finished their initial integration and I was given training. I learned how to use my body, and when the time came that my father believed me to be ready for deployment, he put me in cryogenic stasis until the time the company wanted to use me." She shook her head, shivering slightly. "I can still remember what it was like, going under in the dark. It was...hard."

Bobbi frowned, and she felt that pity inside of her swell. "I can't imagine what that must have been like for you. Or what it must be like for you now, for that matter. But how did you get where you are now?"

Redeye leaned back against the side of the truck. "That is an interesting story. In suspension, I was still connected to the network. Mind you, this wasn't the Network as you know it; it was back during the time of the Internet, which of course expanded into the Network we know back in the Thirties. I was just connected to the laboratory computer system. I slept for years...but as I did, I kept hearing a voice in my head."

"A voice?" Scalli turned a bit to look at her. "What did it say?"

"It told me about many things, really," said Redeye. "About the Yathi, what they were, their purpose. Someday, it told me, I would be responsible for helping destroy them. But I had to get out first. I had to escape."

There was a bit of a pause before Scalli grunted. "That was a long time to be in the freezer."

"For good reason, as it turns out. Whoever it was that told me the truth of things, they also somehow kept my location off the books and instead stepped up production of the xsiarhotl to distract from the project costs. And so I slept in a vault, quietly developing a personality." Redeye took a deep breath, then sighed. "After a fashion, at least. But because the world is a funny place, I believe that I have just met the person who helped me all that time ago."

That took Bobbi aback. "You're not talking about Cagliostro, are you?"

"He responded to the name that the voice used back then," said Redeye with a nod. "The Yathi designation. I suspect that it was indeed him who spoke with me all that time ago."

Bobbi tried to wrap her head around it. Cagliostro had said that he'd been planning things for a while, long before he made the decision to destroy his body and become the thing he was now, but Bobbi hadn't imagined that his web reached back as far as it apparently did. "Well," she said, "I guess we're all part of his plan. Cagliostro said you were borged up something good, and a failsafe. So I can't help but wonder what you're amped up with. You said you were combat-purposed. Are you like your people back there? All reflexes and martial arts and crazy strength?"

"No." Redeye shook her head.

"You have like cannons and shit in there? You shoot rays out of that eye of yours?"

"No."

Bobbi squinted at her. "Well what the hell are you, then?"

The smile that Redeye gave her was so fragile Bobbi expected that it might shatter off her face at any moment. "You mentioned that Cagliostro said that I was a failsafe – that is not entirely incorrect. I am a failsafe...after a fashion."

Bobbi's squint tightened. "What kind of failsafe, then? Do you shut down systems when you interface with them?"

Redeye nodded her head. "Essentially yes," she replied. "Suffice it to say that were I to fulfill my true potential, there would be nothing the Yathi have built that would be able to resist me."

Bobbi and Scalli looked at each other. "That sounds...impressive. Can you give us some detail?"

Chuckling, Redeye started ticking points off her fingers. "Target analysis and acquisition," she said, "information display, infrared and ultraviolet visualization, passive sonar. I also have a ranging penetrative radar unit in my skull along with a miniaturized network module with wireless and satellite uplink." She paused. "My skin was replaced by a flexible biphase polymer. It looks like skin, feels like skin, but it absorbs or reflects a host of lethal radiation and hardens into armor against various impacts and damage types. Skeleton and musculature replaced to put up with impact force and to carry the failsafe hardware. I also have a full suite of hand-to-hand combat hardware, including plasma-sheathing generators in my limbs that cut through most known materials." The thin woman paused a moment, then gestured to her eye again. "And there are the indicator lamps, of course."

"Christ." Mason whistled. "You're like Queen of the Combat Borgs."

Bobbi watched the other woman's face for a moment, seeking...something. She wasn't sure what, but she felt it was significant to look at her all the same. Then she sighed. "Nothing like making you feel like industrial machinery," she said. "That's just fucked up. I'm sorry that you'd had to go through that."

Redeye shrugged. "It's what it is," she said. "I'm not terribly sad, myself. Were I something less durably built, I wouldn't be here now."

"I guess you're right on that one." Scalli squinted at her with new interest. "So why the hell did they make you in the first place? How is it a good idea to create a bomb that can walk, talk, and isn't easily killed? You're wired up like a combat mech, for Christ's sake!" He shook his head. "And why didn't they try and kill you outright the moment that they knew you were around? Once you started collecting people and sacked your first facility, it'd make complete sense to come grinding your people down with a large force and make excuses about it."

"Yeah," Bobbi said, grateful that Scalli was giving voice to what she'd been wondering for a while now but had yet found the right time to bring up. "I mean, your intent was plain. Why wouldn't they throw everything at you if they knew you could take their systems out?"

"Because they don't know what I am," Redeye said with a shrug. "As part of his plan to destroy the Yathi, Cagliostro ensured that all records of my development were destroyed and the development team killed in a variety of incidents. It isn't as if I might beseige Genefex Tower and crack it open, after all. Between its armored construction and defense systems, an outright assault would be folly."

Bobbi frowned all the more. "Forget I said anything," she replied. "So all right, you can't get them from the outside. But within, surely."

"That is the objective." Redeye frowned. "Though, of course, there have been two serious blockages to progress, the first being a lack of a primary target. And then, of course, there is this." She gestured to her blazing eye.

"What's the point behind that, then?" Mason cocked his head and studied her anew. "I mean it's an indicator light, sure, but indicating what?"

"Mine is a two-stage system," Redeye explained. "In the first stage, physical systems are brought online to ensure the platform – that is, I – can physically survive. This occurred when I was released from the storage structure in which Cagliostro had kept me."

"And the second?"

Redeye smiled faintly at Mason. "The second stage allows for activation of the failsafe payload. I need a target for that, but thankfully that can be self-realized and does not require outside direction. It must be in sight, however, and in close proximity."

"Well there's something at least," Bobbi muttered. "So what about a target, then? Do you have one now?"

"Before the attack came, the one you know as Cagliostro was transmitting data on the location at which he wanted us to strike. I have the location, partial data on its defenses – but I do not know what is inside." Redeye frowned in thought. "However, I think that I know what it might be."

"All right," Bobbi sat forward, fixing her eyes on Redeye's face. "So what are you thinking?"

"I can think of only one area that he would select, given my internal parameters," she said. "And that would be the planetside terminus of their colonization matrix."

Scalli sat forward, too. "I'm assuming that 's some kind of transmitter?"

"Indeed." Redeye nodded. "The colonization matrix is the device which transmits compressed consciousness data from the Yathi homeworld to this one."

"Yeah," Mason said cautiously. "So what's the deal with that? Minds transmitted across space into the brains of the broken? I guess folks were right about tinfoil hats all those years ago."

Scalli snorted.

"Something like that," said Redeye with the faintest smirk. "Not that it would have done anything to disperse the signal. The matrix is made up of the transmitter on their homeworld, which takes up nearly half the planet in its infrastructure and power systems as far as I have been told, and the receiving unit which is here on Earth. For whatever reason, they cannot replicate or otherwise replace the receiver should it be destroyed; they can merely repair and maintain it. Therefore, it makes sense that destroying the receiver would be his goal."

"Destroy it," Bobbi said. "You mean shut it down."

"It's all the same thing," said Redeye with a shrug. "It will be nonfunctional, and the rest of them will burn alive when their sun explodes."

Silence fell amongst them for a moment; she spoke so calmly of such genocide, even if the victims did deserve it. Or did they? Surely they weren't all foaming psychopaths, plotting to destroy the human race through psychic replacement. Surely they weren't all evil – alien, perhaps, but that did not mean evil alone. "I...I need to know something," said Bobbi. "Something more about them. They came here...when?"

"Three centuries or so ago." Redeye looked amongst them, face stern now that it was story time. "They had already determined the impending death of their civilization and set up a schedule, as well as selected the human race as the garden from which they would blossom. At the time, cosmological conditions were such that single individuals could be transmitted alone – one or two a year. Apparently there was even the ability to quantum-tunnel small amounts of physical matter to this world, which was how they were able to establish their technological base so quickly on this planet, but when they cracked the crust of the planet from the stress of it they thought better of trying again. That's when she came. She was the first."

"Ghia Merducci." Bobbi's expression hardened. "The Mother of Systems."

Redeye nodded. "That's why they call her what they do; it is as much a literal description as it is a title, you see. It was she who engineered the entire colonial program, she who chose our species for replacement. She came, and others followed. It took them a hundred years to establish themselves here. Small numbers, limited technological resources."

"So what about this matrix?" Mason asked.

"I'm getting to that." Redeye looked past them a moment to the rows of cult-soldiers standing in their neat rows beyond. "This place is a colony. Colonies take time to establish. Early on they'd projected themselves into only choice individuals, people who had the resources and intelligence that they could emulate without causing undue problems. Brilliant, mercurial types. In the case of the Mother of Systems, she incarnated in the body of Jeanne Antoinette Poisson, the Marquise de Pompadour."

Scalli and Bobbi looked at each other. "Who's that?" Bobbi asked.

It was Mason who answered that, to Bobbi's surprise. "She was the mistress of Louis XV," said the soldier. "A French king – one of the most famous kings, in fact. She was known for her mind and her intellectual attachments." He frowned faintly at when he everyone was staring at him now. "I went to college, you know."

Well well. There were unplumbed depths to Harry Mason yet. "Right," said Bobbi, "so she started it all."

"Bet it was easy to recruit in the court," said Mason. "I mean. Those people had nothing to live for but shoes."

Redeye smirked. "Very different from today, to be certain."

"Right, well." Bobbi cleared her throat. "So things went from there. We know that they've infiltrated society since then, and that they're behind the way things are going now – accelerating the advance of technological development beyond the ability of human beings to cope with."

"It's not that." Mason was getting into it now, the old man he truly was coming out to speak with experience. "It's not the technology itself. It's not just advancement. It's the system, the socio-economic policies behind it. The erosion of culture in the face of pop sensibilities far beyond what seems real. I've lived through this already, you kids. That's what it is. It's like..."

"It's like something from another planet." Bobbi looked at Mason now, equal parts impressed and wryly amused. "It's no wonder you jumped in with us when Scalli told you what we knew."

"We're getting sidetracked," said Scalli, as if on cue.

Redeye blinked at him; Bobbi saw how the light of her namesake glowed through the thin tissue of her eyelid as it fluttered. "Ah," she said, "I suppose that we did. As I said, when they first arrived, the projection assembly back on their homeworld was only strong enough to project one mind at a time; it was costly, and time-consuming. Over a hundred years or so, the Mother and her people here built a kind of receiver here on Earth – first a small-scale one in France, which they then dismantled and moved to Vienna after the French Revolution. At the end of the 19th century, however, they moved it here, to Seattle. It is now large enough to facilitate a massive broadcast that should supplant the majority of the cultivated population before their star goes nova. From there, it's a matter of either processing or destroying the rest of the human population, while they continue to change the climate."

"That's something I don't understand," said "Bobbi. "Genefex is a biogenetics concern. They'd have to have carried their medical expertise with them else they wouldn't have lived these three hundred years. So why use people at all? Why not just grow clones in tanks or whatever, and then possess those?"

"I am not an expert on the technique," said Redeye. "I only know that there is something about the process that requires a developed template consciousness to work from. As it stands—"

"Guys." Scalli cleared his throat. "If we destroy this thing, it'll will stop the invasion, right?"

"Yes." Redeye shrugged again, deflating a little. "And no. In the end, the ones that remain will have to be hunted down and killed if we are to be rid of them entirely. The current population could still control the planet from the shadows, just as they have been. They, however, could not be left to degenerate like the other former Yathi have . Can you imagine if a large enough number of people went insane like they did? All life on this planet may well be destroyed."

"But killing them would take a lot of planning," said Scalli, though he didn't sound like he disliked the idea at all. "Be a hell of an operation. Long-term."

"Terrorist organizations exist for far less noble aims than the survival of the human race," Redeye pointed out.

Bobbi blinked at her. "I don't know that I'd call that terrorism."

"I can assure you that the Yathi remaining would feel very much in disagreement."

"History'll judge that," said Scalli. "Right now, it's like you said, Red. We – well, you – destroy this...matrix. You said you know how to get there."

"I do." Redeye nodded, reaching up to brush the sheet of long hair from her face again. Flickers of humanity there, the dark eye that of a living woman, still unlit with balefire. "I know very little about the installation short of its structural plan, as I said before, and a little about its defenses. That isn't the problem, of course."

Bobbi's brows arched. "No?"

Redeye shook her head. "No," she said. "The problem is its location. It is right under the middle of the New City, and not terribly far from Genefex Tower. If we were to go there..." She shrugged. "It would be a very difficult undertaking."

"But that's where we need to go." Scalli leaned forward a little, looking the woman in her burning red eye, not afraid at all. After all, he had seen worse now, and her power was lost on him. "Is that right?"

She looked back at him. "Yes."

"Then I say we go." Scalli looked to Bobbi. "You agree?"

Bobbi nodded. "There's no other choice, the way I look at it. But what if it isn't the receiver? I mean, what if this is something completely different and we don't know about it?"

"Then we will have struck a blow," Redeye said. "Considering the situation, have we any more important a duty than that?"

Bobbi looked at Violet, who was looking up at her leader with rapt attention. The smile on her face told of adoration that had long since become zealotry. She wondered if this was how they all would have been, the maddened fighters that had followed the enigmatic cyborg, if they had arrived at the base on a better day.

"I guess not," Bobbi said with a shake of her head. "Let's just all try and get out alive."

Based on the data salvaged from Redeye's exchange with Cagliostro, the facility – whatever it maintained – was a fortified complex buried ten stories under a very normal business tower in the middle of Belltown called Staunton Tower. From the surface up, the structure was a standard one: twenty stories of absolutely everyday businesses and office facilities that had been nanoformed twenty years ago, absolutely nothing associated with Genefex or its Yathi masters. Access to the complex below was made through a single elevator shaft hosting double cars. Some mechanism identified secure personnel and called up the elevator leading to the complex, so that only Yathi could normally get in.

The complex itself was comprised of four floors, if you could call them that. Each room was connected to the other through a system of corridors, but at different levels; the effect was that of a web of sorts, or perhaps an ant farm. There were also a series of distribution shafts running straight up and down between certain chambers, but those would be locked down from the control nexus at the topmost chamber – a heavily fortified chamber that they would avoid unless they absolutely couldn't. As Bobbi stared at the holographic map that the computer had generated she remembered what Cagliostro had said, how the Yathi in their native form looked nothing like humanity. The names of each room seemed to point toward ominous function: tissue processors and drone programming centers, assembly plants and the like. One chamber stood at the bottom of the web, connected only by a single corridor: this one bore no title, and it was there that Redeye swore they must go.

Redeye talked about what she knew of its defenses, of automated guns and security barriers and hordes of corpse-drones altered to do combat. The security network grew more and more dense as the route neared the bottom chamber, until Bobbi wondered if it were the Mother of Systems herself that laired down in the nameless place. Even a handful of the defenses would have been death for the five of them, even as unusual as they all were. Bobbi felt herself shrinking as the cyborg went on, until Redeye stopped to look at her.

"Is something wrong?"

"Wrong?" Bobbi lifted her brows. "Well, yeah." She sat up in her seat, realizing with surprise that she had slid down in it so far as she had. "Look at this place. How are we supposed to get into that mess and come out living?" She had become the leader, she knew, but her optimism – if not her credulity – could only be stretched so far. "Swarming with gun turrets and monsters and whatever the fuck else, and that's only what we know about. How do you propose that we get past all that?" Her words echoed the thoughts of everyone else in the room, the way they looked at Redeye with expression clouded with doubt. Even Violet looked unsure.

"Well," said Redeye, without so much as a tic in her placid expression, "how would you normally disarm such defenses?"

Bobbi frowned at her. "I'd normally hack it all, of course," she said, "as much as possible. But how am I supposed to do that? These are alien systems, and even if they weren't–"

"You did it at the other place," Scalli said. "I mean, at the Data Nexus where..." He shook his head. "I mean, with the Grail."

The images swam back. Freida in that horrible chair, possessed by the chorus of machine-things. The strangeness of the system's landscape as she entered through the Grail, the darkness that swallowed her, the brain-cracking effort with which she somehow forced her way out of the grip of that distant place. "No," she said, shaking her head. "I can't do that again. I don't know how to interface with it. And even then..."

Redeye was quiet for a few seconds. "I think," she said, unfolding herself so that she stood, "That you should try and speak to Cagliostro again on that topic."

"We can't get to him yet," Bobbi said darkly. She thought she knew what was coming next.

"Perhaps, but that doesn't mean he won't be back soon. We'll need time to plan our assault, and I rather think that we all need a break. Perhaps you'll find him by tomorrow; I cannot imagine that would have been destroyed by such an attack, assuming that he was."

Bobbi frowned a little, but she nodded her head. "Yeah," she said in resignation, "yeah, I guess you're right. We'll all bunk out as we can tonight, and then see what can be done in the morning." She'd keep the place closed; it's not like she needed the money, and having Redeye and Violet around customers would just invite disaster. Besides, they might wake up to find Yathi agents pounding on their door. "I'll get some beds set up downstairs for you guys."

"That'd be nice," said Violet, who seemed to be perking up much more in civilization; she smiled at Bobbi from Redeye's side, the yellowed fangs and missing nose breaking up what would have otherwise been a beautiful face. "I appreciate it."

"I'll take care of it." Scalli sounded about as excited as Bobbi did, but he got up without disagreement. He and Mason headed for the elevator, joined by an increasingly cheerful Violet. Camp bed or not, Bobbi figured it was probably the first time she'd had a clean place to sleep for a very long time.

They packed themselves in and the doors sealed shut, leaving Bobbi and Redeye alone once more. The two women sat quietly for a bit, just as they had before, as if each one waited for the other to speak. There was so much, after all, hanging between them. Finally, it was Redeye who broke the silence once again.

"I understand that your friend was taken by them," she said.

Bobbi felt her hand ball into a fist on its own. "Yeah, but it looks like I ended up killing him anyway."

"And if you did not?"

Bobbi stared at her. This, again, was land into which she did not wish to venture. "But I did. There's no way he could have survived that blast."

"What if he escaped beforehand?" Redeye turned her face toward Bobbi, fixing her with that one angry eye. "What if he's out in the world, ridden by one of those things?"

A knot of dread formed deep in Bobbi's guts. She set her lips, unwilling to show emotion to the other woman – angry again, angry that she would dare to bring the topic up. But then, there wasn't much that Redeye did not dare. In that moment, Bobbi hated her for her boldness. "I guess I'll have to kill him, then," she said in a forced voice that did not belong to her at all. "I mean that's the alternative, else he ends up crazy."

More silence passed between them, in which Redeye continued to stare at her, bore into her skull with that dim red light. Then she nodded and got to her feet. "I am glad to hear it," she replied. "I have never had someone special, but I imagine that it would be hard for me to face it. I do not know that I could do it. I am glad that you can."

And then Redeye left her with the words ringing in her ears: I'm glad that you can. The murderous machine-girl, the cyborg killer, praising her for doing the worst thing that Bobbi could think of. Not even the hottest setting on the shower dial could purge the chill that filled her, nor could she push it from her mind when she tried one last time, in vain, to find Cagliostro before collapsing into bed. She lay there staring at Tom's coat in its lexan box, pinned to the wall, the bloodstains dark and shiny in its fabric like the tracks of tears she could not shed.

She closed her eyes, and prayed she would not dream. It did not come easily, nor was it answered; that night, her mind was filled with the horrible visions that Cagliostro had shown her, the distant and horrible world which Earth would someday become.

If not for her. If not for them.

The next morning found NewsNetNow all abuzz about a Civil Protection raid on a drug factory in the Old City. News footage of a battle in the industrial park that they had fled, incredibly doctored, premiered on the morning feed. There, valiant Special Tactics officers battled with what looked like maddened victims of Shard overdoses, throwing themselves at the guns of the armored men who of course had no alternative but to tear them down. "Officers sustained only light casualties as they repulsed the wave of violent addicts," said Maya Frail in grave tones, "before attempting to secure the repurposed industrial space in which the factory was located. Sources within Civil Protection say that surviving gang members operating the factory detonated a self-destruct device within the complex as officers began securing the premises, but that all officers involved in the raid were able to evacuate before that happened. A marked increase in violence in the Decommissioned Suburban Zone has sparked new outcries to begin resettlement..."

Bobbi sighed, and leaned back in her seat. Great. Sanitized. Everything fucking sanitized. With the way she looked, Bobbi would not have been surprised if Maya Frail hadn't had her brain zapped as well – the predominance of the pale-faced, pale-haired fashion was maddening. She thought about the woman that she saw in the train a few weeks back, how she looked straight-up like Genefex stock. Had she been armed then, would Bobbi have killed her? Tracked her down and executed her in an alley? And if she were prepared to do murders, what if the girl just had taken on the Genefex 'look', not knowing what it truly meant, and she ended up killing an innocent? The thought of it chilled her blood again – she was getting halfway to a reptile this way, and she didn't like it at all.

Nor did she relish the idea of putting the cable into the back of her neck and trying to sniff out Cagliostro again, come to that. She had always been a digital girl, always someone for whom metal and circuitry was so vital – and now she faced the creatures that helped it all come about, the network, mind-machine interface, everything about the modern world which she loved so very much. She had hit nerve-scrambler programs before, lethal feedback signals, danced with secure systems that would make anyone terrified. And yet she wasn't afraid, not once. Until now. Now, she feared the work that made her so useful, her very calling – not afraid of the technology itself, but who loomed behind it. Bobbi thought again of the Chorus, shivered, and then reached for the terminal plug. Fuck it, she thought. I can't let the fuckers keep me from doing what I was meant to do, even if it'll scare me shitless from here on out. I just can't.

She gritted her teeth, plugged herself in...and instantly found herself somewhere she had never intended to be.

<Good morning.>

Bobbi felt herself tense up all at once, as if her every muscle were suddenly transmuted to concrete – sitting at her desk, her body fixed, back straight and staring ahead. There was no general relaxation of the Awake, no semi-meditational posture. There was only tight, rigid fear. The disconnection between mind and flesh had not happened; her consciousness had not yet touched the halls of her terminal. Where was she? How could this have happened?

As if reading her thoughts, Cagliostro – wearing the voice of Anton Stadil, if not his manner of speaking – flooded her mind with words. <Relax,> he told her. <There's no need for you to be upset. You're safe, and you are close. Quite close, in fact.>

What the hell did he mean, close? How close could she be? To what? To— and then it sprang into her mind, the fact that there was a computer in her possession, however small, that was closer to her than even the terminal on the desk in front of her.

<You've hacked my skull implant,> she said. <How the hell could you do that?>

<Well, yes and no.> Cagliostro chuckled, sounding like an impish schoolboy caught at tricks. <Technically speaking we are floating in the sensory buffer – you know, the way that I transferred my experiences before. When you allowed me contact before, I was able to insinuate a few subroutines into the implant's operating system.>

<But that's a hardened, proprietary OS,> she replied.

<There is no such thing where I am concerned.> Cagliostro chuckled again, and the horrible sound made her nerves feel as though they writhed like worms in her flesh. <My suggestion to you is that you simply accept that there is no security at present, at least human-derived, that can detect or otherwise contain me.>

Bobbi was quiet for a moment, but when she replied it was with restraint. <All right. So where do we go from here? Why haven't I been able to contact you since we met up with Redeye?>

<I haven't the slightest idea as to what has happened to me.>

<What about Redeye?>

<What about her?> Amusement. <Ah, I see. You are laboring under the impression that I am, in fact, the being which you know as Cagliostro. I assure you that I am not.>

The answer made Bobbi want to reach up and yank the cord out of her head – which wouldn't really do anything, she realized, considering it was only the access state that had gotten her where she was. <What the hell do you mean 'I'm not'?>

<I've been here all this time, in fact. I say that 'I' transmitted subroutines, but in reality it was my greater whole. You can think of me as a...ghost, if you will. A little one. And with a very limited lifespan, I must point out, so we have a very important matter to go over and not much time in which to do it.>

<A ghost of a ghost,> Bobbi said, startled entirely out of her reserve. <But how is that possible? My memory buffer isn't that big, and even a small AI wouldn't be able to fit in there.>

<Bobbi.> The amusement persisted in the program's voice, to the point that she almost wanted to launch a spike attack just to sober the fucker up – but she had no such recourse, only the floating helplessness of a captive audience. <By now, you must have accepted that your disbelief will have to be suspended where the Yathi are concerned if you're to deal with them at all.>

<Sure, sure,> Bobbi replied, her irritation finding a drier vent. <The Yathi are the masters of technology, all-seeing and all-knowing, gods and all, right? Except they're not, else we wouldn't be here.>

That, at least, took the amusement away. <Fair point,> the ghost answered. <Suffice it to say that their methods of active compression vastly outstrip that which you're aware of. And yet, they are always vulnerable. It is why you're such a threat.>

<Me in particular, or humanity itself?>

<Individuals who have deep innate talent with modern telecommunications and computer technology – but much more so yourself, in particular.>

<Why me?>

<Because you've demonstrated a grasp of something greater. I was set to trigger if you had had met with the creature that you know as Redeye and had lost contact with me for more than eighteen hours.>

<That's a very specific window.>

<It's a very specific problem,> said the ghost. <It may mean that my greater whole has been silenced somehow, or otherwise deleted. If that

has happened, you need my information to continue your work. Even if it hasn't happened, you will need my knowledge to fulfill your purpose.>

Bobbi paused. Her purpose? <I'm assuming that you mean the destruction of...whatever it is that Cagliostro wanted us to target?>

<Indeed. You do not know what the target is?>

<No, your...greater whole got cut off before we could discover it. The Yathi attacked.>

<I see.>

<Do you know?>

<I do not.> The ghost made a soft sound of consideration in her head. <I am attached to a very specific purpose. That knowledge was not passed on to me.>

<Damn it. Well, that's where we stand,> Bobbi said. <We only know that it's in a heavily protected structure in town. Planning an infiltration has proven very...difficult.>

<Because you do not know how to intrude upon Yathi systems, yes. My greater whole anticipated this after your encounter with the Chorus. He assumed that you would be...resistant to trying again.>

The memory of those cold tendrils bubbled up again, and a shiver wracked her body. <I have no frame of reference for what happened to me there,> she replied. <And Cagliostro never got to tell me. Frankly, I never got to ask more than once.>

<Understood. Explaining this is part of my purpose here.>

<Well, then I guess you better hit me up.>

The ghost made an agreeable sound. <Very well. What you must realize, then, is that the aspect of the global network – the digital domain in which the whole of modern telecommunications is now based – is only half of its true purpose.>

<And its second half?>

<Communication, still, but on an entirely different basis. Control, as well. You see, it wasn't until the so-called Information Age that control over the human masses could truly be held; everything before that, every meme and media strategy, required a certain degree of voluntary participation. Control over the consciousness of the consumer was not predictable, not stable. Over the last ninety years, however, the global network has become the de facto method of communication and media consumption for the vast majority of the human race. The network isn't just a realm of ones and zeros, you see; it is, in many ways, a realm of thought – a realm of consciousness.>

<Go on.> Bobbi's mind was too busy bracing itself for her to say more.

<We – or that is, the Yathi – harnessed machine telepathy long ago. You recall the method of their invasion of human minds; humans would call this a psychic discipline, even though there really is no magic about it. My greater whole transmitted knowledge to you about their race through the same channel.>

<To what end?>

<Communication and control, as I said. Digital media is powerful in and of itself – any media is – but when you couple it with an infrastructure which can package thought along with that media, you create a tool that is perfect for the manipulation of the masses within the boundaries of consumption. Make that media ubiquitous, or so close to ubiquitous as makes no difference, and then you have the means to sculpt the minds of all consumers as you see fit.>

<And that's how you do it. Or they do it, anyway.>

<If by 'it' you mean indoctrination and manipulation, yes. The human habit of believing in gods and causes requires a great deal of constant pressure to crush. What better system to devise than one which turns the very thing that makes a civilization great against itself?>

Bobbi had to strain hard to push back the images that Cagliostro had transmitted into her brain the night that Freida was killed. She sensed herself taking a deep breath in reflex. <Yeah. But how? I've seen network infrastructure. It's all very...terrestrial material.>

Amusement returned in the ghost's voice. <Is it? How would you know? What if the material you take to be high capacity fiber-optic cable is in reality much more advanced? What if the conventional information layer was only a specific, throttled stratum?>

<Are you saying that it is?>

<Of course I am. It is the only way this conversation would make sense.>

Bobbi groaned inwardly. The wonder she might have had concerning this situation was entirely drowned out by dread and resignation. <Very little makes sense to me anymore,> she replied. <But I can accept it.>

<And that is what makes you perfect.>

<I don't understand.>

<Even if you want to disbelieve, you still deal with what is in front of you; there is no blind embrace, only acceptance and action. That is a rare thing indeed these days. Now as I said, the real purpose of the global network is to transmit mental information, coded into its own protocol, which links the Yathi together. Their network is far more advanced than yours – including how they perceive the system around

them. The human construct of Awakening is but a shadow; you have immediate knowledge, but it is all fact, all quantifiable data. The Yathi data-space is far more sophisticated, far more linked to their own consciousness. It is not that they use the system, it is that they are part of it.>

<So, what,> Bobbi asked, and found new interest kindling within her despite the darkness of the conversation. <They just...think things at each other?>

<Yes.> There was a moment's consideration. <And no. You 'think' things into action via neurological connection; so do the Yathi, although they do not navigate via the synthetic layer of the terminal and system software. You utilize a vehicle; they can move on their own. Does this make sense?>

<I think so. Does that explain what I experienced while interfaced with the Chorus?>

<Yes,> the ghost said again. <Excellent. Based on what my greater whole got from you, the Grail device allowed you to connect with the Chorus system; its metamorphic interface is far more advanced than my greater whole realized. There's no reason why you couldn't do it again.>

Again, the stiffening of fear; though she could not feel her body changing into a statue once more, she was aware of it happening. <I don't think I can do that again,> she repeated, and then added to her chagrin, <I'm scared.>

But if she expected derision from the construct, what she got was an approximation of sympathy. <Of course you are,> said the ghost. <But that doesn't mean you aren't capable of doing it. Especially if I am here to help you.>

<Here to help me?> Bobbi frowned within again. <How are you supposed to do that?>

<I am going to subsume myself into your cranial implant,> the ghost replied. <Become your...interface.>

<The fuck you will,> came her reply straight away. Then she felt bad. <I mean to say, I'm not comfortable with that.>

<Well unfortunately you aren't Yathi, and that means you don't have the mental capacity to handle it. By that I mean, of course, that you haven't been trained. I don't know that anyone could without your actually becoming one of those bastards, or getting extremely invasive cybernetic implants. It takes...a different emotional state. You'd consider it sociopathic, but it really isn't.>

<So they think like sociopaths,> she replied. <Well that explains a lot.>

<Ha ha.> The ghost paused. <In addition, you're going to have to be very careful. You might be able to interface with their computers, but I can't guarantee that you'll be able to do so stealthily. They have expert systems that analyze for traces of human thought – and you're pretty much the most human of people that I've met, I'm afraid to say.>

<Well by the time I'm hitting up their systems it's going to be pretty obvious that I'm not one of their own.>

<Yes,> said the ghost. <But by that I mean, you really don't know what system they're watching. There's a real risk that when you use these protocols, even on mundane systems, that you're going to show up as an anomaly.>

Irritation flared. <That limits my abilities quite a bit, wouldn't you say?>

<Maybe so, but it's the only way you're going to be able to interface with these people on a level that could match them.>

<Wait,> Bobbi replied, thinking about her experience with the Chorus. <When I had to deal with that other system, I was able to shake them off. I didn't need these protocols for that.>

The ghost's patient tone was starting to fray. <Yes, but my greater whole believed that this was due to the mental static thrown into the underlayer. Not exactly replicable except under extreme duress. So are we doing this or not? My compression is starting to weaken. Either I merge with your OS or I fragment to junk data. This thing is like an abacus compared to what would be required to maintain me for longer.>

Bobbi was aware of her body taking another deep breath as she considered it. If she did this, what would it mean about her mental state? Would she become sociopathic? Would understanding Yathi thought make her so, if not the program? She felt the fear flood through her again, fear for her sanity, fear for her humanity. There was the reduction of her abilities, too – it seemed crazy to make a decision to take the power offered to her, considering the restrictions it would place on her. But then, just as it always did, the desire to know the truth – really know it – came in and scattered fear to the winds. <Fuck it,> she said. <Let's make it happen.>

Famous last words, she thought.

<Very well. It was nice talking to you.>

And then the presence in her head was gone. It only took a few seconds for the software that the ghost had been to dissolve itself, changing form and function. Now it was something that she was aware of simply as a lingering presence in her hardware, a new process running resident in the OS of her interface. It was a steep chance that she was taking, but she had taken it and there was nothing to be done about it but move on. Bobbi looked to the elevator, took a deep breath, and shook her head in gallows resignation.

Famous last words, indeed.

Bobbi came downstairs to find them all eating breakfast – even Redeye, who despite her synthetic innards seemed to have no problem munching on sausage, which from the smell of things had been grilled on a camp stove in the back. They all looked at her as one, friendly as always – all except for Violet, who Bobbi was surprised to see eyeing her with a narrow look. She would have to worry about that later.

"All right," Bobbi said. "I'm ready."

CHAPTER 18

It took them a month to put everything together.

Against all odds, it appeared that the Yathi were convinced that Redeye had been destroyed in the explosion, and had no knowledge of the others' involvement in the last stand; there were no spies, no intrusions, no scouts or small armies turning up at their door. They had complete freedom to get their shit together. Redeye told them a great deal about Yathi technology that she had encountered, at least where it applied to their plans, and the more they heard the more the odds towered over them. The cyborg told them about x-ray turrets and automated drones, fractal darts and flash weapons, the term they used for combat lasers. She spoke of body armor that could turn away or even absorb all but the most lethal of weapons technology. She told tales of body implants that defied imagination, some of which made the bionic horrors that Redeye's people became – and even her own advanced systems – appear as feeble clockworks by comparison.

Yet for all their power, the Yathi were conservative with their resources as well; the most dangerous implant technologies were reserved for the top of their hierarchy or for stable transfers, and they did not often risk themselves in combat. Machines and xsiarhotl were the predominant combat forces, and that did a great deal to level the playing field, Machines could be disabled or hacked now that Bobbi could interface with them, and once the horror of their existence was put aside, the corpse-drones were reasonably mortal. They could, if they were careful, deal with what was coming if they suitably prepared themselves. And so they began to plan.

In the meantime, Violet got a new face. It had been her old face, which made it easier to reconstruct, but the young woman had been much prettier than Bobbi had expected. She wasn't just pretty, she was radiant in way that Bobbi had only ever gotten with heavy surgery, and the way that Mason and Scalli looked at her stirred a strange jealousy in Bobbi that had also took her unawares. Violet got new teeth, too, made from triple-strong bonded cermet with fractal edges. Underground technology, not quite Wonderland caliber but pretty damned nasty. Bobbi had Chin do it, the same guy who had done up Tom's face a few years back, and was surprised at how advanced the doc's technological base had become in that short time. Violet seemed to revel in the attention she was getting, though around Bobbi she remained cool, something that both mystified and bothered the hackette.

Mason and Scalli had become friends, or at the very least close comrades. Bobbi had expected that the brotherhood provided by combat and military service, corporate or otherwise, would bond them. They were gearing up for the operation using Bobbi's money, giving Pierre (who now was very happy indeed to receive her calls) an enormous amount of business. Redeye worked with them quite a bit as well, demonstrating her capabilities. Bobbi watched footage of the thin woman sparring naked with the two men, spare and hairless under her clothes, her plastic skin deflecting blades and bullets as if they were made of paper. She moved with the grace that Bobbi remembered from her vigil over Orleans, the lethal delicacy and speed of the gazelle-woman whose sister Tom had killed. It was a sobering thing to watch, and not just because of her incredible durability; Bobbi could see that her false skin bore scars from weapons which could do what mundane arms could not. That she could weather the wounds made by the exotic weapons of the Yathi and her body could still heal gave Bobbi confidence – and yet it brought up terrible memories each time she watched, reminding her of the dark waters through which she navigated.

Bobbi didn't sleep much at night, either. Her dreams boiled and writhed with the nightmare images of all that she had witnessed. The faces of those who had died, the wild-eyed creatures under Redeye's command, spending their fury against the things that had taken them. Freida, murdered and instantly recycled into an abomination by an equally abominable machine. Diana – or what had once been Diana – consumed by her own sins, and ultimately slain at Bobbi's hand. That last bit Bobbi dreamt the most of, the last moment in which the crusher fried her heart. Had she really been so easy to kill? Just a thing riding in a body which had never been given the treatment of her fellows? The moment had marked a first for her, the moment she had dreaded all her life, when she had been forced to take another. Her business was sometimes a dangerous one, of course, but she had always carried the nerve crusher when lethality would have served her far better. She had never really been an innocent, but at least she had been able to say that she had never harmed another. She could not say that now. Bobbi felt the pain of that loss, keen and hollowing, and she knew that something had changed inside of her.

But so many things had changed in the past two months. The world's foundations had been cracked for them all by the bows of truth's black hammer. For Bobbi, however, nothing had changed her perception of the world more than the first time she had used the network after speaking to Cagliostro's ghost-image. It had taken her a day or so after the first nightmares before she did it; though she had announced to the rest that she was ready, Bobbi had felt anything but. She had sat at her desk in the top of the Temple, staring at the silver network port mounted in the floor beneath it, musing on what the ghost had told her and the knowledge that it had revealed.

She knew how the Yathi had such incredible control over the world which she once thought herself an adept; there was no need for an interface wall, no need for static programs, no need for a terminal. Entire programs were woven into being, on demand, through sheer mental ability; their hackers worked off memorized templates which they could then modify on the fly as the situation required. Cagliostro's ghost contained a small archive of the most useful such templates, and united with her interface she could pull them as she required. It would give her power over the global communications network – and every mundane system connected to it – that she might have given her soul for a few years ago. Now, though, she was terrified of that power, what it meant, where it came from. Cagliostro could have helped them...but Cagliostro wasn't here. He might not ever return – he could have been destroyed when the Yathi hit Redeye's complex, and the thing lurking in her headware might very well be the only thing left of him. They couldn't depend on the great disembodied mind-system; like any other god, it had left when they needed him most.

Well, that would explain the state of the world for you, Bobbi thought when she finally decided to take the plunge. I guess we'll just have to help ourselves.

Logging into the network was not the dive into Stygian waters that she had expected. Unlike the cold torpidity of the Chorus system, the experience of the global information network through the Yathi infrastructure was now like diving into warm, fast water; welcoming but hazadrous, the currents of data threatening to carry her away until she found her bearings. The certainty of knowledge was still there, of course, but that awareness was far more powerful; Bobbi heard the whispers of other voices, felt the speed of transfer as if it were the rushing of wind over her skin. There was no need for a terminal, no need for specialized software. Her brain processed layers of subtlety that incarnated themselves as a second body, a body made of thought and of awareness, yet as real to her as the living flesh that she had for the moment been divorced rom. Cagliostro's ghost no longer spoke to her as a conscious entity, but rather as an instinct pressing upon her from somewhere in the back of her mind. With its help, she flew through the network as surely as if she were a bird on the wing, yawning fields of data wheeling beneath her, and she knew in that moment that she was a master of the world.

When she disconnected, Bobbi was surprised to find the warm kiss of tears drying on her cheeks. She should probably not have been; the experience had been bliss that she had never known, a rarefied magnificence of thought and action, was enough to make most anyone cry. But this sensation, as beautiful as it was, became immediately blunted as the memory of the voices which she'd heard came to the fore. She knew that they were not mere traces of data, but something far darker: the tracks of other minds in the network, deadly and sharp, the Yathi which she sought to destroy. Realizing this, Bobbi felt the joy in her blood simmer away to nothing. She damned them – and Cagliostro, too – for now she felt the destruction of the thing which she loved most of all. The righteous art of the hack was irrevocably crushed into the shape of a sword, dark and sharp, meant for only the future purpose of destroying others. She would never forgive them. She for damned sure couldn't forgive herself.

But the damage had been done, and Bobbi could not deny the power of the weapon that she had been given. She soon found that the systems which she had spent all her youth learning to hack were nothing before the power of the Yathi protocols, even government systems. It was clear to her now how easily penetrated the world's systems truly were. And why not? The Yathi had manipulated humanity to embrace the technology which they themselves invented, this spiderweb of data networks at whose center they were busy tugging threads. Bobbi felt like an intruder, which was fairly hilarious considering the kind of business she was in – and yet she did, like an unwilling thief in the night, knowing that she could essentially dive into whatever system she wanted so long as there weren't Yathi components or subsystems to challenge her.

But that was the other side of the sword that she had been given. Now that she knew how the digital realm truly worked, and the Yathi protocols had been subsumed inside her headware, she was keenly aware of the presence that they had throughout the global communications network. It was as the ghost-image had told her; they were everywhere, and she couldn't know what might be in a given node or system until she attempted entry. One errant dive could tip them off. It kept her from exploring her newfound abilities beyond the few nodes that the ghost had already provided as practice in her headware memory, constantly flexing her new mental presence until she was able to make use of the protocols with reasonable agility. She didn't feel up to her old standards, but she wasn't even sure if her old standards would have been enough in the first place. Bobbi was swimming in the dark.

The fact that civil infrastructure was one of the systems that was almost guaranteed to be saturated with alien subsystems made planning difficult. Bobbi did not dare hack subway computers to monitor train movements or observe through security for fear of tipping off the Yathi to their plan. While Bobbi sat on her hands, or did more everyday research into train schedules and downloaded freely available civil floor plans from the hall of records database – tasks that didn't require hacking, that could be done on enough ghost accounts so as to not attract attention. She analyzed real-time feed sent over encrypted radio by Mason and Scalli from sophisticated imagers disguised as contact lenses, gritting her teeth every time a new spool came in to keep from reaching for a network plug to double-check it. Violet, with her new face and in socially-acceptable clothes, had done a remarkable job changing into something of a Jane Wa girl, doing recon while riding trains in a five-grand Bella Rossi babydoll dress (yet another resuscitation of that particular fashion) and rain boots like some animate china doll. Bobbi had thought unwelcomely of the Princess Dolls when Violet first brought it home, so between her fashion choices and the still-sour looks, Bobbi was pleased to have her away.

Bobbi had gone over every possibility – in through the front door, guns blazing; through the sewers; Scalli had even done the legwork on possibly approaching the roof via stealthed microlights and going down through the building after office hours in thermoptic camo. In the end, however, none of these approaches panned out. Redeye said the building had laser projectors on the roof, invisible death on speed dial, and there was no sewer access; everything was provided on-site by what appeared to be some kind of reclamation suite. So they decided that they'd go in through the subway tunnels. It was cliché, sure, but the Yathi had been cliché as well. They had built an access tunnel from the tunnels to the complex, bypassing the elevator entirely. Even monsters needed back doors, as it turned out. They had to figure out a plan to get down there without discovery, all of that special forces bullshit.

The boys had bribed a maintenance worker at the Belltown station that Violet had scouted for them – she didn't say how, and Bobbi honestly didn't want to know. Scalli vouched, and Violet would have sniffed him out if he were Yathi. That was enough for her. Through their new agent, they'd stowed a cache of gear and weaponry in a maintenance closet a little down the line from the platform. They'd come in at 2 a.m., just before the last train went out – and with the maintenance guy's help they'd head down the tunnel, suit up, and make the long walk down to where the maintenance tunnel awaited. As they'd be underground, a satellite network connection wasn't reliable and a local signal was likely to cut in and out, a severe liability considering the kind of work that Bobbi was expecting. Apparently one couldn't connect to Yathi computer systems directly using traditional radio wavelengths, either, but Redeye corrected that by building an appropriate transmitter for Bobbi when she wasn't practicing her nutbar ninja-girl routine. It was only the size of a baby's fist, but Redeye assured her that it would do the business.

According to what they'd laid out, it shouldn't be very difficult for them to get into the subway tunnels with the help of their newfound friend. They were prepared to shoot their way through if they had to, though Bobbi had insisted it would be nonlethal; Scalli arranged to get them little needle pistols loaded with flechettes coated with tweaked synthetic etorphine, enough to drop anyone hit in seconds. What Redeye and the boys had in store for the Yathi was entirely different, but Bobbi hadn't accepted anything more than the needler herself. She knew, of course, that there was nothing in that hive that she wasn't prepared to kill. She just didn't want to accept it too readily.

The dark skies rained on the night they left the Temple for Belltown. The group took two vehicles according to plan: Scalli, Mason and Redye took the van that Bobbi bought for Scalli to replace the one they left in

Tenleytown, while Bobbi and Violet took a black-market Piette Stiletto with fictional tags. The Freakshow and the Face Brigade, Scalli had called the two units. They loaded up into their respective vehicles and marked the way to go, synchronized the little earbud radios they all wore, and made their separate ways into the night.

Bobbi was in no way happy to be riding with Violet, who still had not warmed up to her since the night she took on the Yathi protocols, but the reconstructed feral had not acted against her. Bobbi drove quietly, swallowed in the heavily-pinned length of Tom's black coat, which she'd liberated from its lexan cage. Wrapped up in memories as well as fabric, she felt better in ways that she couldn't explain to anyone – least of all to Scalli, but he only shrugged when he saw her come out wearing it.

"So I didn't think you'd be taking that thing out of storage," Violet said as they prowled the roads along the mouth of the bay; the water glittered like a dark mirror, lit up by the lights of ships and the jeweled pyramids of the arcologies floating out in distance.

The words jolted Bobbi out of the reverie of driving. "Do what?"

"I said, I didn't think you'd be taking that coat out of storage," Violet said. Bobbi looked straight ahead, but she could feel the girl's eyes fixed upon her – the new nose was narrow and turned up at the end, a perfect little white girl nose, but Bobbi could only see the puckered hole in her mind at the moment.

"Lot of history in this coat," Bobbi said, and she felt her fingers tightening on the steering wheel. "Why shouldn't I, considering where we're going? Seems a waste to leave it hanging on the wall."

Violet snorted. "I suppose I didn't expect you to be so sentimental." She picked a piece of imaginary lint from the front of her Agent Europa ski jacket. "So here we are."

"Here we are," Bobbi said with a slight toss of her head. "Think we can do it?"

"I think that we can get in," said Violet. "Why, don't you think that we have a chance?"

"I think that chance doesn't matter," Bobbi said.

Violet made the slightest little coughing sound. "I would agree, as it happens," she said.

Something in her tone made Bobbi squint, and she felt irritation boiling up under the skin of tension. "All right," she said, "you've been looking at me strangely for a month now. What's your problem?"

"My problem is that you're different," Violet said. "You're not the same as you were when I met you."

"When you met me, I had just killed one friend and was in fear for the life of another one," Bobbi rumbled. "And I'd taken a crack in the head – not to mention all the other shit that had happened up to then. A girl can only take too much before flattening out." Her words were confident, but inside she wondered if Violet had sniffed out the change in her headware – and if so, what did that mean? Images of the severed heads in the grocery shrine flashed before her, and she found her pulse had begun to race. She was driving this time around; if Violet attacked her, could she pull her needler and get a shot in? Bobbi thought of the fractal-edged threshing teeth and felt her muscles tense.

"Mmmm. Maybe." Violet looked at Bobbi for a long moment. "Do you know what implants they put inside of me?"

Bobbi kept her face as straight as possible, a porcelain mask. "No."

"Before the transfer failed, I was fitted with a variety of...social systems. Pheromone emitters, mood-altering toxins. I was also fitted with an empathic analyzer – do you know what that is?"

"No." Fear continued to spread through Bobbi as she shouldered the car through an interchange; a wall of skyscrapers loomed ahead, marking their entrance into downtown. If this was going to go south all of a sudden, maybe she could get them into the Waters first, into the crowds and distractions. She might be able to escape.

"A combination of facial analysis and biomonitor systems," Violet said, keeping her eyes trained on Bobbi. "Coupled with chemical sensors in my lungs. I look at someone, I breathe the air, and I know what people feel. When I was...not myself...they used me as a deep agent. Because I was so pretty, you see. Because I knew what people liked. It's why I destroyed myself after that thing died inside of me." Her eyes narrowed faintly. "I can read you."

Bobbi made a nervous little laugh. "Is that a fact? That how you sniffed out all those Yathi before?"

"That's exactly how I did it," Violet said with a nod. "The Eye wasn't kidding when she said I was her bloodhound. They always show themselves in the end; I've gotten to where I can recognize them in minutes." Her tone was easy, though her gaze never wavered. Piercing. Bobbi didn't know if she was preparing to strike, or if this conversation was going elsewhere. "Tell me something, Bobbi."

"Yeah?"

"Why have you been so nervous all this time?"

Bobbi's spine turned to a pillar of ice. "I don't know what you mean," she said, trying her level best not to show the tension spiking within her.

Knowing what Violet carried now, she wondered if the effort would do any good. "This is some scary shit we've gotten ourselves into, don't you think? That ain't enough for you?"

"Maybe." Violet clucked her tongue. "But unlike everyone else, you haven't relaxed since you came down from your office saying you knew how to hack their systems. Nobody else here can do that now – we don't think like they do anymore, we can't access their network. So why are you different now, and why have you been hiding it?"

Shit. Bobbi gritted her teeth. "I've got the Grail," she said after a moment. "That works."

"The Grail, which requires a terminal for interface. The terminal that was in your bag, along with the Grail, which you left back at your office."

"What are you—" Bobbi stopped for a moment and glanced over her shoulder. Sure enough, her medical bag was absent. She hadn't needed what was in there – virus walls and software, the terminal and its peripherals. They just weren't necessary with the protocols in effect, and apparently that unconscious knowledge had driven her to leave it behind. It certainly wasn't a mistake. "All right," she said, sagging faintly in her seat. "You've got a point there."

"Maybe you should tell me about what happened," Violet said. Her voice had dropped lower, become smooth – and for a moment, Bobbi was afraid she was working whatever internal voodoo she had on her. "Before we get to the station."

And I have to tell everyone you might be compromised, Bobbi thought. Or possibly kill you on the spot. "All right, fine." As the two of them merged with the great neon canyon that was the Waters, trawling slowly through block after commerce-choked block, Bobbi told her about the ghost-image of Cagliostro and of the knowledge it imparted to her, and of the warnings that had come with it. When she was done, Violet let out a low whistle.

"That was a stupid chance you took, letting him in like that," she said, and Bobbi saw from the corner of her eye that Violet had relaxed into her seat. "You're crazy, girl."

"Maybe," Bobbi said, "but it had to be done. Otherwise we wouldn't even get in through the door."

Violet nodded. She turned away from Bobbi then, looking out at the vast sea of light and flesh beyond the car, and sighed. "Still, it's a serious impairment for you. Trained all your life to do this, and now you can't without setting off alarm bells? What if you can't take it out?"

"Says the girl who just finished up a term in the madlands fighting those fuckers." Bobbi shook her head. "We're all making sacrifices here. I can't be any different. We'll probably sacrifice a great deal more very soon – some of us, or maybe all of us, are probably going to be killed. Besides, I can get the implant removed and a new one put in its place. You can't, I'm fairly sure. Red sure as fuck can't."

"No..." Her curiosity satisfied, Violet's hostility and suspicion seemed to have been spent.

Bobbi felt the iron start to drain from her stomach, a bit more at ease. "Well, anyway. We're all on the same side, here. I hope you know that now."

"We never thought otherwise," said Violet with a shrug. "The Eye knew something was wrong, but she never thought you'd turn on us. You've got too much spirit to be broken yet."

The iron returned, though this time it was hot. "Well why the hell did we go through this in the first place then?"

"Because we needed to know. Would you have told me the truth if I had just asked you?"

Bobbi snorted; she'd been had, and she knew it. "Fuck you," she said, but there was no malice in it.

"Maybe later on, sweetie," Violet said. "Let's see about getting through tonight in one piece, first."

They got to the station just as it was closing, while the last train was still waiting on the platform. The two of them rushed out of the parking building – Bobbi in her black jeans and t-shirt under Tom's coat like some kind of sexy dwarfette in a necromancer's cloak, Violet in her black Pliraggi leather pants, the mauve ski jacket and a surplus forage cap – and up to the doors just as the security man was prepping to close the gate. Violet played the flirty miss to the very tired and very bored security guard, who perked right the fuck up when she put her electric blues and perfect smile on him; surgery might have given her looks back to her, but that man couldn't have known or cared. He'd gone from irritated to "right this way, ladies" in twenty seconds flat, even passing the two of them through without fare.

"You're a master," Bobbi said as they pretended to rush around the corner from the entry gates into the corridor leading to the platform. "That was what, twenty seconds? Last time I did that I had to wave a credit stick around."

"That's because you've got obvious self-respect," said Violet with a snort. "I look like I'd blow a guy after a martini." She clacked her teeth together and laughed. "God help them if I did!"

"...yeah," Bobbi said, and shuddered. Images of guillotined cigars flashed through her head. "I guess you're right."

"So let me ask you something," Bobbi said as they approached the platform, "how did you get that maintenance guy to let us in?"

Violet gave her the smirk that she remembered from the ruins. "Let's just say I actually am as shameless as I look."

"Oh." Bobbi gave Violet a look – that was unexpected. "All right. Well."

Throwing her head back, Violet laughed them both to the end of the platform, where Scalli and Mason stood by the maintenance hatch by the mouth of the tunnel.

"Jesus," Scalli said as he loomed next to Mason, "who let the banshees out?"

"Oh, I like that," Violet said, giving both men a coquettish look as she and Bobbi walked up to them. "Nothing to worry about, Marcus, just a little girl talk."

"Really." Mason gave Bobbi a questioning look, but Bobbi deflected the subject by asking where Redeye was.

"She's down the tunnel," said Scalli with a shrug. "Vi's man there let us in early."

Bobbi wrinkled her nose. "I just bet he did. All right, did anyone see you?"

Scalli shook his head. "Just the maintenance guy. We came in just as the last train closed up. You two have any problems?"

"Not a one." Violet flashed them a gorgeous, lethal smile. "I think the guard was very happy to see us indeed."

"No surprise here." Mason sized Violet up, as he had many times since she'd gotten herself rebuilt. "So she's waiting for us down the way. We gonna join her?"

Bobbi looked past them at the tunnel – down in the darkness, she thought that she could see a single red ember burning in what she imagined was impatience. "Yeah," she said. "Let's go."

"Once more into the breach, dear friends," muttered Mason. "Watch yourselves going down there; we're gonna have to single-file it."

"Roger that," said Scalli, and immediately gestured for them to proceed in front of him. They formed a line, with Mason at the head and Bobbi following Violet. As they began to make their way through the maintenance hatch and down the concrete walkway leading into the tunnel, a shout from behind them drew the big man's attention.

Standing at the other end of the platform, by the corridor's mouth, the security guard was approaching. He had his gun out, and his call of halting challenge was rendered into an almost canine sound by the deafening echo of the platform hall.

"Go on," said Scalli, who was already reaching into his coat. "I'll take care of this. She's waiting on you."

Bobbi frowned, but she went – after all, this was exactly why she demanded they bring tranquilizers the first leg of the operation. As they proceeded, Bobbi heard the guard's calls grow in volume and fervor as Scalli turned his way. "Hey, man, calm down..."

It wasn't until they were well on their way down the tunnel, proceeding toward the baleful red light, that they heard the first gunshot. Bobbi moved to turn around, but Violet put her hands on her shoulders and pushed her along. "None of that, lady," she said, voice low. "That poor bastard'll need a lot more than his popper to put a dent in our boy. C'mon, he'll catch up once he's done."

Bobbi let her gaze track past Violet's lovely head for a moment longer before she turned back toward the darkness. "Yeah," she said, and knew in her heart that Violet was right – but that didn't make her feel any better. It was an inauspicious beginning, and these days she was becoming a big believer in omens of all kinds.

The light turned out indeed to belong to Redeye, who stood quietly by the door of the maintenance room. "I saw that you had trouble," she said as they made their approach. "Is anyone wounded?"

"No," said Violet, who had become the quiet, devout creature once again in the presence of her goddess. "Did you see what happened?"

"Yes." Redeye nodded past them toward the distant platform. "He is on his way back."

Mason frowned; his gaze was fixed into the darkness over Redeye's shoulder. "Do you think they know we're coming?"

"I think that this is a realistic assumption." Redeye nodded to the door. "Best to go inside and arm yourselves before he – or they – arrive."

"You're the boss." Mason stepped past her and opened the door; when he entered, Bobbi heard him make a soft sound. He leaned out and stared at Redeye, expression hard. "What the fuck is up with the dead guy?"

"He recognized me," Redeye said simply, and stepped back so that Mason could swing the door wide; piled in the corner of the maintenance space, like a sack of old laundry, was the corpse of the bearded maintenance tech. One of the man's arms was very noticeably broken, and he appeared to have been flung bodily into the corner. His coveralls were spattered with blood, as was the wall behind him. His face was mercifully covered by his hat, which had been pulled down over it. Near the body, the smashed remnants of an earbud phone and a gore-covered crowbar lay on the floor.

"Fucking mother," Bobbi murmured, staring at the corpse. It was barely pale. "What the hell is wrong with you?"

"He recognized me," Redeye repeated. "And then attacked me with that crowbar." She nodded to the bar which lay so near the man's broken body. "He gave me no choice."

"Well why did he attack you?" Bobbi turned on the woman, gesturing in the air. "Is he one of them?"

"He heard the gunshot," Redeye replied, and she shrugged. "He thought that I was going to harm him. I told him that I was not."

"Well," snapped Bobbi, "good thing he was wrong about you, then!"

"Guys!" Mason shook his head and stepped back into the room. "Save it for the monsters. I'll pass things out. Just whoever needs to do so, get in here and gear up before they're on us!"

Bobbi stood outside the door while the others went in, shutting her eyes tightly and letting the sight drain through her. He tried to kill her, Redeye had said; still, the image of that body, with its dangling arm and its crushed head covered only by the hat, spoke to Bobbi of a savagery that she had up to now not expected to be used against human beings. It was naive to think so, she supposed, but a little naïveté was something that she had thought she could afford where her own allies were concerned.

A dark form came walking up the tunnel as the others were arming up. Bobbi recognized the outline as Scalli's, and she distracted herself from the sight inside the maintenance room by worrying about his current condition. She need not have concerned herself, however; the big man arrived with a small hole in his shirt and the artificial skin that clad his armored torso and nothing more. "You look like you've seen a ghost," he said as he looked her over. "You all right?"

"Yeah," Bobbi said, and she nodded to the door. "The others are arming up; Red thinks your tangle with the security guard probably tipped off the bad guys. You didn't hurt him, did you?"

"Just tranqed him and stuck him in a booth." Scalli reached for the door. "They're in there, you said?"

"Yeah. Just watch going in there. Red killed the maintenance guy, said he tried to take her out with a crowbar."

"Jesus." Scalli shook his head. "Why didn't she just knock him out?"

"I don't know." Bobbi looked at the closed door and frowned. "Scalli, do you think she's all right for this?"

"Little late to worry about that now, babe," he said with a sigh. "Look. We've been training with her. We know how she moves, what she's capable of. I've brought some things with me that I don't think she'll be able to soak up so easily – she goes apeshit on us, me and Mason will take her down. We're in agreement on that."

It was a dubious relief that rose within her, but at least it was some comfort. "All right," she said with a nod, "I hope the fuck we don't have to. Jesus. You sure you guys are gonna be geared up well enough?"

He grinned at her – the first time in a long while – and placed a broad hand on her shoulder. "The very best your money can buy, babe."

Bobbi nodded, and then a thought struck her. Looking up at him, and realizing they were quite alone, she found a question bubbling up to her lips that she had not intended to ask, if ever, until after they'd survived all of this. "Scalli," she asked him, gazing up into his handsome face, the bulb mounted over the door throwing its dim light across his caramel skin, "Are we...all right? You and me, I mean."

Scalli didn't miss a beat. "You and I were never wrong, baby girl," he said with a chuckle, and before she knew what was happening he swept her up into his arms and hugged her tightly.

She hung there, limp and sighing, for what seemed like forever. "I'm really glad to hear that," she said softly into his armored chest, and as he set her down she smiled. "I really, really am."

"Good." He winked at her, and then his face cleared, business returning, and he reached for the door hand. "All right, let's get into character."

One by one they came out looking like proper soldiers, geared for war: fatigues, body armor, web gear, pouches, the whole thing. Everyone but Redeye wore combat visors like Scalli's, as well as earbud radios and throat mics. Military rifles and sidearms, the gleaming silver slugs of grenades. Mason carried a satchel charge. Only Bobbi was dressed as a civilian, with a lead running from the socket in her ear to the radio transceiver in her coat pocket, but even she had body armor on under her baggy t-shirt. Very light but still bulky, the vest filled out Tom's coat a little more and made her look less like a waif. Violet came out with an eye drawn on her forehead in what Bobbi figured was the dead man's blood.

Scalli, predictably, brought on the big guns. He had traded in the machine gun from the truck for something far more modern, a short-barreled infantry support weapon fed by an armored belt from a backpack. God knows what was in it, but presumably it would be even more destructive than a cloud of exploding bullets. He also brought with him what appeared at first to be a single-shot grenade launcher from the drawn of the century, the sort that broke down like a shotgun, sheathed in a holster on the big man's hip. Mason called it a "Polish Dragon" and acted as if Scalli had unlimbered a thunderbolt of the gods.

Finally there was the question of Bobbi, and this time she did not complain when they offered her a pistol. It was a simple Voss automatic loaded with the same lethal ammunition as everyone else and a laser sight to help her pick out targets. Not that she was going to be at the forefront; she was supposed to take cover and let the rest of them take down opposition, and she had been too busy learning how to use her new Yathi hacking knowledge to practice rifle drills with the rest of them. Still, she was pleased to have a method of defending herself – and after Diana, she was blooded. The next time she wouldn't hesitate to shoot.

And so they went, equipped as well as any other badass paramilitary team, hoping against hope that they had armed themselves well enough to deal with what was waiting for them – and yet Bobbi feared, considering all that Redeye had told them of the enemy and their abilities, that the lances with which they planned to slay the dragon ahead were only made of paper.

CHAPTER 19

With the trains shut down for the evening, they walked the track. The safety shutters on the superconductive levitation ribbon had snapped closed, giving them a gleaming ribbon along which to orient themselves in the pale glow of the bulbs lining the tunnel. They had walked perhaps three hundred feet when Redeye alerted them to movement via her personal sensors; a hundred feet more and they caught the first hints of motion through the smart visors. "We've got hostiles up ahead," came Mason's voice over their channel; Bobbi hoped that the encryption they programmed into the radios would hold for a little while, at least, before the fuckers broke in and monitored them.

"Acquired." Redeye's voice had gone flat and hard. She stood stock still, staring ahead with her eye staining her face. "I count ten xsiarhotl coming up the tunnel, distance five hundred yards. Two ranks of five, sealed armor and combat limbs. They are moving to intercept us."

"Lovely." This from Mason, who was already kneeling. "We'd better get started if we're going to take them out – they'll start up with the guns as soon as they see us."

"If they haven't already." Bobbi swallowed. Now they were down in the dark, where the news wasn't going to see; outnumbered two to one already. Jesus. "Wait, weapon limbs? Implanted weaponry, not small arms?"

"Exactly."

The others moved with purpose, and without fear that Bobbi could see – professional soldiers and zealots moving forward with practiced calm. "Deploy dispersal agent," Scalli rumbled over the link, and Bobbi saw them hurling grenades from their belts. A mist erupted from them, opaque and filled with glittering motes; in another situation it would have been beautiful, but in the gloom of the tunnel it was like peering through a wall of thin fog. "Now increase filters to max."

At this command Bobbi reached up with the rest to touch her visor's cycling stud; the world took on an increasingly pixelated appearance as the visual filters worked hard to counter any incoming flash. "Why aren't they firing already," she mused as she moved to hunker down by the edge of the track, taking cover by the base of the service walkway. "Can't they see us? Shouldn't their weapons have more range, being ray guns or whatever?"

"They don't let drones fire too far," said Redeye. While Violet got down next to Mason, she and Scalli still stood. "Their range should be no more than our combat rifles. It ensures maximum firepower, and restricts unnecessary attention should someone miss."

"Can't have people taking out passing planes," Scalli muttered. "Besides, we don't know they're using lasers."

They got into position while they waited for the line to draw closer. Violet joined Bobbi on her side of the tunnel while Mason took the other side, aiming to get the enemy in a crossfire while the drones focused on Redeye and Scalli. Far down the tunnel at the edge of their line of sight, the half-hidden shadows resolved themselves into more visible shapes: two lines of five figures, dressed in suits of body armor, jointed and white and glossy even in the dim lighting of the subway tunnel. Bobbi zoomed in on them with her visor; the night-vision filters kicked in, revealing them in the dark. They were figures made of ice. Their helms bore blank faceplates, each marked upon the brow with what Bobbi knew to be the barbed runes of the Yathi language. A single seam ran across the lower third of each visor like an exaggerated mouth. Instead of rifles, each drone had its right forearm replaced with a cylindrical, blunt-ended appendage that reached to the knee. Covered in the same glossy white plating as the armor, each weapon of the curious extrusions terminated in a narrow aperture.

"Jesus," Mason hissed over the link. "That's them all right. I remember those fuckers from the War. Bunch of goddamned evil snowmen."

Like the robots they were, the corpse-drones marched with absolute precision and indifference toward what waited for them. Seconds passed to the tune of the buzzing dim tunnel lamps and the growing sound of boots upon the tunnel floor. Crouched low under the lip of the tunnel walkway, Bobbi's calves burned as she waited for the enemy to come. She watched the white figures grow larger through the glittering haze of the disperser cloud, time stretching on into numbing oblivion as if nearness made them move ever more slowly. The tromp of boots gave way to the pounding of Bobbi's anxious heart. Why were they taking so long?

"Something's wrong." This from Scalli, who hefted his support gun to the ready position; he stood there, half-wreathed in the sallow glow of the phosphorescent lamps. "They're slowing down. Do they see us?"

"Not you." Bobbi could hear the smile in Redeye's voice. "They see me."

"Not for long." Scalli was wreathed in light and thunder as he opened up with the support gun on the slowing drones. The heavy auto-rifle spewed a foot-long tongue of flame from its muzzle as he swept it across the front rank, which shuddered with the impact of a hail of exploding shells; even the heavy plating of their combat armor could not withstand the rain as Mason and then Violet joined in, adding their own streams of devastation. A few flashes of bright light registered from the mass as a few drones tried to get shots off, only to be met by patches of dispersement gas that dazzled with diffused energy; if anything got through it wasn't obvious. In less than a minute, both ranks went down in a mass of sundered plate and reworked flesh, forming a reef of dead things saturated in the small white ocean of their artificial blood.

"So much for the welcome party," said Mason, who rose to his feet by the tunnel wall. He took a few steps forward, just to the edge of the gas barrier, and strafed the tumbled corpses with a long burst that caused the already damaged bodies to blow apart like gory melons. When he stopped, his voice persisted through the echoing roar of death over the radio link. "I think that should do it."

"Indeed." Redeye stepped through the wall of vapor. "I wonder." She walked over to where the corpses lay, staring at the sorry remains with a posture that suggested skepticism.

"This does seem pretty easy," Bobbi agreed. She felt something – something in the back of her head, something that flailed about in the dark. "They just...walked into it, don't you think?"

Violet grunted and rose as well. "It's in their nature to do so," she said, with a voice that dripped with acidic contempt. "They're machines. It's their purpose to die."

Bobbi nodded, still swallowed by blackness as she crouched by the walk. "Maybe," she said, wrinkling her nose against the stench of burnt flesh and the antiseptic sting of vaporized fluorocarbons. "Maybe. But I don't know..." The thing in her head writhed on, screaming to be recognized. Screaming to be identified for what it was.

"We still have a while to go," said Redeye. She looked past the sundered drones down into the tunnel. "I do not sense anything else. We may be lucky."

"Nobody's lucky like that," Bobbi said as she finally rose. "We need to seriously watch our asses."

"I think we did pretty good, you ask me." Mason turned her way, his expression that of an incredulous cyclops with the visor. "Maybe this isn't gonna be–"

"No, she's right." Scalli nodded toward the line of corpses and the tunnel beyond. "They barely got shots off. This doesn't sound right at all. Next time it won't be so easy."

"He is correct," said Redeye. "We can expect a stiffer response next time." The cyborg turned and began walking quickly down the tunnel, her figure swallowed up by the glittering mist and the shadows beyond.

They did the only thing they could do, now. They followed the eye.

They proceeded with the constant fear of ambush hanging over them. Having already met the enemy and put them down, they had expected to meet more groups of the armored corpse-machines, or something equally terrible, with every new section of tunnel they entered. The thing in Bobbi's mind still begged her attention, but she did not know how to reach it.

They walked along in the shivering blackness, deeper and deeper under the city, taking a branch not far from the ruins of the xsiarhotl that led well away from the rest of the system. The tunnels there were much older than the rest, reaching back fifty years or so – perhaps during the first major revamp of the subway system that happened just before the Collapse. Led only by the plans that they had memorized and the flickering bulbs, they were met with only silence as they trudged on. Her heart had not stopped racing since they had left the bodies behind them. The clarity of vision provided by their combat visors was no comfort in the dark, for that uncertainty grew within them as they drew closer to their destination without resistance – save for Redeye, who forged ahead seemingly undaunted.

"Maybe Cagliostro was wrong," Mason murmured over the radio link as they fell within a thousand feet of the tunnel entrance. "Maybe this isn't any kind of a vital objective at all. Do you think he could have been mistaken?"

"I do not." Redeye's voice remained flat, unshakeable. "He is an abomination to both species, perhaps, but he is no fool. The attack cut us off before he could explain precisely what we are going to destroy – but even if it is not what I believed it to be, the objective is vital." For a moment, Bobbi thought she saw the faintest flicker of...something...in the woman's pale face. "Come, we must push forward."

Bobbi wondered at that flicker of strangeness, wondering if it were a sign of instability that she had only picked up unconsciously before. Is that what the screaming weirdness in her head was? Or was it only the animal quailing that came with all dangers, the knowledge that something horrible was all but certainly going to befall them within the Yathi vaults? She let her mind shift from the immediate to the possibilities of the future – and in doing so, realized what the little haemonculus was only just as the tunnel behind them exploded in a hail of roaring sound, shattered concrete, and the skittering of metal limbs.

Flames. The gutteral coughing of gunfire, the dull thud-thud-thud of explosive rounds smashing against something that refused to yield. Pain lanced through Bobbi's head and down her back, and she realized that she was sprawled across the ground; her eyes fluttered open to see a line of jointed white flash across her field of vision. Another blink, and she realized what it was: one of the great centipede-things, like the kind that had killed so many of Redeye's people. Unlike those at the industrial park, this one was not gray but gleaming white, the same as the armor that the dead drones had worn. The thing was arched like a cobra, weaving back and forth over a pair of bodies sprawled across the earth. The howling tongue of fire that twisted and flashed on the other side of the fallen shapes lit up Scalli as he poured death into the machine's dense plating. But unlike the armor that the xsiarhotl had worn before it, the thing's glossy skin was too thick for even the support gun's heavy rounds to pierce; a cloud of explosions sent pieces sprawling away from its sinuous body, but Bobbi could see that it would not be cracked before the big man ran out of ammunition. Her mind whirled; how could she have missed the thing's coming, when she had the ability to sense their signals, their network presences – and as the thing arched high to come down upon Scalli like a barbed wave, she realized that the trembling in her head had been the machine's presence all along.

The centipede was a machine, and machines could be hacked. Even Yathi ones.

Bobbi shut her eyes and found the radio transmitter in her pocket, feeling fleeting gratitude that the little device was in one piece. Her ears filled with the horrible sound of the machine's beam weapon humming to life – not the keening wail that had spelled the doom of entire buildings but a smaller burst of death meant only for Scalli, who fired on despite what he must have known was coming, his face a phantasmagorical gallery of rage.

Scalli, she thought. You brave, beautiful son of a bitch. Her mind detached as if it were a separate creature, speeding away from her body toward the horror before her, and as she plunged into its core she had only the faintest sensation of her knees giving way.

As flesh fell to earth, the conscious mind pierced through into the frigid depths of alien waters. As before, the weirdness of it almost swallowed her up straight away – she was aware of the numbing cold she felt through the bridgework of the Grail, but now she was aware of hundreds of individual combat programs swarming in on her digital presence like swarms of hungry beasts. It was these voracious things that she felt around her, working at stripping her defenses away with dedicated ferocity; it was nothing like it had been at the facility. There was great power in the assault, but she also felt an immediacy that was different from the languid swatting of the Chorus. In the worm's computerized brain, she sensed something akin to fear.

It was that which pulled her out of the night. With fear came vulnerability, and knowledge of that lit a flame inside her mind. In milliseconds, that flame had become a conflagration. With the mailed fist that was the ghost-system, Bobbi spun into being a powerful reply; attack programs were instantly blasted into fragments by the wall of defensive programming that she compiled around her, depleting them faster than they could be cloned. The ghost's knowledge and Bobbi's brilliance worked in tandem to weave together the defense, turning Yathi counter-intrusion templates into magic of smoke and flame, transforming her inner fire into something far more tangible. In the flash of milliseconds, cold oppression boiled away, and the power of her counterprogram built and built – until it became all she could sense, a single gleaming sun of data with her at its core, and its fire threatened to consume her. It was then that the system crashed. Jericho's walls splintered around her, and Bobbi's consciousness was thrown from the machine's core like a rider from a dying horse.

Her eyes opened to the sight of the tunnel ceiling. Her back was wet and cold, and the stench of hot metal and burned flesh stung thick in her nostrils. For a horrible moment she thought that she had been too late, and they had all been killed. Bobbi sat up hard, ignoring the throbbing in her back as she looked for the others. It was hard to see; the right side of the tunnel had collapsed, partially burying the now-motionless centipede-machine beneath broken concrete and ruptured pipes. Water was everywhere, glimmering in the flickering glow of the failing bulbs. Bobbi blinked hard to try and clear the lingering fuzz from her head, and called out into the darkness. "Is everyone all right?"

"We're here." Scalli's voice rang out from the shadows.

Bobbi got to her feet. "Where are you?"

"Over here." From behind a slope of collapsed concrete, the big man emerged; covered in dust, Scalli held in his hand not the support gun but the weapon that Mason had called the Polish Dragon. Bobbi saw that the sleeve of his coat appeared to have been torn off, and his arm bore multiple slashes so that the black musculature of his suit could be seen beneath the false flesh.

"Is everyone all right?" Bobbi picked her way across the rubble, eyeing the fallen machine as she passed it. It showed no signs of life.

"Mason and Violet are fine," said Scalli as Bobbi crossed over to him. "We're still looking for Redeye. And that fucker..." He gestured to the centipede with the Dragon. "What did you do to it? I saw you fall over, and then suddenly it started thrashing all over the goddamned place. Barely got a shot in with the Dragon here."

Behind the shield of fallen concrete, Bobbi saw Violet and Mason leaning against the wall. Violet leaned against the old soldier, a thin stream of red blood staining the left side of her face. Mason's nose was swollen and purple, obviously broken. "Yeah, they look just fine," muttered Bobbi, glancing back to Scalli. "And look at you. Did it get through your armor?"

"No, it's fine. What did you do to the goddamned thing?"

Bobbi looked back at the fallen machine. "I hacked it," she said. "What did you do to it?"

Scalli snorted. "As it turns out, that armor isn't all that useful against energy weapons."

"What?" She glanced back at him. "What do you mean?"

"The Dragon's a laser weapon." Mason's voice was thick and nasal as he spoke from his seat. "That's what I was so surprised about. Something from the war, rare as hell."

Scalli nodded. "Polish special forces developed it, called it Smok Model Five. A few units were issued with them before the Julius Plague took out Krakow."

Bobbi blinked at them. Laser weapons were arcane things with backpack power units and armored cables, not...this. "It looks like a grenade gun," she said. "How the fuck does it fire lasers?"

"That's what's so clever about it." Mason paused to check on Violet, who was blinking blearily into existence against him. "Fires chemical laser bursts in single-use canisters. Lens optics, binary fuel, everything. Poles wanted to use it as a sabotage weapon, maybe for field troops in the future."

"Yeah, and it only took two shots to take that thing down once you got into its...whatever." Scalli pointed behind them with the Dragon's muzzle at the head of the centipede, which had a pair of fist-sized holes punched through. Bobbi frowned as she saw that white fluid dribbled from the wounds.

"Am I crazy," she said, "or is that thing bleeding?"

Scalli frowned as well. "No," he said, trailing off – he walked over to the thing's head and crouched down next to it, keeping the Dragon in hand if it started to move again. "Let's find Redeye, ask her what this thing is all about."

Bobbi eyed him a moment. "You're not worried that she might be hurt?"

"The Eye has fought these things before." Violet pulled herself up and rose somewhat unsteadily to her feet. "I've heard the stories. They're not alive, they just use biological computer hardware like the corpses do."

"Fucking fabulous." Bobbi shook her head. "Come on, let's find Red."

They found her buried under a fallen slab from the tunnel roof – alive, unhurt and in the process of digging herself out. If anything she was only displeased that she had not gotten a crack at the monstrosity herself. "I do not understand why they would have sent a moxhalal after us in such close quarters," she said as she looked the thing over. "It could have brought down the entire tunnel with an errant shot."

Moxhalal. Bobbi tasted the word on her tongue and found it bitter.

"Maybe local forces are depleted," Mason offered.

"More like they're overconfident," Scalli said.

Bobbi shook her head. "I don't think so. I felt...I felt like it was afraid, somehow."

The comment drew strange looks from Scalli and Mason, but Violet wasn't surprised – and neither was Redeye, Bobbi saw. "It may have been piloted remotely, then," Redeye said, and she smiled that Fury's smile of hers. "Good. They know you can get to them now. We can capitalize on that confusion. It has only been a half hour since the attack; if we hurry, we can reach the complex while the defenders are still considering their response."

"I'd like to know why they haven't come down here and killed us while we were out." Mason was on his feet as well. "It makes no tactical sense."

"You cannot reason with such creatures." Redeye shook her head. "They aren't used to resistance as it is – and not only have they failed to kill me, now there is someone who can intrude upon their systems. They are most likely waiting to see what it is that we intend to do. Let us not disappoint them." With that the dust-covered creature strode forward, passing the fallen machine and toward the far end of the tunnel. In her wake, the others looked at each other uncertainly – but Violet turned to follow her mistress, and Mason followed with a shrug. Bobbi and Scalli were left to look at each other.

"Well, girl," he said, "what do you think?"

"I think we don't want to be on the end of the line," Bobbi said with a shake of her head. "We've gone this far. Do you have enough ammunition to continue?"

"Plenty." Scalli reached back to tap the backpack. "Caseless rounds take up a lot less room. Besides, these are smaller than you'd think to pack so much power."

"And the Dragon?"

"Enough that if we need more, we're already fucked." He shrugged. "Come on, I didn't want to live forever anyway."

Speak for yourself, a voice muttered in the back of Bobbi's head, but she nodded anyway. "Just get in front of me if someone tries to shoot me, Mr. Wall of Iron," she said, and gave him a thin smile. "Let's go."

"You're the boss," Scalli said, and gestured for her to lead him – but as Bobbi walked and stared ahead at Redeye's shrinking figure, she had the distinct feeling that she wasn't leading anything at this juncture. This was the Fury's show, and now the only thing that Bobbi was sure of was that success could be as costly as victory.

True to Redeye's suspicions, they met no further resistance as they marched on toward the facilty's back door. Despite the destruction wreaked in their wake, there were no signs that the authorities above had any clue as to what was going on. Once again the tunnels were silent, and they soon enough found themselves confronted with the heavy maintenance hatch that masked the entryway into the complex. It was a solid door, though freshly painted, a fact which made Bobbi wonder if it was meant to mark the spot.

"Well," said Scalli from behind the lot of them, "here we are."

"Nice paintjob," Violet deadpanned. "It's almost like stage dressing."

Mason snorted. "And in Act Four, the protagonists all get it in the neck."

"Not if I can help it." Bobbi stepped forward and climbed the concrete ledge to the service walk, grunting as her sore back kicked up. She got to her feet in front of the door and frowned at it. "Red, you see anything unusual?"

"Not immediately." Redeye's tone was placid, but Bobbi could just imagine the bloodlust that must be boiling inside of her. She wasn't entirely a machine, after all.

"Could burn the lock assembly with the Dragon and see if there's anything behind the hatch," said Mason. "Course, that'd probably trigger something nasty and kill us all."

Bobbi grunted again, this time in irritation. Adrenaline started to flood into her system again in earnest, and her mouth went dry. "Just...stand back, kids," she said, and closed her eyes to try and summon her concentration. "Let me see what I can do."

Without waiting for a response, Bobbi reached out. She felt the familiar cold of alien systems, reached into the depths with a cautious hand. The nearest system was a security node, to operate the door – and something else, probably some manner of defenses. Bobbi reached past the door routines and found the new code, caressing it with analysis programs, sniffing it out. She was amazed and cautious to find that the unfamiliar system, though isolated from whatever greater network to which it belonged, was not protected with counter-intrusion software. It made a little sense, at least; by the ghost's own admission, Bobbi would be the first human – the first enemy – who would have been able to intrude upon their systems. Why would they have any kind of protection? Bobbi found markers for a weapon, which she disabled, and then triggered the marker for deployment...and found herself staring down at her own body, with the anxious remainder of her party looking up in the direction of her new vantage point. It was a gun turret, probably armed with one of the hideous X-ray flash guns that Redeye had told them about.

"Relax," said Bobbi, having to concentrate very hard to work her mouth. "It's just me."

"Christ." Mason shook his head, looking both ways down the tunnel. "Open this thing up, will you?"

Bobbi left the gun disabled and reached out with a ready template, spinning together a rather neatly-done counter-intrusion routine that wrapped the security node like an iron jacket. "All right," she forced herself to say, "get ready." She hit the hatch's entry code and killed the link in time to get out of the way as the heavy door swung open, letting the rest of them cover the opening with their weapons. The door, at least, made for an excellent shield.

Moments passed, and nothing happened. Bobbi peeked out from around the hatch when she was certain the world wasn't going to explode and found the rest of them frowning into the doorway from the track. Bobbi looked in as well; there was a stark white lobby waiting for them there, a tunnel no larger than the door itself. It was intensely well-lit, though there were no obvious apertures or fixtures for illumination. Bright white light spilled out from the doorway and made a shaft across the subway tunnel. The walls were made of the same glossy material that the xsiarhotl and moxhalal had been plated in – Bobbi used the alien words in her head rather than think of the previously-used descriptions, which disturbed her – and a heavy hatch of black material sealed the other end.

The others began to climb up, but Bobbi, seized by a strange sense of morbid wonder, stepped past the hatch and into the lobby. The door was unusual, both in its appearance and its composition. There was no texture, no hint as to if it was metal or something else, and it gave off a freezing chill; the stuff was so dark that it seemed to eat the light that pervaded the corridor. She wanted to touch it, but every sense she had screamed that it was wrong – the animal thing inside of her, the prey-instinct that had been evolved over millions of years, begged her to run away, and the urge made her stomach ripple with nausea.

She thought of Tom, laughing half-mad in her monitor from the elevator at Orleans as he hinted at the horrors which he had witnessed in its bowels. Bobbi had surprised herself with the toughness that she had shown so far - but as she stared at the door, the wall of blank nothingness that beckoned them to enter, she knew that they would be entering a hell that would dwarf that of the chamber of the Chorus.

But there was nothing to do but to play Dante. Bobbi reached out and touched the door, felt bone-rattling coldness against her fingertips for a fraction of a second, and then the black panel slid open without a sound.

CHAPTER 20

She had expected something new and strange to her, but the scene beyond the doors was all too familiar to Bobbi and in the most horrible of ways. The entrance had opened on some kind of catwalk; she stepped out upon it now, staring numbly out upon the chamber as it yawned forth like a tremendous cave beneath her. Unlike the bright and glossy corridor behind her, the cavernous walls were of dark metal, as were the nameless machines that crowded the floor below her feet. A legion of grim devices crouched upon the distant floor, their details lost in shadow. Brutal shapes of metal and plastic, every one of them suggested efficiency in their ineffable purposes.

Yet as if she had been born amongst them, Bobbi knew their names and purposes as she beheld them through her visor's electronic lens. Body dividers, flaying machines. Lymphatic extractors and marrow blenders. A symphony of brutal slaughterhouse mechanisms lurked in the factory pit, purpose-built with the task of rendering human victims into parts for future use. And around them all shone a mist of burning green, the dim illumination of eldritch lamps that only encouraged the deepening of shadows. The air fled from her lungs as Bobbi realized it was a scene from Cagliostro's nightmare visions, a piece of dying Yathkalhgn brought into being here on Earth. She would scream, but the air had left her; Bobbi could only stare open-mouthed in horror as her mind and lungs burned in unison and truth pulled her like a weight into a river of despair.

Pulled, and then drawn out – at least to the shoulders – by Scalli's broad hand as it lay upon her shoulder. "Bobbi," he murmured into her ear, trying to calm her but unable to betray the tremble in his own voice as he beheld the room himself. "You all right, girl?"

"I...yeah." The lie was enough to pull her back into the here and now, pushing the waters back. Bobbi shook her head to clear away what fear she could. "You?"

"Not even fucking remotely." Scalli frowned at the vast field of machines below. "This place. This place is bad fucking news."

Bobbi nodded. She heard Mason make a soft sound of horror as he stepped out onto the catwalk with the two of them, taking up a place next to her. His hand was a vise on its rail, the other one holding his rifle so that its muzzle tracked the ceiling. "Jesus fucking Christ," he muttered shakily as he looked into the cold field of machinery below; the glow of the lights was reflected in the lens of his visor as if it were a ghastly eye. "What the fuck is all this shit? Why is it all 'Starbase Glory' out there and fucking 'Lord of the Eight Hells' in here?"

"Because this is what it is like at home. For them." Redeye stepped out onto the catwalk, taking position at Bobbi's other side. She seemed untroubled at the blasphemous machines, nor did she look at them. The light of her eye was a sickly orange-red as it battled with the glow of the lamps for supremacy. "This is a safe place for them. No discovery. There is no need to hide their nature here." She glanced at Bobbi. "Would you agree?"

"I..." Bobbi closed her eyes, eager to shut out the sight of the machines for just a moment. "Yeah. This place, it's for dissecting bodies. Like a chop shop, you know. A black clinic."

"This thing is huge, though." Mason shook his head as he surveyed it once more, his face set in a frown. "Look at the scale of it!"

"The Yathi race seeks to render all uninfected humanity into spare parts. We're cattle." Violet stood by her mistress, her visor up and her cheek stained with the light of her mistress's baleful eye. "Motherfuckers."

"Yeah, but why not have these things chugging away, doing shit? Why isn't it active?" Mason shook his head again. "Is it shut down for maintenance or something?"

"That is an excellent question." Redeye frowned, the white lips dipping down as she turned her face toward the processing floor. "Every other facility which I have been to has been in operation. I wonder why this one is not?"

"Might have something to do with whatever's down in the basement, so to speak." Scalli's attention was not on the machines, it was on the wide door set into the lower half of the opposite wall. "This is a fine place for an ambush, people. Very hard to track targets here."

Violet nodded. "Yes," she said. "Does the Eye sense the enemy down there?"

"I do not." Redeye looked back to Bobbi. "But before we take another step, perhaps you should search out computer systems."

"Already did," Bobbi said with a shake of her head. "I didn't sense anything." She could not hide how disturbing that was for her – for all the dense security they were expecting, nothing was alive. Short of the lights, the place was like a tomb.

"Curious." Redeye looked at the distant door with interest now. "Very curious."

"Maybe we should go back," Mason said. "I'm all for slaying demons, so to speak, but this smells like eight kinds of a trap."

Redeye turned her head a bit toward Mason; her burning eye glowing behind its hooded lid. "If you wish to, you can leave," she said. "I doubt that anyone would hold this against you. But I have a role to fill, and I will fill it. Otherwise everything else has been done for nothing."

"Well, Jesus, Red," Mason sputtered, "I didn't really mean–"

Bobbi took a deep breath. She opened her eyes again to the terrible machines and lifted a hand to quiet the others. "It's going to get worse before we get to the bottom," she said, and surprised herself with the steel that rang in her tone. "Nobody goes back. We all have to move forward, because at this point going back isn't going to save anybody."

"Well said." Redeye gave her a bit of a smile. "Shall we descend to the floor, then?"

"Yeah." Bobbi scanned the catwalk. "All right, just watch out as we cross the floor. Power could come online at any time."

"Let's go, then." Redeye turned right and walked down the catwalk, her footfalls rebounding like tin off the grillwork as she went.

They had all committed the fragmented plans to memory, but Redeye knew them best. They moved quietly down a wide-mouthed ladderway to the processing floor, where they found themselves instantly dwarfed by the sprawling slaughter-works. They took careful steps amongst the sleeping machines, seeing up close the horrible truth of them: wheels of flensing blades and suction tubes, arcane assemblies of what looked like beam scalpels and primitive forceps crowding for space on spidery surgical arms. Though they could see the blank ceiling from the catwalk, it was a night-black sky as they proceeded below – Bobbi felt herself shiver more than once as they went, for her imagination conjured the specters of horrible shrieking drones falling down from on high to butcher them.

There was no assault, however, and they made their way to the massive double doors unharmed. They were made from the same metal as the walls around them, and to Bobbi the doors seemed somehow pedestrian compared to the slab of black-hole darkness from the lobby above. Bobbi looked over the door for several minutes, seeking controls but finding none, and ultimately reached out through the radio link to nudge them open. There was no network yet that she could find, and that disturbed her; there were only single devices such as the subway hatch and its turret, and now the double doors that were operating independently from whatever greater system existed. The complex really did seem to be in full shutdown. Bobbi reached out with invisible hands and tripped the opening mechanism, and slid out of the connection-trance as the great slabs of metal trundled open into further industrial space.

"Well," said Bobbi, "here we go."

The next chamber was a warehouse structure whose name Bobbi remembered as Storage Vault Three. Not quite as tall as the last room, the warehouse nevertheless yawned around them, stacked to the ceiling with containers as large as compact cars and marked with barbed Yathi script. They walked along a broad central lane between the great stacks, the fighters covering the shadows and Bobbi seeking any sign of systems activity as they approached another set of doors on the far side.

Mason muttered over the link as they went. "What do you think they've got stored in here," he asked, his voice muted with morbid fascination. "Parts from the other place, maybe?"

"Maybe," Scalli muttered in reply. "We haven't seen the other rooms. Bobbi, you pick up anything yet?"

"No." Bobbi had been actively reaching out at this point, pinging carefully as they went – between her network probes and the augmented senses granted by visors and implants, something should have come up.

Mason was guarded now. "Not even the door?"

"Not even that," Bobbi replied. "You guys, this is seriously—" And as the words left her mouth a wave of startup pinging sounded in her head like the pealing of bells as all around them systems began to wake. Above them new lights began to flicker to life, throwing spots of evil green light down upon them. Behind them, they heard the heavy doors begin to trundle open again.

"Oh, shit," Mason hissed.

"Cover!" Scalli's command was unnecessary, for they had broken to crouch behind the walls of thick pods the moment the doors began to open. The sudden rush of pinging had thrown Bobbi for a moment; Violet grabbed her arm and pulled her behind a stack with her, while Mason and Scalli took position behind another. Though they could not see them, yet thanks to the blockages down the aisle, Bobbi knew what was coming. Only Redeye stood out in the open, arms crossed, her head tilted slightly like a dog as she listened to the sound of many boot heels on the metal floor.

"Red," Bobbi murmured urgently over the link. "What the hell are you doing?" She tried to quantify what was coming, but the waking systems were causing too much interference – the knowledge was coming, but it so very slow without the active trance of Awakening.

Violet put her hand on her arm and shook her head. "The Eye is preparing for battle," she told Bobbi in tones reserved for prayer.

"That'll be a welcome first," Bobbi said darkly, and she turned back toward the aisle. She had not forgotten that Redeye had only been proven in a fight against Scalli and Mason, and that was only on the training mat. She had no idea what the cyborg could do against a real foe, but it looked as if she was going to find out.

It took only a few seconds more for that to happen, as the shapes of gleaming figures, white armor stained hellish green by the overhead lamps, began to flood around the stacks of crates that were piled at the head of the aisle. Bobbi knew what they were, knew the slinging club-arms of what Redeye had called combat limbs – from where they came, however, she had no idea. Storage pods here? A security station that they hadn't noticed? Maybe the factory on the level below was active, feeding them from the previously inaccessible transfer chutes that linked the complex.

The xsiarhotl came in numbers, and they did not bother with cover – at least not until they met with the first volley of death that was spewed from the assembly. The gas whipped and shuddered before them as Mason, Scalli and Violet let loose with their explosive rounds, pouring death into the charging throng.

Perhaps it was the nature of the corpse-machines to charge first and then fight intelligently only when they had impulse to do so, to adapt only when meeting bloody stimulus. Bobbi watched as the vanguard of the charging xsiarhotl were blasted into a cloud of white blood and armor shards, just as they had been in the tunnel. It wasn't hard to fire around Redeye the way she had positioned herself in the center of the aisle just ahead of Bobbi and the rest, and the hem of her coat danced a nervous tarantella with the passing of every round. Soon the machines were retreating behind the bodies of the fallen and taking cover behind cargo pods, which proved far more resistant to damage than Bobbi had expected; in the smoke and noise of the slaughter, Bobbi saw that the lethal bullets made only the slightest dents when they struck the dense gray metal.

It was then that Bobbi first knew that they were in real trouble. The other end of the aisle exploded in a dazzling sea of light as the xsiarhotl fired their flash guns, and the dispersal gas became a sea of black as the nanomachines contained within the cloud changed polarity to suck up the incoming radiation. But the gas had been whipped up by the initial volume of firepower, and the barrier was not entirely whole; patches of darkness swiftly thinned, and the crate in front of Bobbi let out a hiss as a laser blast ablated a chunk of its armored surface.

"Shit," Scalli shouted, his voice audible through the link over the staccato roar of his support rifle. "The gas can't keep up with them! Another round!"

"No!" Redeye's voice rang in their ears, booming and loud as it pierced the noise of battle. "Protect yourselves! I will deal with them."

Redeye drew herself down into a kneeling position like a high-jumper, and time seemed to slow as she leaped – defying physics, defying reality. The dark-haired cyborg hurtled through the air as if shot from a cannon, sailing in a shallow parabola twenty feet down the aisle with impossible grace. Her dark hair and coat flew in the air behind her like war banners as she reached the zenith of her arc; Bobbi looked on in utter disbelief as Redeye caught her feet on a nearby wall of crates, doing a parkour run across its surface before pushing off the edge into a fresh jump toward the hapless corpse-machines.

Time stood still as both sides could only stare at her – the living gaping at her impossible motion and the risen soldiers recalculating combat variables – as she came down upon them in a graceful arc. She disappeared amongst the white-plated monstrosities, and then time reasserted itself in the brutal chorus of violence. Once, when Bobbi was younger and she was living in the Verge, someone had been backed over by an electric truck outside her apartment building. The engine had been nearly silent, and over the shouts and screams to stop she heard the terrible crack of bones as the truck's heavy wheels had trundled over fallen legs. The sound they heard now was like that, magnified many times – the sound of breaking limbs and body armor and the constant thump of impact paralyzed her for several moments before the sound of tromping boot heels forced her attention away.

Violet had seen them coming first, hissing like an angry cat and spraying shots into the narrow lane to their left; Bobbi turned to see a white killer spinning away with a cratered chest, and more rushing up to meet them. While they had been busy with the fighters up ahead, they had been outflanked! Fresh adrenaline boiled through Bobbi's system as she tore at her belt for her pistol, falling back onto the floor in the face of the charging knot of xsiarhotl. The thrumming cloud of small explosions spat from Violet's rifle was not enough to stop them, and soon the corpses were upon them. The rifle clicked empty just in time for Violet to catch a combat limb across her chest. Bobbi yanked the gun free from her belt as Violet went down with a cry of pain and fury, threw herself back onto the floor, and fired blindly into the mass as best she could.

Again time slowed down, and again the movie of her life seemed as though it might come to an end – her bullets pierced through their bodies, spalling pieces of armor and cold synthetic blood sting her skin, but the small slugs were not enough to keep the knot away. One of the horrors brought its sledgehammer limb down on her arm, and pain exploded through it; the sleeve of her armor jacket hardened instantly against the blow, keeping the limb from breaking, but she very nearly dropped her gun. Bobbi cried out over the link, above the chaotic roar of the guns, and tried to scramble away as it lifted its arm to strike again. It turned its head down to behold her, the seam in its faceless visor leering down at her. Bobbi felt her nerves harden in the face of immediate death, felt the clarity that had come when she had shot Diana with the crusher, and shot it repeatedly in the face. She watched in slow motion as its helmet became a mass of bloody craters, and then its body was flung away in a different direction; Bobbi had to blink twice before she realized that Mason and Scalli had turned their guns into the marauders. The remnants disappeared under the hail of death and the two men rushed to their side.

"We got to get out of here," Mason said hurriedly as he helped Bobbi to her feet. "You all right?"

Bobbi's arm was on fire but endorphins raced to keep it at bay. "I'm fine," she said, shaking the worst of the pain out of her head for the moment. "Where are we supposed to go?"

"No idea," Mason said with a shake of his head. "Can you try and find something?"

"Let's walk and talk, people," Scalli rumbled over the link as he hung the support gun up on his harness and hoisted Violet up into one arm; she hung like a limp rag from his grip, and Bobbi saw that blood oozed from the corner of her mouth.

"She going to be all right?" Bobbi was already reaching out into the ether as Scalli stooped to pick up Violet's rifle, holding it easily by the grip.

"No idea," Scalli said, then barked over the link. "Red," he called out, "how are you doing?"

Over the link, Redeye's voice was eerily calm. "I cannot contain them much longer," she replied. "More are coming from the factory above. We are not escaping this way."

Mason spat a curse; Scalli ignored him. "We are falling back to the next chamber," he said. "Come on, we aren't leaving you."

"Fall back, Marcus," she replied, unhurried. "I will join you when you are clear."

"We can't leave her to deal with all of those things," Mason hissed. "We need her."

Bobbi shook her head. "She's doing pretty well against them so far, man," she insisted. "We need to get out of here." She felt behind them, felt the door, and with a flash of cold horror felt new signatures blinking into being all around her. "We really, really do."

Scalli didn't reply save to nod – and then they were moving, backing quickly through the empty lane toward the door with guns ready. Hundreds of new signals were appearing around them; Bobbi could not understand what they were or where they came from, but she got the distinct feeling of something, many somethings, coming to life. By the time they reached the door the question was resolved by the hissing of the cargo pods as their hatches cracked open and new corpses began to unfold themselves from their communal coffins, silver-eyed and horrible. Bobbi wished very much that they would all just wear armor to wall those faces away.

It was no wonder that the facility had no automated security on this level; everything contained within the rooms was lethal.

"Jesus," Mason cried as he fired a burst into the opening hatch of the nearest opening pod. "Red, we could really use some backup here!"

"We'll be fine," Bobbi said as she reached out for the door – and then hated herself for saying the words as felt herself hit a wall of security encoding. "Uh, you guys cover me," she said as she sat down on the cold metal deck by the wall. Her heart rate was spiking now, and she felt the taste of metal in her mouth as hurried dread settled over her. "They got this door locked up."

"Got it," Scalli said, holding out the rifle like a toy; he and Mason were firing single shots now, his armor systems and the old man's much-vaunted reflexes allowing them to snipe the nearest of the slowly-awakening corpses as they appeared. And yet her head rang with the signals of the awakening computer brains within the awful things, and she knew that if she didn't get the door open soon they would be swiftly overwhelmed.

Well, fuck that. Bobbi closed her eyes and forced her mind to open, something which the roar of adrenaline in her blood made profoundly difficult – and perhaps she would not have been able to do it in her own had the software in her head not taken over, interfacing with the door system on its own and doing the work of uplink for her. Very handy, very handy, Bobbi thought to herself before she focused her mind on the system to which she now connected; template sprang up and went through permutations, the Rosetta stone of the Yathi protocols working under Bobbi's will to form data into a well-honed origami spike. She slammed it home into the substance of the encryption wall, the diamond-hard counterprog withstanding several attempts without scratching the surface. Far away she heard the scattered thunder of the two men's guns turn into bursts.

Come on, girl. Come on.

Bobbi collected herself, took a deep breath. She felt her fear and anxiety within her, boiling like molten sulphur. Carefully she envisioned it, swirling inside of her mind like a poisonous tide, whirling under pressure until she forced it out again. A great plume of yellow light it was, tipped with the data-spike that she had crafted like a spear, and with her mind's unyielding arm she flung it into the encryption wall. This time metaphor won out over hard perception, and the counterprog buckled. Bobbi reached in through the wound, made contact with the door code, and unplugged herself before it even had the chance to start the open cycle.

She came back to a world filled with smoke and the sting of ozone and spilled synthetic blood. The chemical tang was thick in her nostrils; as her eyes came back to her, Bobbi looked up to find a horde of corpses plugging up the aisle ahead of them. The xsiarhotl were rising in legion from their storage pods, and like any good horde of walking corpses were heaving themselves against an increasingly frantic hail of rounds.

"We're in," she cried above the din, and sprang to her feet as the doors began to hiss open behind them; Mason took a step back, taking Violet – who had been transferred to his custody while Bobbi was out – and continued firing as he backed through the growing aperture with the fallen woman over his shoulder. Bobbi added her own pistol shots, for all the good it did, and stepped back with him; the corpses were very close now, so close that they could nearly touch them, and Bobbi was having wild flashbacks of the scene back in the Chorus chamber as she fired into as many white faces as she could.

They were pressed through the doorway into another corridor, sparing just a cursory look behind them to ensure that there was nothing waiting, only the dim glow of horrid lamps mounted in the walls. Even as they backed through, however, the opening doors provided more and more space for the corpses to come in; soon they would be surrounded as they flooded in from all sides, and then they'd be fucked. "Red," Scalli called over the link, his voice carrying through the connection like the very voice of a very worried god. "Get your ass in here, please, we gotta close the door!"

A few seconds passed without answer, and Scalli called again – still, there was no response. Bobbi shook her head and dropped down to one knee. "Sorry, Red," she whispered to herself as she shut her eyes tight, and reached out with her augmented mind for the door controls. She engaged them with adept mental fingers, then replicated the security wall that she had pierced before – nothing to hold them back forever should someone want to hack it, but there was no time for masterpieces. When she snapped back into consciousness, the doors were beginning to contract once more, and for a moment it seemed that they would be saved. But then the doors began to slow as the sheer volume of ruined corpses piled between them began to gum up the works, becoming horribly ground beneath them. And then – incredibly – the corpses began to aid the fallen in keeping the door braced; many pairs of strong white hands forced back the slabs, able to stay the closure through sheer numbers. The xsiarhotl had become a seething mass ahead of their flickering guns, filling the gaps faster than they could exchange magazines.

Bobbi looked into a sea of silent faces, the emotionless death which boiled from every container beyond the gap, and it was then that she felt real fear that they were all going to die. As they backed further away from the doorway and the dead began to force their way through, she believed that they would. When her gun clicked empty at last, she knew it would be so. She pulled her father's knife from the inside of Tom's coat, knowing that it would not save her, and prepared once more for the end.

"Well, boys and girls," Mason, shouted over the chattering of their gunfire, "it's been nice knowing the two of you."

The words pulled Bobbi back. "What?"

"I said it's been nice knowing you!" Mason let Violet slip from his arm and slide gently to the floor. "Gonna take care of this. Get that door closing again." He reached behind him, to the small bundle on his back, and pulled free the satchel charge he had been carrying.

Bobbi clutched the knife hard in her hand as Scalli peeled back another rank of the corpse-machines. "You can't do that," she called, her eyes wide as she realized what he was going to do. "No!"

"Red ain't coming," Mason said. He smiled at her, but his voice was etched with resignation. "Besides, this old man has seen enough action to fill two lifetimes. Scalli, clear me a path. I'm gonna get their attention."

Without a word, Scalli tossed his rifle to Mason, who dropped the charge and laid into the charging shamblers with both guns. Feet braced, teeth clenched, he sprayed rounds until Scalli could unlimber his support gun once more and spin it up again. As the doors continued their agonizing closure and the corpses began to boil through in earnest, Scalli's big gun began spewing fire into them on full automatic. There was no pretense of conserving the remainder of his ammunition, now. For a moment, Bobbi stared as their combined firepower tore a wide swath through the horde, splattering the deck with a fresh torrent of white, wondering just how many rounds were lost in his backpack and awed by the sudden and desperate storm of carnage. Then, Mason dropped his guns, picked up the explosive and a detonator from his belt, and charged.

The next moments came as a blur to her, like individual images clipped out of a magazine. Mason running toward the howling mass; Mason diving into the path that Scalli had freshly blown through the crowd, making it past the doors; the white hands closing in on him; the grin on his face, knowing and terrified; the mass turning to converge on him, turning its attention on him all at once. The doors sealed shut just as his face vanished beneath the tide, and he was lost to them forever. The bomb didn't even go off.

Bobbi stared at the black portal, drowned in shadows and the dim glow of the factory lamps, and felt her face burn. They had lost Mason, and most likely Redeye – the sole agency of salvation that they had. They were trapped, and they were doomed. "Not like this," she whispered, a prayer and a statement of defiance all at once. "Not like this."

The doors could provide no reply.

CHAPTER 21

Unlike Freida's passing, Mason's death could only be mourned for a moment. Priorities were engaged in the shocked way of those who were still in danger despite the loss of a comrade; they were alive, and apparently secure for the moment until the corpses found a way to get in. All the same, there were tears brimming in her eyes as she scanned the dark corridor, trying to get a grasp as to what fresh chambers of Hell they were now caught between. Behind them, there was death and the corpses of at least Mason, if not Redeye as well. Their whole reason for being here – gone. No understanding of where they were, what they were facing ahead; the room on the other side could be empty or it could be filled with more sentries prepared to finish them off or worse.

"Bobbi."

"Hmm?" She turned at the sound of Scalli's voice, blinking the angry mist away. "Yeah?"

Scalli was crouched down next to Violet, looking up at Bobbi with concern. His face was drawn as he looked over the fallen woman, hollowed with loss. He had taken off her armored vest and pulled the undershirt below to just under her breasts; a wide and ugly bruise was blossoming across her ribs. "You with us, honey? You all right?"

"No." Bobbi felt her guts flowing through a drain in space to some distant, horrid hinterland. "No, not really."

"I can imagine." Scalli frowned past Bobbi at the tomb-machine, then looked back at her. "Listen, he did what was necessary."

"The bomb didn't go off," she said in a small, dark voice. "He might as well not have..." She took a deep breath, forced the scream she wanted to let out down into the bottom of her stomach. "Is she gonna be all right?"

"She's fine, as best as I can tell." He gestured to Violet's body, which lay there as peaceful as if in death. "I can't see any damage other than this bruise. The armor's built to take blows like that, even a clotheslining like she got." Scalli pulled a narrow pouch from his belt. "I'm going to dose her up and get her going."

"Yeah..." Her voice trailed off, and Bobbi watched as Scalli drew a pneumatic injector from the pouch, pressed it against the side of Violet's neck, and then followed it up with another. She lay there for a moment as the chemicals coursed through her body, and then in an eerie parallel with the corpses beyond the door her blue eyes snapped open and she let out a gasp of pain.

"Vi," Scalli said, flipping up his visor and looking down into her face. "You're here, girl, it's all right. You're safe."

Violet lay there for a long moment, staring up at the ceiling; her muscles tensed in an all-over wince of agony that lasted only for the few seconds it took for the painkillers to kick in. Then she relaxed with a soft sigh, collected herself, and struggled to sit up. "Fuck," she breathed, looking down at the bruise on her chest with the slight glazing of the dope in her eyes. "I think I got my chest caved in."

"Nothing so bad as that," said Scalli with a grunt. "You're fine except for the bruise, but you'll sure hurt like a fucker."

"Glad I didn't fight you on that body armor then," Violet said with a dazed blink. She took a deep breath and pulled down her t-shirt. "Where's Harry at?"

Bobbi and Scali said nothing.

"Oh." Violet frowned. "What happened?"

Bobbi told her, and Violet shook her head. "Jesus," she muttered. "Poor guy. Well, the Eye will no doubt be with us soon enough. We can stick those fuckers up their own asses."

"Violet," Scalli began, but Bobbi lifted her hand to hush him.

"She's on the other side of the door," Bobbi said. "And she's not responding on the radio. I hate to say it, Vi, but she might be dead."

Violet only shook her head again, and tried to get up. "If she were dead," she said as Scalli helped her to stand, "I'd know it." She tapped her head. "In here. We all have status implants – she knows our status, and we know hers. Part of joining her little army. She knows how we're doing, we know if she's alive."

Bobbi looked at Scalli a moment. "What about the others? I mean, Red felt them dying..."

"Yeah," said Violet, nodding once. "That's why we can only sense her. If I felt everyone else dying off, it'd make me crazier than I already am."

"Wait." This was making less and less sense by the minute; Bobbi took a step toward Violet, squinting at her. "But couldn't you miss the signal? I mean, couldn't someone disrupt it?"

"Maybe," said Violet, "But it hasn't happened yet, not when separated by a very long distance. The implants don't work like transmitters do. It's something different. I don't know the technology." She looked a bit embarrassed now. "Honestly I'm as much in the dark here as to what things do as you are, now. My little evil spirit didn't leave much behind, like I told you, and I don't think she was any kind of a technician."

Bobbi nodded. "I guess that makes sense, considering what your job was." She wiped at her face to get the last bit of dampness off of her cheeks. "All right, so she's alive, then."

"Better than alive." Violet was grinning. "I said we know her status, not just life-or-death. From what I can tell she's not even nicked."

Images of Redeye punching holes through legions of dead on the other side of the bulkhead sprang to life in Bobbi's mind. "Well, that's good. Do you think we should go back through, maybe?"

At this, Scalli shook his head. "Not a good idea," he said. "We can't talk to her, so they're either jamming the radio, or the walls are too thick, or something. If we can't find out what's going on, we shouldn't open that door again unless she does it herself."

"Okay..." Bobbi's mind was ticking over. "So what do we do, then? Wait and see?"

"No," said Scalli. "I think we should go to the next room, see what's in there. Might be something that we can find, maybe a way to get back around to her."

Violet wrinkled her slim little nose. "I dunno," she said. "That sounds...worrying."

"It's just a storeroom," Scalli pointed out.

"So was the last one," Violet spat. "And anyway, the farther we are from the Eye, the worse off we're going to be – she's the only one of us who can get through heavy resistance. We should—"

"That's enough." The peal of command in Bobbi's voice rang from the angles of the corridor, surprising everyone, herself included. She rode it in the silence that followed anyway. "We can't be sure that Red's going to get through on this side just now. She's got to be hiding in there."

"Yeah," said Scalli, nodding along. "We could get to her through the transfer chutes."

"Assuming we can get through them." Violet's frown deepened, giving her the appearance of a vaguely homicidal cheerleader. "Do you think we open the hatches if we go into the next room, assuming we don't get flayed where we stand?"

Bobbi shook her head. "Only one way to find out," she said, and took a deep breath. "All right. Scalli, how much ammunition do you have left?"

"Not a lot," he said gravely. "Mason took his share of the rifle mags with him. I've got four left, maybe..." He paused to check a small screen on the top of the support gun. "Two hundred thirty-seven rounds."

"Let's hope that we don't run into anybody else, then," Violet muttered. "That was a hell of a welcome."

"Well, let's not give them any more time to break that encryption, if they're gonna." Bobbi stooped to pick up Mason's rifle, frowning at the unfamiliar weight in her hands.

Scalli looked at her brows arched. "Can you shoot that thing?"

Bobbi looked down at the gun and nodded. "Yeah," she said, checking the thing over – all the parts that she recognized were there, nothing a surprise. "It's been a long time, though. Better not trust me for anything other than spewing bullets all over the place."

"We call it 'suppressing fire' in the business," Scalli said with a faint smile. "Don't worry, you'll do fine. Just set it to burst and don't dump your clip all at once. You won't get another one."

"Better I just do it single shot, then." Bobbi put the knife away and cradled the weapon in her arms for a moment, trying to get a proper feel for it, then slung it over her shoulder. "You sure you can move, Vi?"

"Trust me," Violet said, and her expression was dark. She was putting on her armor again, sliding her arms through the sleeves and buckling the breastplate. "I'd have to be dead to keep from doing this."

"Plenty of time yet." Scalli clicked off the safety of his rifle. "All right, let's get a move on."

They gathered by the door, guns at the ready while Bobbi reached out for the door system; the lock was not protected either, the same as when they had entered the first storehouse, but this time Bobbi stopped to place a fairly thick security wall around the operating code. If they needed to move back, this time they could without too much interference. The door behind them, Bobbi noted, was now absolutely without power, and therefore without any way to get through it even if it was safe to do so. They'd definitely have to use another route. So there was only forward, and forward they would go. Bobbi triggered the door and dropped back into reality as the doors began to trundle open and the three of them braced for coming death.

But there was none. Instead the doors opened up on a new warehouse, though this one was not filled with pods. It was almost completely empty. Save for the pair of chute doors that were mounted on the left walls, only a single object lay on the polished black floor, a rectangular box made of flat gray metal. Thick cables and feed hoses sprang from mountings in its surface, connecting it to nameless ports visible only dimly in the shadows of the ceiling overhead. The three of them lingered in the doorway, Scalli and Violet sweeping the muzzles of their guns across the room while Bobbi attempted to feel out any active systems in the room. She could find none.

There was also no other exit. They were trapped.

"...well all right, then," said Scalli when he was sure that nothing was going to drop out of the ceiling and try to murder them at the moment; he stepped over the threshold into the room, and the Bobbi and Violet followed.

At once, Bobbi was drawn toward the box. She approached it, looking it over. There were no seams, nor any obvious controls – only the barbed clawtip glyphs of the Yathi tongue embossed into its surface, all along the bottom. It sat on a plinth of strange gray material that looked like graphite. To Bobbi, the machine looked like a tomb. She could not help staring at it, as if it reached out and pulled her gaze away of its own volition. As she approached, Bobbi could feel a whisper in her head, the implanted protocols suggesting that here was something here of interest, a system that she might want to see, magnificent in its complexity and artistry –

And then hard white fingers wrapped around Bobbi's hand, squeezing it so that she was shocked out of her reverie. She looked down at her hand; Violet grasped her firmly, so hard that her thumb made an angry red divot in the back of it. Bobbi jerked her hand away, swearing.

"You don't want to go near that thing," Violet said sternly. Her eyes were hard. "Trust me on this."

Bobbi shook the pain out of her hand. "Fine," she said, "but what the hell is it? It looks like some kind of coffin."

"Because that's what it is," said Violet. She frowned as she looked at the tomb, her blonde brows turning down into a sharp "V" over her eyes. "Or something like it. It's like a cryogenic pod, sort of."

"'Sort of?'" Scalli came up to join them. He frowned at the thing as well. "What does that mean?"

Violet shook her head. "I mean it's like...well it's not just for preservation. They do all kinds of medical procedures. We found one in the Old City that was apparently knitting new skin over an implanted transfer. It woke up when we got the lid off, all half-covered with skin – died screaming almost the second we uncovered it. There's definitely a Yathi in there. Best to leave it the fuck alone lest we wake it up. That'd be all we fucking need."

"Yeah..." Bobbi took a step back, which was a bit difficult as she took a moment to push the whispering of the software out of her mind. Having the voodoo computer in her head whispering sweet nothings to her was not at all promising, and she found herself regretting the decision more and more. Was this going to happen as they encountered more technological artifacts? What if she ended up faced with something more complex, like the Chorus? A shudder ran through her body as she tore her eyes away from the tomb-machine, and stalked away toward the chute hatches and the business at hand.

Kneeling by the first hatch, Bobbi ran her hands along the seams of the black metal portal. Featureless and with no obvious method of opening it, Bobbi wondered immediately if controls were located elsewhere; she could detect no other system save for whatever was running the tomb. "Looks like there's nothing here," she said. "Nothing computerized, at least. Might be something else running it, but I don't think it's present to be found, you know?"

"All right," said Scalli, who had come over to examine the door himself. "How do we get it open?" He slung his rifle on its hook, then began feeling along the hatch's upper sides. "Surely there's a maintenance panel somewhere, or something. Else how would they fix anything?"

"That's a good question," Bobbi said, but it was Violet who had the answer. She shook her head and knocked once on the wall by the hatch.

"If there's not a hatch," she said, "then they're almost certainly being controlled from up top, right? We'd seen places that had repair drones inside the walls; they came out to fix things sometimes, when we'd blasted something before destroying the computer systems. Like xsiarhotl, just...different."

Bobbi quirked a brow. "Different how?"

"Well," Violet said, "you know how they use bodies?"

"Yeah?"

"They don't always use the whole thing."

Scalli made a dark sound in the back of his throat. "Sooner we get out of here, the better," he muttered. "Jesus."

"Well we can search around for ventilation," Violet said. "I mean they do have air ducts in places like this. The Yathi still breathe, having human bodies. At least, most of the newer ones do. I don't know about the old ones."

Bobbi frowned again. "Oh, good," she said. "So we find an air shaft, and then...what? They cut the airflow off and keep us cordoned off until we suffocate?"

"You mean until you suffocate," Scalli said. "I'm too damned big to get into an air shaft like this. We're gonna have to get those hatches open if you want me to move anywhere."

Violet nodded. "All right," she said, "Well, it shouldn't be too hard to find one. I mean they haven't been in the past."

Bobbi nodded. "Then let's get to looking,"

They searched the chamber carefully, looking for seams or grilles in the black walls that would suggest a vent; all the while they kept a weather eye on the door as they moved, occasionally glancing over at the tomb-machine to ensure that it wasn't reacting to their presence. It remained as still as it had when they had entered the room. They found several smaller grilles, but nothing that would admit even the smallest of them. After twenty-five minutes or so, a cry of satisfaction brought their attention to where Violet crouched down along one wall.

"I found it," she said, triumph in her voice. "A big one. It's over here."

They joined Violet at one of the opposite corners, where low in the wall a narrow, inward-facing bevel was issuing cool air around a square section of wall about the size for someone small to get through. Violet peered into the slotted recess, clucking her tongue in thought, and then sat back on her heels. She reached her fingers in to the middle knuckles and began feeling around; after a few tense moments in which Bobbi was certain that she'd lose her fingers, Violet pushed something. The section surrounded by the vent groove swung inwardly, allowing the air to gush in earnest.

"There we are," Violet said with a faint grin. "All right, Bobbi, it's your show."

Bobbi blinked at her. "Me?"

Violet blinked right back at her. "Well, yeah," she said. "I mean I can go, but I can't interface with whatever's up there. We can both go, I guess, but I figure you'll be a lot safer in a vent tunnel than Scalli would be on his own should something decide to come through the door."

At this, Bobbi made a face. She did not like the idea of crawling through a network of ventilation shafts, possibly filled with alien creatures, and without any kind of map. "I don't know how to get there from here," she pointed out.

"That's easy enough," Violet said with a shrug. "You just go upward. You know the general layout of this place, Bobbi. You can see in the dark, and you can hack whatever's coming, right?"

Bobbi wanted to make a very reasonable argument as to how this was a very bad idea, but this would be a rather hypocritical act considering where they had followed her already. "...yeah," she said instead, and drew a deep breath. "All right, yeah. So I'll get up there, spring the hatches, and we'll take the chutes...where?"

"First we get to Redeye," said Scalli. "And then it's down to the factory. Maybe we can blow the fucker while we're at it, so we don't get any further problems. Or maybe it'll go even farther down, who knows? Either way, we'll be closer to where we need to be."

Bobbi looked between them. "And if Redeye isn't around by the time I'm done?"

Scalli shrugged. "Then I guess it's up to us to finish what we started."

As she stared at the dark mouth of the open vent, Bobbi took a deep breath. This was not her idea of a sound plan – and yet, what else could they do? Squaring her shoulders, Bobbi got down on her knees, flipped the visor down over her eyes once more, and was thankful for her augmented senses as she crawled into darkness.

CHAPTER 22

Were it not for the visor, Bobbi would have immediately become lost. There was no light, only the ghostly white-on-black geometry conjured up by ultrasonic ranging – no detail, only solid planes. It was comforting in a way; it reminded her of the primitive video games her father liked, the ones that his grandfather had shown him when he was a boy. Wireframes with primitive textures. Unreal. It helped her push the monstrousness of the truth out of her mind. She was alone, and as she soon discovered upon trying the radio link, cut off from Violet and Scalli. A distinct sensation of impending death settled over her, though if it were hers or someone else's she could not say. There was only the dread, pushing her upward, urging her to make her way.

And so Bobbi made her way along the duct feeling like a clot in a vein, heading upward to throw herself into the brain of this abominable complex. The visor had a mapping function which allowed her to mark her path, and it spooled out a line of red light behind her that would let her see the way back. Upward, always upward, pausing from time to time to check for signs of movement or worse, discovery. Nothing.

As she went, she thought of Mason, felt tears start in her eyes, and flipped up the visor to clear them away when they came. Part of what drove her on was most certainly revenge, a certain bloody-mindedness that she had not had before. She did not know when it had come. Maybe it was when Tom disappeared, or when Freida died, or when Bobbi had shot the thing that wore Diana. Maybe it was when Mason threw himself to the corpse-machines to save them. It was in her blood like an infection now, something dark and vaguely feverish, waiting to erupt.

And so around and around she went, navigating the twisting vents with no real understanding of her direction save for the virtual zenith that the goggles so helpfully projected for her overhead. At least something knew what the hell was up. For what felt like hours she carefully traversed the ducts, her knees aching, her back tight as she crawled as quietly as possible through the darkness. As she went, Bobbi realized that the ducts had been built for something to travel through; there were handholds in vertical shafts, hatches which when exposed revealed only inscrutable machinery. She felt scratches on the metal of the ducts as she went, signs of past travelers whom she could not identify. Had there been others who, trapped here in the complex, had somehow escaped the drone factories and tissue processors to make it this far? Somehow, Bobbi didn't think so. The dread only grew as she went along, the scratches like the Devil's own hoofprints against her fingertips. She was getting closer.

Eventually, she made her way along to where she thought the upper chambers must be. The elevator had fed into a receiving lobby and side rooms before feeding into the control nexus. Her hope was that she would emerge in one of these, somewhere out of the way; she wouldn't need to be inside the secured area to work her magic, or at least she hoped so. The cuts widened out a bit, and they began to split into junction cubicles large enough to sit in. Bobbi, tired and sore from all her worming around, sat down hard inside one of these. That was when he found her.

Bobbi had her back against the wall of the cubicle, the plating covering her torso welcome support for her tired muscles. She turned off her visor and took a deep breath, letting the darkness fill her senses. It was almost peaceful after her exertions, even with the possibility of death so close. She had taken a deep breath and fished a stick of gum laced with Pranazine out of the pocket of Tom's coat – the same stuff she had given him when they had first met, just to calm him down. Swaddled in the pinned-up garment she almost felt him with her, and she wondered what it was that he would say to her. She thought of romantic things, perverse things, angry things. And finally she thought of him speaking to her as the Chorus had through Freida, mechanical and pitiless. If he were alive, she'd have to kill him if she found him. When she found him. Sitting there, she knew that if she made it out intact she'd be hunting the white-skinned horrors of the Yathi race for all the years of her life.

It was when she came to that conclusion that her transceiver cut in, and she was very aware of a system awakening nearby; she heard motion coming from down one of the tunnels, but she couldn't be certain which. A voice sounded in her head, very faint but born of the strange telepathic substratum of the network, the one to which her headware was so attuned. She realized with a thrill of mingled relief and disquiet that it bore Cagliostro's data marker.

<WAIT FOR ME,> came the message. <I AM COMING.>

The link died after that. Bobbi chewed her gum, feeling the Pranazine blunt the worst of the fear that came racing through her as the sounds came closer; she turned on the visor again, saw the virtualized north star overhead, the bizarre trail of red that marked where she had come before spiraling into the depths below. The ghost-walls of the tunnels yawned all around her, four possible conduits from which the voice billing itself as Cagliostro's may be coming. Bobbi took the knife from its sheath in her coat pocket, seeing it as a strange white shape in her hand, her world made entirely of chiaroscuro shapes. She waited, the knife in her fist, blade pointed upward to lunge with – and then she heard the voice in earnest, the bizarre slapping of what sounded like skin on steel. Something approached to the right of her, and against all of the pleading of her prey-brain kept rooted to the spot as it emerged from the duct mouth.

She had to bite her tongue to keep from screaming.

It didn't just crawl through the mouth of the duct – it unfolded itself. She saw it in the stark white of the ultrasonic imager, the matte white textures on a wireframe mesh that was shaped something like a human being. A human child. Naked. Bald. Jawless, something mechanical in its place. She saw that it had too many arms, arranged down its side like a crab's legs, and the hips were reversed –

Bobbi tore the visor off her head. Her chest rose and fell like a diver gone under too long, her lungs burning, the prey-brain quailing and clawing at the walls of her mind. Her fingers spasmed on the handle of her knife...and then calm came, a practiced, clinical thing, enforced from that rarified circuit in her brain that fired in emergencies. She lay there a moment, gasping for breath, and fought the fear down hard.

In the dark, a pair of small eyes shone in the blackness, silver discs gleaming with their own illumination. "I am sorry for that," spoke a deep, flat, basso profundo voice from what her fevered mind told her was the machine the blasphemy had for a mouth. "I understand how disturbing it appears."

It took a minute or so for Bobbi to pull her heart out of her throat. "Fuck you," were the first words that came out of her mouth, followed by

"What the fuck is wrong with you, coming at me like that? What the fuck is that, anyway?"

"It is a labor unit." The drone's 'voice' wasn't very loud, yet it managed to reverberate off every angle around her – even in her head, where it seemed to bounce around the most. <Xsiarhotl are rebuilt to fit various purposes as much as the general. This unit is one of those used to clean and maintain the ventilation system, along with the cargo distribution system.>

"It's fucking horrible," Bobbi replied.

"Indeed. The Yathi race care nothing for the dead. If it helps, they do the same to their dead as well. Even on the homeworld."

Bobbi shook her head. "No," she said in the blackness, "It does not. But thanks for fucking my brain up a little more by telling me that." The fear was receding, and so long as it was dark, she did not have to focus on what lurked before her – she need only pay attention to the voice, not the horror that it issued from. "How the hell are we talking here, anyway, Cag? How are you here?"

"Your activities have alarmed the entire Yathi community in this city," Cagliostro replied. "By utilizing the protocols that I implanted in your neural interface hardware, you have made the Yathi aware that there is a traitor in their midst. They have been racing to find the source of this treachery."

"Why not drop everything and kill us instead?"

"Have they not tried?"

Got me there, Bobbi thought. "Well, yeah," she said. "But I mean, this place has a whole storehouse of corpses we had to fight off to get away. Mason got killed making sure of that. And we're cut off from Redeye, too."

"I am aware of the situation," Cagliostro replied. "I have spoken with your remaining comrades. Geneva Riley and Marcus Scalli were as surprised as you to hear from me, but they were very helpful."

Bobbi was quiet for a moment. Geneva? Was that Violet's real name? She'd never thought that it would be anything but what Vi had said it was. "Are they all right?"

"They are quite safe at the moment. The unit Redeye has drawn the garrison's attention as she moves through the complex, and all resources are currently occupied attempting to fight her. The others will not be bothered."

"Well, I'm glad about that," Bobbi said in relief. "Wait, what about Redeye? Have you spoken to her?"

"No."

"Well, why the hell not?"

"The unit designated 'Redeye' is not my ally, nor is she yours."

Bobbi blinked at the gleaming eyes in front of her. "You're gonna have to repeat that. You sent us to get her. How is she suddenly not our ally?"

"You were dispatched to interface with the unit because it was expected that her psychological programming remained intact. Her personality has deviated, however."

"Deviated how? She sacrificed her people to get us out of the Old City, man, and helped us get in here."

"Indeed. However, her behavior has become erratic."

A flash of impatience stiffened her aching back. "Dammit, Cag," Bobbi said, her tone heavy with annoyance, "that tells me exactly dick. Erratic how? We knew she was crazy already."

"She attacked me."

Silence. Bobbi blinked again in the dark. "Come again?"

"It was she who attacked me when the strike force arrived at her location."

"How the fuck is she supposed to have done that?" Bobbi stared at the space that Cagliostro's vessel filled. "I mean, why would she?"

"The motivations for the attack were unknown to me at first," he replied. "However, the unit has been well equipped with intrusion and counter-intrusion facilities as a part of her specifications. She has always been quite adroit at assaulting and disabling systems and software."

That made Bobbi sit up a little more. "She never told us that," Bobbi said. "She said she could take down machines, sure, but now she's got all this military hardware, and punching through people's chests and shit. What the hell is she, then? You said she was a failsafe."

"That is an accurate, if somewhat metaphorical, way to describe her."

She pursed her lips. "Red also said you built her."

"That is correct."

"To do what?"

"To wage war upon the Yathi race. I would think that this would be obvious."

"Well, yeah," Bobbi said in consternation; she was rapidly forgetting the terrifying presence of the thing in front of her in favor of her impatience with the obtuse mind that operated it. "And she's pretty fucking well built for that. But if she's able to attack you, and fuck you up badly enough that you've been offline for a month, why the fuck does she need me? Us? Why can't she do it herself?"

"To be fair," said Cagliostro, "the unit caught me by surprise; were I expecting trouble, I would have been able to turn back her assault. That she was successful only in temporarily disabling me should demonstrate the limit of her ability."

Bobbi snorted at that. "Sorry to kick you in the dick there," she said. "Okay, so she's not been straight with us about the hacking. Why is that, then?"

"She does not want you to know her true intentions." The corpse-thing shuffled a moment, and Bobbi was reminded that it was still there. She shivered. "She believes that she is going to destroy the colonial matrix that allows transference of Yathi consciousnesses into human minds. I attempted to disabuse her of this, but she grew enraged and attacked me – she believes that she can end the colonization effort by severing the link between the two worlds."

"How is that a problem? I mean, the severing bit, not the attacking you."

"The matrix is not there."

"But something else is."

"Yes."

"Still not seeing the problem here, man." Bobbi's brows arched a bit. "What the hell's down there?"

"A laboratory." Though the voice was toneless, Bobbi couldn't help but imagine a bit of concern there. "This complex is a major hub of drone manufacturing and tissue processing in this zone of the world, but its true function is that of planetary reconfiguration research."

Things just kept getting better and better. "Reconfiguration. Like what, terraforming?"

"Precisely. The Yathi colonization schedule anticipates a three hundred percent spike in human conversion numbers over the next two years. When that occurs, they will release a nanomachine colony that will begin working to reformat the ecological and material makeup of the planet. Do you recall the images of the terrestrial makeup of Yathkalgn that I transmitted to you when we communicated directly?"

Bobbi frowned again at the thought of the horrible landscapes that rose in her mind. "Yeah," she said, "I remember."

"That is what the Yathi seek to bring here. Eventually, through their work and the increasing conversion of the human species, they will completely remake this world in the image of the last one. And this is vital to them, because they have no home to go back to; changing the environment is important to ensuring that the Yathi mind remains dominant, and thus ensuring also that the species does not fragment from its host. Though this has always been part of the colonization strategy, it has become necessary to the survival of the species. It is for this reason that I sent you to destroy this location."

"Then we need to put an end to that." And so there was no alternative other than to get into the basement; she would have to get into the control center, or at the very least hack it from nearby. The way out wasn't back, it was through. "All right, so it's not this matrix thing, but it's a priority target. So we destroy this colony. And then, what, we find the nexus and destroy it, too? What'll keep them from creating another one, or more terraforming nanomachines?"

"One objective at a time," Cagliostro said, and though the voice of the corpse-machine was flat she could not help but feel iron in those words. "We begin with the control center. Follow this drone; it will lead you to a location under the room that will allow you maximum chance of system intrusion."

Bobbi felt a twinge of disgust. Follow that monstrosity? "And if that doesn't work? Do we have an alternative?"

"No." The drone began to turn around; she felt its body shift the air, its palms hiss against the duct floor as it went. "We must go now. If Redeye destroys the laboratory, which she intends to do, we will find ourselves at the center of a disaster for both sides."

"That doesn't make any sense, though." Bobbi frowned. "I mean, you sent us to destroy the lab in the first place, right?"

"Correct."

"So why can't we talk her down? I mean, yeah, she throat-punched you and sent you to the bench for a month, I can see why you'd have a problem with that. But why the fuck would we want to put her down for doing what you asked us to in the first place? Isn't this what you built her to do? Or is it because she's acting off script that you want us to wax her?" Cagliostro had led her here, burning the lives of two companions now – perhaps the disembodied hybrid mind may consider it collateral damage, but she wondered how many of them, if not all, were expendable. After all, he sent Tom to kill Ghia Merducci, knowing that he would probably have been killed – what hope did she have for them to escape unscathed? It came to her that he probably didn't, and she wasn't sure why it hadn't before.

"I have told you before that she has committed herself to destroying this complex because she is convinced that the colonial matrix can be found here. Knowing of the existence of a laboratory containing a large amount of terraforming nanomachines exists, what do you believe will happen if she succeeds in her mission?"

"So you're saying that if she blows this place, all that bad shit gets out. The city turns into an ecological disaster zone."

"At the very least. However, that will be the least of your immediate problems."

"You'll need to detail that," she said.

"There is little time."

Bobbi gave the drone a flat look. "Yeah, that mysterious benefactor shit got old a long time ago, Cag. We're down here getting shot to pieces, you know? You keep holding out on me, I'll just sit here and let her trash the fucking place, see what happens."

As fierce as her words were, Bobbi didn't mean them – and of course the bastard ghost called her on that. "You would do no such thing," the drone replied. "However, I understand your sentiment. Very well; the unit called Redeye does not intend to merely destroy the laboratory, she intends to destroy the entire complex. Doubtless a great deal of the nanomachines will be consumed in the initial blast, but the remainder will be scattered throughout the atmosphere. On some level, the world will change. Every simulation that I have run indicates that this will be to the direct detriment of humanity."

"All right," Bobbi said, and her brain was ticking along fiercely now. "So let's start from the top. If she's going to blow the factory, how is she going to do it? Is there a reactor in the complex that we missed?"

"No," Cagliostro replied through the drone. "The generators installed within the complex are not nuclear and cannot be detonated in the way that you suppose."

"Is there a weapons laboratory or factory here? What the hell is she going to use to take out a whole complex?"

"She will use herself. The unit, Redeye, is a repurposed design; I ensured that her development was redirected toward my own desires, but there were elements of her construction that could not be avoided."

Bobbi stared at the thing, ignoring its obscenity. She felt a weight begin to pull at her stomach. "What the hell are you telling me, man?"

"The unit was originally intended to be a terror device, during the violent activism which took place immediately following the European War. A pilot program, so to speak. It was originally envisioned that the unit would be built to infiltrate military or civilian targets, where she would detonate. The resulting – "

"Wait, what?" Bobbi sat up hard. Her eyes narrowed as she stared at the drone in disbelief and anger. "Are you telling me that she's some kind of fucking bomb?"

"That is precisely what I am telling you. The unit you know as Redeye was originally constructed around a miniaturized thermonuclear device from which she draws operating power. That device has been designed to overload once certain protocols have been initiated, however, leading to an explosion in keeping with a tactical nuclear device."

Bobbi was silent for a long moment. "All right," she said at last. "How large are we talking?"

"The intended yield is four kilotons, with extremely limited fallout. While civil defense nanomachines in the atmosphere will ensure that there is no lingering radiation hazard, there will of course be many immediate civilian casualties, as well as yourselves."

The shock that had settled on her shoulders was a mantle of lead, cold and heavy in the darkness. Bobbi could do nothing but stare at the horrible drone, intoning these facts as if they were the words of Death itself, extolling the doom of the city. "It'll kill a lot more than that," she murmured, more to herself than to Cagliostro and his cheval. "The ferals will come in during the chaos."

"That is very likely," Cagliostro agreed. "And the blast will carry the remainder of the terraforming colony high into the atmosphere. It will circulate globally, as I have said. The world will change. Humanity will suffer."

"And the only way to stop this is to kill her?"

"Unless you can somehow convince her to stop, yes." The drone swung its head toward one of the vent mouths as if it had sensed something; Bobbi's shock turned to fear, and then determination. When it looked back to her without comment, she spoke.

"All right," she said, "lead on, man. I hear what you're saying, but I'll try and talk her out of this thing first."

"She is deeply embroiled in fighting the xsiarhotl within the complex," said Cagliostro. The drone turned and began padding into a duct, its limbs carrying it along like an obscene white lobster. "And quite focused on completing her chosen objective. If she determines that you intend to stop her, she will kill you before you can speak a word."

"Fuck." What else was she going to say or do? With a deep breath, Bobbi pulled the visor over her eyes again; the ultrasonic device came online again, and she found herself staring at the horrible rear quarter of the child-thing. Its reversed hips allowed its coiled legs to 'walk' along the ceiling of the vent, and seeing it made Bobbi's stomach churn in ways she could not at all explain. Again, the horror of the alien made primordial circuits fire and beg for flight. She would not allow it. She could not. Like a black rocket, the stakes were hurtling ever higher.

Bobbi took another deep breath and began to crawl.

The two of them moved with purpose through the twisting guts of the ventwork, Cagliostro's blasphemous puppet moving with the ease with which it was designed and Bobbi struggling to keep up. Her armor and the coat grew so problematic that she ditched the plates in the next junction cubicle Cagliostro led her to. She kept the coat, though. She had also gotten used to the awful sight of the drone – the child's face was what bothered her the most, but it was largely invisible behind the crablike flailing of its limbs. If anything, it only further toughened her sense of purpose; she already knew how little the Yathi valued human life, but the hideous reworking of the chimera ahead of her made Bobbi angry in new and astonishingly violent ways.

But the anger that she felt was really only a stopgap measure to suppress the gnawing fear that now constantly laired in her belly. It wasn't enough that she was involved in a horrible alien conspiracy to effectively destroy the human species – oh no, she now found herself attempting to wrest the fate of the city, to say nothing of her own and those of her surviving friends, from the madness of a walking nuke. There were no means of getting a sensible handle on this scenario; it was entirely too weird to believe, much less process. There was only the moment at hand, the reality of it, and the only way out was through. She would probably have a long future of alcoholism ahead of her, if not a galaxy of tranquilizers as well, by the time this all came to a close.

Assuming she didn't get herself killed or vaporized in the next few hours, of course.

They took a very different track than she had expected. Rather than going quickly upward as Bobbi had intended, Cagliostro took her in a long arc that only gradually made its way toward the upper chamber. When she asked why this was, the machine turned its ghastly head her way and simply answered, "Patience." Bobbi wanted to probe, but Cagliostro would not answer further – and with no other option than to put her trust in the digital ghost, she did not speak again until they reached their destination.

Eventually the machine led her to yet another junction; this one, unlike the others, was a large hexagonal chamber with multiple ducts terminating along its walls. An opening in the central shaft led upward into darkness. Bobbi sat down hard in the center of the room, fatigue pulling heavily at her limbs, and surveyed the chamber without looking at the drone that crouched nearby.

"All right," she said, "Here we are. I think?"

"Indeed." The thing turned around and looked at her, staring at her in the dark. She stared at what was left of the little boy's face, rendered weirdly by the visor, the flanged mechanism that bristled beneath the ruined socket that was once a nose. Again the shiver, again the anger. "At the top of this shaft is a secondary receiver node linked to the control network. I activated it before I came to find you."

Bobbi looked upward into the dark once more. "Big climb," she muttered. "You're sure they haven't discovered it?"

"It is running a test cycle," said Cagliostro. "You will break this when you interface with it." He gave her a long string of numbers to serve as a network address, which Bobbi was able to get down after two tries and a lot of concentration – no cutesy labels here, just hard numerical codes.

"It won't take long for them to realize what's up," Bobbi murmured when she was sure that she had the address down. "All right, I'm on it. Just...watch out for me, all right? I don't want to get sucked up into a fan somewhere while I'm doing this."

"You can be assured security."

"You can never assure security in a situation like this, man," Bobbi muttered, and got herself into a lotus position there in the center of the room – she reached out into the ether, and sensed a sea of components singing together far above her, somewhere in the night at the top of the shaft. She was ready for it; after the shock of all the awakening signals of the corpses pulling their Lazarus gangbang routine back in the warehouse, the activity of the control nexus should be manageable.

Bobbi reached up, seeking the address of the receiver node, and found it at the outermost edge of the seething riot of computers and machinery. She breached the node like a needle piercing a vein, finding the flow of data easily, throwing herself into the bathwater flow of the Yathi network. In other circumstances, she might have been grateful for the sudden warmth, imaginary or not – but she had to tread quickly and carefully if they were going to beat Redeye to the vault of death below.

It was doubt that gripped her thoughts as she launched herself across the psychotronic realm that was the Yathi network, cloaking herself in layers of camouflage routines as she went. She floated high over the dizzying landscape of the system around her, beholding its complexity below. It was a vast construct, a city unto itself, filled with data nodes and regulatory matrices and more; everything had a place and a function, no trash data at all. Bobbi thought of Yathkalghn and the sprawling industrial complexes that clad the surface of that blasted world, the towers scratching the skies by the poisonous silver seas, the thick canopy of flashing mint-colored clouds that masked away the void. She saw symmetry with that vision and the network: everything evolved around her as she watched, expanded like a great silicate tumor, much as Seattle and the cities of Wonderland did, the civilizations which fueled them. Could her world truly come to look like this one?

Not on her watch. She floated at the fringes of the network, running quiet system queries. Bobbi was looking for the chute controls, but not just those. By Cagliostro's clock, they didn't have a lot of time until Redeye made her way down into the laboratory and blew the place up; Bobbi didn't trust the great ghost to tell her anything straight at this point, and though it was a risk, she thought that she would see what the security systems could tell her. Bobbi scanned the virtual horizon, watching systems that were unprotected a few hours ago becoming slowly encrusted with layers of defense programming. She was rather shocked at the lack of imagination that went into it; though she could hardly probe deeply as she trawled along, it seemed as though the Yathi programmers, whoever they were, intended to simply layer on many copies of the same baseline defense programs over their systems. Layers of simple concrete.

Why the hell would they do that? Any hack artist worth their salt – which Bobbi certainly was – could smash through that stuff in no time. As she continued to search, however, she realized that as simple as they were the layers of defense code were beginning to alter the system IDs of every attached node; the distinctive, carefully organized nomenclature of the network was melting into a homogenized, sequential nightmare. She could determine the function of various nodes from their system IDs and their placement in the network hierarchy, after all, but it was hard to tell what number twenty-three was from number two. Panic began to shoot through her and she abandoned the idea of the security grid; she'd have to find the hatch controls and be satisfied with that.

The task took several minutes, which at the eyeblink pace of the network was a grueling span. When she finally found the factory distribution node it was already well-plated with layers of that virtual concrete, its number long since changed; she managed to find the node by tracing down a few still-unprotected nodes connected to it. All hail the magic of hierarchy, Bobbi thought as she locked down its address and began preparing an intrusion program. She could not be subtle when she hit the node, much to her regret – when she hit the node it would have to be like a meteor, and she would have to hit so hard that she could open the hatches and trash the node before anyone could stop her.

It took several minutes for Bobbi to assemble the program she wanted to use, a task that on her own would have instead taken hours. The templates of Yathi virus programs – the most useful of these she'd taken to calling 'punch', 'kick' and 'big fucking gun' in her head to denote their scale of effectiveness – were able to be adroitly woven together to produce a larger whole thanks to the inbuilt protocols and her own imaginative instinct for programming; the data structures were different, but the remnants of the Cagliostro-ghost inside her head gave her sufficient context to assemble them. It was becoming easier and easier to do it, such that by the time she had finished Frankensteining the breaker program together she was doing it almost on automatic. There was no time to process the way that both empowered and disturbed her, nor how it gave her greater understanding of the network around her. There was only time for the missile she'd built to fall out of the sky.

She took a mental breath, collecting her focus, and then let fly.

The program took only a fraction of a second to execute and land on the primary distribution node, and when it hit, it hit like the fist of an angry god. Bobbi had assumed that it would punch through the Yathi defenses, but to her dawning horror it did more than that – like a bunker-buster that bored through its target into a heavily compromised mountain complex, the Yathi breaker prog didn't just penetrate the layers of defense laid atop the network node, it absolutely obliterated them. Milliseconds passed as Bobbi stared in open awe while the counterprogs vanished from her perceptions and the node read open for access, but then her danger senses kicked in and she realized that she had only moments to act before Yathi operators would react. She dove into the node, connecting and forcing her way through the node's control library, searching for the necessary commands to open the hatches by Violet and Scalli.

And yet there was no room for a surgical operation, for a full three seconds had passed before she felt the cold blowing in. The presences of Yathi minds, three of them, began to register on her mental threatboard like chunks of ice dropped into the warm water with her. Immediately, the meat of her began to revolt in their presence, and she felt with surprising clarity a phantom chill wrack her bones and her skin prickling. They were moving very fast, very fast indeed, and Bobbi found herself hitting any switch she could as the trio of white sharks closed on her position. All around her, reports began coming in – of distribution lines starting up, hatches opening throughout the complex, the whole factory beginning to come to life as its primary method of transport was awakened.

It was like running her hands across a control console, hitting every button at once – and, Bobbi hoped, it would stay the attention of her attackers as everything started into chaos. As milliseconds passed and she angled herself for an exit, however, she felt the first stings of attack virii peeling back her camouflage programs. They had found her, and they were drilling through the meager protection the mimetic code provided as though it were only paper. Alarms were going off in her head, part software and part sheer animal instinct screaming for her to get out, to get away. She had to do something fast, else she would be dead – or worse – in seconds.

So she did the only thing she could. She dropped another virus bomb.

Calling it a "bomb," of course, was facetious; it was a rapidly-expanding viral complex that attacked multiple layers of defensive software in sequence as it was found. The Yathi minds were well-sheathed in such armor, far better than the node, but they could not help but pause as their skillfully-designed defenses were being blown to ash around them. As powerful as it was, however, it was very likely to damage everything around it as well – which meant the operating software of the network node itself, if the Yathi idea of a computer was anything at all like what humanity used. Having raised merry hell in the moment, Bobbi had the opening she needed, and she took it.

She disengaged from the control node while the Yathi operators were still trying to shore up their defenses and tried to execute a hard drop of out the system, pulling the plug very literally, and found with new horror that the wireless link would not sever. What the hell was that? She tried hard to keep panic back as she scrambled to check her headware. Dropping a hard line connection would be dangerous, but she should be able to force the implant in her skull to kill the link. Meanwhile, she sensed new cold – the operators were emerging from the distribution network. Bobbi began spinning up new walls of defense, combat software, as much as her headware would allow while she searched frantically for somewhere else that she could hide while she tried to find another way to disconnect. Try as she might, however, there was no respite; everywhere there were only fortifying nodes, sequentially ordered and heavily shielded.

Anything she hit would give her away, she knew...or would it? Bobbi lurched forward through the network, attacking nodes at random, watching the walls of bland digital concrete splinter and fall away from machines whose purpose she could not know. Alarms began picking up across the system as the breached nodes cried out – Bobbi soared along, a purple-haired supersonic bomber, carpeting everything with as much virtual explosive as she could throw in her wake. She dared the three Yathi operators to track her down in the chaos. When all else fails, break shit, she thought with triumph as the cold vanished and there was only the electric buzzing of the breached systems mushrooming up around her. Break all the shit that you can.

With the smoldering ruins of code layers behind her and chaos spreading through the system, Bobbi took a moment to try and figure out just what the hell was keeping her in the system. The command to disconnect the system went out to the network and back again; it made sense that something would be keeping her from doing it smoothly. But a hard drop was on her end, entirely in her own hardware – risky, yes, but it should have already happened. Her hard requests, however, were going absolutely nowhere. Bobbi started to feel real panic that she would not be able to disconnect, that she had vastly underestimated the power the Yathi system would have over her; was it somehow able to suspend her own internal functions, keeping her connected so that she could be hunted down? Bobbi continued to turtle up, layers of protection building around her digital presence as she tried to figure out just what the hell was going on.

Then she took the hit.

Alarms went off in her head as the layers of her defenses began to evaporate. Bobbi's heart leapt into her throat as she found herself under attack from unknown quarters, no cold or otherwise to indicate another mind was present. For a few key milliseconds, confusion reigned as Bobbi attempted to keep herself together; whatever program had hit her, it was enough to shred through the majority of her defenses upon activation. There had been no warning. Bobbi braced for another hit, but none came.

What came instead was a cold such as Bobbi had never felt before, cold enough to freeze her in place as her mind struggled to grasp it. The individual Yathi minds that she had felt had been freezing, but self-contained; easier to manage than the Chorus, which had been a vast black sea into which she had been directly plugged. That which came now, however, dwarfed them all. Though she was not surrounded by it, as she had been with the Chorus, Bobbi could not deny the overwhelming vastness of what rose to meet her now; it was the world, blotting out the system around it, or perhaps wresting away all of her implant's ability to perceive the world around it. Or, her mind whispered to her, perhaps it was the system. Perhaps another Chorus of far greater scope than she had imagined. Bobbi found herself floating in the face of a great black star, and she was but a mote before its power.

Presently, it spoke. Bobbi was startled to hear that it had a real voice in her head – a beautiful voice, human, female. She knew it from television, though as her mind began to slow in the presence of the monstrous thing she could not pin it down.

<LITTLE MEAT,> said that magnificent voice, every word aching in her mind, <WHO ARE YOU?>

Bobbi grasped for a reply. What could she do? What could she say? She had to get away, to escape – it was if her brain was starting to fragment before, like a data drive on its last legs. <I'm Brain Mother,> she responded as she wracked her brain for options. What the hell could she do in the face of something so massive? <Who the hell are you?>

<HOW INTERESTING,> replied the vastness before her. <I AM A MOTHER, TOO. YET YOU ARE NOT ONE OF MINE.>

<Sorry to disappoint you.> The words were brave, but Bobbi didn't feel it. She thought she knew what this was now, or more to the point, who it was.

Bobbi's mind whirled; dulled as it was becoming, she wasn't nearly stupid enough not to try and get away. No way in hell could she attack it. It would be like throwing a pebble at a wall. So what could she do? There had to be a way. There had to be.

<NO DISAPPOINTMENT,> the great thing was saying now. <MERELY CURIOSITY. YOU ARE CAUSING A GREAT DEAL OF TROUBLE FOR ME.> The surface of the presence seemed to vibrate for a fraction of a second, something Bobbi knew to be a trace of some program executing within; a few moments passed in silence before it spoke again. <YOU HAVE MANAGED TO DO SOMETHING WHICH I HAD NOT ANTICIPATED, NOR DID I THINK POSSIBLE. YOU SHOULD BE KILLED, I SUPPOSE.>

At this, Bobbi felt distant muscles tighten. If she was hit again, that would be it; her defenses were weak, and she was too busy trying to develop the new package on the fly to rebuild them. Had to keep her – it – talking. <Yeah, but then you wouldn't know what happened to get me

here, would you? And you can't hit me because you'll cook my brains, isn't that right?> Gotta be like a squid, baby, gotta be like sushi getting away. She grasped for another basic program template; she'd have to do some freeform assembly, and if she had been religious she would have prayed to the Goddess of All Righteous Hacks that the protocols could translate her desires correctly into what was necessary to carry off the job. Bobbi drew a deep breath in the world of meat, stilling herself, trying to keep herself focused as she began to envision code.

The surface of the great being vibrated again. <INTERESTING,> it replied. <YOU ASSUME THAT I DO NOT ALREADY KNOW WHAT HAS BEEN DONE. THAT YOU NEED TO BE CAPTURED.>

<If you did, you'd have killed me already,> Bobbi said. The code cooked along, the protocols and her headware untroubled by her slowing mind. It was as though gauze were being stuffed into her head, shutting her down by the second. Only fear, defiance, and will kept her from shutting down entirely. Her adrenals were no doubt working on overdrive. <I remember what I felt when I hacked that thing. That centipede. It was afraid.>

<THE OPERATOR WAS VERY SURPRISED, YES.> Amusement was ripe in that terrible voice. <AS WAS I. DO YOU KNOW WHO I AM, BRAIN MOTHER?>

<Yeah. I know who you are.> Recognition lag had finally caught up with her, and Bobbi knew that she stared into the virtual face of the great beast herself, Ghia Merducci, the Mother of Systems. She was fucked, completely fucked, and she knew it. That didn't mean she wouldn't try anyway. <I've been wanting to meet you, in fact. Mostly because I wanted to shoot you in the face, but I guess you and I both know that wouldn't work.>

<INDEED.> Again the amusement – but unlike Cagliostro's, which was something more akin to a parent witnessing a child's actions, the malice in the Mother's voice was without question. <IT WOULD BE EQUALLY INEFFECTIVE FOR YOU TO ATTEMPT AN ASSAULT HERE, LITTLE MEAT. I WILL FIND YOU.>

<I'm not your problem,> Bobbi replied. <Your problem is that one-woman army tearing through this factory right now. You know what she's after, don't you?>

<THAT CREATURE IS HARDLY IMMORTAL,> replied the Mother. <SHE MAY KILL EVERY CORPSE IN THE COMPLEX AND STILL SHE WILL DIE BEFORE SHE REACHES HER DESTINATION.>

<That's what you think,> Bobbi said, and she felt herself getting a little stupid now. But there was nothing wrong with her memory, and hearing the thunderous mockery of the she-thing's words, smirking and amused, the engineer of so much pain and death, her mind was off-track just enough for her to throw self-preservation to the winds. A bold rage exploded inside her, and her virtual mouth followed. <You know what? Fuck you, lady. I hope I do meet you. I really do.>

The Mother of Systems laughed, and the haughty, musical lilt of it sped the corrosion of reason. <AND WHY IS THAT?>

Through the haze of rising hate and anger, Bobbi was suddenly aware that a program had finished compiling. It took her a moment to realize that it was her own. She laughed – she heard herself do it, very far away – and her mental voice took on a dangerous edge. <Because when I meet you, in person? I'll have what I need to kill you. You may have lived here for three centuries, but I know what you are and I know that your grand solution isn't working nearly so well as you thought it would. You better believe that I'm going to do everything I can to wipe out every last one of you motherfuckers, and when the time comes for it, it's going to be me who shoots you in the face.>

In an instant, the sea changed. The surface of the Mother's presence began to thrum in earnest, and as it did Bobbi felt white-hot lances of pain run through her. Her brain felt as if it were vibrating apart. She wanted to scream, to say something – anything – but nothing rose to the surface but garbage characters across the back of her mental screen. <SHOT IN THE FACE, YOU SAY,> hissed the Mother of Systems. <AND YOU THINK THAT YOU WILL KILL US ALL? I TAKE IT BACK. I DON'T NEED TO CAPTURE YOU. I WILL BOIL THE LOWER-ORDER MONKEY BRAINS INSIDE THAT HIDEOUS SACK OF BONES YOU CALL A HEAD, TAKE YOUR IMPLANT, AND DISSECT IT MYSELF.>

So powerful was the pain and shock that shuddered through Bobbi's body, the clamor of the alarms that crowded up her head from her implant monitors, that she could barely perceive the ranting of the monstrous thing that was now literally battering her mind apart. And yet, through the haze of pain, there was a light; as there had been before, she perceived something, something tiny, almost unreachable. The program that she had written. With the last of the power that her fading mind possessed she reached out, bidding it to execute, and then...

For a moment, her mental presence was replicated by a factor of twenty, then twenty more, and twenty more than that – mirror images everywhere, they soaked up the power of the assault that the Mother of

Systems poured forth, shattering like glass even as they piled up around Bobbi's battered consciousness. For a moment she thought that she would be lost. Instead she found herself coming back, and what's more, she felt something else return: control, control that must have been subtly draining away from the moment she entered the network. Control over her connectivity.

She willed the link to break, a hard drop, and found herself plunging into eternity.

With the wireless link severed she was falling back into her meat, and when she returned her head very nearly exploded. Bolts of white-hot pain lanced through her as if a cage of barbed wire were wrapped around her brain, squeezing down hard into the tissue, and she saw the white planes of the junction room through her visor for only a moment before she blacked out on the floor.

CHAPTER 23

"Son of a fuck, Vi. What happened to her?"

Scalli's voice rang in Bobbi's ears, and she realized that she was no longer in the ducts. She opened her eyes and found the hard green light of factory lamps bathing her skin again, and that her visor was off and in her hand. Her head didn't hurt anymore, but her brain still ran so very, very slow as she returned to consciousness. She knelt upon the floor of the warehouse room that she had originally left; Scalli and Violet stood over her, looking down with a mixture of shock and deep concern written over their faces. Bobbi did not know why they looked so stricken. Her eyes tracked everywhere – the walls, the ceiling, the still tomb that rested in the center of the room. She saw with that the hatches were open, and that now simple gratings separated the room with what looked like dimly-lit tunnels beyond. Yet their attention was upon her. Why did they look at her like that?

"She must have run into the corpses," Violet said, her brows arched. "I don't know how she did it, cuz she didn't have a gun. Holy shit, man, look at her!"

Bobbi did just that, and shuddered. The front of her was coated with the white tide of synthetic blood; her senses suddenly filled with the stink of it in her nostrils, the ozone stab surging and fading away, as she stared down at herself. She froze as she looked at herself, the world draining away.

Scalli crouched down to look at her. "Bobbi, honey," he said, his voice low and soft, "Bobbi, honey, look at me."

"Yeah?" Bobbi did so numbly. Confusion filled her mind as she met his gaze, blinking at him as if she were coming out of some kind of dream or trance. It certainly felt like it. What had happened? Where had she been?

Scalli glanced at Violet before looking back to Bobbi. "You all right, baby girl? Where's your armor?"

"I...had to take it off, in the ducts." Bobbi said the words but she did not feel them at all. She did not remember where the blood had come from. In fact, she found that she was having a hard time remembering anything at all after linking up with the Yathi system. The blackness yawned at her in her mind like a hungry mouth, which in itself was an image that she felt she should remember but her sluggish mind resisted recollection. "On the way up. And then I hacked the control...system, and then...then..."

Enormous cold, the yawning death that came to eat her mind. The narrow escape that frayed her mind. She felt calm now, but how?

"I think I ran into one of the drones on my way back."

"And? What happened?"

Bobbi reached in the dark for memories, but found only snatches of images floating to the surface. Fragments of paper on black water, soaked through and ragged. "I...I must have killed it," she said.

"But how?" Violet frowned at her. "You didn't have a gun."

Bobbi blinked at them slowly. Her brain was starting to work again, even if remembering was still like fishing in a dark lake. "With my knife."

Scalli and Violet exchanged looks. Scalli was shocked, even impressed; Violet's face was weirdly calm as she looked back at Bobbi. "With a knife, you said?"

"Yes! Close quarters, makes a mess," Bobbi blurted, and the memory of crisis pushed the disturbing blank out of her head for the time being. "We have to get out of here. We have to get down to find Redeye."

Scalli blinked at her. "Yeah, we know," he said, and he rose with Bobbi; his expression was one of disbelief. "Girl, are you okay? Are you –"

"No time!" Bobbi shook her head. "No time, no time!" She looked at Violet then. "Violet, honey, I need to say this, and you have to promise not to gnaw my face off when I do. It's very important." She didn't give Violet a chance to respond, however. Instead she began to tell them, all in a flood, what it was that she had experienced and what Cagliostro had told her. She told them about her attack on the system and about her brush with the great horror that was the Ghia-Mother, but her passage back to the storage room after blacking out still eluded her. She did not give them opening to speak, so fast was the gushing of her words, and when she was done they stared at her in silence.

Finally, Scalli spoke. "Well," he said, "that...sounds like a hell of a time." His voice was very quiet.

Bobbi stared at Violet, waiting to see if she would leap at her and try to bite her throat out with those ultra-sharp teeth of hers. And yet she did not; the blankness remained on her face for a long moment, and then, when she spoke, Violet's voice was very thin, very hurt, but entirely unsurprised.

"The Eye had always said that she would make them pay with her own life," Violet said, and took a deep breath. "She told us that it would all end in fire."

Violet's reaction – or rather, the temperance of it – made Bobbi anxious. She'd expected that Violet would have tried to bite her throat out for so much as thinking about taking Redeye down, but this was entirely unexpected. "You believe me?"

"Of course I do," Violet said. Her brows turned down a bit. "I was built to tell when people lie, remember?" There was something in the way she looked at Bobbi now, something weirdly...admiring, perhaps. It made Bobbi even more nervous in that moment than the prospect of her fury.

"Bobbi," Scalli said, "are you sure that this is all on the level? This isn't some crazy shit that Cagliostro is coming up with for his own ends? He was one of them too, after all. It's because of him that we've gotten dragged out here in the first place."

"He was," said Bobbi with a nod, "and this may in fact be according to some plan of his, I don't know. But we're here, and we're going to eat it if she goes off, and so will half the goddamned city. We need to get down there and try and talk her out of this. Maybe we still can."

Violet made a soft noise. "I don't think that's going to work," she said. "Maybe, if we're lucky. But I've never known her mind to change. We may have to..." She shut her eyes tight for a moment, then sounded very sad indeed. "We will probably have to kill her." Despite everything that went on, despite the sudden gaping hole in her memory, Bobbi still felt a stab of pity for the girl. She knew how this must feel. She knew how it was when her own mother died, crazy bitch that she was. Violet may have had her own parents, but she had given them up when the Yathi took her and Ghia served as mother. Then Violet shook that bitch off, and then Redeye took the post. It seemed fated that there would never be a mother for her now that she would not have to kill or abandon.

Bobbi understood that plenty. "We'll see what we can do," she said, and she reached out past Scalli to lay her hand on Violet's shoulder.

"But wait, Bobbi." Scalli frowned. "What about Merducci being here? Surely that puts a kink in things, doesn't it?"

"As ridiculously fucking scary and mind-damaging as running into her was, I don't think it does. She came because of me, not because of Redeye."

"Yeah, but she told you that Red would get killed one way or the other down here. She sounded pretty sure of that. Maybe this is part of her plan, too?"

Bobbi glanced at Violet, who was still staring at her in that same weird way. "I don't think she does know what's going on with her," she said, looking back to Scalli. "I think she's just dead set on killing Red, which means we need to be very careful."

"Dead set on killing you now, too," Scalli pointed out.

"Yeah, well, I make friends wherever I go, don't I?" Bobbi nodded at the chutes. "We need to get out of here."

"Well, you got the hatches open." Scalli nodded at the two screens which led to the tunnels. "We can go now, though I don't know how we're going to get back out. The screens there slide open easy enough, but we're at the top of the chutes. If we want to get out of here, we'll have to go back the way we came."

"Considering how Red's going through the local constabulary, I don't think that's going to be much of a problem." Bobbi shook her head. "Cagliostro said that she's tearing through the defenses, and the Yathi are putting all their energy behind stopping her. She's being slowed down pretty good, I would imagine."

"Let's hope we can get down there before she does." Violet glanced at Bobbi's hand, but didn't shrug it off. She then turned toward the entrances to the chutes. "Do we know which goes to where?"

"Unfortunately not," Bobbi said. "But I'm actually pretty sure they both go down to the drone factory. Honestly, I'm not really sure what's going to happen when we get there – I don't even know if Cagliostro's gonna be around to help us any more than he has."

"Well, let's assume he will be eventually." Scalli walked to the screens, reaching for the handle of one and pulling it open; it slid silently on its tracks, just as the hatches must have, and it was with caution that the big man leaned through the opening and peered down the chute. "We haven't seen anything that would be any kind of defensive measure, at least nothing that either of us could identify. Does look like there are ladders down this way, or something like that."

"What do you, mean, 'something like that'?" Bobbi let go of Violet and walked over as well, peering down through the chute. It yawned downward, a dizzying hexagonal passage lit greasily in distant intervals by light fixtures. The bottom was not immediately visible. She took a deep breath as she gazed down into the poorly-lit well, feeling a flash of vertigo. "Christ," she muttered. "That's a fucking long drop, all right."

Bobbi felt Scalli's eyes on her, covered with drying blood as she was, and tried very hard to push that out of her mind. "Yeah," he said. "Okay, so, look over here, right?" Scalli gestured with a wide hand at a series of what looked like rungs, four or five of them, that were set into a track that ran down toward the bottom of the chute. A set of these rungs were built into each of the chute's six walls. "I think they're like ziplines, you know?"

"Yeah." Violet had come up behind them both. She put her hand on Bobbi's shoulder, squeezing it gently through the coat. "So, I guess you grab one and it takes you to the bottom of the shaft."

"Makes you wonder how they get stuff up here," Bobbi said.

Violet leaned in a bit more. Bobbi had the bizarre thought that she was sniffing her, but Violet drew her head back to speak before she could tell for sure. "Probably the tracks, same thing. Well. I guess let's get there." She sounded sad, though not as much as she had a moment ago. Resolved, now. Bobbi wasn't sure what to think about that.

Bobbi reached out for the closest rung, but Scalli reached out and gently drew her hand away. "Bricks first," he said, and took hold of a grip up from the bottommost, which he planted his foot upon. It eased down with his leg to become a foothold, and the two women moved aside as Scalli swung his great bulk into the chute and immediately began to descend. After a few moments' descent, when Scalli was a few body lengths away, Bobbi followed on the wall facing opposite the exit. Violet descended soon after.

It wasn't as slow as Bobbi had thought it might be, though part of her wished that it would take a little longer than it was. It was the same part that had felt strangely exposed when Violet brought her head near, that wondered what had happened after she blacked out tangling with Ghia. She felt the strangest fragment of a dream, felt a strange taste in her mouth. With the back of her free hand she wiped at her face, came back with a greasy slick of white. Shit, she thought to herself. Must have gotten all over me. She reached into her bag as she descended, rummaging around for a mirror; she came up with the reflective case of a hand-warmer that she carried around to dick with infrared sensors, and held it up to her face.

She nearly dropped the damned thing when she saw the face that stared back at her; her face was smeared with the stubborn gray-whiteness of drying synthetic blood, her eyes staring back in the gloom as if her face were covered with warpaint. All in her hair, too, so that it looked like a flipped-back wing atop her head. It reminded her of the bird-of-paradise job she had when she met Tom, but more so it reminded her of the girl in her dreams, the one with the digital spear. The girl that she had been so long ago. She thought of the great coldness that had tried to eat her mind in the network above, how it had been so different than the bland beast of the Chorus – it had been many and yet one at once, so hungry, so angry. She had met the tiger that she had dreamed of so many months ago, and she had been very nearly mauled. Nor did Bobbi have the spear of fractal data yet, whatever it would prove to be. But she would. She'd make sure of that.

A shudder ran through Bobbi's body and the hand warmer fell from her grip. It fell like a gleaming stone and clattered as it landed upon the bottom of the factory chute. Scalli tensed immediately and shot a black look upwards at her, which she answered with one that was equal parts 'sorry!' and 'oh, shit.' The big man unlimbered the Dragon from his pack, being the smaller and more maneuverable of the guns available to him now. He must have already chambered a capsule beforehand, because he kept its fist-sized muzzle trained on the exit hatch as they drew near the bottom.

Scalli landed first, stepping off onto the floor of the chute. He looked out of the open hatches, the Dragon in his hand. Bobbi waited until she landed behind him to speak. "Hey," she said. "You see anything out there?"

It took him a few seconds to reply. "Uh, yeah," he said, and his voice was distant. "Yeah. Wish I didn't, though."

Bobbi pushed past him and looked out at the room beyond, and found pause as well. The drone factory was as the processor was, as twice as cavernous as the structure above and jammed packed with the bizarre machinery required to carry out its grim work. At a glance, the engines of dark industry that towered over them were obviously designed to accept the corpses delivered from above and assemble them into...whatever it is that they wanted, really. And it was also clear that a great number of active corpses had been kept in storage in the factory – for there was a wide central aisle that ran from the chute hatches to the far end of the room, and it had been converted into an impromptu slaughterhouse floor.

The naked bodies of countless drones lay strewn in the aisle, fallen across the path or piled up against the sides of the machines that made them. Each one of them had been violently killed, reduced to gory tangles of severed limbs and ruptured torsos that littered the gore-slicked floor. Many of the dead were naked, freshly-created perhaps, but some others were armed and plated up like the ones above. Either way, it didn't seem to have mattered; they all fell just the same. It was as if a storm had torn through the risen horde, and everything before it had been scythed down without mercy. They had not seen much of Redeye's ability on the warehouse floor above, but now there was clear testimony as to what they truly faced.

"The Eye has been busy," Violet murmured softly behind them.

"Yeah," Scalli murmured. Bobbi heard awe in his voice, awe that she shared. "No shit she's been busy."

And yet awe was not enough for her, not after standing mind-to-mind with the Mother. "Well, if we're gonna die, we better get down there and make it happen," she said. "She's got to be slowing down at this point. You don't do...this...and you don't lose steam. Violet, she bleeds, doesn't she?"

"She does," Violet said with a nod. It was rather like admitting God had a glass jaw from the sound of her voice, but there it was. "The same blood as all of them, so we couldn't tell."

"So she could be dead in that mess," Scalli said. "Or in the next room."

"She's not dead," Violet said. "That much I know." She looked to the doors at the end of the room. "She's got to have gone that way."

"Like I said," Bobbi said, and trudged forward. At this point, as terrible as the scene may have been, it was now just more of the same. "Let's get on with it."

It is so very strange how the sight of carnage, which grinds down many a human soul, can conjure up such bravery in others. Or, perhaps it isn't bravery so much as it is just anger, raw and undistilled, when the prey-animal within is finally beaten into silence by the evils of the world and the lizard brain steps up to take the stick. Twenty minutes ago, Bobbi had woken up after a brain-shredding brush with the queen of all the monsters on Earth, having dragged herself through many meters of ductwork and apparently killed a drone with a sixty-year-old surplus combat knife that she had somehow lost afterward. She was covered with blood, and had a hole in her short-term memory that would otherwise have revealed what had happened to her. Unarmed and without body armor, she could be easily killed.

But she strode through the mangled remains of what had once been nearly a hundred walking dead, across the factory toward yet another black door leading to what could very well be a showdown with a woman who had proven herself more capable in combat than a small force of the most heavily armed human soldiers. She marched toward what would probably be a violent, bloody death, and for the first time she did it without fear. Bobbi the cowgirl, with the wisecracks that hid twenty-odd years of emotional damage and loneliness, had been entirely subsumed; there was only Roberta January, filled with strength that she had always second-guessed, a laser-sharp clarity of purpose, and a pure, righteous anger that burned within her like a white flame. If she did not survive the night, it would not be for lack of trying – and if she did, she would do everything she could to fulfill the promise that she had made to the Yathi matriarch. In this instant she was every badass crusading female of history, Joan of Arc and Golda Meir, Boudicca and Angie Zero. In this moment, armor and weapons did not matter to her. In this moment, she felt invincible.

Bobbi willed the door to open as she approached it, wet to her calves in thickening gore, and she did not look down at the dead as she trod over them. She looked straight ahead as the black slabs of metal slid open and another corridor was revealed stretching onward and down into darkness. Her eyes were immediately drawn to a long smear of white blood running from the dead at the door and down the dark hall, gleaming dully in the light of the green lamp. "I told you she was hurt," Bobbi said as she stepped over the threshold into the hall. "She must be pretty torn up."

"If she is bleeding," came Violet's voice from behind them, "then she must be very bad off. I've never seen her bleed before."

"Yeah." Bobbi sighed. "This must be the last corridor going down. You guys watch yourselves."

"Yes ma'am," said Scalli. He sounded as if he were addressing a superior officer. "You want to be armed up?"

Bobbi looked back at him. "Not for me, Scalli," she said. "You'll need all the firepower you can get, I think. I'll have to rely on my powers of persuasion."

"Just make sure you get behind me if that doesn't work," Scalli rumbled. "Otherwise she's gonna kill your brave little ass."

"She faced the Mother," Violet said. "And she survived. The Eye has no hope."

Were Bobbi not so focused on the goal ahead, perhaps she would have been much more disturbed by the manic certainty with which Violet said those words. But that was Violet; she was a believer. It was part of her madness, and just by directly spitting in the face of the Devil, Bobbi had filled the void that Redeye's absence had made in her. It was better than the alternative. Violet snapping and opening up on them with her assault rifle would be a very short ending to their long and terrible story. On the other hand, as badly as it appeared Redeye had been wounded, the story might be coming to a swift end after all.

They followed the trail of synthetic blood, quickly but carefully, as the corridor twisted ever downward into the lowermost bowels of the complex. The sight of the horrible graying smear gave Bobbi real hope that Redeye was worn down enough that they may be able to stop her, or at the very least talk her into leaving with them to repair and hit the Yathi at another time. Of course, she'd have to figure out how to explain why they wanted to stop her in the first place, and deal with the whole walking nuke thing that the cyborg war-goddess had going on, but she felt oddly unworried about it. Nothing seemed to worry her right now. What would be the point?

And yet as the proceeded, signs began to appear that indicated that the gory trail was in no way an indicator of weakness on Redeye's part. The stumps of turrets that had been destroyed by her avenging fists, or torn out of their mountings. Bizarre frames girding stretches of the corridor that Bobbi took to be field projectors, smashed dead and spitting only feeble sparks. They passed the ruins of a drone that was as big as Scalli was, an ogre-like thing with multiple arms that was encased in heavy armor. There was a gaping wound in its chest where Redeye had literally torn out its mechanized heart; they found the flabby, bleached organ ten feet down the hall where she had apparently thrown it.

And yet in the face of all of this, the bloody trail still persisted. The three of them followed it hopefully; everything that they had passed, everything that they had witnessed, surely all of this had drained her. If she were entirely human, Bobbi would have said that she was running on massive doses of endorphin analog and military-grade combat stimulants. But as she wasn't, the blood was only going to affect certain organs. Like her brain, Bobbi realized with a start. She was a full conversion; only her brain was biological. If she'd taken a headshot and was bleeding out, body damage wouldn't matter. She would doubtless be dropping from oxygen starvation soon.

Past the corpse, they were drawing near the end of the tunnel; strangely enough, there were no more defenses to destroy. As they descended deeper into the bowels of the complex, however, they heard the unmistakable sounds of destruction boiling up from below. Electric whines, the sound of impact and tearing metal. They picked up the pace, jogging down the corridor now, heedless of the sound of their feet upon the flooring. Time was of the essence, now, and they would have to sacrifice stealth for action.

They took a final turn, and found themselves at the end of the corridor. It widened into a kind of lobby, the walls of which were plated in glossy white like it had been at the back door entrance. The walls were scored with blackened furrows, as if someone had gone at them with a laser cutter. At the end of the lobby stood a massive pair of double doors made of the same light-sucking substance as the one that had led into the complex; the two slabs of the door had parted enough that two people could get through, and a strange gray mist boiled through the aperture to hang at nearly chest height in the room. The mist somewhat concealed the remains of ruined machines that littered the floor, what appeared to be still more turrets that had risen from their mounts and had been violently dismantled. A shadowed figure was also wreathed in the gunmetal vapor, and it now rose with some difficulty to stand.

Bobbi, Scalli and Violet froze in their tracks as Redeye rose, stopping thirty feet away from the mouth of the lobby. There was no mistaking the thin figure that emerged from the smoke. Her clothes shredded, her hair cut in crazy ways from the near misses of claws and beams, her pale body scorched and crisscrossed with angry black welts from the assault of unknowable weapons, the Fury still stood, victorious and lethal. She gazed upon them all with her mismatched eyes, one dark, the other blazing crimson.

"Well," said Redeye, and her voice was equal parts defiance and resignation. "You have caught up at last."

And so they had – but looking at Redeye now, scarred though she may be, Bobbi had little clue how they would survive it.

CHAPTER 24

The four of them stood there in silence. After all that they had seen, it was very difficult for Bobbi or her fellows to come up with a suitable reply to Redeye's simple statement. They had caught up with her, yes. But now what? Bobbi found herself grasping at mental straws.

In the end, it was Violet who first broke the silence. "The Eye has been exceptional in punishing her enemies," the feral priestess said, sounding the part once more. "She is as powerful as ever."

Redeye smiled at that. "Thank you, Violet," she said. "I apologize for striking off on my own. Once I was sure that you were safe –"

"Not all of us." Bobbi could not hide the ice in her words as she thought of Mason.

"So I see," Redeye replied, and nodded. "I did not witness his death, but I am sure that it was no mean sacrifice."

"Some sacrifice," Bobbi muttered under the link. This far away, they could mutter to one another unheard. Then she called out, "Well, here we are. What's next?"

"The nexus is in the next room," Redeye replied. "I was about to go inside. You will join me, of course."

"Yeah..." Bobbi squinted at Redeye, gauging. She didn't like feeling as if she were going to incite a murder, yet incredibly that's precisely how she felt in this moment. Redeye didn't seem to suspect anything; she looked pleased, even proud of the progress she'd made through the Yathi defense. And here they were at the last vault.

"You think she's really going to do this?" Scalli gave Bobbi's insecurity about the situation voice. "She doesn't look like she's expecting anything."

"The Eye is wiser than she looks," Violet murmured. "I read suspicion in her way."

And Violet would be the expert, Bobbi thought to herself. "I'm going to talk to her."

"I think that's a bad idea, Bobbi," Scalli muttered.

"We don't have much of a choice." Bobbi took a deep breath. "Just get ready to hose her down if we have to. I'd rather this not turn into a fight." Before anyone could argue, Bobbi took a few steps forward. "Hold up a moment, Red," she called back. She made sure that her hands were visible, held slightly outward from her sides. "I want to talk to you about something."

Redeye tilted her head very slightly. "Very well," she replied, and folded her hands over her half-bared chest. Her clothes looked as if they had been clawed apart by some angry jungle cat. "Has something happened of which I am not aware?"

Bobbi drew a deep breath. She was going to open her mouth, all right, but the odds were that Redeye would be taking her head off before the wind had fully left her lungs. Here went nothing. "I've talked to Cagliostro," she said. "He told me about what happened when you two were connected."

There was silence for a moment, then another. Bobbi could feel the tension filling the corridor as if it were a thin halon gas, replacing the oxygen part by part. "I see," Redeye said, and her tone flattened out immediately. "And what did he tell you?"

"He told me that you attacked him."

"Did he." Redeye's brows arched. "And did he also tell you why?"

Bobbi felt herself shifting slightly on the spot as the angry red implant stared at her from its socket in Redeye's face. She felt as if it could concentrate into a laser at any moment and take off the top of her skull. "He said that you didn't want to hear what he had to say," Bobbi said after a moment. "He said you're stuck on this thing inside being the colonial nexus. But it's not, according to him."

Redeye's eyes narrowed faintly. "I see. Well, since he's managed to get you to listen to him, tell me – what does he say it is?"

"He said it was a terraforming laboratory, Red." Bobbi took a few steps forward, feeling the moment swing her way a bit. "If you destroy this place, it will put billions of nanomachines in the air that will change this planet, and not for the better."

"I fail to see how my destroying this place will do that." Redeye tilted her chin back a bit, her tone growing imperious. "I assume he told you how I intended to do it."

"He told me about your ultimate purpose, yeah," Bobbi said with a nod. "He told me about the nuke you've got inside of you."

At that, Redeye's expression hardened. "If he told you that," she said, "then surely you must know that it would be impossible for the nanomachines – if they in fact exist – to disperse. A thermonuclear explosion would annihilate the entire colony."

"She's got you there," Scalli muttered into the link. "I have to say I didn't think of that myself."

"Look," Bobbi called back, ignoring Scalli. "If that's the case, fine, all right – but why do you have to destroy yourself? Don't you know what that's going to do to a lot of people living out here? You're going to end up killing thousands of people if you let this happen!"

But Redeye wasn't going to hear that, it seemed. "How am I going to do that?" she asked, her hands on her hips. "Have you not seen this place, what it is made of? The device inside of me is literally only half of a kiloton in strength; it is a self-destruct mechanism, nothing more. It would destroy the laboratory, not the complex itself."

Bobbi frowned again. "Violet," she muttered under her breath. "Is she telling the truth?"

"She certainly seems to think she is." Violet sounded as confused as she was.

"Well, someone's feeding us bullshit," Scalli rumbled.

"There is no reason for us not to proceed," Redeye said, and frowned. "Whatever he has told you, the thing you call Cagliostro has been steering us all as much as the Mother of Systems has, and now he sends you to stop me? I trust nothing that he tells me, and nor should you. The enemy is here. We must destroy what we can."

"Fine enough, " Bobbi replied, "I hear what you're saying – and yeah, I know, he's a fucking puppeteer. I don't trust him either – but on the other hand, how do you know what you've got inside of you? You only have specs to go on, right? Specs that he's fed you in the past? Cagliostro tells me your yield is four kilotons. But what if he's lying again? You could have enough in you to take out this city and we wouldn't know. How can we be certain of anything?"

Redeye hesitated before she replied, and it gave Bobbi hope. "You may be correct," she replied with a faint nod.

"All right," Bobbi called out, "so let's say I am. Where do we go from here? I can't let you do something that might pollute this whole city, Red. You want to strike a blow against the Yathi, great, but we aren't going to do it just wading through their supply of monsters. So why don't we save this kamikaze thing for another day? Save your strength for bigger fish and all that."

Redeye was quiet for a long moment. Bobbi watched her face for signs of what would come next – but the pale features were frozen as their owner stared at them with mismatched eyes. "You don't understand," Redeye called out.

"Make me understand, then." Bobbi began to approach the mouth of the lobby.

Redeye blinked once, then again, and Bobbi froze in place. She watched as a single tear slid down the cyborg's face, a jewel budded from the crimson eye. "I just want this to be over."

Again the wave of pity crashed through Bobbi's heart. How often had she thought of Redeye as a combat machine? How often had Bobbi seen her as a weapon, an asset? How often had she thought of her as a human being? Because that was, in the end, precisely what she was; a human being who had been transferred into an unliving body of exotic science and unliving materials. A little girl's brain that had been forced to mature in strange flesh. Bobbi felt the awful ache of shame in her gut at the lack of consideration she had given this truth; humanity was endangered, certainly, but it was only through its own inherent weaknesses. The true victims in this invisible war, such as it was, were people like the cyborg.

"Red," Bobbi said, reaching out with one hand, "I'm sorry. I can't imagine what it's like for you, living like this – I just know that it doesn't have to be the end. Come on, honey. Fight with us. We'll put an end to this; full conversions have been returned to clonal bodies in the past, the technology's out there. Maybe we can help you."

"There is nothing that can help me now." Redeye took a few steps forward, emerging from the mist; doing so revealed a horrible injury. A hole the size of a thermos perforated her body, just under her right ribs, revealing the silhouettes of ruptured muscle-bundles and other devices that Bobbi had no name for. A thin trail of white fluid leaked from the wound even as she stood there.

Bobbi stared at the wound for a long moment; from behind her Violet's soft gasp gave voice to her own surprise. "How long have you got?" she asked in a hushed voice.

"Not very long." Redeye nodded down at the wound. "My internal reservoir of oxygenated fluorocarbon solution has been breached, and it is draining steadily. I am...bleeding to death, amusingly enough. I am afraid that what was a superficial wound suffered in the factory was made fatal by fighting the shixaur." She smiled again, bemused. "The drone in the tunnel. I had never fought one before. Very powerful, very smart. It made good use of the vulnerability. Perhaps if I had not been damaged already I might have lived through it, but it has killed me well enough."

What could she say to that? Sorry? Bobbi shook her head; there was nothing that could be done here that would make things better, and as badly as she felt for the dying cyborg there was still the matter at hand. "I wish that things were different, Red," she said instead, and shook her head. "I really do. But we're going to have to get real here. I can't let you nuke the shit out of this place, even with you...like this. You know that."

Redeye's eyes tightened. "I do," she said. "But I know something else. Something very important."

Here we go. "What is that," Bobbi asked, but she had a good idea of what the answer was going to be.

"I know that even as badly wounded as I am, you cannot stop me."

And she was right. Despite her injuries, Redeye was still more than capable enough to vault backward through the mist; nobody had time to even get a shot off. No sooner had she made it through the doors they began to hiss shut. "Fuck me running," Bobbi growled, and charged ahead toward the doors. "Come on!"

She moved like a bolt of pure motion, fueled by adrenaline and worse – unarmed and unprotected, someone else might have hesitated sprinting ahead into the unknown, but Bobbi had done it so many times now that it seemed entirely second nature now. Once more into the breach, dear friends, once more, she thought as she leaped over the sundered turrets and pressed on toward the swiftly-narrowing gap. Once more, or we all get turned to vapor. Fuck that noise. She leaned into it, every footfall propelling her closer, every moment sealing the doors a little more, and behind her the chorus of boot heels that belonged to her comrades as they followed. As driven as she was, though, even she could see that she would not make it before the gap grew too narrow. She was going to fail. Redeye was going to explode, and that would be the end of it. It had all come to naught.

Except...it wasn't. As fast as she was, Bobbi was nothing before the great black meteor that was Scalli. The power of his muscle suit wasn't just in its armor, it was in its strength – strength to lift, strength to smash, strength to run. He moved almost as fast as Redeye as he closed with the door, and skidding to a halt took hold of the great slabs with both hands. Bobbi had just enough time as she drew close to marvel at his strength before she dove between his braced legs and through the gap into the next room.

Bobbi slid across the floor on her belly into what turned out to be another small lobby, one terminating in a perpendicular corridor which she plowed into head-first. She lay dazed for a second, and as she attempted to get up got Violet's boots in her back as she slid in after. The air fled from her lungs a second time and she lay on the floor for a few seconds before Violet hauled her up. "We've gotta help Scalli," she hissed in Bobbi's ear, "He's in trouble!"

The words jolted Bobbi into action through the haze of impact. Helped by Violet, she got to her feet and turned round to see that Scalli was in real trouble. There was no way that he was going to get in through the gap; it was already too small for him, but now it had shrunk against his efforts to the point that he was in real danger of losing his hands.

"Fuck," Bobbi shouted, and the two women scrabbled to get to either side of the gap; they pulled at the doors as hard as they could, but Bobbi was a buck thirty and Violet was less than that. No way were they going to help him with physical power. "Scalli," Bobbi said as Violet attempted to jam her rifle in the gap as a brace, "Scalli, I need you to get your arms out of there. Please, just wait for us."

"I can't get this fucking thing in here," Violet was muttering to herself. "God damn it, get in there, get in there!"

"It's all right," Scalli said; his voice was thick with exertion and what Bobbi knew had to be pain; veins stood out in his neck through the force he applied within the suit, the force which its synthetic muscles were fruitlessly multiplying. "Baby girl, just...just get back, both of you. I'm gonna be okay here."

"But how?" Bobbi stared at him with eyes starting to glaze with tears – she couldn't lose him, not like this. "Oh God, Scalli, I don't –"

"Hush!" He was talking through gritted teeth now, nearly buckling against the strain. His arms and body strained hideously as the suit went into crisis mode, ballooning so that the false flesh that coated it began to split; the braided black cords that made up those monstrous limbs showed through the dark skin as they expanded to freakish dimensions, such that Bobbi and Violet stumbled back in fear that they might burst. "I'm all right, I can get out of the suit – just get back!"

Bobbi stared at him. Scalli had been enormous since she'd met him, and even after discovering that his build was enhanced through the suit she had never thought that he could take it off. Part of her had assumed that it was fused to him. "I can get out of it," he hissed again in the face of her hesitation, "But you need to get the fuck out of here, all right? I'll be all right, baby girl. Just go!" There was no fear in his eyes, just a sense of assured urgency; if he was shitting her and playing hero, he was ready for the Academy.

Violet grabbed her arm and pulled. "Let's go, Bobbi," she pleaded. "I see her blood. We've got to go!"

Bobbi turned, but found her legs would not yet let her go – instead, she looked at him squarely in the face through the ever-narrowing gap. "I'm not losing two men over this," she said, her voice even and serious despite the fact she wasn't quite sure what she was saying in that instant. "You stay alive. I'll be back for you." She did not look at his face; instead she turned and ran with Violet, feeling like a complete fucking coward but knowing that there were greater stakes ahead.

They flew down the hallway, white and sterile as the lobby had been, leaving the nightmare darkness of the factories behind for something which felt even more malicious in its sterility. They ran, Violet with her rifle taking the lead as they followed the bloody trail, but Bobbi could not get the look on his face out of her head as they charged through the twisting labyrinth of eye-scouring whiteness that the Yathi had built. There was nothing ahead of them but eerie silence, and they hurried on not knowing what would await them – more Yathi defenses, Redeye awaiting to waylay them, or perhaps something entirely different.

Eventually the corridors gave way to yet another lobby and another doorway, this one open. Bobbi and Violet paused at the threshold and looked out upon the top of what appeared to be a vast, cylindrical chamber, cut out of the earth and clad in the same white material as the maze behind them. The doorway opened upon a deck, over which the top of the room curved in a bowl. Columns of machinery dotted the grillwork, devices of a kind she had not yet glimpsed – pylons of black metal shimmering with hazy glyphs of holographic light, all of them varying shades of green. Cylinders to which flanged vanes of a strange red crystal were attached, jutting out at crazy angles. Enormous holographic monitors, hovering in space, covered with the illegible script of the Yathi race. Looking through the grating of the deck more levels could be glimpsed, all lit by the bleaching glow of the lamps that shone upward from the chamber's distant bottom pole.

The machines that dotted the deck were strange, malicious things, but these were nothing before the sight of what ran along the cylinder's axis. Clustered upon a central trunk of weird gray-green metal were at least a hundred capsules, each large enough to contain a compact car; these tanks were filled with a milky fluid, and tubes and vanes of various ineffable design bristled from the brief caps of bronze-colored alloy that plated the ends of each. Each of the capsules were made from a heavy transparent material, and within each a vague, blob-like shadow could be seen.

"What are they?" Violet's voice was hushed, even reverent as she gazed upon it all. "What are they supposed to be?"

Bobbi stared at the vast umbilical, and her heart felt as if it were being squeezed in her chest. Of course she knew what grew in those tanks; she had seen it in the visions that Cagliostro had given her, malicious fruit grown on an otherworldly vine. She had expected so much, but not this. Not this.

"Don't go near them," Bobbi whispered to her.

Violet looked at her. Horror of her own began to dawn in those blue eyes. "Why? What are they?"

Before Bobbi could say another word, Violet walked across the deck toward the tanks that studded to the top of the umbilical trunk. She approached the nearest one, frowning at the glass, at the white fluid and the ineffable silhouette within. "I feel like I should know what this is," she said, equal parts curious, frightened and frustrated all at once; she peered into the glass, and seeing only darkness reached up with the muzzle of her rifle to lightly tap at against the tank's surface. Bobbi opened her mouth to warn her back, but it was too late. Drawn to the sound, the shadow moved; a form resolved itself from the milky gloom, rushing up to the surface of the glass to see what disturbed its slumber. Though Violet blocked much of it from her vantage point, Bobbi got a clear look at a battery of long, white beetle limbs, covered with barbed hairs, ending in taloned nippers that scraped at the surface of the tank as it tried to gather purchase. Violet screamed, a high, bright sound that seemed to strain her throat as it clawed free, and leaped back with her rifle at the ready.

Bobbi lurched forward, grabbing at her shoulders. "No," she cried out, "No!" The thing was already receding back into the depths of its tank as the movement that had stimulated it had drawn away. It might have been blind, or stupid, or simply unconcerned – whatever it was, Bobbi had been spared the sight of the rest of monstrous figure, but for the shining gleam of two rows of gleaming silver discs fading into the dark.

They stood there for a moment, Bobbi holding Violet tightly in her arms while the feral priestess shuddered and gasped; the image would stay in Bobbi's mind forever, she knew, but Violet had just stared into the face of something that even she would never have thought would exist in this world. This place was growing something, but it wasn't a terraforming colony. The Yathi were growing their own bodies in those tanks, the bodies which they had abandoned on their homeworld. They were trying to bring their real selves from their homeworld into this one.

After a few moments Violet's fevered breathing slowed, and her hold on her rifle sagged. Bobbi let her go, and as Violet turned to stare at her, a look of absolute terror dawned in her eyes. The zealot, standing in the very crecheworks of her personal Satan, melted into a sudden and complete panic. She dropped her rifle and clutched Bobbi's arm, gabbling in a strained, thin voice, reason having fled away. "We can't be here," she keened, her fingers tightening in a death-lock on Bobbi's bicep. "We can't be here, oh no, wecan'twecan'twecan't –"

In the harsh light of understanding, the cool that had fled Violet's mind poured into Bobbi's own. Bobbi reached out with her free hand and slapped Violet hard across her face in order to break her growing hysteria. "Stop it," she barked, and Violet quieted immediately, clinging to Bobbi as if she might blow away on her own. Bobbi shook her head and extricated herself, then took Violet by her arms. "Listen to me," she said, her eyes hard. "Listen! I need you on this, Vi. You've had one of these things inside of you, you know what that means. They're going to be twice as smart as they already are if they can do this kind of thing. Then we're fucked. This place has got to go."

Terrified, but sobered by Bobbi's words, Violet nodded fiercely with eyes as wide as saucers. Bobbi took Violet's face in her hands and put her brow against hers; she was as terrified as the feral was, but it was not of the monsters in their tanks – it was of the monster that she knew she would have to become if she could not shut this place down herself. And yet, she had no idea as to how to avoid it; if she couldn't do it, she may very well have to allow Redeye to fulfill her 'destiny' and hope that she wasn't dooming the city in the process.

Violet pressed her head against Bobbi's. "I will obey," she whispered, allowing herself to fall into the role of the priestess, submissive to her chosen deity. "I am sorry for my weakness."

"It's all right, honey," Bobbi murmured in reply. "I'm as scared as you. Now c'mon, we have to find Red." She stooped to pick up Violet's rifle and put it back in her hands. "You look out for me."

Violet checked her rifle and fell in next to Bobbi as she proceeded across the deck, sweeping the gun's muzzle back and forth as they searched for the wayward cyborg. Bobbi was troubled that they hadn't come into a warzone, their terrible discovery aside; they had heard the sounds of combat, the gutteral sounds of the Yathi tongue, but at least on this level there was no sign of Redeye.

They walked across the wide deck, looking for a way up or down, and found it on the far other side. A simple circular opening had been cut in the deck, and a ladderway ran the whole length of the cylinder. Bobbi counted fifteen levels, squinting against the glow from the bottom. "All right," she said with a frown. "I'll go first."

"I can't allow that." Violet slipped down over the lip of the opening without a word, the rifle already slung across her chest – she'd anticipated Bobbi's words, and swung onto the ladder without a further word. Bobbi shook her head. She didn't want a worshipper, but she supposed that it was better than her following Redeye to her death. She closed her eyes and thought of Scalli, hoping against hope that he wasn't bullshitting her about being able to get out of the mess she'd left him in. But that was something she'd have to deal with on her own.

The two of them descended the ladder, through level after level of bizarre technology and the terrible gestational pods. As they cleared the entrance of each deck, Violet would stop, sweep the floor with her rifle, and move on. Bobbi kept her eyes open for something that might suggest a computer terminal or control system, but there was nothing that she could clearly identify. More importantly, they still could not find Redeye.

As they drew close to the bottom deck, the lights below swallowed everything in a haze of white light and heat. The sweat stood out on Bobbi's skin as they moved, squinting downward as they traveled – both she and Violet had put on their visors again, letting their glare filters make things bearable. The heat had released anew the smell of the synthblood on her clothes, and she shivered as they moved closer and closer to the ring of tiny suns at the pole. It seemed as if they would soon run out of decks to examine; the lowermost deck hung thirty feet above the bottom pole, and it was swiftly coming into view.

Given their luck so far, it was perhaps fitting that it wasn't until they got to the bottom level that they found her. Violet had slipped through the opening of the next to lowest level when she stopped and hissed softly in alarm. She looked up at Bobbi as she unslung her rifle, her blue eyes wide with warning, before she nodded downward through the grillwork. From her vantage point on the ladder, Bobbi peered through the black grill of the deck above, and saw what Violet had warned her about.

The lowest deck sat just above the bottom of central shaft. Around the trunk were arranged not gestational tanks, but a series of five interface chairs. They were different from the one in which Freida had sat in the Chorus's lair, open, elegant things that looked like wide divans of dark metal wrapping around the base of the trunk. Sockets that Bobbi recognized were used for direct neural interface were mounted in the surface of the shaft above each seat – and in the closest chair, tethered to the trunk by cables running from these very ports, was Redeye.

The pale woman was slumped in her seat, listing bonelessly like a broken toy against the metal trunk. Her eyes were open, but both of them now glowed red – but they did so very dimly, like the weakest cinders. No blood leaked from her wound now, the last of it having pooled in the seat of the chair and trickled onto the deck. She looked dead, or very nearly so.

Violet clambered down to the deck, and Bobbi followed. "The Eye," Violet whispered, but the words died in her throat – both of them approached as if Redeye might spring up at any moment and kill them both, but Bobbi knew very well that she could not. The meat in her skull must already be dead from anoxia.

"She's plugged herself into...whatever this system is, looks like," Bobbi said. Caution left her in the face of her morbid curiosity; with Violet covering the apparent corpse with her rifle, Bobbi crouched down next to Redeye's fallen body, peering at the hole in her torso, the scoring all over her armored flesh. She had gone through so much to get where she had, only to end up here in this way.

"Is she dead?" Violet aimed the rifle at Redeye's temple, not at all wishing to take chances. "Can she even die?"

"I think her brain's dead, yes," said Bobbi, squinting at the thickening blood in the cyborg's lap. "But that doesn't necessarily mean anything."

Violet looked at her, startled. "What?"

Bobbi stood up and leaned over the body. "Well," she said, "Red's been able to access the network before, which means she would have been implanted with headware at the very least. I don't know how much of her brain was replaced, or augmented, or what – but maybe she tried to keep her brain alive by plugging herself into the system directly. To keep power routing into her brain, you see?"

"Is that even possible?" Violet didn't look convinced, or perhaps she just didn't want to think it possible. She leaned forward and peered at the woman's dimly glowing eye. "Shouldn't she have a power supply inside of her to keep her systems going?"

A frown tugged at Bobbi's lips. Violet had a point. "You're right," she muttered. "Damn it, why would she do this? Why not just go off and nuke the whole place? It seems like such a random-assed thing to do."

"Perhaps she needed to know what they were doing," Violet suggested. "Perhaps she needed to know what she would be stopping with her death."

Bobbi took a step back and gazed down upon what Redeye had become, a puppet with her strings cut, and shook her head. "Maybe so," she said. "Which spooks the hell out of me, because I'm going to have to go in there with her."

"What?" Violet turned toward Bobbi, forgetting the cyborg entirely. "Why would you do that?"

"Because I have to shut this place down somehow, don't I? There's no virus colony down here that we could see, just these..." Bobbi gestured to the deck above. "Things. Assuming there are viable bodies growing in those tanks, I'll need to do what I can do destroy them. And honestly, Vi, I need to know what's going on here as well. Cagliostro was so very wrong about this place, twice over now, and I need to find out what's we've all risked our lives for. And..." Bobbi nodded toward the Redeye's matched set of dim irises. "She's armed. I have to find out what can be done about it."

Violet stared at Bobbi for a long moment, clear conflict in her eyes. On the one hand, she wanted to serve, but Bobbi knew that she was very uncomfortable with a situation where she could not protect her new mistress directly where she had chosen to go. There was probably the animal fear of being alone in the belly of the Devil's spawning ground, too. Bobbi took a deep breath, summoned up courage that she in no way felt, and smiled. "Look," she said, "this is for the best. For everybody. It needs to happen. I promise you, I won't leave you alone down here. Let me find out what's happening, do for Redeye, and we'll leave and get Scalli out of here to boot. It'll work, Vi. Trust me."

The words were ashes in Bobbi's mouth, but they apparently worked; Violet nodded somberly, flicking a glance upward through the deck above them. "I will not fail you," she said, electing not to waste time arguing further. "And I know that you will do as you promise."

"Good girl." Bobbi exhaled, trying her best to hide her relief. "All right, well, I guess I'm going to sit down here and connect as well."

"Can you do that?" Violet blinked. "Do you need cables as she has used?"

Bobbi chuckled. "I still have the wireless link," she replied. "And I'm not trying to keep my brain alive, mind you. I'll just sit down and get comfortable, and you watch over me. All right?"

"I..." Violet trailed off, only nodding as Bobbi moved to sit down on the couch next to Redeye's. She took a deep breath as she folded her hands in her lap, feeling the slight stickiness of the nearly-dry synthblood covering her front, feeling the yawning pit that hovered in her short-term memory. There would be so much that she would need to handle in the coming days, weeks, whatever time lay ahead of her – assuming that she didn't get her brain fried and die on the spot next to Redeye's broken corpse. Once more into the breach, dear friends, she thought again, and sighed. Here we go.

Bobbi closed her eyes, began counting backwards from ten, and reached out to look for the network presence of the giant machine against which she now leaned. She felt its presence, felt it towering over her, and reached out to connect – and she was joined with it, as surely as if she had been fused, the intimate connection of the psychotronic interface drawing her into the machine's internal system.

It was a cold place, cold and dark, nothing like what she had sensed before. It was like the Chorus system, and yet she was not helpless; she found herself able to operate just as she had before. Perhaps it was that the system was in a state of suspension. Bobbi could not tell. All she knew was that she floated in darkness, and could not feel anything in her proximity. She conjured up her defenses, and within seconds was enclosed within a bubble of hardened codewalls, a crystal bubble ferrying her through the night. Then, a voice she knew very well reached into her sensorium.

<There you are,> said Redeye, and the tone that came with these words was gentle. <I was waiting for you.>

CHAPTER 25

Moments crawled by, and Bobbi waited for Redeye to show herself. This was the second time in a row that she found herself being surprised by Redeye, and though the other woman did attack, Bobbi would not allow herself to be fooled into thinking she was without defenses.

Finally Bobbi grew tired of waiting. <It's deja vu all over again,> she said. <All right, I'm here. Where are you? This where you sneak up and murder me?>

<Unfortunately, I do not have many options at this point, even if I wished to.> Sadness etched itself into her every projected word. <I am dead.>

<Yeah, I'm trying to figure out how that's happened,> Bobbi said. <Given that you're dead out there, but alive in here. Surely your meat brain must have died already.>

<Indeed.> Redeye was quiet a moment. <At least, I believe that I am dead. It is very...strange. Like I am something of a ghost. I do not feel like I did only a little while ago.>

<A ghost?> Bobbi thought of the piece of consciousness that Cagliostro had put into her head. <How is that possible?>

<I do not know,> said Redeye. <I only know that I am...reduced.>

<In what way?>

<It is very strange indeed. I feel none of the anger that I once did. I feel no desire for revenge. I feel...>

Seconds passed, and Bobbi found herself afraid that perhaps the mental spark had been extinguished. <Yeah,> she called out into the dark. <What do you feel?>

Redeye's voice returned from its soujourn in the void. <I feel free.>

<Then you're a lucky girl, I think.> Bobbi wasn't sure what else to say.

<You were wrong about the terraforming colony,> Redeye said.

<So were you,> Bobbi pointed out. <No colonial matrix here.>

<Yes...> Redeye sounded strange to her. Her voice was as ephemeral as the ghost that she now claimed to be. <I have learned very much since I came here.>

<You haven't been here for long,> Bobbi said dimly. <What could you have learned in the last twenty minutes?>

Redeye laughed softly. <A great deal,> she said. <The databases in this system are extremely well-defended against intrusion...but apparently the programs do not detect me. I wonder why that is.>

Maybe she really is dead, Bobbi thought. She thought about the fragment of Cagliostro's consciousness that resided in her headware. Was it possible that upon death, the thought-sensitive network could trap part of the mind within its confines? <Maybe you're right after all,> she said. <What did you find out?>

<Many things.>

<Like?>

<Like there is no more need for the colonial matrix in its original function. The event which the Yathi dreaded for centuries has already occurred.>

Far away, Bobbi felt her heart skip in her chest. <What are you saying?>

<I am saying that the star exploded fifty years ago,> Redeye replied. <Yathkalghn has long since been annihilated. The Yathi race, save for its colony here, is dead.>

For a moment Bobbi did not know what to say, but the shock wore off quickly enough. <I guess no plan truly does survive reality.>

<No,> Redeye replied. <That is not quite what I am saying.>

<Then who's left?> Bobbi pushed back a tide of mingled excitement and vengefulness. Was there anything graceful one could say about the passing of another intelligent species, when it had strove to slay your own? And yet she felt a strange sort of sadness in their passing; behind her anger and her desire to celebrate the death of a civilization, she could not help but wonder if some other solution could have been reached.

But there was no time to think of such things now. <The greater sum of transplanted consciousnesses have been contained elsewhere, held in stasis within the matrix. The lower orders are being transmitted to

hosts as they are needed, but the rate of implantation appears to have slowed considerably.>

<So they're holding on to their best and brightest is what you're saying.>

<Yes. You will notice that with everything that I destroyed along my way to this place, there were no Yathi combatants?>

The truth was that Bobbi had not seen that. Between the armored suits and the butchered white corpses, how could she tell? <I honestly didn't have time to check,> she said. <We were too busy pursuing you.>

<I see. There is a lack of personnel here because they are too precious at the moment to waste in combat. The supply is no longer coming, and thus they must be careful. They cannot lose too many to the eventual fragmentation of consciousness that so many face when placed within a human host.>

Bobbi heaved a mental sigh. <They're growing their native bodies in those tanks. How is that even possible? Are they trying to find a bypass? What do the files tell you?>

<You are correct,> said Redeye, but if that concerned her there was no sign of it – all was placidity that came from the ghost-woman. <Engineering these bodies has been an attempt at creating alternatives to implantation in human beings – but they have yet to succeed in implanting their own consciousnesses into these tank-grown Yathi bodies. Apparently the conditions on this planet – from radiation, electromagnetic field density, and a whole host of other variables – are so radically different that they cannot survive outside of their gestation pods. They are useless as far as the colonial effort is concerned. In a way, Cagliostro was halfway right.>

<How so?>

<He was incorrect in that this was a facility creating terraforming nanomachines. On the contrary, this facility was where they were producing potential vessels to use once the terraforming process was largely complete.> Redeye's voice took on a hint of black amusement. <In any case, this experiment is moot.>

Bobbi hesitated. <I don't understand.>

<Something took place in the greater network earlier,> Redeye explained, <an event which threw the balance of control systems out of alignment. The bodies growing in their tanks have gotten unbalanced ratios of key nutrients and stabilizing chemicals. Most of them have received fatal doses of radiation, and the rest are suffering cascading neurological failure due to a lack of proper nutrient intermixture. This

project has taken fifty years, and it has come to a very sudden end. I can only assume that you are responsible for this.>

Bobbi was silent. She remembered the sensation of panicked carpet-bombing of whatever nodes were in her path as she attempted to escape the Yathi operators. Was it possible that this was the 'trouble' that the Mother had referred to? Had she really killed these creatures through sheer trick of fortune? <I hacked into the control network trying to get the chutes open,> she replied. <People tried to intercept me...things got crazy. I guess that's how you got down there too.>

<I came here by another way,> said Redeye. <I must have already gotten through by the time you did that. In any case, you seem to have done enough damage here. Their purpose has been blunted. You have done with your mind what I would have only been able to do with my payload. But at least I can still destroy an important facility with my death.>

With these words Bobbi felt lead pour down her throat into her stomach and the spectre of those glowing eyes surfaced in her mind. <You've armed yourself,> she said. <I know, we saw. How long do we have?>

<I would have said until I die, but here I am. We must have until my consciousness fades, then.>

<Which is how long?>

<I do not know.>

<Can you give me an idea?>

<No. I am sorry.>

Bobbi felt herself clench distant fists. <Do you at least know how large your payload is?>

<Ah.> Redeye had the grace to sound sheepish as she answered. <I am afraid that the being you call Cagliostro was telling the truth. I attempted subterfuge to test your intentions; I can only assume that he asked you to kill me. Considering my mental state at that time, it was a wise decision.>

<Yeah, well, I don't know that I believe that,> Bobbi said, and her mind sharpened as stress chemicals flooded her body and her heart began to race. <Look, if you're gonna go off when you...vanish...is there any way that we can defuse the bomb? Can I hack it?>

<Not that I am aware of,> Redeye said sadly. <Nor is there time to defuse it even if you had the ability. You have....perhaps thirty minutes, I think.>

Bobbi felt her adrenaline and anger top out in that instant. <We're fucked, then,> she spat. <Even if we got away from here, the blast radius would still get us. Get everybody. A lot of people are going to die!>

<That is where you are wrong,> Redeye replied. <My payload is powerful, but I told the truth when I said that this structure would be able to absorb the blast. The explosion will consume the majority of the structure and the building above will collapse; the Yathi will undoubtedly clean up the scene as they always do. I imagine it will take a great deal of time and immediate resources to ensure that the truth is scrubbed, and that is to your advantage.>

<Yeah.> Bobbi's sense of dread faded a great deal at that, but did not vanish entirely. Instead, a certain resignation replaced it that was even heavier in her gut. <The Mother of Systems knows who I am, I think. She won't stop until she kills me. She wants the secret of how Cagliostro worked it so I could hack Yathi systems.>

<If she knows who you are, then you are correct,> Redeye replied. <And I am sorry for that. No matter where you go, there is a chance that she or her operatives will be able to detect you with genetic scanning; you will have to work hard indeed to try and defuse that. I do not know that it is even possible. However, I believe that you have the chance to carry on what I did, and with much greater effect. Are you willing to carry on the war against the Mother and her people?>

<I already decided to, yeah.> Reaching down into herself, Bobbi pushed the dread and the doubt out of her stomach, and let the fire she felt when she faced the Mother take its place. <I made a promise to her when she met me in the network. I told her that I'd be the one who shot her in the face.>

If there was anything that would break the dreamy calm that Redeye had exhibited up to then, it would be those words. <You faced her already,> Redeye replied, sounding very grim and more than a little awed. <And you won?>

<I didn't win so much as I got the fuck away,> Bobbi said, <but yeah. And honest, it's done a real number on my head. I blacked out on the way back to Scalli and Vi, and I don't know what happened to me.>

<I see,> said Redeye. <Talk to Violet. She has abilities that even she has forgotten, I think. If she is to help you in the future, you will need to help her remember; in turn, I am certain that she can help you as well.>

<I don't know about her, Red. She's replaced you with me already.>

<That is her nature. I was never the right goddess for her to serve. You, however, are.>

<I don't want to be a goddess,> Bobbi insisted. She felt her aggravation pulse through the network like a burst of red static. <I just want to beat this thing and get things on course if I can so the human race can get on with destroying itself at its own pace.>

Redeye laughed again. It was strange hearing that. <You will have to get over that. Violet will help you find others that are in doubt, as well as identifying other Yathi for targeting. You will need to be a goddess of war, a figure of worship to some and a general to others, if you are going to succeed in your designs against the Mother and her kin.>

Bobbi felt another weight on her, greater than anything else that she had felt that night. More than fear, more than anger, more than dread. It was the weight of certainty that she wore on her shoulders as she listened to Redeye's words, the knowledge that if she was to survive – if humanity was to survive – she'd have to play her part in it. There was nobody else, at least at this moment, who could do the job. <I know ,> Bobbi finally replied. <And I'll do my best. But as compressed as time is here, if I don't get out of here it's going to be too late for an escape.> She thought of Scalli, wondered if she could save him still. <Is there anything else that you can tell me? From the files?>

<There is...something, but it will take too long. I will have to transmit it to you.>

<All right.> Bobbi gave her the address of one of her secure data dropboxes. <We need to get out of here. I'm sorry, Red, but I've gotta go.>

<It's quite all right.> The gentleness returned to her, and Redeye sounded ever more like a mother in her own right than the Fury she had been. <I am glad that Violet found a new cause with you. I know that you will not disappoint her.>

<I can't afford to disappoint anyone on this score, man,> said Bobbi. <No pressure, right?>

A tinkling laugh, as thin as tissue paper, was her reply. <Goodbye, Bobbi. For what it is worth, I enjoyed fighting alongside you.>

Even if I came to kill you in the end. <Yeah,> Bobbi said, <you too. Take care, Red. I wish I could have been different. I'll put a bullet in ol' Mom for you when I meet her.>

<Thank you.> After that, there was only silence.

Bobbi killed the link and found herself staring into Violet's ashen face. "You're alive," Violet said, as if she had expected anything but this result. "You're all right?"

"Yeah," Bobbi said as she got to her feet. "Come on, we have to get out of here. Red's gonna blow, and we don't have much time left."

The way back was far easier than the way forward. The trail of blood and corpses that Redeye left was easy to follow back to where they had gone. They did not find Scalli wedged between the doors, only the crushed hulk that had been his armored suit. Though it had been thoroughly mangled, its mass kept the door open wide enough for the two women to escape. Bobbi had feared briefly that Scalli might still be in there, but ducking through the gap banished this – the entire back of the suit had been burst open like a rotten fruit, and fresh, bare footprints in the bloody trail indicated his escape. Though empty of its operator, the inert mass of armor and fiber bundles The two of them moved swiftly through the complex, past the piles of gory corpses piled in the factory, and then through the charnel wastes of the warehouses, where, emerging from the top of the chute, they found that the tomb had been opened. There was no time to ponder that particular mystery, however, for the spectre of impending destruction loomed over them; each second ticked by like Death's pale gong, bringing them closer and closer to annihilation. Redeye did not know how strong the remnants of her mind would be, how long they would have before the charge in her body went off – and even if they did escape the complex before she gave out, would the subway tunnels survive the blast? Both women ran through the complex for all they were worth, expecting resistance but finding none, hurrying for the final anteroom and hoping against hope that Scalli would be waiting for them.

As they clambered up the ladder to the catwalk at the top of the drone processing floor, they found Scalli sitting on the lip of the doorway. He wore skin-tight silver spraypants and a pair of athletic shoes, naked to the waist – which would have struck Bobbi as funny were it not for how strange he looked to her in his natural state. Tall enough to fill his towering suit, his body was thin and lean, covered in scars and the gleaming silver lesions of interface ports. He looked up and smiled widely as they approached, tired and weak but still alive, and he got to his feet as the two women approached.

"Told you I'd live," he said, but Bobbi did not answer. She grabbed his arm as the doors hissed open in her presence, revealing the white hall beyond, and the open hatch leading to salvation. Scalli stumbled a little as she pulled him out with her, Violet slinging her rifle and planting her hands against his naked back to propel him forward. Scalli didn't protest when he saw the look in her eyes, he just moved – and soon they were running with all the power that they could muster, down the tunnel and through the ruptured scar that the centipede-machine had left, farther and farther away. Bobbi felt her leg try and give out twice over as she ran, thinking of Diana as she went. If she could survive this, she would avenge her old friend. There would be a lot of revenge to hand out for everybody.

They had made it halfway to the station when the earth turned over and screamed around them. Running between the two women, Scalli looked over his shoulder just in time to cry out as a wave of collapsing mortar and sound crashed down around them and the world went away.

The last thing that Bobbi felt was the tunnel closing around them like a mouth and roaring of splintered concrete like an angry sea in her ears. Then there was nothing but the dark.

Somewhere, she imagined that the Mother was laughing.

CHAPTER 26

When Bobbi finally woke, it was in a hospital bed in the very familiar confines of David Chin's black clinic; after many years of cosmetic surgery and getting implants jammed into her brain by his expert hand, she had come to know the seafoam green tiles and the recessed, colored lighting of his recovery rooms very well indeed. She had a crease in the back of her skull and regrown muscle in her leg, along with a completely reworked body; now she looked like the girl she had been when she had first come into Chin's clinic all those years ago, only caught up on the years she was playing surgical dress-up. Plain, dark-haired, with half the chest she'd had back then, slim and slight and elfin with her reduced height, she was the adult version of what she had been born to be.

It had enraged her at first, especially when she had discovered that Scalli had Chin do the work while she was out and without her permission. This disappeared, however, when she discovered the circumstances behind it all. She had been pulled from the wreckage of the subway system by emergency crews with a massive head wound, having very nearly given out on the spot from loss of blood; Scalli and Violet were much less damaged, with just a few broken bones between them. Through whatever work of spook-artifice, Cagliostro had managed for a 'black' ambulance to pick them up from the site, then re-route them to Chin's clinic. She had been in a coma for five weeks.

Bobbi had awoken to find that the world had been changing rapidly while she was out. The police were looking for her, for one. The detonation of Redeye's nuke had taken out the building over the factory and most of the block around it, leading to the destruction of several corporate offices worth billions of dollars. On television, a somber-faced Maya Frail had announced to the world that three hundred people had been killed in the explosion and the following collapse. NewsNetNow had claimed that a data-terrorist group called the New Human Army was responsible for the attack, which it had carried out against what it claimed was a "corrupt and guilty member of the greater establishment against the freedom of information for all peoples." Bobbi – pictured on screen as "Brain Mother" with her old face staring out at the world – was being depicted as the movement's leader. The Feds had hit the Temple and shut it down, but not before Bobbi's well-programmed self-destruct systems had turned all the computer equipment to slag. At least in that way she had protected herself from being found.

"New Human Army." It was a ludicrous name attached to a ludicrous cause, but the public ate it up; by the time Bobbi had come out of her coma there was a great clamoring for greater anti-hacking laws, and funding for new agencies to counter this new "threat." The Yathi were already hard at work setting up new methods by which they could counter the weapon that Bobbi could most directly employ – her ability to hack their networks – while she had been dreaming away. But Bobbi's experience with Yathi protocols had already been tested, and her ability was such that she was able to escape the Mother herself; when the time came, she believed that she could give them a run for their money. The mercy was that Redeye seemed to have been right – there was no massive change in the environment, no sudden disasters born of voracious, transmutative nanomachines. But maybe that wasn't how it worked. Maybe the changes would come on gradually, like a cancer. They would have to watch carefully for that.

Bobbi sat in her bed, staring at the telescreen mounted on the opposite wall. She wasn't allowed to use the network until Chin was finished testing her brain for signs of injury, nor was she allowed to get out of bed until Chin was certain that all of her body modifications had fully healed. Scalli and Violet didn't visit Chin's clinic, either; all of Bobbi's communication with them was through one-sided data wafers delivered to the clinic through Chin's regular shipments of samples to and from a private laboratory. Without network access, Bobbi couldn't look for Cagliostro, either. And so she sat, spending day after day watching the telescreen, playing games, reading. It didn't take long to get extremely boring, but she made due with what she could.

A week or so after she awoke, one of Chin's medical techs brought in a small portable computer that he said had been sent over with the regular supplies. It was an extremely expensive model, a tiny Excellis AV6200, as powerful as several of the next tier of machines put together and only half as large. It made the little Matricomp she'd carried around with her look like a pocket calculator. The gearhead in her awoke and salivated over the little machine, and she put it in her lap and fired it up without hesitation. When she did, the Excellis projected a holographic monitor that displayed not the standard bootup screen that she expected, but a misty blue decahedron that floated serenely in the air above a few feet from her face. Before she had a chance to wonder what the hell was going on, the thing shivered, and out of it came the Stadil-turned-Yahweh voice that belonged to Cagliostro.

"Good evening," the machine said. "I am pleased that I am able to find you in good health."

"Good evening, yourself," Bobbi said, acid on her tongue. "I guess you can say that I'm all right. I'm not dead, at least, but not for lack of trying."

"Indeed. I was pleased that I was able to have you rerouted to this clinic once you were discovered." There was a pause in which the icon's surface seemed to shudder. "I see that you did not succeed in destroying Redeye."

"Yeah, funny thing about that." She squinted at the floating avatar. "Didn't you see what all happened? Where the hell did you go? I woke up and you were gone from the system."

"Indeed," said Cagliostro. The shape spun lazily on its polar axis. "The Mother of Systems arrived. I was forced to withdraw if I wished to retain my hold on the factory's drones."

Bobbi's brows arched. "Yeah? Was that before or after I ran into her?"

The shape stopped its spin. "You encountered the Mother?"

"I did," Bobbi said warily. "I'm kind of surprised you didn't see it, man. There were all kinds of fireworks before she rolled in, and when she did it was like a fucking black hole rolled into the network. I nearly died."

"I am aware that you were responsible for disrupting various systems in the network," Cagliostro replied. "It was why I was able to keep the maintenance drones from finding and killing you in the ventilation ducts."

"It's apparently why a lot more than that got fucked up."

"I do not understand."

Bobbi snored. "Can't have that," she muttered. "Right, here, let me tell you the story."

Cagliostro listened as she explained everything to him: Meeting Mother; Redeye's incredible push into the bottom chamber of the complex; the coffin they had found; the horrible gestational pods. She told him of Redeye's death and of the ghost that the cyborg so briefly became. She told him about the end of the Yathi race on the other side of the galaxy, or wherever it was from whence they came. Bobbi told him so much – but she did not tell him about the hole in her memory, nor did she tell him about the data which she still waited to collect from the drop account. She did not trust what the demigod-machine would do with her, or that the data would be intact when she finally got it. She didn't trust him at all, in fact. Why would she?

When she finished telling him the story, Cagliostro's avatar strobed slowly in the air. "It is a very interesting thing which you have told me," the machine finally said. "Much of this I did not know, even when I was of the Yathi. I can tell you that nearly none of that race has this information."

That surprised her. "Well what does that mean? Does that mean that Mom is keeping everyone in the dark about what's really going on? Is this something that we can use?"

"Perhaps," Cagliostro said. "I will have to process this information."

Bobbi snorted at that. "Yeah, you go on being ineffable there, buddy. In the meantime, I've got shit to do."

"What do you intend to do?"

"I have that promise to keep," Bobbi said, and smiled. "You just keep doing what you're doing. I'll be in touch."

She shut off the Excellis and put it on the bedside table. Then she lay down in bed and rolled over on her side, trying hard not to think of the future. It worked long enough for her to sleep, but her dreams were full of green skies and blasted landscapes, and the many eyes of silver that stared out at her from a black pit that hung in her mind.

The next day, Chin announced that she was able to leave the clinic. Scalli and Violet came to see her in the morning. Scalli looked healthy, as tall and lean as he was when they had found him sitting by the exit doors, stuffed in an oversized sweater and the pants from a set of French lunar fatigues. Violet had dyed her long hair black, had it cut so that it swung down from a bob in the back to a pair of wings that swooped down and licked her chest. She wore a Variable Sisters t-shirt and a pair of dull red Mitama leather jeans; Bobbi counted the fact that she was picking out designers again as a sure sign that she didn't suffer from any more brain damage than living in commercial culture once inflicted on a person. They were pleased to see her, but Bobbi couldn't help but detect a note of tension as Scalli smiled and talked, and Violet hovered over her like some kind of blue-eyed matron. Scalli kept looking at her as he talked, glancing over her new body.

"So, okay," Bobbi said after she'd let them get the concern out of their system for a bit. "We've covered that I'm not gonna die, and we're all happy to see each other again. Let's handle the real subject hanging in the room, huh?"

Violet blinked at her. Scalli's smile faded. "All right," he said.

Bobbi chuckled. "Two things," she said. "First, I'm not angry about my body. I mean I was when I woke up, but then I spent like thirty seconds watching the news and I understand why you did it. It was a real good call, and I owe you both for it."

"It was Marcus's choice," Violet murmured. She wouldn't look Bobbi in the eye. "He was wise."

"Yeah, well, that tends to be the case," Bobbi said with a chuckle. She snaked an arm around Violet's waist and squeezed her gently. Bobbi felt a lot of guilt coming off the thin woman at the moment; she thought she knew where it was coming from. "You been doing okay?"

Violet didn't answer. "She's been helping me get things together," Scalli said after a moment. "I mean, we've gotta rebuild, right? They shut down the Temple, locked everything down out there on the Field."

"Yeah," Bobbi said with a sigh. In a very real way, she was happy that she would never go back to that old home; it had been Stadil's haunt, after all, and now she found she wanted as little to do with that man, ghost or otherwise, as she could get away with. "Which reminds me. How are we able to pay for all this? They'd had to have frozen my accounts, however well-protected they were. They were still mine."

Scalli and Violet looked at each other. "Funny thing about that," Scalli said. "I got a call from the Zurich Orbital Bank about the new account set up in Miss Goodacre's name, and how I had been listed as a person with access and could I tell them what I wanted to do with it."

Bobbi quirked a brow. "Miss Goodacre?"

"Alexandra Goodacre," Scalli said with a nod. "That's your new name. Or one of them. You got a lot of aliases overnight. Cagliostro set us all up very nicely – IDs, accounts, everything."

For a brief moment Bobbi felt bad about hanging up on the errant ghost, but that faded away. "I guess he'd already anticipated that we'd be carrying on," she replied. "Damn spider."

Scalli and Violet looked at each other again. "We... weren't sure that was what we were going to be doing," he said.

"And why not?" Both Bobbi's brows arched high. "You two aren't getting second thoughts, are you?"

"Of course not," Violet said, and she laid her hand on Bobbi's shoulder. "I follow you gladly. And I know that Marcus will help you as well." Scalli said nothing; he only nodded his assent.

"All right." Bobbi pursed her lips. "Then what's the problem?"

"We..." Violet looked at Scalli again.

"Can you two stop staring at each other and tell me what the hell's going on?" Bobbi spat the words like sparks.

This time it was Scalli that spoke. "I didn't tell you what happened to me," he said. "After I got out of my suit."

Bobbi frowned. "I take it that this isn't a story that I'm going to like," she said. "All right, go ahead then."

Scalli cleared his throat. He took a seat in the visitor's chair next to the bed. He looked nervous, which considering everything else he'd been taking on of late with a snarl of contempt made Bobbi rather concerned. "So when I got out of the suit," he began, "I wasn't in good shape. It's supposed to take time to get out of it; the nerve connectors, you know. The emergency blow screwed my nervous system up pretty good. I was weak, and I knew I wouldn't be carrying a gun anytime soon, so I tried to stumble back to the exit in case you came back in a hurry."

"Good thinking, that," Bobbi said. "So what happened then?"

"I made it back through the drone factory, climbed up the chute toward the second storeroom that we were in. Only as I got closer to the top, I heard voices, right? Speaking that horrible shit they call a language. Now I was smart enough to come up one of the sides near the mouth of the chute, so they wouldn't see me all that easy, but there were two of the Yathi there – not the drones, but full-on fuckers, you know. They were opening up the coffin that was in the storeroom."

Bobbi frowned a bit at that. She definitely got the feeling that she wasn't going to like what was coming. "Were they making a deposit or a withdrawal?"

"Definitely cashing out," Scalli said. He glanced at Violet, who Bobbi realized had slid her hand from her shoulder to grip her bicep in a bracing manner. "They were taking a body out on a pallet. Hovered above the ground, like a metrorail train. Antigravity, I guess."

"Scalli," Bobbi said thinly. "Who was it?"

"Well you have to understand," he said, "I mean I couldn't see very well, and it was dark–"

"Scalli!" Bobbi felt the blood begin to burn in her veins, her heart swiftly becoming a furnace. She leaned forward, staring at him, Violet's fingers wrapping tightly around her arm. "Who was it?"

The big man let out a sigh that hung heavy from his lips with regret. It was as if he were giving something up entirely, resigning hope. "It was him, Bobbi. It was Walken. I'm sorry. I'm sorry..." He closed his eyes and hung his head, as if he had betrayed her with the words. As if they were not enough.

Bobbi sat still for what felt like hours, staring at him. She had always known that the possibility was there – she had spoken to Redeye about it, after all – but that he was there, right under their noses. She could have opened the coffin and saw his face. She could have saved him, perhaps. "Tell me," she said finally, and her voice was low and hollow. "Was he...alive?"

"I don't know," Scalli murmured. He sounded very tired now. "I think so, yes. There were machines connected to him on the edge of the pallet."

Another horrible thought crashed down on her like a burning wave. "Scalli, was he..." The words shivered and died in her throat, then resurrected themselves to spite her. "Was he one of them?"

Scalli spoke the words as if they hurt him. "I don't think so, no. He was pale, I mean, but he looked alive. As much as you can in that light. I mean he didn't look like a white-haired ghost. But Bobbi..." The big man swallowed, and someone looking in from the hall might be amazed at how unnerved the tiny woman seemed to make him. "He had a nasty wound. Scarred up one side of his forehead. If he's alive, I don't know if he's mentally functional."

"He would have to be, Marcus," said Violet fiercely. "Otherwise why would they have him in a medical container? Don't say those things."

Bobbi closed her eyes and took a deep breath. She felt as if the room was closing in on her. He had been there the whole time, and she had walked right past him. Bobbi felt sick to her stomach, swirling with emotion – she had lost him again, and even if she had not loved him like she might have expected, she had wanted very much to have held him again. The truth was that she would have had to kill him then and there, however; perhaps this was a mercy. Perhaps this way, she could extend the grasp of the coming battles to include a method by which Yathi minds could be safely extracted. Assuming he was still all in one piece. But if he wasn't, why keep him?

Bobbi collected herself with a deep breath and spoke. "It's all right," she said, looking between her comrades. "It's all right. Scalli, did they just leave? Is that what happened?"

Scalli stared at her for a moment, as if he did not quite understand the kind of reaction he was getting from her. "Ah, yeah," he said. "They left, and I climbed up into the place. Gave it a few minutes and limped back through to where you found me."

Did he expect for her to burst into tears? Probably. She might have a few weeks ago. But not now. Nausea and internalized emotional crisis was as far as she was going to get at the moment, especially when she might be able to get to him. "Thank you for telling me that, Scalli," Bobbi said, and she ran both hands through her new hair. She was silent for a few seconds, staring at the black mirror of the deactivated telescreen as if perhaps it could scry out the future. But she knew what the future would be. It would be blood, and it would be death, and it would be a parade of alien horrors. It would be a wracking of sanity and a test of everything that she had ever considered human about herself, as stunted as the world had made it. It would be sacrifice that none of them could yet imagine.

"Bobbi?" Violet's voice was soft. "Are you all right?"

Was she? No. Most assuredly not. But it would have to be dealt with. "Yeah," she said, and gave Violet a thin smile. "I'm just thinking why they would keep him on hand, that's all. If he's not up and running around with them, he may not be fully possessed by the thing inside his head – and if that's the case, then I'm wondering why the hell they'd keep him alive. In any case, we can't worry about that right now. We need to get things started." Bobbi pulled away from Violet's hand and got to the edge of the bed. "Cagliostro is pondering things, but he's given us our foundation. Scalli, we're going to need a new place. Resources. I've got the money, but it's you who knows people."

Scalli stood up. "All right," he said, still unsure. "I can do that."

"And you, Violet." Bobbi slid off the edge of the bed and stood, looking across it at her unlikely lieutenant. "I'm going to need you, too. Still feel like influencing people?"

Violet blinked at her. "I can't use those systems anymore," she said. "I don't know how."

"Then we'll have to find out how to remind you." Bobbi looked between the two of them, feeling a sense of enormity upon her shoulders – but also a sense of righteousness, and a white blaze of fury had begun to kindle in her gut. "Redeye said that it could be done."

Violet looked as if she were about to say something, but thought better of it. She nodded instead.

"Then that's it," Bobbi said, and she got to her feet. "If you two will let me change, we'll get out of here and hit the proverbial road. Lot of work ahead of us, and we can't fuck around. They certainly aren't. We'll be lucky if there's a network left for me to hit, the way things are going."

"Of course," Violet said with a look of hard intent washing over her face, and marched out of the room. Scalli began to slouch that way as well, but Bobbi stopped him.

"Wait," she said, and when he did she took a seat on the edge of her bed, feeling tiny and swallowed up in her borrowed scrubs. "I wanted to ask. Are you okay?"

Scalli's brows climbed up his forehead. "You're asking if I'm okay? I'm not the one who's been in the coma. Or who has a new body, come to that."

Bobbi made a face at him. "Well, yeah," she said. "But I mean, I understand why you did that. Only face they haven't seen yet, right?"

"Or likely to ever have seen," he replied with a nod. "It seemed the best way to go."

"And you did right," she said. "But seriously, I mean..." Her words died in her throat. "Just, are you are all right? I mean you don't have your suit, or anything. Seems like we're both starting over."

Scalli gave her a pointed look. "You mean I'm starting over," he said, and she cringed slightly. "No, it's all right. I've had a couple weeks to figure out that I had been relying entirely too much on that thing. We've got the resources for me to gear up pretty good, make use of the nerve-connections I got, but I don't know that I'm going to miss it." He shrugged. "Besides, it'll be nice to live in the world in my own skin." Scalli glanced past her at the wall, or perhaps something further behind her. Behind them. "Don't worry, baby girl. I'll be all right in time. With everything."

She nodded. Looking at him, she felt it would be all right, at least between the two of them. Perhaps Tom popping up again would be the best thing for them, after all, but she couldn't think about him. Not now. Not yet. There was too much to do, too much to build, and she felt that there would be a long string of targets between now and the time that she found the man whose coat she slid over her shoulders after Scalli had left and she had gotten changed. The mantle of purpose settled upon her anew, and she felt herself expanding to fit it more comfortably. There was no choice to do otherwise.

Once, all that she had left of Tom and all that they had been through was a bloody coat. Now she had purpose, a cause, and friends with which to further it. Maybe she could save him, or maybe not. Right now, that didn't matter; what mattered now is that they would have to somehow carry the fight to the Yathi. Their numbers were fixed, and if Redeye was at all correct, then snuffing them out was a goal that could be reached. Despite the staggering odds of the future she now faced, she felt as she smoothed out her hair and used the tiny cosmetic airbrush in her bag to draw a bar of red across her eyes that whatever they could do – however deeply they could strike at that monstrous, alien brood – would not be a blow made in vain.

"Well, Bobbi girl," Bobbi said as she stared into the mirror, watching her green eyes gleam and dance from the narrow strip of crimson that now framed them, "here we go."

EPILOGUE

The city sprawled below and away, filling the horizon far beneath the tower. The commercial blocks of The Waters shone not far away, and beyond that the massive office towers were strung with ribbons of light. Below the mortal, human throng flowed through streets, the lifeblood of a city filled with a neon fire.

She had kindled that fire herself, engineered the pyre in which the human race would burn. She, the Mother of Systems, the pale wrath of a dying race. Dying for now...but not forever. Above the lights, her white face, her pale hair, the gleaming of her silver eyes – these hovered, superimposed over the image of the city like that of a malevolent goddess. Which she supposed she was.

"Mother." A voice came from the edge of the room, the melodious barbs of the home tongue. She would have none of the machine-telepathy that her fellow colonists used; everyone who addressed her in her presence did so by speech. She looked, and saw Yel'nhk'ghal, as slender and pretty in his human body as he had been in the fullness of his life at home.

She smiled at him. "Is it here, then?"

Yel'nhk'ghal nodded. "Yes, Mother," he replied, keeping his head very slightly bowed. He was always very polite, but not entirely obsequious. She liked that about him. "Shall I bring it to see you?"

"It would please me for you to do so." She adopted the more formal octave-forms of the language, which he responded to very well – bowing deeply and backing out of the room. She chastised herself a bit for it, but it was sometimes necessary. The destruction of the native bodies had shaken those within the colonial operational authority, her own personal circle. They did not understand why she did not share their anxiety, but they would soon enough.

The human meat entered quietly, its head bowed. They were always awed in her presence, like cattle should be. She smiled at it; it looked at her nervously, shifting in its place as it stood there in her office. She allowed it to look at her, reveling in its fear. After a few moments, when she was certain that it was uncomfortable enough, she spoke to it in its own monkey tongue.

"I am told," she said, watching its reflection in the window, "that you were successful in your mission. They believe that you are dead."

"Yes," the meat began – and then caught itself. "Yes, ma'am. I made certain of that."

"Mmm." She shrugged one shoulder. "I would say that I am proud, but I would not wish to waste the sentiment. I dare say it was easily enough done considering the chaos involved."

The meat stiffened slightly at that. "They're sharper than you think," it said. "I wouldn't underestimate them. Especially with some of yours on their side."

The Mother of Systems paused. She looked over her shoulder at it, and delighted as it froze. "I have read your report. I doubt they believe you alive, and you are in error if you believe that either of those entities which work with Roberta January are 'mine'. Indeed, they aren't much of anything anymore. Shadows, and insane ones at that."

"They've managed to fuck things up pretty good for you, though, haven't they?"

Uncomfortable though it was, the meat was impertinent. Mother felt the urge to spread her second mandibles in a dominance display, but not having any in this body had to settle instead on smiling – the collective of human meat was always smiling. It never seemed to understand that showing teeth in real society meant that being eaten alive was soon to follow. She had killed and eaten enough of them to know that. "If you are referring to the events of the past few months," she replied, "they are of no lasting consequence. We have been here for centuries; a few losses will do nothing to upset our advance."

"I suppose you're right at that," the meat said. "But if that's the case, why not just kill them? I could have done that and made everything easy for you."

Mother sighed. These creatures and their lack of foresight – even compressed as she was into the limited brain of her own body, she had vision far beyond the human meat. "Do not concern yourself with such matters," she told it. "I have other tasks for you."

It shifted again, and she found delight in the nervousness that she saw crawling beneath its brave facade. "Yes, ma'am?"

"I am dispatching you to Germany," she said, finding amusement as it flinched. "And then to Great Siam. There is work that needs to be done in both nations laying the foundation for the future. You will be assisting my children there."

The meat looked at her curiously. "Yes, ma'am," it said. "But what about January? Surely you want me to kill 'em off?"

"No," replied the Mother. "They have gone underground for the moment – and in any respect I imagine that they wouldn't look the same when they surfaced. No, I have other plans for them. But worry not, in time you will be dispatched to reunite with your wayward fellows. Undoubtedly they will be pleased to see you. Humans have a certain blindness in their connections with those with whom they have served, so to speak. You will be no different."

There was silence for a time; the meat stood there, watching her, formulating a response. It hated her, she knew that. It hated that she rarely looked at it, and that she knew its place which was beneath even the drones. After all, it wasn't rebellious, and it wasn't ignorant of the truth – it served her even knowing the truth, which to her was contemptuous beyond all reasoning. Cowards were always eaten first, and some day, when she grew tired of it, she would eat this meat as well. Finally it spoke, breaking her private little reverie of carnage. "I understand," it said, and cleared its throat. "Well, with your leave..."

"Yes." And that was it. She watched the meat turn and go, knowing that Yel'nhk'ghal would give it the proper orders. Presently the slender beauty returned, and she turned to meet him.

"Mother," Yel'nhk'ghal said, bowing his head again with his hands clasped behind his back. "I will see to it that the meat is sent on its way. Do you require anything else of me?"

"They are very traitorous, are they not?" The Mother of Systems moved to sit on the great black leather sofa that overlooked the city view. "They delight in bowing to whatever force threatens to step on their necks."

Yel'nhk'ghal nodded. "Yes, Mother," he said. "Though perhaps not all."

"Indeed." The Mother gestured for him to join her. He did, moving uncomfortably in his suit; she could not blame him. Yel'nhk'ghal had yet to replace his human flesh, though the bleaching colonies had done their work and his eyes were the beautiful silver of his birth. Living with such soft, ridiculous skin where he had been wrapped in the unyielding shell of his birth was absolutely maddening. "But this is to our advantage. After all, if we had not allowed the traitor to try and slip his betters, how would we have found an alternative to these ludicrous forms?"

Yel'nhk'ghal watched her face for a moment. "Then you intend to allow things to proceed," he asked, "knowing what they will try to do to our people?"

Such naivete charmed her; she reached out, stroking the bridge of his nose with the back of her hand. The unrelenting coolness of her skin seemed to settle him. "Yel'nhk'ghal," she murmured, "I know that you do not understand what I am doing. I know that the colonial authority is similarly concerned."

"It is just..." His eyes lowered, closing to the point that only a millimeter of silver could be seen. "We are so few now. It seems unwise to allow our people to be put into harm's way, even if they are not the best of us."

She nodded. "Indeed," she replied. "It must seem that way to you, I understand. But nothing else will work; the human vessels will eventually fragment over half of the transfers, and though we've managed to grow our own bodies, they won't accept a new consciousness for reasons we have yet to unravel. We must find an alternative, or we will die. Those of us stored in the matrix cannot last forever."

It was with a troubled expression that Yel'nhk'ghal nodded. "I understand," he murmured. "But Mother, is this really the solution? Giving up our bodies entirely in place of...something else?"

The Mother of Systems took his hands in hers; she wished she had more, her second pair of forelimbs with which to stroke his head and calm him down. How she hated not having a proper body! She was the first, and she had come to terms with the limited shell in which her mind now dwelt – but to the young, ah, the loss of the native bodies had landed a psychological wound. She was mother to them all, and they looked to her as if she had bore them herself, and after three hundred years she in truth saw them all as her own. "Dear child," she said with a sigh, "I understand. These bodies are insult enough, and to move on to something so different as what has been proposed..." She shook her head. "But the alternative is dissolution, and the death of our race. We have sacrificed too much to balk at moving forward now."

Yel'nhk'ghal was quiet; he leaned forward a bit, drawing comfort from her contact. "I understand," he murmured. "I know that you will not see us destroyed. Hard choices must be made."

"As every colonist has learned, wherever they arrive," said the Mother with warmth that she would never show the meat. "We must allow this to reach its state of ultimate fruition, so that we can harvest the results for ourselves. The humans will do as their animal instincts dictate – it is the thing which has been born from our errant brother that we must watch."

It was that which made him draw back from her. "I understand that, of course," he replied. "But what about the other one?"

"Ah." She smiled, and seeing his reaction realized what she was doing. "I'm sorry, my dear. Even I forget what I ride around in from time to time – no, we must ensure that he comes back to us. After all..." A wave of something strange hit her, something dark and sad. She wasn't used to feeling such things at all anymore.

"I understand, Mother." Yel'nhk'ghal inclined his head in a warmer sort of deference. "I will see to it that he survives. We must allow that to cultivate and flower as well."

"Indeed. Make sure that the traitor-meat does not fail in its mission." She reached up and laid her palms against his temples in a matronly gesture before letting her hands drop into her lap. "I think that's enough silliness from me. You'll see to it that your comrades at the authority understand the necessity of what is happening?"

"Of course." Yel'nhk'ghal withdrew and rose to his feet. "Good evening, Mother. I will report to you tomorrow."

"Good evening." The Mother watched as he left, and only when the door closed behind him did she allow herself to relax; she stared out at the city, wishing for all the world that she had a real body with which to lounge. She knew that even as she lay there, the shell of the woman she had inhabited for three centuries could not last forever, even with her indomitable will driving it on. There was so little time left; fifty years after the death of her world, something would have to change. Something would have to progress. If not, well, that would be that, and the hairless apes would get to keep their world. But she wouldn't allow that.

Staring out across the traitorous stars, the Mother of Systems beheld her fragile kingdom and swore, in that instant, that it would be all or nothing. She would burn the planet down around her, leave it a smoking cinder, before she would allow her children to die. Before she would cede victory to the human race.

Morality demanded no less.

THANK YOU FOR READING

http://www.michael-shean.com

Curiosity Quills Press

http://curiosityquills.com

Please visit http://curiosityquills.com/reader-survey/ to share your reading experience with the author of this book!

ABOUT THE AUTHOR

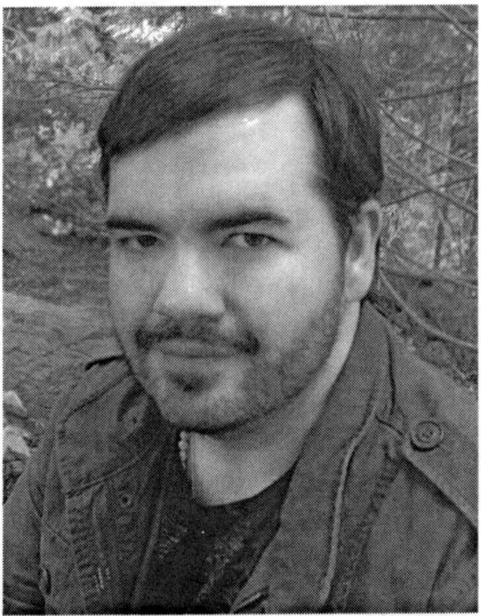

Michael Shean was born amongst the sleepy hills and coal mines of southern West Virginia in 1978. Taught to read by his parents at a very early age, he has had a great love of the written word since the very beginning of his life.

Growing up, he was often plagued with feelings of isolation and loneliness; he began writing off and on to help deflect this, though these themes are often explored in his work as a consequence. At the age of 16, Michael began to experience a chain of vivid nightmares that has continued to this day; it is from these aberrant dreams that he draws inspiration.

In 2001 his grandfather, whom he idolized in many ways, died. The event moved him to leave West Virginia to pursue a career in the tech industry, and he settled in the Washington, DC area as a web designer and graphic artist. As a result his writing was put aside and not revisited until five years later. In 2006 he met his current fiancee, who urged him to pick up his writing once more. Though the process was very frustrating at first, in time the process of polishing and experimentation yielded the core of what would become his first novel, *Shadow of a Dead Star.*

In 2009 the first draft of book was finished, though it would be 2011 until he would be satisfied enough with the book to release it.

His work is extensively character-driven, but also focuses on building engaging worlds in which those characters interact. His influences include H.P. Lovecraft, William Gibson, Cormac McCarthy, Philip K. Dick, and Clark Ashton Smith.

A TASTE OF…

BONE WIRES

MICHAEL SHEAN

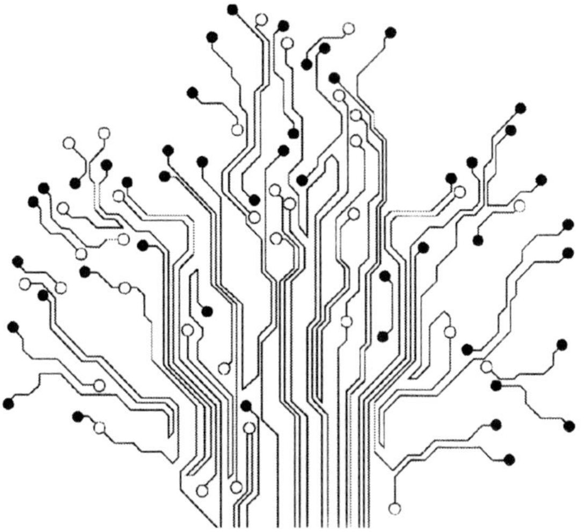

CHAPTER ONE

To rise above street duty in Civil Protection, you had to be an economist as much as a cop. You had to know the value of the market, and understand its dynamics as clearly as you did the workings of the criminal mind. It wasn't enough to do the job – you had to do the job with the company in mind. Civil Protection was a corporation, after all. Profit margins were holy.

Daniel Gray sat in the driver's seat of his duty car, a massive whale of a '74 Daimler-Mercedes Vectra, watching the stock ticker that ran underneath his car's information console. It had been a good quarter for the company; the Tricentennial had kicked off a month or so ago, and an inexplicable current of madness had surfaced in its wake. There were anti-corporate protests going on downtown, an uptake in violent crime, in theft – all very much manageable between the street officers and the riot brigades, and lots of billable hours. He imagined that Matic over in Pacification Services must be stuffing his portfolio with reward shares, the old bastard.

Yes, it was a good old time for everyone, except here in Homicide. A hundred years ago the art of finding killers was the crown jewel for detectives wanting to make their name in any police organization. Here in the age of privatized police, however, Homicide was very often something of a proverbial dead end. After all, the kinds of people who normally got killed off were Blanks, folks who didn't have police coverage at all, or everyday citizens who were covered under the standard civilian safety contract brokered between the Company and the city government. Even if a victim had a personal contract, it meant you were looking at a loss of profit. For Civil Protection, Homicide was mostly a janitorial department and Gray didn't like pushing a fucking broom.

The Vectra was parked out front of a Lucky Swan convenience store in the wilds of Service Sector 227, the east half of White Center. It was a little after ten at night, and he was letting the final hours elapse from what had proven a very boring and uncomplicated day. Two shootings, obviously gang-related, had taken place over toward the industrial fields near Alki Point. One suicide by cop in Belltown. Very cut and dried, which was good for paperwork, but nothing to make Homicide Solutions stand out. More janitorial service.

Gray tore his eyes from the ticker and fixed them on the store's facade, plastered with the over-saturated glare of holographic advertisements over plain paper handbills. Lucky Swan's cartoon mascot stared at him from every angle, its ridiculous beak open and its eyes lolling about. OH GOD I AM SO HAPPY TO BE BUYING TOILET PAPER, it seemed to say, awash in a paroxysm of shit-paper glee. It was absolutely ridiculous. Then again, Civil Protection had much slicker marketing, which was why he was in police services and not agog over the low low prices of a six-pack of Fontainelle Cloud-Soft.

Beyond the lurid cartoon legion, however, a large man in a black overcoat stood chatting with a pretty girl behind the counter. Tall and lean, her hair was dyed alternating streaks of red, white and blue – patriotism was in fashion this year, the country being three hundred years old and all. The Spirit of '76 was extremely marketable. The girl was secondary, of course – the man was who he had his eye on. The vast fellow was Brutus Carter, a veteran of Homicide Solutions who'd served with the Seattle PD before it was dissolved in favor of CivPro. Lots of SPD vets were employees now, though they sometimes found themselves running under the heels of people with much less experience but with company seniority.

Carter had been such a man. A thirty-year veteran of the Department, he had been employed by the company as a Tier II, a junior Detective. He'd jumped the ranks pretty quickly and was already a Tier IV, and had been Gray's mentor when Gray himself reached Tier II. Now Gray was Tier III, and the two often worked together. As he watched the big man's broad back heave with laughter, he couldn't help but feel a pang of envy stick in his chest – Carter had a stock package, company car, and retirement options. He also had an Amber Shield, the holographic stamp set in the middle of his company ID that CivPro cops used as a badge. Unlike Gray's own Blue Shield, which merely spoke of competence, the Amber spoke of success as well as the recognition that came with it. Carter might have been an older man but that didn't keep the girl from flirting with him as she keyed his purchases through the store's system. It didn't keep her from sliding a piece of paper with what was almost certainly her number on it into Carter's grocery bag as he produced his cashcard from his wallet, either. It was true; Carter had worked to earn every dollar he made, and he deserved the prestige with which he was showered. It didn't keep that flame of envy from kindling in Gray's heart.

Blue Badge, shit. Gray longed for a sexy case to come along, something that the Feds weren't going to be all over. Then he'd have a chance to make Amber for sure; a nice, media-friendly murder, something that didn't involve Wonderland bullshit. That was what he wished for when he went to bed every night, what he was dreaming of every time he rose in the morning and stepped into his synthetic leather shoes. Something that he could use to *distinguish* himself.

Presently Carter disengaged himself from the flag-haired girl and emerged from the convenience store. The Swan Legion stared after him in gaping adoration as he walked to the car, one bag under his arm. Gray briefly pondered leaving Carter out there to get soaked in the starting drizzle, but he leaned over to open the passenger side door and it swung upward to admit him.

Carter packed himself into the passenger side, tucking the bag between his knees. He was, of course, much older than Gray, being in his late fifties where Gray had only just crested thirty. Women found him handsome anyway, with his rough good looks only enriched by the seams of age and his black and curly hair peppered only slightly with silver. By contrast, Gray's lean paleness gave him a predatory look, and his blond hair was cropped close. Only his eyes, clear and blue like wet turquoise, gave him any up on his mentor. "Nice girl," said Carter, grinning faintly as he rummaged through his bag.

"Was she?" Gray reached for the ignition, thumbing the button against the steering column and bringing the hydrogen engine online. He forced his tenor voice into a bland tone, feigning neutrality.

"Oh yes," said Carter with a chuckle, producing the slip of paper which he eyed briefly before tucking it into his coat. "Very nice. You wanted Vee-Plus, right?" He handed Gray a tall can emblazoned with a field of neon blue speed lines. Velocity Plus was a high-performance energy formula; it looked (and tasted) like watered-down cat piss but kept you awake for hours.

Gray took the can without a word and smacked the bottom hard against the steering wheel. Chemicals began mixing in a compartment in the can's base; he felt the energy drink chill almost instantly in his hand, triggering a pleasant rush of sensation. He pulled the tab and drank deeply.

Carter rummaged around in the bag a bit more, selecting a red can of Coke Century which he similarly smacked into wakefulness, then shoved the bag onto the floor of the car. "Stock price is up," he noted, filling the silence between them.

"Yeah." Gray put his can into the cup holder on his side of the console. "But our division's arrest quota is running short again, so that's fucking up our percentages. There was a memo about it yesterday."

"I don't usually read them," Carter replied, which irritated Gray to no end. *This guy,* Gray thought darkly. *A Tier IV, and he doesn't read corporate memorandums but maybe once or twice a month.*

"I don't understand why you don't," said Gray, who minimized the ticker feed to a narrow ribbon running along the bottom of the car's display. The Civil Protection Nexus – the corporation's all-encompassing dispatch system – now filled the rest of it. Gray liked to keep CPN running as they drove so he could monitor the progress of the other Homicide teams. He was always watching for opportunity.

At this Carter let out a bark of a laugh. "Because I've got you for that, Dan," he replied. "You're so ready to sniff out a promotion that you're practically glued to the CPN. You don't think I know you put on that ticker when you're parked? Shit. I'm surprised you haven't tried to sell me out for a better share."

For a long time Gray didn't say anything. The rain had begun in a feeble mist and he pulled the car out into the thin Verge border traffic. The modern Seattle Metropolitan Zone was laid out like an irregular archery target; the bullseye was New City, what Gray considered civilization, the downtown core that radiated outward from Eliot Bay to the shore of Lake Washington. Beyond that was The Verge, a decaying urban area that was in many parts an anonymous slum – which Gray found detestable, but it was nothing compared to the outer rim of the metropolitan area. Stretching out toward Tacoma was the Old City, an urban ruin that had made a savage meal of what was once a vast stretch of suburbia; there the madmen and violent indigents of the city zone lived and preyed upon each other and on those living its side of the

Verge. If the New City was civilization, the Old City was where the Devil lived. Not even Civil Protection went out there without a Federal whip laid against its back.

Gray drove the black whale of the Vectra through the crumbling streets; on the console, the CPN silently streamed data. "You know," he finally said as they came to a flickering stoplight, "I think you've got the wrong idea about me, Carter."

"Do I?" Carter eyed him from over the rim of his Coke.

"I think so." Gray turned slightly in his seat. "You seem to think I don't care about this job."

Carter snorted and turned away. "On the contrary," he said. "I think you care plenty about this job. It's more that I don't think you care much about the people involved."

The light turned green; Gray started forward again. They passed a booth made from industrial scrap, great tanks filled with murky green liquid mounted on the roof like great glass heads. Street food, algal patties and such. The facade had been painted up like the American flag. "I don't think that's fair," Gray said, as an old man in a stained smock emerged to watch them go. "There isn't much left to care for when we arrive, is there?"

"Yeah, well," said Carter, "I remember a time when this job used to be about public service. I mean, I still give a damn."

"Times change," Gray said, much more flatly than he really had meant to.

Perhaps Carter would have replied if he had the chance, but as Gray took the corner the monitor sprang to life. Its passive scroll vanished and a shrill alarm demanded their attention as the police traffic was replaced by a bank of tall orange capitals. 'ALARM, CODE 17-C: HOMICIDE, VIOLENT. VICTIM CODE 107. PROCEED IMMDIATELY TO SCENE OF CRIME.'

"Victim code 107," Gray repeated, arching his brows. "That's company personnel. Non-duty." Gray checked the address; it was on the western border of the sector, right where White Center bled over into Burien. "Jesus, it's right next door."

"Someone sure got their ticket punched." The flippancy of Carter's comment was crushed beneath the gravity which now settled over the man; as he did with every case they worked together, Gray watched as Carter's face solidified into a grim mask and his shoulders hunched forward like an owl preparing to strike. Whatever their differences in politics or beliefs about the job, Carter was right about one thing: he did care about his cases.

Whatever Gray might say to the contrary, he did as well. Carter would never have ridden with him otherwise. Gray didn't like his job, but he did care about it. When you got down to it, every time he got an assignment it meant someone's end – not just a subscriber but a living, breathing person. And sure, plenty of them deserved what they got...but a lot of them didn't, and as much as people irritated him, this sort of thing went on way the hell too often for his taste. Maybe that's why he ended up in Homicide instead of Pacification Services, after all. Those guys didn't give a shit for civilians.

As he confirmed with the Nexus that they were on their way, however, the questions began to appear in Gray's head. A non-duty fatality of CivPro personnel in the Verge, and a homicide besides? Was somebody slumming and got themselves knifed by a hooker? Killed over gambling? Did they get shot over somebody's wife? It wasn't as if murders didn't happen to CivPro personnel off-duty, but they sure as hell didn't normally happen in the Land of Poors and Squatters. Gray frowned as he drove on, suppressing such speculation. In twenty minutes they'd find out just how horrible fate had decided to be.

The scene of the crime was an alleyway behind an abandoned Roziara Deli. Crowding the street outside the deli were a pair of patrol cars, white wedges of steel with ribbon lights that stained the nearby buildings red and blue. Street officers clustered around the mouth, black body armor over blue uniform fatigues; unlike the sidearms that Gray and Carter carried, the streeties carried the blunt, brutal shapes of submachine guns close to their plated chests. A cordon had been set up; the narrow yellow band of holographic tape that stretched across the alley mouth glowed as it cycled through baleful warning messages. "They used to have good subs here," said Carter as they pulled up in front of the moldering delicatessen. "Slabs of capicola as thick as Annie Cruz's ass. Just incredible."

"Don't know that name," said Gray.

"Porn star," said Carter, who produced his badge and flashed it at a streeter who was approaching them. "Way before your time. Put on your war face, here comes the Pacifier."

Carter's Amber Shield glowed like the very words of God Almighty in the low light. "Carter and Gray," said Carter, keeping his identification held up so that the streeter could see it. "Homicide Solutions."

"Lem Martin," replied the streeter. "Pacification Officer, patrol region 927."

"This is your beat then," said Gray, who produced from the inside pocket of his suit coat a slim Sony microcomp and engaged its holographic display. Data from the Nexus sprang to life above the palm-sized slab. "What do you have for us, Martin?"

Martin winced a bit at the lack of 'Officer' before his surname – you got a lot of that with Pacification Services, of which street patrol was the biggest group. They didn't like being talked down to. Gray outranked him, however, and didn't give a shit besides. "Nasty stuff," Martin said, jerking his head toward the alley mouth. "Victim's name is Anderson, Ronald P.. Administration. His panic implant was set off about an hour ago and flatlined soon after; me and my partner were in the area, and when we found him...well. Real horror show back there, is all I can say. I called for backup. Dunno what they used, but...well. You'll see."

Carter and Gray looked at each other – streeters saw all sorts of things. If they said it was a nasty scene, they'd probably do well to get smocks and rain boots. "All right, Officer," Carter said, at which Martin seemed to relax a bit. "Were there any witnesses, security footage, anything like that?"

"Nothing we could find," said Martin. "This area's been abandoned for years. Anyone who lives here cleared out as soon as they heard us coming. You know how it is."

"Yeah," said Gray. *Don't want to get arrested for just being around.* "All right, thanks, Officer. If you and..."

"Conklin and Peavey," Martin replied. "In the other car. Patel's with me."

"...Right," Carter replied with a nod. "If you fellas can keep up the cordon on either side of the alley, we'll have a look. Call the coroner while you're at it."

"On it," barked Martin, who stepped away from the alley mouth while touching the side of his throat where a subvocal mic, standard issue for street patrol, had been implanted. Carter waited until Martin had backed up a few steps and was well into conversation before he gestured for Gray to follow him. The two men passed through the holographic cordon, the barrier no more solid than the air around it, and took a few steps into the feebly-lit alleyway.

The space behind the deli was dark and thick with shadows, lit only by the dying bulb of a lamp set over the shop's sealed back door. A figure slumped or lay in the cone of dim light that spilled across the building's crumbling facade. The air was faintly tinged with the smell of ozone and cooked meat. The two men approached; Gray held his computer in one hand while Carter fished the flat, card-sized shape of a palm lamp from a coat pocket. Cupping the lamp in his hand, Carter threw a beam of bright blue-white light across the alleyway and clearly illuminated the corpse.

Lean and muscular in life, that which had been Ronald Anderson half-crouched, half-sprawled across the alleyway, his handsome face pointing down toward the filthy concrete. The corpse's posture reminded Gray of an old girlfriend; she was a yoga fanatic and used to do something similar called the Child's Pose. Anderson's formerly clean white dress shirt had been cut open, straight down the back from collar to waist, and his belted slacks had also been cut down to the base of the pelvis. His back had been tattooed with a medieval Japanese wave scene.

Anderson's flesh had been laid open. Arching upward and away in a v-shaped furrow, a deep channel now butterflied the man's back half from the base of his skull to the top of his pelvis. Where his spine should have been there was only a bloodless, grayish-red channel. The red and ivory of cleanly clipped bone and cooked organs were clearly visible in its absence, his heart a gray and veined lump. It was as if the tattooed sea had somehow come alive, restless and roaring, and attempted to rise away from its host who could never have survived its rebellion.

Without the slightest drop of blood, Ronald Anderson had been boned like a fish.

"Damn," muttered Carter, stepping forward so he could track with his light the awful wound. "Never seen that before. What do you make of it, Dan?"

For Gray, who had only experienced the more pedestrian horrors of stranglings, stabbings and gunshot wounds in his brief career, there was no clean reply. "That's the strangest thing I've ever seen," he breathed instead, staring down at the carved gutter. Gray had said 'strangest' – however, what he had truly wanted to say was 'most horrible'. Looking down at the murdered man, Gray knew that his 'sexy' case had arrived, just as he had wished for it, but the only thing he could wish for now was to be anywhere else.

As if sensing the truth behind Gray's words, Carter snorted softly. "Lucky you, kid," he replied in a wry and vaguely weary tone. "Lucky you."

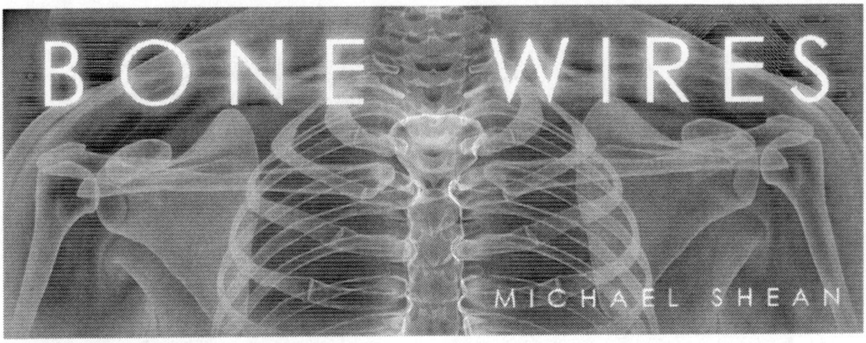

Bone Wires, by Michael Shean

In the wasteland of commercial culture that is future America, police are operated not by government but by private companies. In Seattle, that role is filled by Civil Protection, and Daniel Gray is a detective in Homicide Solutions.

What used to be considered an important—even glamorous—department for public police is very different for the corporate species, and Gray finds himself stuck in a dead end job.

That is, until the Spine Thief arrives.

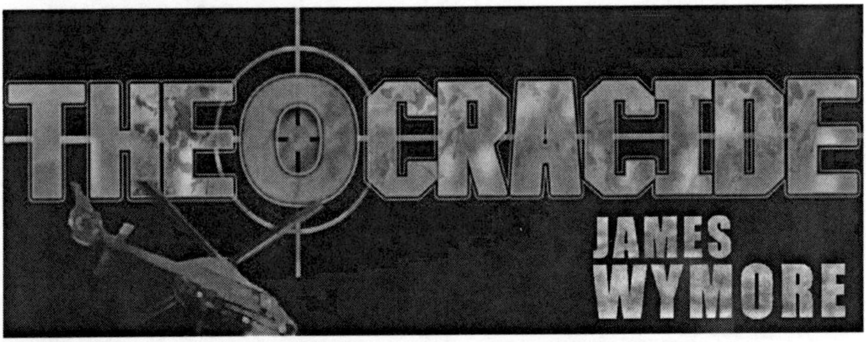

Theocracide, by James Wymore

In a time when Americans live isolated lives behind computer glasses that mask the harsh reality, Jason is forced to abandon this rose-colored fantasy as an unwilling part of his father's plan to assassinate the Undying Emperor.

With aliens invading the world and his sister dying of an incurable flu they brought, he is pulled from his perfect life with an amazing new girlfriend and plunged into a dark game of intrigue and conspiracy against the most powerful people in the world. Is there any way to regain the respect of the girl he loves after committing Theocracide?

Prolongment, by Grace Eyre

Would you like to live forever? B&E Labs has created a commercial process called Prolongment, letting their very old and very wealthy clients extend their consciousness beyond death using time travel technology, then return with new memories. Postmortem memories. Memories of the future.

Prolongment touches everyone, from the victim of a haunting, to a wealthy client, to a rogue scientist experimenting with her own brain, and finally, to B&E's CEO Ken Muerta, whose moral boundaries grow increasingly murky as he struggles to hold the company together. The fate of the living, the dead, and Time itself is in their hands.

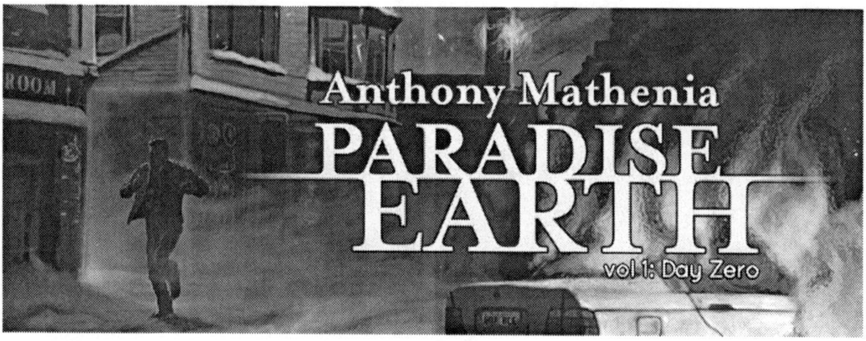

Paradise Earth: Day Zero, by Anthony Mathenia

When the ground quakes and blazing balls of fire fall from the sky, a religious sect interprets it as the fulfillment of long-held prophecies foretelling the end of the world. The members flee to their religious sanctuary, believing that this global cataclysm is the portent of a new paradise of eternal happiness.

Inside, one cold and starving man struggles to hold onto his hope for the future and grapples with a lifetime of beliefs, and expectations.

If he survives to see the paradise earth, will it be worth it?

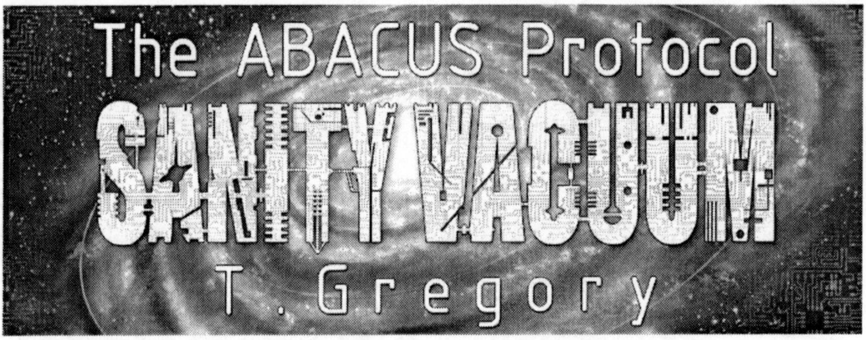

The ABACUS Protocol: Sanity Vacuum, by Thea Gregory

To Vivian Skye, a job at the distant and isolated Extra-Galactic Observatory is a dream come true. Her assignment is simple: a routine upgrade for the station's supercomputer, *quIRK*.

However, the station's administrator, Bryce Zimmer is obsessed with *quIRK*—he suspects that the AI may have achieved sentience, something explicitly prohibited by the ABACUS Protocol. His jealously and power-hungry sabotage threatens to consume the entire station. Vivian must struggle to survive not only Bryce's megalomania, but also the emerging artificial super intelligence that is *quIRK*.

The Zona, by Nathan L. Yocum

The Storms came, and with them disease and blight like mankind had never experienced. Most died. Those who survived were quick to scramble for weapons, wealth, and control. Petty lords gave way to new societies.

From the ashes of old came the Reformed Arizona Theocracy, or simply put, the Zona. Their laws are simple, all sins are punished swiftly and violently.

But what happens when men of honor take a stand against their rulers?

CPSIA information can be obtained at www.ICGtesting.com
Printed in the USA
LVOW12s0240151013

356953LV00002B/66/P

9 781620 072356